· T H E ·
P E R F E C T
F A M I L Y

· THE ·
PERFECT
FAMILY

SHARON DALEY

E. P. DUTTON NEW YORK

Published in the United States by E. P. Dutton,
a division of NAL Penguin Inc.,
2 Park Avenue, New York, N.Y. 10016.

Published simultaneously in Canada by
Fitzhenry and Whiteside, Limited, Toronto.

Library of Congress Cataloging-in-Publication Data

Daley, Sharon.
The perfect family / by Sharon Daley.
p.   cm.
ISBN 0-525-24628-2
I. Title.
PS3554.A432P4   1988
813'.54—dc19
87-25186
CIP

Designed by David Lui

1 3 5 7 9 10 8 6 4 2

First Edition

Excerpts from "We've Only Just Begun", lyrics by Paul Williams and music by Roger Nichols © 1970 Irving Music, Inc. (BMI), all rights reserved, international copyright secured, reprinted by permission of the publisher.

Excerpt from T. S. Eliot's "The Love Song of J. Alfred Prufrock" from *Collected Poems 1909–1962* by T. S. Eliot copyright 1936 by Harcourt Brace Jovanovich, Inc. Copyright © 1963, 1964 by T. S. Eliot. Reprinted by permission of the publisher.

To Harry Barovsky

ACKNOWLEDGMENTS

I want to thank friends like Alice and Dick Powell, Paul Mantee, Ed Lipnick, Judy Bustany, Roger Hyde, Dick Greenberg, and Susan Daley for giving freely of their time to read, correct, and offer advice; to Sharon Haberfeld for explaining the difference between a plaintiff and a defendant, knowing a metaphor when it's mixed, and allowing me to share space in her law office with Marilyn, Gail, and Diane, who made my writing cubbyhole a quiet haven. And finally, special thanks to John, who with constant patience provided everything from practical advice to minute research.

My only regret is that my late friend, the novelist Barbara Betcherman, will never know how much I owe her. It was she who insisted I begin this book and made it possible for me to meet Henry Morrison, an agent willing to take a chance on an unknown writer, and who in turn sent the manuscript to Joyce Engelson, whose editor's eye landed gently on every problem I was too blind to see.

The thought of our past years in me doth breed
Perpetual benediction: not indeed
For that which is most worthy to be blest;
Delight and liberty, the simple creed
Of Childhood, whether busy or at rest,
With new-fledged hope still fluttering in his breast;—
       Not for these I raise
       The song of thanks and praise;
     But for those obstinate questionings
     Of sense and outward things,
     Falling from us, vanishings;
     Blank misgivings of a Creature
Moving about in worlds not realized,
High instincts before which our mortal Nature
Did tremble like a guilty Thing surprised:
     But for those first affections,
     Those shadowy recollections,
    Which, be they what they may,
Are yet the fountain light of all our day,
Are yet a master light of all our seeing;
      —WILLIAM WORDSWORTH
       "Ode on Intimations of Immortality"

The ode was intended for such readers only as had been
accustomed to watch the flux and reflux of their inmost nature, to venture at times into the twilight realms of consciousness, and to feel a deep interest in modes of inmost
being, to which they know that the attributes of time and
space are inapplicable and alien, but which yet can not be
conveyed save in symbols of time and space.
      —SAMUEL TAYLOR COLERIDGE

Part One

Whither is fled the visionary gleam?
Where is it now, the glory and the dream?
—WILLIAM WORDSWORTH
"Ode on Intimations of Immortality"

1

Judith Gregory sits in the Superior Court of Santa Monica listening to the attorney plead her case. Since she too is a lawyer, Judith appreciates his problem and almost feels sorry for him. When she declined to enter a plea of temporary insanity, she knew the state would have no choice but to charge her with second-degree murder. But Judith had no choice either: she refuses to pretend her mother's death was the result of a moment's uncontrollable hysteria. Death deserves more respect than that.

Watching with professional detachment, Judith is fascinated by her attorney's cross-examination. He is good, the best her father could buy. But as far as she can tell, nothing he is suggesting is true; she certainly can't identify with the despondent, grieving daughter he wants to portray. As a matter of fact she remembers, not without pleasure, the excellent meal she treated herself to just before her last visit to the hospital. She had concentrated on ordering carefully, a dry chardonnay to complement the hearts of palm salad, followed by a full-bodied cabernet for the steak Diane. She cannot picture the bottles and tubes the lawyer is asking the jury to imagine; she can only visualize the perfect, fresh raspberries and champagne she had chosen as her final course. She is grateful to her parents for teaching her to enjoy a good meal. But she is sure her attorney would not point that out in his opening statement.

After the meal that night, she had just time enough to drive to her parents' house, move out, and then, around midnight, walk to the hospital. It was one of those touted California winter nights—with the faint smell of salt and seaweed riding on the breeze from the Santa Monica Bay. Remembering the rest of the night is a little more difficult. Judith isn't sure how long she sat on her mother's bed holding her hand and looking at the plastic tube funneling a clear, sweet fluid from the ubiquitous bottle into a withered, desiccated arm. She does have a vague recollection of watching the faint glow of dawn insinuating itself through the dark hospital windows and of speaking to her mother, not in the expected hushed, soothing words usually reserved for the dying, but in almost fierce, animated tones. "It's okay, Momma. I'm here." Barely disturbing the stillness of the white sheet that covered it, a pathetic figure turned slightly and moaned. Judith has no doubt her mother had heard. She cannot afford a doubt.

Her mother died around 5:45, which was good, because the morning nurse might have reversed Judith's decision.

Now her attorney, in rebuttal to the prosecutor's opening statement, is suggesting she had entered Saint John's Hospital in a crazed, grief-stricken state. Judith feels a wrenching pressure in her chest, and for an instant she has difficulty breathing. She doesn't want her daughter, Emma, to hear this nonsense. It hadn't been like that at all. Indeed, when Judith entered her mother's room that night and dismissed the night nurse, she thought she did so with politeness, assuring the lady she would be paid for the entire evening.

That same nurse is testifying now, recalling the evening much as Judith does. Obviously that doesn't help the case, but Judith is confident her attorney will persuade the nurse to agree that she was confused about the sequence of events. The witness is already eager to volunteer that she wasn't there when Mrs. Gregory died, so she will probably admit there is no way she can be sure what happened.

Judith turns and looks at her daughter sitting rigidly in the front row of the courtroom. My god, Emma's lovely, Judith thinks. This is not the first time Judith has been struck by the resemblance between her daughter and her own mother. It had taken years for Judith to appreciate her mother's strong, sharp features. Looking at Emma, she regrets it had taken years to notice a lot of things.

Emma meets Judith's stare as though she can't quite remember where they met and isn't sure she cares to be reminded. For an instant Judith has an insane urge to take the stand and plead guilty to compounding the sins of motherhood: guilty to caring too much; guilty to acting as if she didn't care enough; guilty to confusing protection with custody. She could only plead innocent to the single count of not loving.

Emma's image wavers and begins to recede farther and farther into the misty haze of Judith's rising tears. It's all happening again, she thinks. No attorney in the world can outwit the justice of life coming full circle. Taking a deep breath, Judith wills the pain in her chest to subside and then forces her attention back to the proceedings. She hopes she will not need to testify. She is content to let the attorney lie about the last night she spent with her mother. His story is so much more dramatic than hers.

Christine Wolfe's hands are shaking slightly, but she sounds sincere as she responds "I do" and takes a seat facing the table where Judith sits next to her attorney. I won't be asked the right questions, Christine thinks, so thank God I won't have a chance to tell "nothing but the truth."

"Just tell us in your own words what happened on the morning your mother died," the lawyer says sympathetically. Christine knows he means, "Just use the words we agreed should be spoken, no more no less."

"My sister called me at six-fifteen from the hospital and . . ."

"When you say your sister, you mean the defendant, Judith Gregory?" the lawyer interrupts.

"Yes. Judith called me at six-fifteen and told me she was at the hospital and that Mother had died."

"Did she sound upset?" he asks on cue.

Christine had not recognized her sister's dead, flat voice that morning when she called, saying "It's over. I need you. Please, come to the hospital as soon as you can." There was no hint of the confident authority she automatically expected when her sister spoke. Instead, Judith sounded resigned, almost submissive, not desperate or despondent, which is what the attorney is hoping to hear. But he doesn't know Judith as well as I do, she thinks. "Yes, she was upset," Christine answers.

The lawyer follows the script perfectly. "How could you tell? Was she crying?"

"No. But when she said she needed me and asked me to come to the hospital right away, I knew she was upset. It was the first time in my life I ever heard Judith ask for help."

"And did you go?"

"Yes."

"What did you find when you arrived at the hospital?"

"I went right to Mother's room and found my sister sitting on the bed next to my mother, holding her hand." The memory of that morning came flooding back. Her green-eyed sister, nearly seven years older than she, still beautiful, tall, slim, and always in control, was sitting next to their mother's lifeless body. "I'm going to need some help. I have to go home—Emma's alone," Judith announced, as though her major concern was a shortage of babysitters.

Now, Christine notices her sister looking at Emma and is surprised to see Judith's hands clenched, white with tension and her eyes brimming with the beginning of tears. Christine wonders what her sister might be feeling apprehensive about, since from the moment she was arrested she has offered no defense, her silence as guilty as any plea she might have entered.

Judith's attorney moves slowly away from the table where his client sits and approaches the witness stand, suggesting he is reluctant to leave Judith alone, but indicating Christine's response to his next question demands his full attention. "Would you say that your sister was a devoted daughter?" he asks.

"Yes, my sister was devoted." Christine is tempted to add that they were all afraid of Judith and her determined devotion. In fact, she considers the entire trial a ritual affirming Judith's authority over them. Why else would her sister sit there silently, not lifting a finger to defend herself, almost defying them to learn the truth. It is exactly like the time Judith came home pregnant. She wouldn't answer anyone's questions then either.

"Was anyone else present when you arrived at the hospital?" he continued.

"No, Judith didn't notify anyone but me. I arrived about six-forty-five; the morning nurse wasn't due until seven o'clock."

"And what state was your sister in?"

"She appeared exhausted and detached, like a soldier suffering shell shock."

"Are you familiar with shell shock?" he asks with apparent surprise and interest. "Do you have medical training?"

Christine pauses. Here it comes, she thinks. The appeal for sympathy and the demand for respect. Now they will have two sisters to pity instead of one.

"Mrs. Wolfe?" the lawyer prods gently, as though he has no idea what the answer might be that she so painfully hesitates to give.

"My husband returned from Viet Nam suffering from shock and delayed stress syndrome. Over a period of time, I became acutely aware of its symptoms and effects." Christine looks down at her older sister, whose still beautiful face shows no hint of the haunted stare or the wounded soul she associates with her husband, Bill.

"So you would say that your sister demonstrated that she was under great stress at the time of your mother's death?" the lawyer prompts.

"Yes."

"Would you say that your sister gave rational thought to the consequences of her actions?"

"No."

Christine's answer comes just before the prosecution's objection that the question calls for a conclusion. The attorney looks appropriately chastened and withdraws the question. When the judge instructs the jury to disregard the answer, Christine thinks, They probably won't, but they should.

Christine tries not to think of the day Bill closed the garage door, started the car, sat on the cold cement floor, and wrote her a letter that called for a conclusion. He had given quite a bit of rational thought to the consequences of his actions.

While his daughter testifies, Robert Gregory sits next to his son, Edward, on a low, bare oak bench outside the courtroom. No one had advised him that witnesses were not permitted in the courtroom until they had given testimony, and he envies Edward's foresight in bringing a book.

It occurs to Robert, as he gets up to stretch his legs, that he had awaited life's most important events while sitting on torturous furniture. He remembers almost two years ago sinking into an overstuffed chair in the hospital to wait for the results of his wife's surgery. Within minutes, he felt an undercurrent pulling him down deeper and deeper into the feathery sea, until he realized he had no hope of surfacing without help.

His two daughters had waited with him that day—Judith, sitting in an austere, modern chair, maddeningly in control; Christine, pacing the floor, visibly nervous and upset. They were so different—Judith, fair-skinned, blond, still sleek and trim, suggesting the champion athlete she had been; and Christine, small, dark-haired, and delicately rounded in a way that conveyed an unused sensuousness. Actually, Robert couldn't remember spending this much time alone with his daughters in years, and he was surprised to find they annoyed him. He wished both of them would go away and leave him alone and was thankful that his youngest child, Edward, had not been able to fly in from New York for Margaret's surgery.

Robert and Margaret had been married over thirty years. He had always considered his marriage conventional, even good by today's standards. In all those years he had never been unfaithful to his wife, probably, he reluctantly admitted, as much out of fear as love. He hated imbalance, and jeopardizing his marriage represented the greatest imbalance he could think of.

After sitting silently for over two hours, Judith had urged him to take a break. "Dad, go have a drink. Chris and I will wait here." He was startled when his younger daughter snapped back, "I don't think Dad wants to be alone right now." Robert thought Christine's reaction to Judith's suggestion sounded more like contempt than concern. Guilt pushed away the pleasant thought of having a quiet drink alone in some comfortable bar. He smiled at Judith and said, "Thanks, darling, but I think we should all stay here until the doctor comes." The triumphant look on Christine's face confirmed Robert's suspicions that his daughters were engaged in a war he hadn't heard declared.

When Dr. Davis finally appeared, Robert felt Judith grip his arm, and, obeying her wordless command, he allowed himself to be fished out of the downy cushions that engulfed him. When the doctor gently but professionally pronounced Margaret's death sentence, Robert's first thought was of disruption, followed of course by guilt, remorse, and impending loss. At Robert's age, he knew that death, perhaps more than life, demanded careful planning and appropriate preparations. "Do you think we should tell her?" he asked the doctor, who had presided over his children's birth and was now overseeing their mother's death.

The doctor looked weary. How many times, Robert wondered, has he been asked this question?

The answer was practiced. "That's your decision to make with the children. But I think she's strong enough to handle the truth. Besides, if I know Margaret, she won't let us get away with less."

"How long?" Robert remembered trying to keep his voice steady.

"A year. Perhaps a little longer. We can never be sure about these things."

Now, almost two years later, Judith is accused of walking into the hospital and deciding that it was time for her mother to die. Yet, in spite of the evidence, Robert refuses to believe his daughter could act with such premeditation. Regardless of how maddening Judith can be, he can't imagine her intentionally harming anyone. For just an instant this morning, she reminded him of the old Judith, or the young Judith, he should say. She had smiled at him, her eyes fixed on his, and said, "It's going to be okay, Daddy, don't worry," in the same open, trusting way she had as a child. Had he imagined tears in her voice, or was he listening to his own memories?

Why can't she just admit she was temporarily out of control, unbalanced? If she did, this trial would be no more than a formality. After all, she has her own daughter to consider. What will Emma do if Judith ends up in jail? But Robert knows his daughter would never admit to an irrational act. It was the same when she came home a husbandless mother, offering no defense, refusing to discuss the matter.

This time Robert knows Judith's silence is much more serious. Her attorney has warned that her refusal to reveal what happened that night makes it almost impossible to defend her not-guilty plea. Suddenly Robert feels an uncharacteristic rush of rage. Damn Judith! I should go in there and tell them what I really think. That she knew exactly what she was doing and didn't give a damn what others might think or feel. Of course, he knows he won't do that.

Robert watches Edward intent on his book and feels shut out. His son, so quiet and watchful, has always been a mystery to him. Robert considers him more Margaret's child than his, perhaps because he was the baby, and a male. Nonetheless, he is proud of his son, especially since he has become a fairly respected playwright, or so the critics have said. "Would you like to come for dinner tonight?" he asks his son.

Edward looks up from his book just as a bailiff appears, commanding, "Mr. Robert Gregory." Before his son can answer, Robert turns and enters the courtroom with grim determination. He will do what is necessary. He is, after all, head of the family, regardless of what his children think.

Edward Gregory watches his father disappear into the courtroom and wonders at his youthful appearance. At fifty-seven, Robert Gregory still resembles a boyish Van Johnson, his manner conveying an innocence that warned against lubricious jokes and corrupting temptations. His father is every inch the respected citizen, the honest managing editor of the local newspaper. Edward puts his book down. There is no need to go on pretending that the pages interest him. Does he realize how much of this is his fault? Edward wonders.

As the youngest member of the Gregory family, Edward has always felt distanced from the others, a member of the audience instead of a participant in the play. He experienced their pain, even when he suspected they were unaware of it themselves; knew their motives, even when they didn't think they had any. Witnessing so much love falling so far short of its mark had almost destroyed him. He had fled his family and California, seeking refuge, first as a student at Columbia, then as a teacher at NYU, and finally as errand boy at a theater so distant from Broadway that even "off-off" didn't adequately describe its location. During those years, he had returned home to attend mandatory, ritualistic ceremonies: Christine's wedding, her husband's funeral, and the final Christmas to acknowledge their mother's impending death. But this was one family gathering that defied protocol.

Only Judith had known about his shameful departure from teaching. She had even abetted it, breezing into New York, sweeping him up from his alcoholic haze, and pushing him in the direction he was too inert to travel. She introduced him to a producer who was willing to take chances with unknown writers. Edward wasn't sure how he knew that the producer was the father of Judith's child and that Judith's silence had kept even the producer unaware of Emma's existence. He also knew that Judith was aware of his discovery and with an unspoken command had forbidden him to reveal her secret.

Good old Judith, so sure the world couldn't run without her. And in some ways, she's right, he thinks. He tries to imagine how the world he ran away from might have survived if Judith had never existed. He couldn't. And he tries to understand why he feels such resentment toward her. He can't do that either.

When Judith called him in New York to report the results of his mother's surgery, she sounded as if she were giving a weather report. He could almost hear her saying "Cloudy, with the possibility of rain, and Mother is dying." Naturally, he offered to fly out, but Judith insisted there was no reason. "She'll be out of the hospital in a week, and she'll be fine for the next several months. There's nothing you can do, so there's no point in your coming home. You know that's what Mother would say, so let's do what she would want." After he hung up the phone, he had to admit he was relieved. It was always easier to let Judith handle things, and then resent her for it later.

Two months after Judith's call, Edward did go home for the holidays, and nothing seemed different. His mother cooked a big Christmas dinner; Christine's little boy was patted and paraded; Judith's beautiful young daughter watched thoughtfully; family jokes and insults were given and taken with equanimity; everyone oohed and aahed over their presents; and Robert passed around his special eggnog that no one liked but everyone drank because it seemed imperative to observe past rituals. Edward wondered if he had somehow misunderstood Judith's report.

But there was no misunderstanding the call he received almost two months ago. His father's usually amiable voice sounded tense, almost angry. "Your mother's dead. And you may as well know now, Judith has been arrested. She won't even defend herself. It's all so stupid, your mother . . . she wouldn't have lived much longer. I just can't understand why your sister . . ."

Edward had wanted to say, "I think I understand," but he realized there was no point. It wouldn't occur to his father that the facts didn't always speak for themselves. It was easier to believe that Judith had simply acted precipitately to prevent their mother's further suffering. His father would consider any other motive unthinkable. But Edward couldn't see Judith playing "Angel of Mercy," with or without premeditation. Something was terribly wrong here. "I'll be there as soon as I can," he had said and hung up without saying goodbye.

This morning, his sister had entered the courtroom as though she welcomed the expiation of a guilty verdict. But guilty of what? The responsibility of her mother's death? The interference in her sister's marriage? Emma?

Sitting on the uncomfortable bench where his father had appeared so at ease, Edward wonders what prompted his father's dinner invitation and is relieved that he didn't have the opportunity to respond. It isn't that Edward dislikes the woman his father has chosen to replace his mother, but he feels he owes Judith at least a gesture of loyalty. He knows his father wouldn't be able to understand that. "We're all on trial here," Edward says to an empty hallway. And he knows his father wouldn't understand that either.

Part Two

There was a time when meadow, grove, and stream,
The earth, and every common sight,
    To me did seem
    Apparelled in celestial light,
The glory and the freshness of a dream.
                    —WILLIAM WORDSWORTH
            "Ode on Intimations of Immortality"

2

Judith stood on the edge of the pool, legs tensely bent, eyes clenched, fiercely determined to plunge miles into her father's waiting arms. Through the darkness, she heard his voice, "Come on, baby, I'm right here."

She peeked out and saw her mother standing out of the sun, watching with more concern than encouragement. It was Judith's first visit to the public pool, and she had heard her mother call her "only three years old" and say she was afraid of someone named Polio. But her father said not knowing how to swim was more dangerous than what her mother was afraid of, and Judith was happy her father made her mother listen.

Now she looked down at her father, half buried in the water. There was no question that she would be safe when she landed. It was the falling she feared. "Come on," he en-

couraged, "I'm right here. Jump!" Taking a deep breath, Judith
sailed out toward trust.

A new world opened up, cool and pretty to look through.
There were bubbles everywhere, on the wavy legs that ran
up into a wavy red cloth, on the tips of her fingers, and big
ones right in front of her nose. When she laughed, she heard
a funny growling sound like the noises her father made when
he pretended to be like the wolf in "Little Red Riding Hood."
Then the laugh stopped, and everything became silent. She
tried to cry, but she couldn't hear that either. She could only
feel the surging pain pouring in behind her breath.

Water pushed past her face and rushed down her body,
dragging her legs straight out behind her. Suddenly she was
high in the air and heard her own cry at last. "Where were
you, Daddy? You weren't there."

"Sure I was, every minute," he laughed, hugging her and
then tossing her back into the air. "Okay, here we go again."

She wanted to scream, but before she had the chance,
he laughed, and his strong arms caved in. Again the watery
door slammed shut, and the laughter from the world above
ceased. But before the underworld noises started, she felt
herself lifting again, and crashing through the surface she
continued her journey in rhythm to her father's "Uuuuuuuuuup
we go. Isn't this fun?"

She heard her mother's quiet reproach. "Robert, I think
that's enough. She's frightened."

Judith found herself rising high in the air where she
could look down at the top of her father's head, and through
her coughing and wailing, she noticed for the first time that
he had a little spot in the middle of his head where all the
hair was gone, just like where one of her grandmother's birds
had pecked her mate. She laughed.

"It's okay, Margaret," her father said. "She likes it. She's
going to be a great swimmer."

Judith felt the strong hands rotating her fat tummy back

and forth a hundred feet in the air. She squealed with delight. "You'll win a gold medal someday," he said.

As she relaxed and let her body fly back down into the water, she thought she would like to win whatever her father wanted her to. But on the way down, she knew she had to be quiet and hold her breath.

The stars were brighter than she had ever seen them. Pointing at an entire galaxy, Judith asked, "How far away is that star, Momma?"

Her mother glanced up in the general direction indicated by her six-year-old daughter's finger. "I don't know, honey."

Judith looked to her father. "Daddy? How far?"

Robert Gregory pondered the problem for a moment. "Let's see, I can't be exact, but I'd estimate the one you're pointing at to be about four billion, six hundred million, three thousand, two and a half miles and nine inches away."

Judith lay back on the blanket and tried to see all the way to the other side of the stars, but the distance kept slipping away from her. She loved Lake Arrowhead, with its Christmas tree smells and the sudden silence when people stopped talking. Even when the noisy birds called her out of bed in the morning, she could still hear the gentle lap of the water against the dock. There were lots of things here that she didn't have at home, like stars at night and pancakes in the morning. The mornings were best. After breakfast her mother went for long walks, while she went swimming with her father. The cold lake water sat so still she could swim as far as she wanted, not like the ocean that tossed her up and down like a horse that didn't like its rider.

Judith's mother never knew the answer to the really important questions. Of course she knew where the Monopoly game was stored or where last year's Scotch plaid woolen skirt was hung, but it was her father who kept untangling the mysterious threads the world was weaving around her life. She asked her mother questions, partly because she didn't want to hurt her feelings and partly to dramatize the special relationship she enjoyed with her father. "Momma, why don't we see stars like this at home?"

Margaret looked at her husband and smiled. "I don't know, but I'm sure Daddy does."

"Daddy?" Judith didn't bother to repeat the question. Her father had heard and would answer.

"Well, honey, our house is surrounded by a big city, and at night, when everyone turns on the lights, they outshine the stars. Up here, the stars don't have to compete with other lights."

Judith always wanted to let her father know she understood his answer, even when sometimes she didn't. "Is that why you don't light up the car inside when you drive at night?"

Her father nodded his head. "Exactly. That's an excellent analogy."

Judith didn't know what that meant, but she saw her father was pleased, and that was her only concern. She didn't want to say something silly, because that always reminded her parents that it was past her bedtime.

Judith moved over and put her head on what her father called "Margaret's condition." She envied the bulge for being able to breathe without air. Her parents told her that she began in the same place, but she didn't believe it because, as hard as she tried, she could only hold her breath underwater for two lengths of a pool. Her mother had looked like this once before, a long time ago, but whatever was inside died. It must have drowned, Judith thought. "Momma, am I going to have a brother or a sister?" she asked, moving her hand across the mound under her head.

This time Margaret spoke with unusual authority. "I don't know, dear. And neither does your father."

"It'sway imetay orfay edbay," her father announced in that strange, wonderful language that her mother and father alone could speak. But she recognized what the sounds meant and regretted asking the question that ended the evening.

Years later, when Judith returned to Lake Arrowhead, the silent, crystal air she remembered had fled with the invasion of the Los Angeles smog. And the suburbs, which had crawled out of the city and wrapped themselves around the mountain's foothills, cast a glow in the night sky forcing the stars into competition. The stars were losing.

Usually the warm sounds from her parents' bedroom soothed her back to sleep, but tonight her father's voice stopped, and she heard her mother's soft cry. Judith listened for a reassuring quiet, but doors opened and slammed shut, and she heard an outsider speaking. "You go on. I'll stay with her tonight." An engine started and lights swept across her wall as though seeking hidden intruders. "Momma," Judith screamed into the dark room, but no one answered.

What had she done wrong in the middle of the night that would make them leave her with a strange voice? She stared at the little clown with the tiny light in its nose, and she tried to remember the words to the song she had learned in Sunday school. Her grandmother told her that if she believed in that song nothing could happen to her. So she sang until the clown grew dark and she couldn't hear her voice anymore.

The daylight noises were different too. No "rise and shine" commanded her out of bed, and the kitchen didn't send any smells to make getting up easier. Then her door opened, and her father moved quietly to the end of her bed. "Time to get up, honey."

"Is Momma home?" Judith asked, trying to remember last night.

"No. Remember, we talked about how the baby would be born? Well, last night we went to the hospital, and the doctor helped your mother have the baby. In a few days, you'll get to meet your new baby sister. Now you have to help me take care of things until your mother comes home."

Judith wasn't sure how she felt about having a new baby sister, but she liked the idea of taking care of things. "Can I fix breakfast?"

"Sounds good to me. I'm starved." He sounded just like he was talking to her mother, and she liked the way that made her feel. "By the way," he added, "your grandmother wants to come over and keep you company when I go to work. She thought you might like some suggestions on how to run things. Okay?"

Judith loved her grandmother. On Sundays, while Judith's parents slept late, Grandma Rose would always come and take Judith to church. Her grandmother sang the best of anyone in church, and Judith loved standing next to her and listening to her sing her favorite song about an old rug and cross on a hill far away and how she loved the cross and Gladly, the cross-eyed bear.

Everyone, even the minister, called her Sister. "It's like a great big family," her grandmother told her.

Judith couldn't figure out why her parents didn't seem to be part of the family. "If you're all sisters and brothers, why don't Momma and Daddy ever come to visit their relatives?" Judith asked.

Her grandmother made a little clicking sound, like the one she made when she wanted her parakeet's attention. "When your mother was a little girl like you, she came every Sunday. But your father hasn't accepted Jesus into his heart yet." Jesus was just a little baby, and Judith couldn't see why her father wouldn't like him.

Judith walked into the kitchen, where her father was pouring a cup of coffee. "Do you like babies, Daddy?"

"Of course. Don't you?" he asked.

"Then why don't you like Jesus?"

Her father looked annoyed. "What are you talking about? Who told you that?"

From the sound of his voice, Judith sensed she should

keep her grandmother out of the conversation. "You don't go to church. And my Sunday school teacher says that's where Jesus lives. So I thought maybe you didn't like him."

"Judith, I'm tired. You have to be a big girl and help me get the house ready for your mother and the baby. And mind your grandmother."

"If I get to take care of things, why do I have to mind Grandma?" she asked suspiciously.

"Because I said so," he said. That was an answer other people like teachers gave, but this was the first time her father sounded like them. Judith suspected having a baby must change people. She began to understand why her father didn't like baby Jesus.

As her father backed out of the driveway, Judith stood stock still on the porch, her hand thrust palm out, her mouth frozen open in that annoying way even bright children have of appearing slightly retarded. She was trying to warn him that the puppy had sneaked out the back door, but he just waved back at her as he eased the car down the driveway, turned out onto the street, and headed for the center of town.

Judith carried the puppy's limp body from the driveway into the kitchen, where Margaret Gregory was not so much cleaning up the last of the breakfast mess as she was attacking it. Judith's mother was fond of saying that when you hated housework as much as she did, cleaning should always be an act of revenge. So she constantly avenged herself on dirt and chaos, the result being a spotless, well-ordered house.

Judith watched her mother move around the kitchen with military precision, driving back the enemy, wiping tabletops, storing cereal containers, and whisking milk, butter, and jam into the refrigerator. Judith's three-year-old sister, Christine, was trying unsuccessfully to slow the assault by catching at her mother's skirt. At ten, Judith still had not forgiven Christine for entering the world. She made allowances for Edward, the baby born twelve months after Christine, but it was Christine who had first burst through the barricade of Judith's safe, uncontested province. After that, Edward hardly mattered.

Judith wasn't sure if it was her mother's "Oh my God" or the sight of blood trickling only slightly from the puppy's nose that brought Christine's piercing wails. In an instant, her mother took Christine by the hand, moved without panic to sweep Edward from the playpen, and headed for the door. "Get in the car," Margaret ordered.

Strapped in his car seat, her baby brother supported Christine's hysteria by sobbing mechanically. Judith could hardly hear her mother's instructions to hold the puppy gently and not to move him more than necessary. But feeling the puppy against her arms, Judith knew there was nothing more for her brother and sister to cry about.

That afternoon Judith invited her friends to the puppy's funeral. Margaret dug a hole under the pine tree they decorated each Christmas, and Judith solemnly placed the little shoebox coffin in the ground. After replacing the dirt, her mother leaned the shovel against the tree, looked at the small group of mourners, and asked, "Who wants to go into the kitchen and have a wake?"

"Have what awake?" Judith asked, knowing sometimes her mother didn't bother to explain things clearly.

Her mother's laugh seemed unfair. "I mean we can have a party for the puppy."

"But the puppy can't come." Judith could feel the throat ache that always comes just before the tears.

Margaret leaned over and picked up Edward. "That's true, but we have lots of parties where we don't see the one it's for. Like the Easter Bunny at Easter or Santa Claus at Christmas." Judith had stopped believing in the Easter Bunny and Santa Claus a long time ago and suspected that the explanation was more for Christine's benefit than hers. For a change, Judith regretted being smarter than her sister.

After a cookie and milk wake, Judith followed her playmates out into the yard, where they circled Christine, taunting "The worms crawl in and the worms crawl out / And ants play pinochle on your snout." Christine sat on the ground screaming. As Judith joined in, she wondered if the others were as frightened of the words as she was. It seemed only her little sister had the sense to understand that the words they sang were frightening. But the more Judith felt fear, the louder she sang.

That night her father came home with a box that made noise through the holes in the top. "This is for you," he said, setting the box on the floor. Her father lifted out a squirming duplicate and held it out to her. "I'm really sorry, honey. Can you forgive me?"

Judith wanted to reach out and claim the tiny substitute, but instead she said, "Give it to Christine. She's the one who cried all day." She was sorry her father looked hurt, but she didn't know how to explain that it was her fault for leaving the door open. If she accepted this newcomer, it would be like she never cared about her own puppy, not even enough to be punished. But she didn't want to hurt his feelings. "I'm tired of having a puppy. Christine wants one of her own, anyway," she said.

Christine reached up, begging to take the little animal. Judith took it from her father and put it into her sister's arms. "Don't squeeze it, or it will die," she warned.

Later in the darkness, Judith crept into the nursery. Her brother slept soundly in his crib, and her sister was spread out on her bed with her arm across her new pet. Judith carefully moved Christine's arm and picked up the sleepy dog. "You don't belong to me. But I'll take care of you anyway," she whispered.

Margaret Gregory moved at a steady pace, setting the table, wrapping last-minute packages, then ducking back into the kitchen to make sure no dish had the temerity to cook more slowly or rapidly than dictated. The scent of cooling pies and cloved ham trespassed into the living room and mingled with the pine fragrance. Judith shut her eyes and breathed in Christmas.

Christine circled the Christmas tree, stalking the brightly wrapped boxes piled under the tree. She picked up one and shook it, but its secret was secure beneath the blue snow-flaked paper and the tightly drawn red bow.

Her mother detoured to the Christmas tree on her way to the kitchen and reached for the present in Christine's hand. "If you know what's inside, it will spoil Christmas," she warned her younger daughter.

"I wasn't trying to peek," Christine protested.

Judith flopped down on the floor to play with her little brother. "Can I take Eddie and Christine caroling tomorrow?" she asked.

Christine still clung to the package, more to hold her mother still than to defy her. "Can I go with Judith?" she pleaded.

Her mother gently lifted the little box from Christine's hand. "Yes, if you promise to mind her and not to wander off." Then Margaret turned to Judith. "You can take Christine, but I think Eddie is too much for you to handle."

Judith pushed Eddie's toy car back and forth in front of him, blowing noises across her vibrating tongue simulating the sound of a race car with a defective motor. A large, scruffy dog splotched with black, brown, and white patches began growling and pulling at Judith's skirt. Two years ago, when her father brought this animal home, Eddie began calling it Puppy. Now, even though Eddie was four years old and the dog had outgrown his name, no one had attempted to change it.

Eddie laughed and grabbed for the car, doing a nearly perfect imitation of Judith's car noises. "I can handle both," she told her mother, who was continuing her journey to the kitchen. "I want to take him. Besides, Grandma is going along with the whole Sunday school class."

Margaret looked down at Judith, who was now lying flat on the floor letting Eddie run his car across her body as though it were an obstacle course. "I don't think he's much of a singer. But if you really want him along, I guess it would be all right," her mother said, but her eyes flashed the worried look she wore when her children were not within reach.

A few hours later everyone was there. Her father had come home early to make the eggnog, and her grandmother arrived with an armload of gifts. Judith knew that most of her friends waited until Christmas morning to open their presents, but she liked doing everything on Christmas Eve. First, they would all gather while her father poured the eggnog. Then, they would sit down to an early dinner. And finally, when dinner seemed like it would never end, her father always said, "I think there are a few things under the tree that should be opened."

It was the one night that her mother would leave the dirty dishes sitting on the table and settle comfortably on the sofa to watch her young demolition squad wreak havoc on the carefully decorated scene. Red paper showing Santa Claus and reindeer landing on houses, blue paper with children playing in the snow, gold ribbons, silver bows—all went flying as boxes were torn apart.

Eddie screamed with delight as he zoomed around the room on his first three-wheel bike. Christine ran to kiss her grandmother for granting her wish—a shapely, red-haired Barbie doll. "She doesn't look very respectable to me," her grandmother said, examining the doll. The smile on her face assured Judith that her grandmother was secretly pleased at seeing Christine so happy.

Judith watched Christine and Eddie playing with their gifts and was surprised to find that toys no longer interested her. Instead, she was content just to watch her brother and sister having such a good time. She had no memory of a time when she resented sharing her home with them. In fact, sometimes she pretended they were her own children. She could dress them up, play with them, and even boss them around when she thought they misbehaved. They were better than dolls.

Then her mother was standing beside her. "This is for you," she said, handing Judith a plainly wrapped box.

Judith unwrapped the package slowly, enjoying the suspense. When she removed the lid and folded back the tissue paper, she saw a beautiful, pale green cashmere sweater. She had seen this sweater when she was shopping with her mother and had reached out to stroke its smooth green softness. But when she saw the price tag, she hadn't dared to ask for it. "This is just what I wanted," she said, kissing her mother on the cheek.

Judith ran upstairs, unbuttoning her blouse as she went. Standing in front of the mirror, she slipped on the sweater. She loved it; it matched her eyes perfectly. The only thing that bothered her were the two, almost imperceptible protrusions underneath. She hoped no one would notice them.

When she showed off her sweater a few minutes later, her father said, "You look lovely," and her grandmother commented, "You're getting to be a big girl." Judith liked the idea of growing up.

"I love my present, Momma. How did you know I wanted it?"

Margaret Gregory smiled at her daughter. "I was paying attention," she said.

"Big girls don't sit on their fathers' laps," Robert Gregory said, gently easing Judith onto the seat next to him.

Judith felt her father's new rule had something to do with the talk they were having. Her grandmother had brought her home from church and then had taken her brother and sister for a walk. Now her mother sat silently while her father looked serious and explained how men had penises and women had vaginas and breasts. Judith knew about those things, of course, but her father was so serious she didn't want to interrupt him. She already knew that Christine and Eddie had come from her mother's stomach and got fed from her mother's breasts. Only a few days before she had stood in front of the mirror and put her own new soft swellings in the palms of her hands. She was examining them when her father walked in to tell her dinner was ready. She couldn't understand why he kept apologizing to her. What had he done wrong?

Judith tried to pay attention when he started talking about how penises worked. She had seen one often enough when she helped change Eddie's diapers, but she thought it would fall off after a while, like the cords he and Christine had on their stomachs when they came home. But one day, when she walked into the bathroom while her father was soaking in the bathtub, she saw it floating on the water. That was when she realized that Eddie would always look strange. Now, as her father explained that penises carried little bugs that got loose and swam around in a woman's tubes, she was glad she didn't have one.

"This is nature's way of letting men and women love each other and have children. Do you understand?" her father asked.

If it was nature's way of making people love each other, why was he pushing her away and acting differently toward her? It had something to do with the bugs getting inside her, but she couldn't figure out how that could happen. She didn't want to know what she didn't understand, because she was afraid if she knew, she would change too.

"Yes, I understand," she said.

3

Christine surveyed the room she had always wanted. This was where no one ever came without knocking first, not even her own father. It had its own phone, which sat on the old oak desk that used to be in her father's old office at the newspaper. An overstuffed chair, passed down from grandmother to daughter to granddaughter, stood in front of a large bay window that framed the Santa Monica Mountains in the distance. For years Christine had watched Judith sit here and read, letting the natural light from the window fall across her book. And in the evenings when she passed by the closed door, she could hear her sister's murmured words as she exchanged secrets over the telephone with unseen friends.

Now that Judith was going away to school, this room was hers. Christine had grown tired of the wallpaper birds and butterflies in her room. She could hardly wait to hang her posters on these bare, white walls and rearrange the desk so that she could look out at the sharp mountain ridges as she worked. Christine curled up in the old chair that had never lost her grandmother's scent of lavender and watched Judith pack. "When will you be home?" she asked, pulling her legs under her body until she resembled an adolescent amputee.

Judith tossed a pink flannel nightgown into her suitcase. Then she began checking closets and drawers to make sure she hadn't left anything important behind. "I don't know. Why, will you miss me?"

Having Judith around was like having a second mother, only her real mother never did things just to be mean. Once in a while Christine still had bad dreams about the time Judith marched around her, screaming about worms crawling in and out. "Of course I'll miss you," Christine answered.

Judith stopped moving around and for the first time seemed to pay attention. "I didn't realize until now how much I'm going to miss you and Eddie. If it weren't for the scholarship, I wouldn't have gone so far away. Maybe I made a mistake. Maybe I should have gone to school here."

Christine considered the scholarship another prize Judith had won, like all the trophies she received for being a good swimmer. She hoped Judith wouldn't give it back, because otherwise she might not move away, and Christine would have to stay in her old room. "Are you sure you don't mind if I move in here?" Christine asked, trying to make up for being glad Judith was going.

"Why should I mind? It's your turn. You're almost eleven years old now, and you'll have to help Mom with Eddie and the house. So you deserve the best room. Besides, when I come home, I can stay in your old room and pretend I'm a little girl again. I remember the night you were born; that light kept me company all night," she said, pointing to the little clown's face that was plugged into the wall beside her bed. "I brought it with me when I moved into this room. Do you mind if I take it with me to Berkeley to remind me of you? You can do anything you want with the rest of the stuff in here."

Christine didn't know what her sister was talking about, but she had noticed a long time ago that Judith always talked to her like her father did, with long explanations. She preferred the way her mother just gave a simple yes or no.

"You can have your room back after you finish college," Christine offered reluctantly.

"When I leave Berkeley, I'll get a job and have a real place of my own. Then you and Eddie can come and visit me whenever you want. Would you like that?"

Christine thought she would rather stay right here. "Maybe I'll come up and visit you at school."

Judith closed a small suitcase. "Mom and Dad can bring you up for the first swim meet."

Christine used to like to watch Judith swim. The water had a magic power to make her sister's blond, wavy hair turn long, dark, and straight and to change her everyday green eyes to deep blue. Christine would catch her parents' pride and clap with delight when this tall, thin, dripping wet stranger climbed out of the pool and reached for her gold trophy. But that was before Christine learned to hate swimming. "Can I put these in the closet?" she asked, indicating the trophies that sat on the shelves, little patches of dark metal showing beneath the peeling surface.

Judith studied the mementos for a minute, then shrugged, "Sure, why not. With luck, I'll win some new ones next year."

"Do you know who your roommate will be?" Christine asked, trying to imagine sharing a room with a total stranger.

"I don't know. It's the luck of the draw. But I'm sure we'll get along. I just hope she's quiet. They say the first semester is the hardest."

Christine didn't think her sister had ever been afraid of anything. She would plunge into the water like she was sure unseen hands were there to catch her or walk into a room as though she thought everyone wanted her there. And Christine guessed everybody did want her, like all the boys who called to talk to her. Sometimes the phone rang so much that Judith asked her to say she wasn't home, even though she was sitting right there. Her parents usually punished Christine when she lied, but it was okay to say Judith wasn't home, even though she was.

Judith snapped her suitcase shut. "Can you help me carry some of this stuff downstairs?" she asked. Without answering, Christine untangled her legs and jumped up with youthful agility. Picking up two small cases, she followed Judith downstairs, where her parents were waiting by the front door.

Her mother looked up as they descended the stairs. "You'd better hurry or you'll be late," she said. Without a backward glance, her mother led the way out the front door and headed toward the car. She already had the trunk open before the rest of the family was out of the house.

It was funny how different her mother and father were. Her mother was always busy doing something. Almost before dinner was over, she would start clearing the table and cleaning the kitchen, as if sitting down was the same as being lazy. But her father would sit and talk to the rest of them until it was time to do their homework. And then, while her father read the paper, her mother would either sew, or iron, or work in the garden if there was still light. Just before time to go to bed, her mother would give them a worried bedtime kiss and stay downstairs while her father followed them upstairs to read a story. Christine remembered that when she had her tonsils out, her mother acted like it wasn't important. But when Christine woke up in the strange bed surrounded by a curtain, her mother was sitting next to her, gently stroking her hair and very softly humming one of Grandma Rose's church songs about Jesus calling her home. Her mother never played, or laughed, or even cried. She was just there, like she was waiting for something bad to happen.

But her father was different. He laughed and teased and

played games. While she was in the hospital, he brought a whole gallon of her favorite ice cream and dared her to eat it all by herself. When the cold burned her throat and made her cry, he announced he was giving a "sore throat party" and invited all the other kids in the room to join in. He went from bed to bed, dishing out ice cream and making silly faces, until she finally stopped crying and started laughing. That made her throat feel worse, but she didn't mind anymore.

Her father talked a lot too, always explaining the answer to a problem like a teacher in school. Usually, he would end his talking with "Do you understand?" and she would say she understood because her brother and sister always said they did. But there were times Christine didn't think he meant what he explained—like saying people should be themselves, and then saying Judith was a good example of what happened when you studied hard because she got to go to college free, or trying to make Eddie and her learn to swim. "Just look at Judith," he would say. "She's an example of how easy it is." That's when Christine decided she hated swimming.

Christine leaned against the car as her father finished loading the last of Judith's belongings into the trunk. She thought Judith looked sad when he reached out and shook her hand. "We're going to miss you, honey. Just remember, we're all proud of you," he said.

Her father always shook Judith's hand when she won a contest or got good grades or, like now, when she was going away. But when Christine got the "Good Citizenship" award at school or went away to camp, her father kissed her or hugged her shoulders and said, "That's my girl" or "Be a good girl." He only shook hands with Judith, never with her or Eddie, or even their mother for that matter.

Judith held her father's hand and said, "Can I give you a kiss good-bye?"

"You're too big for your old dad to kiss," he laughed. "You should save your kisses for all the handsome young men who will be after you at school. Just don't pass them out too freely," he said, giving her hand one last firm shake.

Judith turned, bent slightly, and kissed Christine lightly on the cheek. "Be a good girl and study hard. I'll write to you as soon as I get settled," she said. Then she turned to her brother, dropped down on one knee and embraced him. "Bye, baby. I'll miss our 'go out nights.' Plan a good one for my Christmas vacation."

Eddie seemed pleased that Judith had chosen him to plan the next family outing. Each one in the family took turns planning one evening out a month. Her mother usually found a flower show or just settled for a drive in the foothills; her father always chose a symphony; and Christine could be depended on for the latest movie. But with Eddie it was always a different choice—one time the zoo, another time a walk on the beach, and once even a trip to the downtown library. When Eddie was just a baby, he started calling them his "go out nights," and Judith said it was a perfect description of their monthly outings.

"Can I come visit you at Berkeley?" her brother asked.

"I wish you could come with me now. You'd probably be able to help me with my papers," Judith laughed. Christine knew her sister was talking about the "go out night" her family went to see *King Lear*. It was about an old king who lost everything because his daughters didn't help him. Judith had insisted they go to see it because she was reading it in her English class. After the play, Eddie argued with Judith when she said the king's daughters were monsters. He claimed the old man got what he deserved. Christine didn't like the play, but Eddie said she just didn't understand it. Maybe she didn't, but he didn't have to be so stuck-up about being smart. Besides, her mother must not have liked it either, because when the king carried his dead daughter on the stage and started screaming, her mother cried.

As Judith opened the car door, her mother stepped forward and handed Judith a small box wrapped in yellow paper with a white bow in the middle. "I bought some blue stationery with your name on it. Be careful driving," she cautioned. Then she leaned over and gave Judith a bedtime kiss on the cheek.

Judith smiled. "You shouldn't have told me. It would have been like a surprise waiting for me when I got to school."

"There will be plenty of surprises waiting for you. I don't think you'll need any from me. Just remember, we're here if you need us."

For a moment, Judith's face wore the same hesitant look it did when her father shook her hand, and Christine was afraid she might not leave. Finally, Judith smiled and got into the car. "I'll miss all of you," she said, waving before she had even started the engine.

As she watched Judith pull out of the driveway, Christine waved back, trying not to think about how nice it was going to be to have the best room in the house all to herself.

Judith's first letter started a family ritual. Her mother waited until dinner was finished and then brought the bright blue envelope to the table. Her father reached for it. "The envelope please." And opening it, he proclaimed, "And the winner is..." Then he read:

October 2, 1962

Dearest Family,

I love everything about Berkeley. The campus is beautiful, and my classes are all interesting. My roommate's name is Karen. Dad, you'd hate what she plays. Hi-Fi—Elvis Presley. I can't get much work done in my room, so I go to the library to study.

Everyone is talking about what happened at the University of Mississippi. I can't believe that two people actually died just because some colored student wanted to go to school.

I met a Negro girl named Sara who is studying to be a doctor. She went with the Freedom Riders on a bus trip to Alabama and tells some pretty grim stories. She probably exaggerates just to make what she did sound dangerous. We have a lot of Negroes here, and no one seems to pay any attention to them.

I have to study for a chemistry test so I better sign off. (Why do they make P.E. majors take the same courses doctors do? It's stupid.)

I love and miss you all,
Judith

P.S. The pool is terrific here. I can't wait until I see you for the first swim meet.

P.P.S. Christine, Thank you for your letter. It sounds like you had a special feeling for what you saw. Get Dad to take you to the Huntington. It has a good collection, and, as I recall, Mom loves the gardens.

Love and xxxes

Her father handed the letter to her mother. "It sounds like she's off to the right start," he said.

"What are Freedom Riders?" Christine asked her father.

"They're a group of people from all over the country who go to states in the South and work so Negroes will have a better life."

It sounded like fun, and Christine wished she could take a trip like that. "Is Judith going to go with them?" she asked.

"I don't know. But if she did, we should be proud of her."

Her mother took the folded letter and slipped it back into the envelope. "It sounds a little dangerous to me," she said, starting to clear the table.

As her father finished his coffee, he asked Christine, "What did Judith mean when she said 'you had a special feeling for what you saw'?"

Christine could still see the vivid colors in the picture of a woman who had two faces pointing in different directions and a body that had breasts where they couldn't really be. She wanted to describe it to him, but the picture's sharp lines didn't translate into words. "Our art class went to see a Spanish painter. I can't remember his name. One picture looked like a woman who had been broken up into pieces and painted back together the way he wanted her."

"Sounds like Picasso," her brother said. When Eddie said something, it sounded like he had just read it in a book. She almost felt sorry for him since they advanced him into her grade, he was so little compared to everyone else. She and her brother used to be about the same size, but in the past few years he stayed little as she grew, until now her friends had begun to call her "Fatty." Each day she vowed she would never eat again, but by dinnertime hunger obliterated her resolve, and she ate more than ever. But at least she wasn't a shrimp like her brother. All her friends admitted that he was the smartest boy in school, but she knew they thought he was strange.

The next week, her father took the family to the museum. As they walked across the grounds, her mother stopped and knelt in front of a deep red rose. "I wish I could grow mine to be this beautiful," she said. "You go inside and look at the pictures. I'll stay here for a while."

Christine was disappointed. She wanted to show her mother how lovely pictures could be too. "Come with us. I'm sure they have pictures of flowers hanging all over," she teased.

"I'm sure they do, dear. But the pictures will always be there, and this rose won't."

Everyone in the family knew that her mother didn't know a lot of things that they learned in school. Christine wanted to teach her. "But Dad says some of the pictures are on loan, and he said that means they won't be here forever, so that's the same thing as this rose," Christine explained patiently.

"Perhaps, but they will always be someplace for people to see them. This will be gone soon," she said, pointing to the perfect flower, "and no one will ever see it again. When something can't last, I think it's very important to pay close attention to it while we can." Her mother smiled and gently pushed Christine toward the museum. "You go enjoy the pictures. I'll stay here and look at the real thing."

For the next two hours, Christine went from room to room with her brother and father, while her mother walked in the gardens. In one gallery, Christine was startled by a picture of a field that was plowed into long, straight, yellow-and-green lines. Inside, the furrows were filled with violet and blue. Cutting across the field, an even deeper trough of blazing colors crashed violently forward like a wave. The only thing holding it back was a brick wall in the distance. Beyond the wall loomed dark mountains and trees. And above everything, a burning sun beat down on mountain, tree, and field, radiating so much yellow heat that it was painful to look at. Everything in the picture's world was divided. The field, mountains, sun—all looked like they wanted to touch but couldn't. There was something about this picture that frightened Christine. Suddenly she was aware of her brother and father standing next to her. "I don't think I like this painting," she said.

Eddie looked at the painting. "When Van Gogh painted it, no one else liked it either. Maybe that's why he killed himself a few months later."

"That's what I call taking art seriously," his father laughed.

Christine didn't like her father's joke. She couldn't think of a good enough reason for anyone to kill himself. It almost made her sick to think about it, especially when she had already decided that she wanted to paint pictures when she grew up. She hated it when her younger brother spoiled things by saying what she didn't want to know. Christine thought about her mother waiting outside, enjoying the fresh spring flowers. "Maybe Mom's right. Some pictures don't look very real."

Her father appeared to agree. "I have to admit it doesn't look like any landscape I've ever seen," he said.

Eddie continued to study the painting. "I think if Mom saw this, she'd say it was the real thing."

Her brother never agreed with anyone, no matter what. "You think you're so smart," Christine said, moving away from the painting.

"My God, where did my little sister go?" Judith said when she came home for the summer. "Someone introduce me to this beautiful young woman." Then Judith held Christine at arm's length and examined her more closely. "I hope you're not dieting too much. You've lost a lot of weight."

Christine had made everyone promise they wouldn't tell Judith how she was changing. She wanted to surprise her. Her body was taking shape, as though it were the material of an invisible sculptor's hand, tightening the waist, filling out the hips, shaping the breasts. She knew she would never be as tall as Judith, nor as slim, but that was all right. Her darker, fuller beauty was her own, not like her sister's. Suddenly, she realized she was glad to have Judith home again. It was nice having an older sister to confide in. As Judith carried her bags upstairs, Christine asked, "Would you like your room back?"

"Of course not. It's your room now. I don't belong there anymore. Besides, the wallpaper in your old room keeps me company." But Judith didn't act like she really wanted company. It wasn't that she was quiet exactly. It was more like she was watchful. When Christine told her about the dumb boy who asked her to the junior high dance, Judith appeared to be listening with her eyes. "The world is so different from what I thought it was. Not everyone is as lucky as you and Eddie," she said. Something about the way she said it made Christine feel like she shouldn't be happy about being lucky.

*   *   *

In August, Judith said she wanted to visit her friend Sara. "You remember her, Dad. She's the girl you met when you came to the swim meet this spring."

Christine hadn't seen her sister's last competition because she had the flu and had to stay home. So her father and Eddie went alone. When they returned, both were strangely quiet. Eddie acted like he had returned to a house full of interesting strangers who invited careful study. And although her father reported that Judith had come in first in the freestyle event, he didn't smile his usual proud smile. He just said, "I met Judith's Negro friend. I don't like what's going on."

Now Judith stood facing her father, waiting for him to answer. "I remember," he said, as though it were a memory he didn't want.

Judith waited for her father to say something more, and when he didn't, she continued, "I have another month before school starts, and I want to work on some projects before I return to the old grind. You don't mind, do you?" Christine sensed Judith wasn't really asking for permission. It was more like she was being polite.

Two weeks later her father opened the envelope her mother handed him. "And the winner is . . ."

August 20, 1963

Dear Mom and Dad,

I won't be coming back before school starts. Sara and I have decided to room together this year. She has a great little place just off campus. I'm going to be busy moving my stuff into her apartment. Then I'm going to Washington with her and some other friends who own a van. Martin Luther King will be there and he needs all the support he can get. I'll call you from Washington.

Love,
Judith

A few nights later, Christine and her family watched the television and saw what she thought must be every Negro in the world standing quietly listening to a man who talked about crossing over into the promised land. She didn't understand why Judith went so far to hear him speak. She could have stayed home and gone to her grandmother's church, where the minister sounded the same.

"Judith's getting a little carried away," her father said.

Judith didn't visit as often as she did the first year, and Christine was glad because, over the past year, discussions had turned into arguments, and eventually arguments had turned into fights. Every time Judith came home it was the same thing. She would rush into the house and hug and kiss everyone. Then for the next few hours she would ask Christine about her art classes and Eddie about the latest book he was reading. But by the time they sat down to dinner, she and her father would already have begun to argue about things Christine thought were silly. Why did it matter so much what was happening so far away to people they didn't even know? It certainly didn't seem important enough for her sister and father to fight about.

On her last visit, Judith accused her father of not taking a stand in his newspaper against what she called "America's middle-class hypocrisy." And he said, "It seems to me you're the living image of a middle-class girl. We have nothing to be ashamed of in this family, and I resent your attitude." There was something in his voice Christine had never heard. The only word she could think to describe his new tone was "mean," but she knew that wasn't quite right. During these arguments, her mother kept silent, her eyes dark and worried. Finally, Christine changed her mind about looking forward to her sister's visits. Now she wished Judith wouldn't come home at all.

She didn't write very often either, and when she did she only wrote about terrible things that seemed to be the family's fault: *My God, last year Evers is murdered on his doorstep, then four little black girls are blown to bits in their church, and now those crazy people in Birmingham are turning fire hoses and dogs on children. How can we just stand by and let these things happen?*

With each letter, her mother's expression became more worried. And her father stopped saying, "The envelope please." Finally, her mother just said, "We got a letter from Judith. It's on the desk."

September 24, 1964

Dear Mom and Dad,

It's worse here than in Mississippi. At least there they don't pretend to believe in free speech. The other day I noticed for the first time the two copper plaques that read: "Property of the Regents, University of California. Permission to enter or pass over is revocable at any time." I guess Berkeley giveth freedom and Berkeley can taketh it away.

I've decided that I would make a pretty bad P.E. teacher, so I've decided to be a lawyer.

J

A few weeks later, Judith's roommate called, introduced herself, and asked to speak to Margaret Gregory. "It's for you," Christine said, handing her mother the phone. "It's Sara."

Her mother seemed to know what Sara hadn't said yet, because she asked, "What's the trouble?" even before Sara had the chance to tell her there was any. And after that her mother only listened until she finally thanked Sara and told her good-bye. After she hung up, she turned to Christine. "Can you and Edward manage the house? Your father and I will have to go to your sister."

But when her father came home early from work, he didn't act like he was going anywhere. "Just what in the hell does she think she's doing?" he shouted. "Do you realize they may not let her graduate?"

Apparently, her mother did not care, because the answer she gave had nothing to do with his questions. "I've made flight reservations. We have to go there, right now."

"The hell we do. She got herself into this, now let her get herself out," he said, pouring himself a drink. "We should never have sent her to that goddamn school."

"Then I'll go alone," her mother said quietly.

Christine felt invisible as she watched her mother move with resolution toward the door. She couldn't remember her mother ever going away by herself, except to go shopping, of course, or to visit Grandmother Rose. It was always her father who went away on business. Christine hoped she had changed her mind when she stopped at the door and said, "Robert, are you sure you don't want to fly up with me? Sara said she would meet us at the airport. I think Judith would want you there."

"No, I'll stay with the children. Do you have enough money?" And then more to himself than to anyone, "My God, arrested."

"She was only carrying a sign, not robbing a bank," her mother said. "Sara said all we had to do was come up and they would release her into our custody."

"I don't think it would help matters if I go. Maybe she'll talk to you," he said.

"You're the one she cares about. She always looked to you. Don't punish her for trying to grow up," her mother said.

"Trying to grow up!" he exploded. "How? By breaking the law? Next you'll be excusing her for acting like a wh—" Her mother's dark eyes narrowed, and the look on her face frightened Christine. Her father must have seen it too, because his rigid shoulders sagged, and he said, "All right, all right. Tell her I love her."

Her mother touched his arm and said, "Christine can fix

dinner for everyone tonight. I'll call you as soon as I can." Then for the first time she seemed to notice her daughter. "Christine, I'm counting on you to take care of business until I get back."

"Sure, don't worry. Tell Judith I said 'Hi.' " Christine knew it was a silly message, but she couldn't think of anything else to say.

After her mother had gone, her father slumped down in his chair. "You go ahead and do whatever you have to, honey. Everything's going to be fine." The way he sounded made Christine embarrassed for him. As she started upstairs, Christine saw him put his head down and sensed his tears. Before she got to her room, she hated her sister.

When Judith came home with her mother, she was wearing an old-looking skirt belted with a thick rope. It dangled unevenly around her ankles. Her long, uncombed hair hung in strings to her shoulders. Nothing reminded Christine of the clean, wet sister who swam for her trophies. Her father didn't even move to shake her hand when she walked into the house. He just looked at her and asked, "What kind of an example do you think you're setting for your brother and sister?"

Christine wanted to tell her father not to worry. She was glad that her sister had changed because now nobody talked about being like her. When Judith tried to embrace her, Christine stepped back and turned her head. She didn't want to be associated with this person who had caused so much trouble. But Judith looked more hurt than insulted. Then Eddie put his arms around Judith and laughed, "You look like Cinderella before her fairy godmother cleaned her up."

Christine held her breath against the embarrassed silence that usually surrounds strangers who are forced upon each other, like people pushed together in an elevator. "I'll go upstairs and change," Judith said the same way someone might have said, "Let me off on this floor, please."

A little while later Judith came downstairs. Her hair, still wet from the shower, was pulled back in a ponytail. She was dressed in clean blue jeans and a plaid shirt that Eddie must have loaned her. Christine had stopped growing, while her brother continued to get taller and skinnier. Now he was as tall as Judith and as thin. But the clothes knew the difference. They made Eddie look like a gawky scarecrow. On Judith, they became sleek and graceful.

During dinner, Christine waited for someone to say how good the food was. She had called her grandmother to find out how to make her Sunday chicken. It was the first time Christine had cooked a whole meal by herself, working all day to make sure everything was perfect. Even the cupcakes with the powdered white frosting had turned out right. But no one mentioned the food. Instead, her father and sister started to argue.

"Just remember, young lady, if it hadn't been for this middle-class life you criticize so much, we couldn't have sent you to that damn school," her father said.

"You didn't 'send' me. I earned a scholarship, and you were proud of me, as I recall."

Her mother got up to pour the coffee. "Maybe we should talk about this after dinner," she said quietly.

Her father shook his head. "No, I think we should talk about it now." Then his voice softened, and he turned back to Judith. "I'm still proud of you," he sighed. "I just don't understand your attitude. Why can't you change the world without condemning ours?"

When Judith didn't answer, he repeated the question he had asked a lot lately. "What are you trying to prove?"

And she gave the same answer she usually did. "I'm not trying to prove anything." But this time she added, "I don't have to. Not anymore."

"What's *that* supposed to mean?"

"It means I'm doing what you used to say was impor-tant—I am being myself."

Her father slammed his coffee cup into its saucer, black

liquid staining the crisp white cloth. "Do you think you're being yourself by looking like a tramp and spouting the latest gibberish from illiterate folk songs?" he shouted as the rest of the family looked down at their plates.

Through the silence that followed, everyone heard Judith's whispered "Fuck you."

It happened so fast, her father out of his chair, her mother's cry as Judith's hand came up too late to stop the slap, and the look on her father's face when his daughter ran from the room.

Judith didn't come home after that.

Her grandmother's voice reminded Christine of dried October leaves. It rustled and never got loud, not even when they were young and she or her brother broke something her grandmother liked. She still brought presents when she came to visit and talked about how big Christine was getting, even though she was fourteen years old and hadn't grown for over a year.

But tonight, when her grandmother came to visit, no one appeared happy. Her father didn't give her the usual light kiss on the cheek. He just said, "Good evening, Rose." And her mother didn't even say hello. Instead she announced, "We'll talk about this in the other room." Then turning to her son and daughter she said, "You go upstairs and do your studies. Your grandmother can come up later and say goodbye."

Christine waited until she knew they had forgotten her, and then she crept out of her room and hid at the top of the stairs so she could listen as her grandmother discussed what she called "Judith's problem." From the sound of his voice, Christine couldn't tell if her father was angry because of "the problem" or because Judith refused to solve it.

"What do you mean, she doesn't want to get married? Has she given any thought to what is best for the child?" Christine heard him demand of an unseen listener.

Her grandmother sounded like she didn't like saying the words. "She says the baby would be better off with no father than a bad one."

Then his voice, louder than theirs, "Her place is here, at home."

"That will only make matters worse, Robert," she said. "There would be too much tension here. She needs forgiveness."

"Rose, you dragged that girl off to church every Sunday for years trying to save her soul. It doesn't seem to have done much good," he said. And then more quietly, "As for forgiveness, I can't imagine her asking for any."

Her grandmother's voice was stiller, and Christine had to lean forward to hear. "She's going to stay with Sara until she graduates in June, then she will live with me until the baby comes. I'm only interested in what's best for Judith."

"And then what?" he demanded.

"She's been accepted into the UCLA Law School. She'll work and go to school just the way you did."

"And just who will take care of the child?" he asked.

"You seem to forget that I raised Margaret by myself. And I think your daughter will do as well."

"That was a little different," he said. "You were a widow. She's a—"

Her mother's voice snapped all the way to the top of the stairs, reminding Christine of the warning it held just before she or Eddie was about to do something wrong. "Robert!" And then, as though some danger had passed, she said, "Judith has made her decision. There's nothing else to talk about. We mustn't do anything to drive her farther away."

"Drive her away? I want her to come home. She's the one driving us away."

Christine could barely hear her mother's "Give her time. She'll grow and forgive."

Christine felt a familiar anger. What did Judith have to forgive? She was the one that was causing all the trouble.

Suddenly she heard a noise behind her and turned to see her brother standing in the shadows on the landing above her. She was afraid he might say something and give her away. Instead, he walked into his room, slamming the door loudly behind him. After that, Christine didn't hear any more voices.

At least once a week after dinner her mother would unwrap some new package, gently lift a tiny jersey nightgown or a little knitted blanket out of tissue paper and present it to the family. "She'll need the basic things," she said.

Her father's nod of approval didn't fit his response. "I don't know what she's going to do," he would say. Or "What would she do if you or her grandmother weren't there?"

Her mother's response was always the same. "She'd manage."

Christine couldn't understand why her mother acted like Judith had done something right, instead of something wrong. When a girl in Christine's class got pregnant, the principal wouldn't let her come to school anymore, and she lost all her friends. Even her grandmother, who was forever talking about sin and evil, didn't seem to be upset that Judith had "gotten into trouble," as they said about the girl in school.

"Why is it okay for Judith to do anything she wants, and I can't even go out on a date in a car?" she asked her mother.

"You'll have plenty of time to decide what you want. And when you do, you will have to live with those decisions for the rest of your life."

"And so will we," her father added, picking up the evening paper.

The one thing Christine wanted was to be able to say what she thought, but she never knew how. It wasn't that she was shy exactly. She had lots of friends at school, and she was usually elected to some class office. She suspected people liked her because she said what they expected her to say, not what she sometimes felt. There were times she wanted to defend her sister when her friends joked about Judith's pregnancy. Instead, she walked away.

Now that her mother was running around buying presents for her sister like she had won some prize, Christine couldn't tell her mother that she had two different feelings running in opposite directions. She didn't want to be like Judith, but she envied her all the attention. "Well, I'm ashamed of her, even if you're not," she said.

Christine stepped back when her mother's eyes flashed dark and angry, and she said, "Don't you ever say anything like that again. She's your sister."

Christine didn't see what being her sister had to do with it. If the girl in her school were her sister, she still would have been suspended and lost all her friends. "It isn't fair," she said. "Judith gets away with whatever she wants. Maybe I should rob a bank or something."

Her brother looked up from the book he was reading. "You don't have the nerve."

Eddie irritated her lately. All he did was make snotty remarks and sulk around reading books he had hidden all over the house. In fact, everybody irritated her lately, but she didn't know how to tell them. "At least I don't sneak around reading dirty books and writing weird stories," she said, not liking the sound of her own voice.

"You should. It might do you some good," her brother said without looking up from his book.

Her father put his newspaper aside. "What are you reading, Ed?"

"D. H. Lawrence," Edward said, laying his book aside. "He's a good writer."

"So they say," his father said and went back to his paper.

Christine had never felt so angry and helpless. She wanted to scream at all of them. Couldn't they see how she felt?

"Christine," her mother said, as if she were answering Christine's unasked question. "We are a family. If none of us had faults, we wouldn't need each other. But that's not the way life is. There may come a time when you have trouble. And if that time ever comes, the only people you can count on to take care of business will be your family. Remember that!" It was the only time Christine could remember her mother making what sounded like a speech.

After Emma was born everything changed again. The arguments and anger stopped, and a new routine settled on the household. Sometimes Christine went to see the baby and help her grandmother, and sometimes Eddie would offer to go along to mow the lawn or weed the garden. But from the night Emma was born, Christine's mother never visited Judith again.

Her father never went either. Every night he asked how the day went, and her mother would tell him about whom she had seen at the grocery store or what new flower had appeared in the garden. But she never mentioned Judith or the baby. Her father listened, appeared interested, but always seemed like he was waiting for something more to be said. One night after dinner, he said, "Sooner or later she will come for a visit." And finally she did.

Her father greeted Judith at the door as though she were a new acquaintance he was nervously eager to please. He reached out toward the bundle Judith carried. "So this is what everyone's talking about," he said, carefully lifting the triangle tip of the blanket that covered Emma's sleeping face.

Christine had to admit Emma was the prettiest baby she had ever seen. She wasn't bald like most babies; her hair was a light curly mass; and her eyes were almost black.

"Would you like to hold her?" Judith asked, presenting Emma to him like a peace offering.

Her father looked embarrassed. "I was never much good with babies," he said. "I'm afraid they'll break."

Judith had changed. She was softer, quieter. "You should have learned by now that they don't," she said.

*　　*　　*

Christine turned east, away from the ocean, dreading the dangerous drive up the narrow, winding canyon road that led to her sister's house. Last month the rain had swept mud and rocks out of mountains, washing away parts of the curving road. She tried to avoid the ruts without getting too near the edge, where she imagined herself missing a turn and plunging miles to the bottom of the canyon. When she finally pulled up in front of the run-down little house where her sister had moved, her hands were sweating, and the back of her blouse was soaked.

Balancing her daughter on her hip, Judith greeted Christine at the door. "Welcome to Shangri-la," she said. "I call it my cabin—it's a nice euphemism for shack."

Inside, the place was clean but disordered. The bedroom was where the living room should have been, and bookshelves separated by cinder blocks lined the kitchen walls. As if she were reading Christine's mind, Judith explained, "I like to read when I eat."

In the middle of the living room, which was really a bedroom, a highly polished, uncluttered desk sat incongruously pristine in its surroundings. "That belongs to people who live in squalor, so I like to keep it neat and shiny for them," she explained. Christine guessed she meant the poor people she worked for, but she didn't ask.

While Emma sat on the floor inspecting her scattered toys, Christine and her sister sat on a frayed sofa drinking tea that tasted like candied apples. Christine looked around and laughed. "Mom would shape this place up in no time."

"I don't hate chaos, so I don't feel a particular need to impose order on it." It was one of her sister's casual remarks that always made Christine feel she was missing some important point.

When Christine told Judith what she wanted to do when she finished high school, her sister made it sound easy. "What's the problem? We could use a famous artist in the family."

"You don't understand. They just assume I'm going to go to college. There's going to be an argument."

Judith laughed. "They've heard arguments before. I think they might be able to survive one more." Then, as an afterthought, she asked, "Have you talked to Mom?"

"I can't talk to Mom. You know she'll just tell me to talk to Dad."

"That's not a bad idea."

But that wasn't easy for Christine. She won her school's Good Citizenship Award every year, not because she was a particularly good citizen, but because she hated to take chances or cause trouble. "I can't stand to upset him," she said.

"Sometimes I think he thrives on it." It was another one of her remarks, and Christine almost asked her to explain it, but Judith went on. "Look, it's going to be your life for a long time. Why don't you just tell him how you really feel?" Christine wanted to say she remembered the time Judith said how she really felt and because of it she never really came home again.

Christine looked at Judith. Her hair was still long, but now it was pulled back neatly in a blond mound, and she didn't wear clothes that looked old and worn anymore. It wasn't that she looked like she used to when she still had the big room and boys called her every day. She simply looked new. Christine wondered if Judith had learned the caterpillar's secret, crawling into a cocoon whenever she wanted to and, presto, emerging first as a champion swimmer, then a ragged campus protester, and now the quiet mother who worked and supported her baby. Christine was tempted to ask her if she felt like the different person she looked like.

Judith leaned down and picked up her baby, who had begun to make whimpering sounds that reminded Christine of a puppy they once had. "Are you asking me to talk to Dad for you?" she asked, as she gently tucked Emma next to her on the sofa.

"Would you?" Christine asked anxiously.

"I don't think I have too much influence with him."

"It's not a matter of influence. It's just a matter of telling him. I'm not like you, Judith. I can't say things that I know will upset people."

Her sister laughed and patted Christine's hand. "Okay, just leave it to Judith de Sade, I'll put the old thumbscrews to him for you."

A few days later, Christine's father knocked on her door. When she answered, he just stood there for a moment looking at her as though he wasn't sure who she was. Finally he said, "Your sister talked to me today. I wouldn't want to think I ever forced my children into doing something they didn't want to do." Christine tried not to think of what Judith might have said.

Christine was glad her father agreed to let her stay at home. She enjoyed working at the art gallery and taking art classes at night. She was content in the familiarity of her own room and the quiet of the whole house since Eddie went away to Columbia. Her father even helped her set up a studio in the room she had as a baby. She painted there for hours, now and then glancing at the animated wallpaper and wondering why she had disliked it as a child.

On weekends her father would wander into the studio and watch her paint. "I always enjoyed going to the museum," he told her. "But I must confess I didn't understand half of what I was looking at. Sometimes I thought you kids could paint better pictures than they did. And now I know I was right," he said proudly.

It was nice living at home, Christine thought. Once in a while she felt guilty for not missing her brother and sister more. Not that she didn't love them both, but Eddie was always so watchful, writing his secret thoughts and never talking to anyone. And Judith still acted like she knew something no one else did.

*   *   *

Judith brought her daughter to dinner at least once a month. The family had grown politely comfortable. The conversation seldom involved more than family business and gossip, as though they had all taken a vow of silence when it came to personal topics. It was only after Christine started dating Bill that the monthly dinners revived old contests.

Ironically, it was Judith who was responsible for Christine's meeting Bill. Judith was working part-time in the UCLA Law Library and had invited her for lunch. As Christine crossed the campus, she found herself caught up in one of the many demonstrations that had become so popular. Pushing her way through the protesting crowd, Christine saw him sitting quietly at a table decorated with a poster that read JOIN THE ARMY. The sad, shy expression he wore didn't seem to fit his uniform as he sat there listening to the names he was being called.

At lunch, Judith had absentmindedly pushed the food around on her plate. "I know it seems unfair to yell at a few lone recruiters," she said. "But when are we going to learn that 'I was just doing my job' is no excuse." By the time lunch was over, Judith had eaten very little. "Doesn't this war bother you at all?" she asked.

Christine resented her sister's tone. After all, it was her friends who were being called and killed. What right did Judith have to try and make her feel guilty? Only last month a boy who had been the football star of her high school class was killed in some place even the newscasters couldn't pronounce. At his funeral, the minister called him a hero, soldiers shot salutes, and some officer handed his parents the carefully folded flag that had covered the coffin. What the hell was she supposed to do, tell his sobbing mother that her sister thought "just doing his job" was no excuse?

Christine reached for the bill. "I can afford to pay the check. I just can't afford to be as sure of things as you are."

After she had left Judith, Christine saw him again in the parking lot. He didn't move like she thought a soldier would. None of his gestures seemed confident—fumbling for his keys, then unlocking the car as though he wasn't sure it was really his. Nothing about him reminded her of the soldier in the picture that invited young men to join him in a new career. Christine didn't usually act on impulse, but she couldn't help calling out, "I'm sorry about the trouble you had today."

He looked up and smiled. "Thanks. I'm getting used to it. But I appreciate the kind words."

Standing next to their cars, they almost shouted their conversation. No, she didn't attend UCLA. She was only visiting her sister. No, he was not from Los Angeles. He was from Chicago. Yes, she lived near here. No, she wasn't involved in the antiwar movement; she wasn't sure who was right and who was wrong. No, he didn't really understand the war either; when it was all over he wanted to be a teacher.

When he finally walked over and stood beside her, she was surprised to find he wasn't much taller than she was. And she was fascinated by the way his short brown hair couldn't seem to decide where it wanted to lie. Eventually, when he asked, Christine didn't hesitate to give him her phone number.

Unlike everyone else, Bill didn't have any strong opinions about the war. He just accepted it as part of the life he had chosen. Like him, Christine didn't have any strong opinions either. She just accepted falling in love with him as part of the life she had chosen.

Now Judith sat across from Christine, cutting Emma's roast beef into minuscule pieces. "My God, Christine, at best he's going to go off and kill innocent people, and at worst he's going to get himself killed while he's at it."

Christine had drawn strength from her feelings about Bill. He knew her, understood her, wanted her to be exactly what she was. "Love hasn't got much to do with occupation," Christine argued.

Judith watched Emma chew her food. "All right, then he's too old for you," she said.

"You know, for a so-called liberal, you have some pretty

old-fashioned ideas. Mom and Dad don't think he's too old. They like him."

"That's because Dad approves of his politics," her sister said, without even glancing at her father for verification.

Her father shook his head. "It's nice having children who speak for me." And then to Judith, "Why don't you try saving yourself and your daughter, and let the world take care of itself for a change? Has it occurred to you that most of your clients are guilty of treason? In any other time they would be shot for burning the flag and running off to Canada."

"Try to understand," Judith said with unusual restraint, "I need to feel that what I'm doing is right—and I wish you would too."

Her father sighed. "Sometimes I think you do what you do just to infuriate me."

Her sister seemed to consider the possibility. "It's an interesting thought."

Christine never understood how her sister could get so upset about things over which she had no control and yet never seem concerned about things she could change. Judith didn't have to live in her canyon shack and drive an old car. She had choices. Her father was still upset because she was content to work for almost nothing as a paralegal in a seedy storefront law office.

Judith went on as though her father hadn't spoken. "Believe me, the difference between seventeen and twenty-four is a lifetime. I've been there and I know."

"I'm almost eighteen," Christine protested. "You always act like you know so much for your age. You're only six years older than I am."

"Almost seven, and I might as well be a hundred years older than you are at this point."

"You think you're a hundred years older than everybody." Christine noticed her father's smile when she added, "Don't you ever get tired of telling people what to do with their lives?" Then Christine tasted the words that had never been said before, and she liked the flavor. "I may not be as old as you are, but at least *I've* found someone who loves me enough to marry me."

"I can't argue with that," Judith said quietly.

The sad look on Judith's face and the worried one on her mother's reminded her of the dinner she had fixed the day Judith returned from Berkeley. Already she regretted the words that a moment ago she had savored.

Finally, it was her mother who spoke. "Judith," she said in an even voice, "let your sister make her own mistakes. After all, you have."

After that, they changed the subject, but Christine noticed no one looked directly at each other as they discussed Eddie's progress in school and the latest indication of three-year-old Emma's precocity.

4

The night of the fire, Robert Gregory found two things he wasn't shopping for—a job and a wife. It was Christmas 1940, and in some perverse way, the threat of war had exaggerated the holiday spirit. It was as if selecting just the right gift and increasing the volume of the most appropriate music would ward off evil spirits and make "Peace on Earth" a reality.

Robert knew the world was choosing up sides, and Franklin Roosevelt was bound to be one of the team captains. To prove he could get good players, the president had instituted the first peacetime draft, and Robert realized it was just a matter of time before he would follow his roommate as one of those chosen by the not-so-Selective Service. "Think of it this way," his roommate had said. "Germany won France, Italy got Greece, and Japan is going after China. If we don't do something, the bad guys are going to win this crap game, and there just won't be any nice places left to visit."

Even though he had no money, Robert chose the diversion of the crowded Santa Monica five-and-dime, partly to avoid boredom, and partly to permit his roommate to be alone in the apartment with his girlfriend.

As he watched the frenzied shoppers, Robert found himself fingering items he didn't even recognize—at the tobacco counter, he examined something that looked like a long bent nail. "That's for packing your pipe," a harassed clerk informed him. Robert wandered over to the housewares department, where he examined a small porcelain jar with a ringed metal top. "Are you interested in an egg coddler?" a grandmotherly type asked. Robert made a mental note to look up "egg coddler" the next time he went to the library.

Finally, without thought, Robert moved to a counter surrounded by eager bargain hunters. In an attempt to be inconspicuous, he picked up a rough, plaid scarf from a pile of woolen items lying about in disarray. "It's a bad buy," he heard her say. He was about to comment on her unusual sales approach until he looked up and saw her. She was unfashionably thin, and her dark eyes, framed by her light, blond hair, were unsettling. Everything about her told Robert that if she said this scarf was a bad buy, he would be a fool not to listen.

And then it happened. That background smell that everyone must have registered and then ignored became noticeable when the word "smoke" was attached to it. The results were instant, but not dramatic. A few people simply put down the merchandise and moved to the exit. Others mentioned, almost in passing, that there must be a fire.

It was the dark-eyed salesgirl who phoned the fire department, helped usher customers from the store, and then went about closing all the doors. Not, as she later admitted while Robert stood next to her outside, that she knew anything about how oxygen fueled a fire or even that she had considered the notion of containment. She had simply memorized the "In Case of Fire" instructions that had been posted in the employees' lounge and followed the instructions to the letter. Outside, as the fire trucks began unloading their equipment, he moved closer to her. "Were you frightened?" he asked.

"No. It was bound to happen sooner or later. It's the high school students they hire for the holidays. They sneak into the stockroom and smoke. I suppose we won't be paid for this time off." It wasn't a judgment, just an appraisal of cause and possible effect. "Anyway," she added, "it kept you from buying an overpriced cheap scarf."

"I would have taken your advice," he said truthfully. He didn't add that he couldn't have afforded it even if it had been a bargain. He wanted to keep the conversation going, but he wasn't good at talking to girls. It wasn't that he was afraid they might not like him—actually they seemed to find him attractive. He was over six feet tall, but his reddish-blond hair, blue eyes, and freckles suggested a boy was hiding in a large man's body. He thought it must be his size that made him uneasy around women—he was afraid that if he accidentally touched them they might break. But this girl was different. She didn't look or sound like the type who would break. She gave the impression that she dealt only in hard, factual life.

"You're a student, aren't you?" she said, more than asked.

"Yes, UCLA."

"What do you study?"

"English."

"I always wondered why anyone would study what everyone knows from the time they're old enough to talk." There was no trace of irony in her voice, just the same matter-of-fact appraisal he had observed before.

"It's a good point," he laughed.

"What are you going to do when you get out of school?" she asked, with what sounded like genuine interest.

"Probably be a soldier for a while."

"And then?"

"Be a writer."

"Do you have talent?"

It was maddening the way she spoke, as though she were

interviewing him for a job that he hadn't even applied for. "I
don't know yet. I've published a short story and some poetry
in the college literary magazine. But that hardly makes me
Tolstoy."

"Do you get paid when you publish?"

"No."

"By the way, I don't know who Tolstoy is," she said
without apology and then continued the interview. "Do you
live with your parents?"

Robert didn't want to go into his life's story, and besides,
there wasn't much to tell. "My parents are dead," he said,
hoping it didn't sound like a plea for sympathy.

She didn't appear embarrassed, the way some are when
the subject of death arises in casual conversation. "You must
work then."

He wanted to know more about her. But he couldn't
figure out how to turn the conversation around, and he was
afraid if he changed the subject, he might lose her attention.
"I work the night shift at the paper."

"Writing?"

"No. Mostly I just run errands."

"Why don't you write about the fire tonight. You were
there. Wouldn't the paper be interested?"

It should have occurred to Robert that he had been
present at a newsworthy event, and he felt embarrassed that
someone who didn't even know who Tolstoy was should be
the one to point it out. "If I write the story, who shall I say
read the emergency procedure?"

"If you're asking for my name, it's Margaret . . . Margaret
Harris."

"May I call you?" he asked.

"I don't have a telephone."

"Then can we meet for coffee sometime?"

"Yes." Another fact stated without comment.

Robert was beginning to regret the attraction he felt for
this strange person who seemed so bereft of words.

"If you're going to write about the fire, you'll have to

find out when the store will reopen. When it does, you can meet me after work, if that's convenient." Again she was simply pointing out what Robert should have logically suggested, and for the second time, Robert felt foolish.

The fire, confined to the storeroom, had caused almost no damage, but when the night editor at the *Echo* agreed to let him try the assignment, he threw himself into it as though it were an epic conflagration. He didn't mind the editor's major rewrite that appeared on the front page. It still had his byline under the headline EMPLOYEE AVERTS DISASTER IN DIME STORE.

"Did you read the story?" Robert asked, as he walked up to where Margaret was methodically folding a woolen sweater that some anxious, last-minute holiday shopper had inspected and then carelessly discarded on the counter.

She looked up. "Yes, I read it."

It had taken only two days for the store to reopen, and during that time, Robert was surprised to find that he thought of nothing but Margaret and her opinion of his article. Now he stood there, irritated that once again she offered no more than a direct answer to a direct question. Finally, her silence forced him to ask, "Well? What did you think of it?"

"I liked it," she smiled.

Robert felt like he had just won the Pulitzer Prize.

Robert memorized Margaret's work schedule and each night waited outside the store to walk her home. She accepted this as if it had been agreeably prearranged. The more he saw her, the more he felt he was trying to unravel some intricate design. Even her looks invited analysis. Her large, dark eyes and almost white, blond hair defied genetic rules and should have looked unbalanced. But with Margaret it worked to such a degree that he noticed both men and women staring at her with startled appreciation. And a woman as tall and thin as she should have given the impression of frailty, except the sureness with which she did everything implied, well, "force" was the only word Robert could think of.

When Robert tried to imagine making love to this paradox, he had the uncomfortable vision of her being larger and stronger than he, but that was probably due to his lack of experience. Only once had he made love to a woman, if it could be called that. His roommate had supplied him a date for the school rival's football game. Robert was no sports fan, but he was usually too shy to seek dates for himself, so he accepted the invitation. After the game, the four of them lived up to the spirit of such occasions by consuming more beer than they were used to or wanted. Then, with a knowing smile, his roommate announced that he and his girlfriend were going to her place "to visit."

Robert stumbled along with the girl to his apartment, undressed, and clumsily fumbled his way to consummation. Afterward, she cried over her lost virginity, which he found incongruous considering that during his unpracticed love-making she complained constantly and made suggestions for improvement. She accused him of seducing her, threatened to kill herself if anybody found out what they had done, and made him swear never to mention what had happened. His vow of silence and the reassurance that he would always respect her appeared to brighten her spirits, but did little for his. After that night, he had lost his desire to seek what others called pleasures.

Margaret was different. She wasn't coy or frightening. She listened to whatever he said, regardless of the subject, and he imagined her taking mental notes. "How did your parents die?" she asked one evening on the way home.

Robert had read all the accounts of how the ship had sunk. It was a ludicrous example of deadly coincidence, stupidity, and cowardice—the captain found dead in his cabin at suppertime; the first wisps of smoke that curled out of the writing room at 2:30 A.M.; the bosun who should have led the fire fighters drunk in his bunk; fire doors left open and equipment missing or inoperable; and the first mate failing to order an SOS until 3:23 A.M. Finally, there was the explosion that condemned one hundred and thirty-four men, women, and children to death by fire or water. The first five lifeboats carried ninety-two crew members and only six passengers. Robert was only fourteen years old at the time, but even then he wondered if his parents were among the passengers who struggled in the turbulent water as crew members steered through them in half-empty lifeboats ignoring their pleas for help. The only hero had proved to be a radio operator who stayed at his fiery post waiting for orders to call for help. And even that one show of heroism proved false. A few years later, that same radio operator was convicted of trying to blow up his immediate superior with an ingenious bomb. After that, there was strong suspicion that he had murdered the captain and set fire to the ship in the first place. "They were on the *Morro Castle* in nineteen thirty-four," Robert said.

Robert expected the usual "How awful" or the standard "I'm sorry." Margaret remained silent, as if she were waiting for further explanation. "They were musicians," he said. Robert pictured his mother and father, clutching their instruments as the burning ship foundered in a heaving sea. "They were on their way home from a South American concert tour."

She seemed to consider what she had heard, then asked, "Who took care of you after that?"

"I was in boarding school when it happened. So I just stayed on there until I graduated," he said, surprised that she didn't ask for details about the sensational tragedy.

" 'Boarding school'—it has an exclusive ring. I've never met anyone who went to a boarding school."

"We weren't rich, if that's what you mean," he said, hearing the hard defensiveness in his voice. He knew that Margaret didn't have much when she was growing up, but she had never indicated she felt deprived. "I don't mean we were poor, but we weren't rich either," he said, regretting his earlier tone. "There was a court case, and the shipping line agreed to pay the survivors. The bank was my guardian. They managed the settlement and paid my tuition and expenses."

They walked along for a while in silence, and Robert

glanced at her. If she was offended by his momentary snap-
pishness, she didn't show it. Instead, she looked puzzled. "But
you couldn't live at the school all the time. Where did you
go for the holidays?" she asked. "Didn't you have relatives?"

"Not many—none that I knew really. My parents were
pretty old when I was born. I did visit my mother's old-maid
sister, but I don't think she liked having me around. I didn't
mind staying at the school. There was always someone around
to talk to."

"I can't imagine not having a family. Weren't you lonely?"

"I never thought about it. I don't think I was," he said,
experiencing the same discomfort he always did when this
subject arose. It wasn't that he still grieved for his parents,
or ever did for that matter. They were concert musicians who
spent most of their time on tour. He loved them, he supposed,
and he was certainly grateful to them for giving him an appreciation of music and literature when he was a child. But
he had no clear picture of them as people. In fact, the whole
concept of "family" held little meaning for him.

"What about you? How old were you when your father
died?" he said, deciding to change the subject.

"Four. I remember a big, comfortable presence and how
awful it was when it was gone. Mother taught herself typing
and shorthand and went to work at the Ford plant. She's been
there ever since."

Robert had come to rely on Margaret's ability to follow
a conversation in any direction he chose to take it. He wasn't
much of a dancer, but he imagined the two of them ideal
partners, he changing steps, she following with perfect ease.
"Why didn't your mother remarry?" he asked.

"After God and me, she didn't have time left for a man,"
she said without a sign of sarcasm.

"Were you lonely?" he asked, feeling the need to recip-
rocate some of her earlier concern for his childhood.

"How could I be? My mother and I had each other to
worry about and take care of," she said without further comment.

When they reached her house, he accepted the customary invitation to come in for coffee. He enjoyed his visits with Margaret and her mother. The house was small, comfortable, and so clean it always made him wonder if they did anything in their spare time except scrub floors and polish furniture. Rose Harris was smaller than her daughter, with dark impassioned eyes and appropriately matching dark hair that was pulled back severely and rolled at the nape of her neck. Robert thought Margaret must have selected the sharpest feature of each parent, regardless of their complementing qualities. He marveled that two women could be so alike in some ways and so totally different in others. Rose was an attractive woman, perhaps, at one time, more beautiful than her daughter. Each emitted signals of submerged passion. Rose demonstrated hers by the intensity of her obeisant praise of God and faith in a better life to come. Margaret's was manifested in an intense drive to organize her temporal life on earth.

Tonight Rose welcomed him and then, as soon as politeness allowed, went to her room to rest and read "her book." Since Robert never saw evidence of reading material lying about the house, he assumed she meant the Bible.

After Rose's departure, Margaret poured more coffee and then curled up on the sofa, tucking her long legs under her skirt so that she gave the impression of some Eastern mystic about to give sage advice. "Are you planning to ask me to marry you?" she asked, as though she were inquiring about the fitness of the coffee.

"Yes." Robert wondered if that were true. "If I did, what would you say?"

"I'd say yes. But only if you're sure of your feelings. I'd want you to think about the difference in our backgrounds. I don't know anything about the things you like. You might want someone better educated than I am."

Robert appreciated her concern, but didn't consider it a big problem. He had come to respect her native intelligence. "You could learn," he said. "Why don't you take some classes?"

Margaret studied her coffee with the look of a student

68

puzzling over unfamiliar material. Usually, Robert liked the quiet moments between them and didn't feel a need to fill in the soundless air with conversation. But this silence had an uneasiness about it that forced him to ask, "What are you thinking?"

"I'm sure I love you. And if you do decide you want to marry me, I'll be a good wife and mother," she said deliberately. "But if you ask me to change, then that might change too."

A year later they were married. Rose invited them to live with her until they could get settled, and they accepted gratefully. Living as a family was a new experience for Robert. He found it not only pleasant, but convenient. Although he sensed an unstated alliance between mother and daughter, he excused it on the basis of his being the only male in what had always been a female empire. He didn't feel uncomfortable. Indeed, he was treated like an honored guest who had to be looked after like a bright but sometimes troublesome child. Both women contributed to making his life easier. Rose was more than willing to type the feature stories he was now writing for the *Echo* and Margaret made it her business to pick up and deliver whatever books he wanted from the library.

The time he saved by not having to attend to everyday needs, like preparing food or making sure he had a clean shirt, permitted him to finish a short story based on the night he had met Margaret. He was especially pleased with his description of her and the way she had handled the fire. Handing it to his wife, he said, "Read this and tell me what you think."

Margaret sat down and read each page carefully, pausing occasionally to look up at her husband. When she was through, her husband asked, "Well, what do you think?"

As if paying a great compliment, she said, "It must be terribly difficult to make things sound more exciting than they really are."

*   *   *

Six months after they were married, Robert joined the army, and a year after that, he found himself standing on the deck of the battleship *Arkansas* where he could see wave after wave of assault boats packed with unseasoned young men lurch toward the beach. Through his field glasses, it appeared more a bizarre ballet than a battle—boats turning over gracefully in the water, men in heavy battle gear sinking below the surface without struggle, survivors in intricately choreographed movements advancing to embrace a few inches of wet sand, and exploding mortar shells providing a kaleidoscopic background. Except for their battle gear, those who plunged into the sand might have been mistaken for young men on holiday throwing themselves down after an exhausting romp on the beautiful French shore.

Retreating to his cramped quarters, Robert inserted the paper into his old Remington. This time, he thought, Margaret is wrong. It isn't difficult to make things sound more exciting than they really are:

NORMANDY INVASION
ROBERT GREGORY
Stars and Stripes

OMAHA BEACH, June 6, 1944—Today Allied troops landed on the Cherbourg peninsula under the command of U.S. General Dwight D. Eisenhower. In the first 25 hours of fighting the American First Army reported an estimated 7,000 casualties . . .

Robert knew he had been luckier than most. He had managed to graduate before enlisting, and then, even with his limited experience, he was assigned to *Stars and Stripes,* the military newspaper. The last time he had seen his wife was two months ago, just before he shipped overseas. It took her last letter a month to arrive, and, as usual, she wrote in a straightforward style most veteran reporters would have applauded. Robert savored her letter like a gourmet eating his favorite meal:

May 1st '44

Dear Robert,

Both mother and I are fine. She is busy working with her church group knitting wool socks for soldiers, although I doubt such warm clothing will be needed, since I don't think the war will last past summer.

Robert smiled. How like Margaret, he thought. She's decided the war is ending; therefore all knitting should stop. If she could, she'd call a conference and demand everyone return to their own countries. Not because she wants the power to dictate, but because further fighting simply isn't practical.
Her letter continued:

Mother has taken on additional hours at the plant. I told her I don't approve. At her age she's doing too much. But she thinks it's her duty to the war effort, and I must respect her feelings.

Mr. Johnson asked if I would be interested in becoming a buyer for the store, but I told him no. I appreciated his offer, but I didn't think it would be fair to accept a promotion and then have to leave because of the baby.

Robert skimmed the rest of the letter for confirmation of what she had just said, but there was only further reporting: *The spring flowers are beginning to bloom;* and then later: *I ran into Mr. Kimbal and he said to tell you your job at the* Echo *was waiting for you.*
No further mention of a child. He read and reread the phrase "because of the baby." Could she actually be making an announcement with such a casual reference, or was it just Margaret assuming that because she had decided it was time to prepare for a family, she would turn down all future offers that might interfere.
The last time they were together she had embraced him in the dark and whispered, "The war will be ending soon. I

want to get pregnant now so we will have a family by the time you get home."

At the time, Robert had wondered why Margaret was so sure the war would end on schedule or, for that matter, why nature would consent to fit into that schedule. He was about to tell her that she was all the family he wanted, but, as she invited him into her arms, all misgivings vanished. Each time he made love to his wife, it was a new, pleasant surprise. He marveled that such soft, smooth skin could give off so much heat. As in everything else, she was a perfect partner, anticipating and responding to his unplanned, spontaneous desire with thrilled ease. He had to admit part of the excitement was the power he felt when, with a light touch, he could bring this normally unanimated woman alive. He imagined himself a conductor, orchestrating her hidden passion and receiving fierce pleasure in her crescendo of fulfillment.

Afterward, as they lay in each other's damp arms, he asked her, "Why don't you ever say, 'I love you'?" She moved closer to him. "I just did. Couldn't you tell?"

When Robert was finally able to put a call through to California, she said, "Of course I'm pregnant. Didn't you get my letter?"

He realized he should have known that Margaret didn't make casual statements.

Margaret had been right, the war was ending in Europe, but she miscalculated the stubbornness of the Japanese. By the time his baby was born, Robert was on his way to Iwo Jima to report the last, fierce struggle of a proud enemy. When Margaret's letter finally reached him, the baby was already three months old: *We never discussed a name,* she wrote, *but I thought you might like to call her Judith, after your mother.*

Robert was vaguely disappointed that it was a girl, and it surprised him that he didn't feel particularly nostalgic about his mother, but he was touched by Margaret's gesture. In the abstract, he was a proud and happy father, passing out the

ritual cigars and accepting the fraternal pat on the back for
one night well done. But in truth, he couldn't get excited
about what he had never touched or held. It was Margaret
he missed.

In fact, he was ashamed to admit that he was almost as
anxious to hear his wife's reaction to the several short stories
he had sent her as he was to receive the announcement of a
birth that had little to do with him. He wasn't sure why he
valued Margaret's opinion, but he felt a need to hear her say
"That's good" in the same unhesitating way she had said "The
war will end soon." But instead she wrote:

> I read the stories you sent me. I enjoyed them, but
> I can't say if they are good or bad. I don't know about
> such things. I only know that if this is what you want
> to do when you come home, then you should do it.
> Mother can watch Judith and I can go back to work until
> you publish something.

Robert believed that Margaret would have supported
him even if he decided to lock himself up in the attic and
write until doomsday, and for some unexplainable reason,
this irritated him more than her uncritical reading of his work.

As Robert looked at the eight-month-old stranger who was
waiting for him when he returned home, he suppressed a
twinge of resentment. He didn't like sharing his wife in the
middle of the night. And the long-awaited talks he had imagined during the dead hours of the war were constantly interrupted by the child's wailing needs. Even Rose, who always
seemed more concerned with his well-being than her own
daughter's, now turned her attention to this infant interloper.
All in all, Robert found fatherhood irritating.

When Mr. Kimbal called from the newspaper and invited
him to lunch, Robert welcomed the chance to escape the
domestic routine in which he felt a forgotten participant. "I'm

going to the paper," he told his wife sullenly and left her sitting on the sofa, nursing her child.

When he walked into the managing editor's office, he was greeted like a long-lost son, although he couldn't recall ever having spoken more than a few words to Mr. Kimbal before.

"Welcome home, my boy," the old man said, shaking his hand and patting him on the back. "Pretty bad over there, wasn't it?"

Robert had viewed most of the war from a safe distance, never considering himself in immediate danger. But he had seen boys, almost fresh from Sunday School, sink their bayonets deep into the bowels of strangers and then celebrate survival by shouting as they yanked the steel up and out. Many of those who had engaged in this grotesque puberty rite came home only to be told they had no experience for employment. Robert suspected his own experience was about to come in handy.

"I just carried a pencil. It was a lot worse for the guys who carried guns." He was surprised to see that Mr. Kimbal regarded this statement as a sign of humility rather than simple truth.

"Don't be silly. Everyone did his part. We read your reports and were impressed by their vivid force. By God, I felt I was right there with you during the D-Day landings. I'd like to think you learned a little about reporting while you were with us," Mr. Kimbal beamed.

Robert didn't remind Mr. Kimbal that the only hard news he had ever written for the paper had been the five-and-dime fire, and even that had been almost completely rewritten.

When Mr. Kimbal finally offered him a job, Robert hesitated. "I'm writing a book," he said, as though that were some sort of normal reply to a job offer.

"So, who says you can't do both?" Mr. Kimbal smiled. "We're a small paper. You won't be out every night pounding a beat. Remember, Hemingway and Dreiser were both journalists, and they managed to write some pretty fine books. What's yours about?"

Robert was tempted to confide that he had started a novel about his war experience, such as it was, but the characters he wanted to create kept slipping out of his grasp. He had a filmy notion of them, but when he tried to get them on paper, they twisted free and drifted away. Each new paragraph sounded more and more like the reports he had filed for the military paper—factual, but lacking sincerity and depth. He wasn't sure what his book was "about" anymore. "It's about the war," he said, avoiding Mr. Kimbal's questioning look.

Again, Robert sensed that Mr. Kimbal read his response as something more sensitive than embarrassment. "Fine, fine. I'd like to read what you've written . . . when you're ready, of course," Kimbal said kindly. "Now, how about my offer?"

Margaret had insisted on returning to work until he finished his book, and even Rose encouraged him by offering to convert the garage into an office so he could work undisturbed. But he felt uneasy about being supported by two women. Besides, he didn't like the way the book was going. "I appreciate it," he told his former boss. "I'd like to give it a try."

Later, when Robert told Margaret that he had decided to go back to the paper, he read disapproval in her disappointed expression. "I thought you wanted to finish your book before we talked about the future," she said.

Robert considered her remark unfair and decided to take the offensive. "What do you want from me? I did it so I could provide for you and the baby."

It felt good to be the aggressive victim, and he appreciated the guilt he heard in her voice when she said, "You know I would never want you to give up writing because of me." But his satisfaction faded when she added, "I doubt anyone ever really gives up what they're good at, even for people they love."

*   *   *

"Come on, baby, I'm right here," Robert said, stretching out his arms to his three-year-old daughter as she stood on the edge of the pool, legs tensely bent, eyes clenched, fiercely determined . . .

Robert stood in the shallow end of the pool watching the diamond flashes of light as they reflected off the water and danced on his daughter's tanned skin. The metamorphosis from drooling, wordless dictator to lovely, adoring daughter went almost unnoticed by Robert until one day Judith advanced like a determined dancer, throwing herself forward to welcome him home with the word "Daddy." From that day on, she was a human being, with words and ability, surrounding him with what he had never known—exuberant adoration. What intrigued him most was this small, beautiful creature's eagerness to please. Standing on the edge of the pool, she looked at him with an absolute trust that frightened him.

Robert waited patiently for his daughter to take her first leap into the pool. "Come on. I'm right here. Jump!" he commanded.

Judith held her breath and jumped into his waiting arms. Robert let her sink gently below the surface of the water. He felt her sweep past his legs as he raised her out of the water and lifted her over his head.

"Where were you, Daddy? You weren't there."

"Sure I was, every minute," he laughed, sensing that she enjoyed the game. "Okay, here we go again," he said, letting her ride down into the water and then quickly lifting her up and over his head. "Uuuuuuuuuuup we go," he reassured her.

Margaret took a step forward. "Robert, I think that's enough. She's frightened."

Damn it, Robert thought. Why can't Margaret just relax? This morning, for instance, Margaret had been afraid to bring Judith to the pool, saying "I don't think we should take the chance on exposing her to polio." But Robert had insisted, "Look, I work all week, and I don't get a chance to spend much time with Judy." His daughter had jumped up and down, pulling on his pant leg, chanting, "I wanna go, Daddy." Encouraged by his little ally, he offered his wife further argument. "Besides, not knowing how to swim is more dangerous than going to a public pool. If my parents had known how to swim, they might be here to enjoy their granddaughter."

He looked at his wife. "It's okay, Margaret," he said. "She likes it." As if to confirm his insight, he heard Judith above him laughing. "She's going to be a great swimmer."

He held his daughter aloft for a moment longer, her little body almost lost in his large hands like a squirming lump of clay anxious to be molded. "You'll win a gold medal someday," he smiled up at her. Robert felt Judith relax, and as he brought her down into the water, he took secret pleasure in the fact that he knew his daughter better than his wife did.

A few nights later, he tucked Judith into bed, kissed her good night, and returned to the dining room, where he was surprised to see his wife still sitting at the cluttered dinner table waiting for him. Usually, by now she would have cleared the table and had his coffee waiting. He had become so used to Margaret's routines that even slight variations made him uneasy. "Is there something the matter?" he asked, afraid he had forgotten something important like a birthday or anniversary.

"I think it's time we had another child," she said.

Robert was startled by his own panic. He was content with the family unit just the way it was. Besides, he couldn't understand why she wanted more children. She didn't seem to enjoy the one she had. From the beginning, she had cared for Judith with grim determination, constantly checking a suspected diaper, stalking a dangerous crib, or feeling for an impending fever. Robert managed a smile. "What's the hurry? How about letting me get used to the one we've got."

"I don't want an only child," she said, refusing to follow the conversational dance step Robert had planned. "When I was growing up, I knew I was the most important thing in my mother's life. She worked so hard, I felt guilty knowing that if anything happened to me, she would have nothing. It's not good for a child to feel she is the most important person in a family."

Robert couldn't follow the mysterious logic Margaret had brought with her from a different world. He was rather glad he hadn't been forced to share his parents' occasional attention with a rival sibling. "Come on, Maggie, Judy's only three years old. I don't think it will hurt her to be the center of attention for a while."

His wife's dark stare made him feel like a child who had just been caught in a lie. "When I was growing up, I knew that the people who called me Maggie didn't want to take me seriously. I don't think we should call her Judy."

Robert recognized the rebuke but refused to acknowledge it. "I don't want to have children I can't afford," he said.

"I don't think that's going to be a problem anymore," she replied evenly. He knew she was referring to his promotion to assistant editor at the *Echo*. And the war had provided more than just a promising career. The GI bill was making it possible to buy a comfortable two-story house not far from the ocean in Santa Monica. It was another opportunity that had moved him one step farther away from his original plans.

At first, he had taken Mr. Kimbal's advice and worked on his book in his spare time. But the old problem of not understanding his characters remained a constant obstacle. He knew how his characters acted, but he didn't know why. It was like describing close friends and suddenly realizing he knew nothing of their past, whether from not caring enough to ask or from not listening when he was told. He had finally handed the manuscript to Margaret, saying, "Put this away. I'm going to give it a rest."

Perhaps Margaret is right, he thought. Maybe Judy would like a brother or sister. But he wasn't convinced that life was a matter of such simple formulas. If it were, he and Margaret would be more alike. After all, they were both orphans, he more than she. Both only children. Yet they were completely

78

different. He considered himself more open to life, less guarded. He didn't agree that crowding extra humanity into a house guaranteed happiness.

His wife insisted he go to work as usual, although every indication suggested she was in the early stages of labor. "You have a paper to put out," she said, as though she were referring to the nightly ritual with the cat. "I'll call you at the office if this turns out to be the real thing."

Actually, Robert was relieved. He always felt slightly incompetent around the house. He put his arm around her shoulder, trying to avoid touching her bulging stomach. He had missed his wife's first pregnancy and had never imagined her as anything but thin and agile. Watching her over the past months had frightened him. Everything about her remained thin, except the area between her breasts and pubic bone, where she had become grotesquely large. It amazed him that such graceful, slender legs were capable of carrying so much concentrated weight, or that such smooth skin could tolerate so much abusive stretching. But despite this assault on her body, she had become more energetic, almost carefree. There must be something to the old wives' tales, he thought.

"All right, I'll go," he said, kissing her gently. "But if you have any more pains, promise you'll call me."

"I promise," she said. Then, putting his hand on her stomach, she asked, "You're not sorry, are you?"

It had taken Robert months to accept the idea of having another child. In fact, even now he wasn't sure how much he welcomed the invasion of another stranger into his life. But the look of pleasure on his wife's face dictated his answer. "Don't be silly. I love you."

She held on to his hand tightly. "It's important for you to know that I love you and that I want to give you everything I can."

He couldn't remember her saying "I love you" since the night he had walked her home and they talked about getting married. Even then it had been a statement of fact, not an outburst of emotion. He had come to expect Margaret's word-less proofs of affection—the perfectly run house, the ironed shirts, the excellent meals, and the still-exciting passion in the darkness. He kissed her on the cheek. "Promise you'll call," he repeated, not knowing how to respond to her sudden articulated declaration of love. He was relieved when she smiled, released his hand, and said, "I promise."

Robert anxiously sought the control he felt at his office. He liked to think the *Echo* was something better than the average small-town newspaper. He knew his subscribers would rather see their own names in print than read about some head of state. But the paper served an important local pur-pose, alerting citizens to worthy causes as well as warning of possible dangers.

Occasionally, he would concentrate on national stories and their implications. This week was especially hectic. The assassination of Gandhi had moved him so deeply that he had ordered a series of editorials on passive resistance. He was aware that his colleagues considered him a bit too liberal, but they were dependable and predictable, and he sensed they liked and respected him. He was working on the Gandhi story when his secretary informed him that Dr. Davis was on the phone. Robert felt his pulse quicken, but the doctor was quick to sound reassuring. "Robert, Margaret's fine."

Robert heard his own breath rushing out toward the phone, easing his tension and assuring the doctor he had heard. "How's the baby?"

Robert caught the practiced silence that followed and sensed it was designed to let the listener prepare for bad news. "I'm sorry, Robert. The baby was stillborn."

Robert couldn't hold on to a specific feeling. "How's Margaret taking it?" he said, hoping to find some emotional guidance.

There was a moment of dead air between him and the doctor. "It's hard to tell with Margaret," he said thoughtfully. "She appears to be more concerned about how you will feel."

Only a sharp wave of guilt kept Robert from blurting

out that he didn't even want another child. "I'll be right there," he said, and hung up.

Robert glanced up at the galaxy of stars indicated by his six-year-old daughter's finger and heard her ask, "How far away is that star, Momma?" He anticipated Margaret's "I don't know" and was ready for Judith's "Daddy? How far?"

"Let's see, I can't be exact," he pondered, "but I'd estimate the one you're pointing at to be about four billion, six hundred million, three thousand, two and a half miles and nine inches away."

He could visualize Margaret's frown hidden in the darkness and imagined her unspoken "Why can't you just tell her you don't know the answer?" Margaret wasn't amused by his technique for ending Judith's question and answer sessions. He tried to explain that it was just a harmless game both he and Judith enjoyed, but she remained unconvinced. "Some day," she had warned, "Judith may not be able to accept the fact that you don't have all the answers." In fact, he suspected Margaret was secretly annoyed because Judith called on her politely, like a teacher giving the slow-witted student a chance to perform before turning to a gifted one for an answer.

"Momma, why don't we see stars like this at home?" Judith asked, remaining true to the game.

Robert heard, more than saw, his wife look up at him. "I don't know, but I'm sure Daddy does," she answered.

"Well, honey, our house is surrounded by a big city, and at night, when everybody turns on the lights, they outshine the stars. Up here, the stars don't have to compete with other lights," he said, relieved that this answer required no creative invention.

"Is that why you don't light up the car inside when you drive at night?" she asked.

Judith's ability to transfer new information to other situations continually amazed Robert. He looked forward to the conversations they would have when she was older. "Exactly. That's an excellent analogy," he said.

Robert watched his daughter's silhouette wiggle toward his wife's pillowed lap. He had occasional misgivings about Margaret's condition, but the doctor had assured him that Margaret was in excellent health and could see no reason not to expect a healthy, normal baby.

Since their son's stillbirth almost three years ago, Margaret had changed. Not that she had become morose or brooding. In fact, the child's death appeared to have had the opposite effect. If anything, she was more intensely concerned with life. She had insisted that they begin taking Judith at least once a month to a concert or a museum. When he argued that a four-year-old was too young for a crash course in Art Appreciation, she said, "I want her to know all the things I missed." So they made regular pilgrimages to the university to see whatever was passing for culture that month. And eventually he looked forward to Judith's excitement with each new adventure. But he noticed that Margaret dozed during the concerts and preferred the museum gardens over the exhibits.

Robert had been surprised when Margaret suggested buying the cabin at Arrowhead. She was hardly the outdoor type. But she said she wanted a place that would give everyone a chance to do what they wanted and still all be together without interruption from the outside world. Now, as Robert watched the moon climb over the pine trees, he was glad she had insisted. It was a pleasant change from his hectic schedule at the paper.

Robert got up from the blanket they had spread in front of the cabin and stretched. He couldn't remember being so relaxed and content. Of course, he occasionally daydreamed about lost opportunities and unsatisfied yearnings. He still thought about finishing the novel or knocking out a short story. Sometimes he even made a mental note to ask Margaret where she had put the manuscript he had long ago given over to her safekeeping. But since Mr. Kimbal's retirement and Robert's subsequent promotion to managing editor, he had little time to dwell on the "what might have beens." Robert looked down at Margaret and Judith and couldn't imagine a more adequate wife or perfect daughter. All in all, he liked his life.

His daughter's voice floated through the evening air. "Momma, am I going to have a brother or a sister?"

Margaret's response was firm. "I don't know, dear." And then, after a pause, "And neither does your father."

Did his wife suspect that he didn't care about having a son? If anything, he wanted another daughter. The night chill pried into Robert's jacket and began to penetrate his skin. He wasn't sure if it was Judith's question that annoyed him or Margaret's answer. Having a bright child had its drawbacks. He could no longer spell out the words he didn't want Judith to hear.

"It'sway imetay orfay edbay," he told his wife.

5

Edward sat between his mother and Christine, watching the ancient, outcast king shake his fist in defiance of the storm and his fate and scream, "Blow, winds, and crack your cheeks! Rage! Blow!" Usually, his family attended simple musical plays that were already vaguely familiar because the songs were played many times on the radio. But this play was very different, longer and more complicated. His father had agreed to attend because Judith was studying *King Lear* in her English class, and he said that seeing a play was always more fun than reading one. Only Christine had objected, complaining, "Why do we have to go to see something just because Judith wants us to?"

Edward suspected there were times when Christine didn't like Judith. Every year when school started, she would sigh, "I hate it when my teachers ask 'Are you Judith Gregory's little sister?' because then they expect me to sound like I know everything."

Unlike Christine, Edward didn't mind being "Judith's little brother," even though he realized it meant people expected him to be active and popular. Instead, he played a game no one knew he was playing. He would guess how long it would take before his teachers and classmates began calling him "a brain," and as soon as they did, he knew they would forget how good Judith was.

Now, watching the play near its conclusion, Edward was glad he had an older sister studying Shakespeare because he was certain he was seeing something wonderful and important on that stage. When the grizzled king stumbled toward the audience carrying his dead daughter in his arms, Edward heard his own heart beating above the old man's screams of agony. Next to him, Christine shut her eyes and put her hands over her ears to mute the pitiful curses of a ruined man; but his mother leaned forward intently, tears running down her face.

Judith always laughed and called these the "go out nights" because that's what Edward had called them when he was still a baby. Everyone's choices were predictable. His father chose musical events, his mother anything that involved flowers, and Christine movies. Last month he was forced to sit through Rock Hudson and Doris Day in *Pillow Talk.* At least he tried to be different, to take the family where they had never gone before. He was searching for one place where they would all be the same, where they would all look at one thing and agree that it was wonderful, where they would all be happy at once.

No matter whose choice it was, each outing ended at the ice cream parlor, with him and Christine arguing which was better, chocolate or vanilla. In the end, they would always look to Judith for a decision, knowing she would judiciously recommend that they order a double scoop, one of each flavor, in order to decide for themselves. His parents never entered the debate, since they admitted grown-ups had no taste when it came to such delights.

Tonight, however, Edward noticed that Christine was content with a single scoop of vanilla, and he had little desire to argue with her about her choice. They walked along wordlessly licking their cones, more, it appeared, to prevent dripping than to enjoy the taste. His father finally broke the silence. "Remind me not to divide up my property," he said.

Judith looked stricken. "I'd never act like that," she said, adding, with complete confidence, "and neither would Christine or Eddie."

Edward didn't understand his sister's reasoning. "It was the king's own fault," he said. "He brought on all his own problems by thinking he could bribe his daughters into loving him. Besides, he was mean to the only one who really understood him."

"How can you say that? Didn't you feel sorry for him?" Judith asked, sounding genuinely shocked.

Even though she was almost eight years older than Edward and a senior in high school, Judith never talked to him like he was the baby of the family. At the same time, he had the feeling that he didn't quite measure up to some standard she had set for him and the whole family. Tonight he sensed that both he and Shakespeare had let her down. "Yes," he said, "I felt sorry for him. But I felt sorry for him because he didn't know how dumb he was."

Edward heard the tease in his father's voice. " 'How sharper than a serpent's tooth it is / To have a thankless child!' "

Edward remembered when Lear said the same thing, and he wanted to tell his father that the old king was just feeling sorry for himself when he spoke those words. But he felt a little guilty and ashamed of himself for thinking he knew more than his father did. "I just meant he wanted everyone to treat him like a king, but he didn't act like one, and that caused all the trouble," Edward said, trying not to sound like the "know-it-all" Christine sometimes called him.

His father smiled at his son. "I think you have given tragedy a new definition," he said.

"My teacher said that to be a tragedy, the main character has to have what she calls a 'fatal flaw,' so I suppose Eddie has a point," Judith said thoughtfully, adding, "But I still think that his daughters were just as much to blame."

Christine walked along quietly. "I didn't like the play. It was too sad," she declared.

Edward admitted to himself that he hadn't understood a lot of what the actors had said, but he was sure he had understood the people without understanding all the words. "It wasn't sad," Edward said.

As they reached the car, Christine challenged, "Then why did Mother cry?"

Edward didn't know the right words to explain why his mother's unusual behavior wasn't a good reason not to like the play. He was sure his mother's reaction was the correct one. "Crying doesn't always mean sad."

"Your brother's right," his mother said. "I think I was crying because at the end, everybody understood each other."

His father put his arm around his wife. "That's a pretty high price to pay for understanding," his father laughed.

Edward looked at the expression on his mother's face, and for the first time in his life, Edward realized that his mother knew something his father didn't.

Edward watched as his sisters came down the stairs carrying the last of Judith's luggage. "You'd better hurry or you'll be late," his mother said as she led the way out the front door and headed for the car.

Edward wanted to tell Judith not to go. She was the only person who made him feel normal. He was the smallest and youngest no matter where he went—at home, at school, everywhere. Even Christine towered over him, and she was only a year older. Since he had been advanced into Christine's class, she avoided him at school as though she were ashamed of him. He had to admit that he did feel odd, not because he was smaller or younger than everyone else, but because he could see things other people couldn't. Only Judith seemed to understand that his thoughts were older and bigger than he was.

He would miss nights like the one last week when his parents went out leaving him and Christine in Judith's care. The three of them had played Monopoly, until Christine tired of losing. "Eddie's weird," she complained to her sister. "He always wins."

"Not always," Judith reminded her. "Remember last month, you won. And he's not weird, he's smart. Someday he'll be famous, and we'll be proud of him."

Edward was grateful for Judith's defense and pushed his victory. "I let you win," he told Christine. "If I had stayed to the end, I would have won."

Christine stuck out her tongue at him. "You think you're so smart."

Judith punched him lightly. "You know, Christine's right. You're getting pretty conceited."

Edward considered Judith's accusation. "No I'm not," he said. "It's the truth. I let her win."

"Maybe," Judith conceded. "But I think we should quit. You're going to win anyway. Besides, I have to study." Judith put away the game. "It's English. You want to help me with it?" That was the kind of question that made Judith special. She wasn't afraid of his knowing things.

Now Judith was going away, and Edward wouldn't see her for a long time. "We're going to miss you, honey," his father said, reaching out and shaking his daughter's hand. Edward knew that Judith was his father's favorite, and that was okay with him. After all, she was Edward's favorite too. But it was strange that his father always shook Judith's hand instead of kissing her. He wondered if Judith thought it was strange too.

Judith gave Christine a hug and kissed her lightly. "Be

a good girl and study hard," she said. Edward thought Christine looked anxious to end this parting. She's glad Judith's leaving, he thought.

Then Judith turned to her brother and embraced him. "Bye, baby. I'll miss our 'go out nights.' Plan a good one for my Christmas vacation."

"Can I come visit you at Berkeley?" he asked.

"I wish you could come with me now. You'd probably be able to help me with my papers," she laughed. He hoped that was Judith's way of saying she would miss him and wouldn't forget him.

Finally, his mother stepped forward and handed Judith a small box wrapped in yellow paper. "I bought some blue stationery with your name on it. Be careful driving."

Edward wondered why his mother couldn't say what she looked like she felt. Then he realized he hadn't said what he felt either.

Edward couldn't help staring at the Negro girl Judith had brought to lunch after the swim meet. She was beautiful in a way Edward had never thought of before. Her face had no sharp angles like his mother's or sisters'. Hers reminded him of the faces carved on the totem poles he had studied in geography class. And her hair was cut shorter than his, framing her head like a tightly curled crown. She's like a warrior princess from a mysterious land, Edward thought. And she's being nice to us, even though she knows she's better than we are.

Only a few hours ago, Edward had watched his tall, graceful sister brace herself in a tense crouch and then with unbroken motion throw herself out over the water, land, and begin her strong steady stroke. Reaching the end of the pool in front of her competitors, Judith somersaulted under the water with the playful agility of an otter and headed back to complete her lap. Now, sitting next to her dark friend, Judith looked pale and uninteresting.

Edward wasn't being included in the conversation, but he didn't mind. It was interesting just to watch the majestic creature in front of him react to his father's words. "Sara, I sympathize with your impatience, but you're trying to move too fast. You can't change things overnight."

The bones under the princess's black skin seemed to harden, and the smile that appeared looked tired, almost bored. "I wouldn't call two hundred years 'overnight,' Mr. Gregory. How much longer would you suggest we wait?"

Edward could tell that his father didn't like the way she had asked the question. "You can only lose support by stirring up trouble, and that will hurt the cause," he said, his voice hardening the way the girl's face had.

"Whose cause is that?" she asked with a faint accent Edward had never heard before.

"Daddy," Judith interrupted, "what Sara means is, we've just talked like good liberals, but we don't really do anything to change things."

His father turned to Judith, and the tight, controlled voice he had used when he spoke to Sara relaxed and loosened into familiar parental anger. "Listen, young lady, I think I've always tried to change things when I thought they were wrong," his father said.

"How did you do that, Mr. Gregory?" Sara asked with accented politeness.

"I've never burned down a building, if that's what you mean," he said, the anger sounding less acceptable when directed at an outsider. "But I don't think I've ever let a bigoted remark go unchallenged, and my paper tries to make people aware of injustice whenever it occurs."

Compared to her effortless movements in the water, Judith now appeared tense and nervous, twisting her napkin and fumbling with her silverware. "Daddy, in Birmingham they turned fire hoses on schoolchildren and put over eight hundred blacks in jail for just marching down the street. Don't you think it's time we stopped talking about injustice and started doing something about it?"

Edward began to feel uncomfortable. His father always seemed to enjoy talking to people. Now it occurred to Edward that maybe his father only liked to talk when he was sure of the responses. Today, his father clearly wasn't enjoying himself. "I suggest you start by not saying 'blacks.' Where I come from, that description would be considered prejudiced," his father said. "And as for 'doing something,' the best thing both of you can do is study hard and become good citizens. That will do more to change things than all the marches in the world."

When Judith didn't answer, Sara said, "Judy says 'blacks' because that's what we are, and we're proud to call ourselves that. But I do agree with you, Mr. Gregory, the only way we will win in the end is by getting educated and gaining political power. Of course," she smiled, "we may have to burn a few buildings before that happens."

Edward didn't think of his sister as "Judy" and wondered if being called a different name made her a different person. He guessed his father was wondering the same thing because he emphasized his sister's familiar name when he spoke. "I don't think I'd approve of *Judith's* breaking the law."

Judith looked down at her plate like a little girl who had been unjustly punished. "Even if the law is wrong, Daddy?"

Before his father had time to answer, Sara turned her attention to Edward. "Edward, Judy tells me this is your first visit to Berkeley. How do you like it?" she asked.

Edward thought Judith's friend had hardly noticed him, and now he was embarrassed to be caught staring at her. He wanted to tell her that from the minute he had set foot on the Berkeley campus, he envied the students who moved from building to building like they didn't really have to be there. But he was pretty sure his father hadn't been impressed by some of the things he had seen. When they were walking to the swim meet, his father had moaned, "My God, look at that pair." Edward looked in the direction of his father's nod and saw a man and woman about his sister's age, barefooted and dressed like poor clowns in a circus. For some reason, Edward liked them and wanted to make excuses for their strange appearance. "Maybe they don't have any money," he said. At first his father had sounded disgusted, but then came the laugh that always meant the subject was not really important. "I doubt that, but if you're right, I'd hate to see what their parents look like, considering the price of education these days."

Edward heard Sara waiting for an answer, and instinct dictated prudence. "Huh, oh Berkeley's okay, I guess," he said, hating his stumbling voice.

His father looked relieved that the subject had been shifted. "Edward isn't interested in swimming," he explained. "But his sister was sick and his mother couldn't come, so I suggested he tag along to see the school."

Sara didn't look at his father when he spoke. Instead, she gave her attention to Edward. "Do you think you'd like to come to Berkeley when you graduate?"

"Edward's our resident genius," his father answered for him. "I suspect he'll be a doctor or professor someday."

Sara's dark eyes met Edward's in a direct, equal stare. "Is that what you want to be?" she asked.

"I haven't thought about it," he lied.

When Judith answered the door, she looked like everything else in his grandmother's house, large and comfortable. "Come on in," she invited. "Grandma just went to the store."

Edward looked forward to visiting his grandmother after school. He enjoyed watching her move around with some unannounced purpose, humming songs he remembered from Sunday school, making sure he had something to eat, finding him old pictures of relatives he had never known, and mindlessly dusting off the top of a spotless table. The house was dressed like its owner, in neat, sturdy, old-fashioned apparel, and the air smelled like peace and safety. Since Judith had moved in, his grandmother devoted less time to entertaining him. That was all right, because in some ways he now felt like a welcome apostate seeking sanctuary.

Judith turned and moved slowly, pushing her stomach toward the living room. Edward set his books down on the old Queen Anne table next to a plate of oatmeal cookies that always awaited him. Edward watched his sister settle into a worn, overstuffed chair, filling it up. "Do you like being pregnant?" he asked, picking up a cookie.

"Would you believe I hate it?" she laughed.

Edward didn't know what to say. All the books he had read suggested women loved having babies. "Then why didn't you go to Mexico and have an abortion?"

His sister looked surprised. "You certainly know a lot more than I did at fourteen." And then with a slight edge to her voice that Edward knew was not meant for him, "But then at fourteen, I didn't know anything." Judith leaned closer to Edward until she looked like she was hiding a ball between her breasts and knees. "Do you think I should have gone to Mexico?"

Edward was flattered that his sister was interested in his opinion. "Heck no. I like the idea of being an uncle. But if you didn't want to have a baby, I just wondered why you didn't do something."

"I didn't say I didn't want the baby. I'm just not in love with being pregnant. It's not all it's cracked up to be," she laughed. "You've been reading too much Hemingway."

Edward flushed, remembering how he had felt last night as he lay in bed reading D. H. Lawrence until the words stopped being words and started being pictures that made his body ache with a fullness that moved the sheet below him. He had shut his eyes and let the book whisper to him about how it should be, how it would be. But until then, he knew he had to content himself with the pictures in his mind and the release that would eventually come as he began to move the covers gently back and forth, pressing them against the ache.

He looked at his sister's swollen stomach and wanted to believe her love affair had been everything he looked forward to. Edward took a chance on breaking the rules of sanctuary by asking a question he doubted Judith would answer. "Why didn't you get married?"

"Probably because I wasn't asked," she said. And then, as if he had removed a protective barrier, she asked, "How are things at home?"

Edward didn't welcome the inquiry. Not that things were bad at home—they just weren't the same. Edward had watched the undeclared war between Judith and their father, and he envied her the respect of battle. He only wished he were taken seriously enough to cause trouble. The other night when he announced he wanted to be a writer, his father told him not to waste time on romantic dreams, as though Edward had just declared he wanted to be Superman when he grew up.

He was tempted to tell Judith about the night he found Christine crouched on the darkened stairs, eavesdropping on the argument between his parents and his grandmother. It was the first time he had ever experienced real anger. He had almost hit Christine for being so stupid, for not being able to understand anything that was going on around her. In fact, he wanted to yell at all of them for acting like everything had changed just because Judith had. Didn't they see that their pain came from pretending they weren't feeling pain. "Things are okay," he said. "You know Dad's pissed, but he won't say anything. He's upset because you don't want to live at home."

"He'd be even more upset if I did. I couldn't give him what he needs, even if I wanted to."

"What do you think he needs?"

Judith shrugged her shoulders. "Atonement, I guess."

Edward had read *Madame Bovary,* but he couldn't imagine his sister eating arsenic to pay for her sins. And he didn't think anybody wanted her to either. A new thought began to form. "Whose atonement?" he asked.

Judith sat back and looked at him curiously. "That's a very interesting question, Eddie. But I don't know the answer."

Edward had received several scholarship offers, but chose Columbia because its distance from Los Angeles offered uncomplicated separation from his family. He still made appropriate visits home, this time to attend Christine's wedding ceremony.

The bachelor party was well underway when Edward and Robert pushed their way into the back room of the smoke-filled bar. Edward was a little uncomfortable with his assigned role. After all, he hardly knew Bill, certainly not well enough to be drafted as his best man. When they finally found Bill, he was proudly displaying Christine's picture to an admiring sergeant. By way of congratulations, the soldier slapped Bill on the back and said, "Looks like you're getting a nice piece . . ."

Bill reddened as he looked up and saw Robert and Edward. Interrupting the sergeant, Bill said, "This is my bride's father and brother." The sergeant turned to Robert. "You should be proud. You've turned out a nice thing for Bill here," he said, slapping Bill's shoulder again. If it hadn't been for the stricken look on Bill's face, Edward would have laughed.

As the sergeant lumbered off to join a small band of his drinking companions, Edward whispered to his father, "That's the kind of guy I want in front of me if I ever have to take a hill." The grim set of Robert's jaw indicated that his father failed to see the humor.

Edward wasn't an expert on insignias, but even he could see that several of the soldiers were seasoned infantrymen probably on their way to a second tour of Viet Nam. Edward felt out of place here, wearing his crewneck sweater over a button-down shirt. He had joined the fringes of the campus antiwar protests, yet he felt vaguely guilty that he wasn't one of this group, that he was seventeen, and that next year he would have a college deferment.

Bill had invited Robert and Edward to the party, explaining shyly, "There'll just be a few of my army buddies." Now, Edward noticed that when Bill introduced his "buddies," he stumbled over their names as though he had just met them himself. He feels more out of place here than I do, Edward thought and tried to picture Bill sneaking through a rice paddy, ready to shoot into the first clump of grass that rustled. Impossible to know who can kill and who can't, Edward thought.

"How do you think the war is going?" his father asked a soldier who was leaning on the bar.

The soldier looked disgusted. "It's going—it's going," he said, walking off and leaving Robert standing alone. Edward watched with interest as the men seemed to purposely avoid conversation with his father. People usually took to his father immediately. All his life, Edward's friends had said, "Your dad's really a nice guy," or women would comment "Your dad's so sweet and shy." Edward felt it had something to do with Robert's resemblance to Van Johnson, with his freckles surrounding a boyish grin and his tall angular body poised to trip over some invisible object. The only person Edward could think of who appeared to dislike his father had been Judith's friend Sara. But then, he laughed to himself, I doubt that blacks are into Van Johnson.

Edward moved closer to his father at the bar and said, "Not your everyday eloquent group, is it?"

"I wish Bill weren't involved in this war. For once I have to agree with Judith. We shouldn't be in Viet Nam," his father said, turning to order another drink.

A few months ago, Judith had sent Edward an article written by their father comparing the Second World War with the hopeless entanglement in Viet Nam. Edward had been moved by his father's closing lines:

> We knew our enemy then. He came in armored hordes, killing our neighbors, stealing their lands, murdering whole races, and destroying our civilization. Our enemy was Greed and Power and Evil, and few hesitated to raise the flag and take up arms. But who is our enemy in that little jungle village? The child who cries for rice? His mother and father pulled from their huts and shot? The young girl slipping into the hills to join her rebel friends? Who, long after this terrible war has ended, will be proud of what we forced our young men to do today?

At the bottom of the article, Judith had scrawled, "*Will wonders never cease?!*"

It was raining when they left a few hours later, and Edward was surprised when his father asked him to drive home. He was even more surprised when he asked, "Do you think Christine's making the right decision?"

Edward was cautious. His father never asked him to drive, and seldom asked him for his opinion. "I don't really know Bill well enough to say."

His father sounded exasperated. "That's my point. Doesn't he have any friends of his own? Why did he ask you to be best man?"

"Probably a little pressure from Christine," he said, although Edward doubted that. Christine was not the type to press things on other people. In fact, he doubted either the bride or the groom had given the decision to get married much consideration, much less the decision to choose a best man. "Don't worry," Edward told his father, "they seem made for each other."

They rode along in silence for a while; then Edward heard his father ask, "What do you think of your sister?"

"I think she'll be happy," Edward said, uncomfortable

with both his father's question and his own trite answer. He wanted to say, "Christine will never be happy because she has never taken a chance on not being." But Edward realized that was probably trite too.

"Happy? She used to be. What's happen t'her?" His father's slurred voice explained why Edward was driving. "I don't know when things started t'go wrong. Remember when the puppy died? Most little girls would have been upset, but she didn't even cry. She blamed me. I brought a new puppy home, an' she wouldn't take it. She wanted t'punish me."

Edward didn't know anything about a dead puppy, but he knew the subject was no longer Christine—it was Judith. Without thinking, Edward said, "I am a man / More sinned against than sinning."

His father roused himself. "Huh? What's that?"

Edward was suddenly ashamed that he felt so little sympathy for his father. He wanted to erase the past few painful years for his father, but at the same time he experienced an unexpected sense of vindication. "Just a line I remembered from *Lear,*" he said.

Finally, his father put his head back and closed his eyes. "Keep up your grades. You don't want to lose your deferment." Then he added, "When she didn't cry, I should have known that something was wrong with her."

The rest of the way Edward let the rhythmic sound of the windshield wipers drift between them and concentrated on the wet road.

The next morning, Edward lay in bed unable to breathe or slow his beating heart. He knew the terror would pass as soon as he was fully awake. It was a familiar routine when he came home for a visit. As he opened his eyes, a bomb burst somewhere in the back of his head, but that too was a familiar sensation. He could distinguish an old-fashioned hangover from an anxiety attack. He had become an expert in both.

He closed his eyes again, trying to push away the dream

he had dreamed with only slight variations since he was six-
teen years old. Actually, it was less a dream than a fairly
accurate account of the night he learned how much books
didn't say. Her name was Barbara Ashton, and, even in his
dream, he never diminished her by calling her Barbie, as
everyone else did. She wasn't one of the brightest girls in his
school, but she certainly was one of the most beautiful. That
was one reason Edward cherished his time with her. He knew
she could have her pick of any boy she wanted. True, she
chose him at first because she needed help with her homework. But as the semester wore on, they began to do more
than just carry their books home, lay them out on her dining
room table, and study. They had actually begun to go to
movies together, and once she even let him put his arm
around her and caress her shoulder.

The dream always began with the evening they were
alone together. Her parents had gone out, and Edward's memory insisted it was she who suggested they skip the movie,
go to her house, and listen to music. Even in sleep, Edward
could feel the all too familiar rush of blood exploding
throughout his body as his unconscious recreated the picture
of him sitting next to her on the couch. He wanted to touch
her, to recite poetry, to tell her he had been waiting for it to
be right.

She invited him nearer and didn't demur as he started
undressing her, slowly, gently. He thrilled at their nakedness
as they pressed against each other, slipping to the soft carpet.
The sound of his heart masked her giggles, which he had been
trying to ignore.

He wanted to experience every part of her, but when
she said, "Hurry up," everything stopped. He tried to bring
it all back, the needing, the imagined wonder, the expected
ecstasy. But the blood retreated to less excitable organs, and
he found himself wishing he were any place but on a soft
carpet, nude, with errant parents about to appear. He had
wanted Barbara, not this strange person named Barbie lying

next to him, looking silly without her clothes on. He pushed her away.

"What the hell's the matter with you?" she demanded.

After that, the dream varied. In one version, Edward responded by suggesting that he would be all right if she would just act like she was supposed to. In another, he imagined that as Barbara arose from the floor, her stomach began to grow larger until she turned into Judith, who smiled a knowing smile and said, "You've been reading too many books." Usually the most frightening variation was his father entering the room, picking up his unfulfilled Barbara from the floor, and carrying her off to satisfy her every need.

All of those versions were preferable to the humiliating truth—the embarrassed little girl who whimpered, "I'm sorry," as she pulled on her blouse, trying to hide herself at the same time—the young boy who turned his back as he dressed, hoping she wasn't looking. That was the first night Edward discovered he could dim his memory by sneaking some of his father's wine up to his room.

Recalling the dream, Edward smiled. He always regretted not telling Barbie (when he was awake he never thought of her as Barbara) that the classics never mentioned what he should feel when the object of his passion giggled and insisted on speed. He had judged her harshly and had long ago decided how he would make up for that. Someday he would write the truth.

Edward became aware of breakfast smells creeping up the stairs into his room. He tried to concentrate on what he had to do today. The guests would start arriving at the church around noon. Sometime before that he was supposed to make sure he had the ring, pick up Bill, and get to the church. The rest was easy. It was his father's job to hand Christine over to her new husband, and it was Edward's to seal the bargain by providing the ring.

Edward took a deep breath and got out of bed wondering which had put him in this foul mood, last night's bachelor party or the dream that followed it. His headache didn't help, and, as usual, he regretted giving in to the urge for immediate escape. Some things hadn't changed. He shouldn't have secreted the bottle of brandy into bed with him last night.

Edward could no longer ignore the smell of sausage cooking, and he envisioned everything that would go with it. His mother pulled out all the stops when he came home to visit, and he wasn't about to suggest that toast and coffee would be more suitable for the hangover that continued to plague him.

In the kitchen, his mother was destroying the last evidence of departed diners. "Where is everybody?" he asked.

"Christine is getting her hair fixed for the wedding, and your father had to leave early. He wanted to write an editorial on the murder of that union leader, Yablonski. Can you imagine, someone shot his wife and daughter too. A child." Margaret Gregory shuddered. Edward was moved by his mother's stricken expression. Before he could think of something comforting to say, his mother went on. "Your father didn't look well this morning. Neither do you. Would you like some coffee?"

Edward wanted coffee desperately, preferably shot directly into his veins. "That would be very nice, thank you."

"Breakfast?" she asked, pouring the dark, life-saving liquid into the cup she had set before him. "Maybe later," he said, grateful when she didn't argue.

"How was the party?"

"I don't have anything to compare it to, but everyone seemed to enjoy himself. Bill's shy. He and Christine seem well suited."

"I'm not sure being alike insures being well suited," his mother said. Turning to the sink, she picked up a dishcloth and began to scrub the counter. Whenever Edward thought of his mother, he thought of her wearing some manner of cleaning cloth, the way some children think of their mothers as wearing a familiar old bathrobe. He was startled when she turned and asked, "Are you glad you went away to school? Are you happy?"

Edward heard more than the need for maternal reassurance. Was it concern? Suspicion?· "I'm okay," he said. "I miss being home." The truth of his answer surprised him.

"Do you?" his mother asked. She stood very still in front of him, wet cloth in hand. "What do you see when you come home?"

Edward felt uncomfortable under her steady gaze and wished she would continue to move around. For years he had been aware that his mother's constant motion masked her quiet intensity. "What do you mean? I see what I always see. Nothing's changed." And in fact, very little had changed since he had left for New York. Judith appeared settled and content with her life. She had finally finished her law degree, found a job as a storefront attorney, and moved into a cabin in the coastal mountains. Although his mother had never said so, he was sure she disapproved of the cooperative nursery school Emma attended each day. But Judith had insisted on Emma's finding out what the real world was all about. Whatever that meant. Judith's life consisted of Emma and her work. Other than her friend Sara, Judith seemed to have no social contact and wanted none. And Christine, rejecting the family's genetic traits, had turned into a small, dark, delicate woman. It was hard to imagine her married and managing a home.

His mother remained motionless, watching him closely. "I know nothing has changed. Sometimes, when you meet an old friend, you notice things you never did before—that he never looks you in the eye, or that he has an annoying habit of running his hand through his hair. You realize he's always done these things, but now he irritates you, and you don't want to be his friend anymore."

From the day he was born, Edward could not remember his mother ever raising her hand to him. She had never needed to punish him. A look, a word had always been enough. Now he felt he was about to be punished for an unnamed offense.

"I'll always be your friend," he said, trying to lighten the conversation.

"You'll have a lot of friends in your lifetime. Some you'll keep and some you won't because you'll begin to notice things about them you don't like. But you have no choice about your family. Take care you notice the good things too—the ones you never noticed but were always there. I'm not your friend, Edward. I'm your mother."

Edward watched his mother bring the dishcloth back to life, lifting the last few dishes from the table with one hand and wiping away the dirt with the other.

Part Three

Thou little Child, yet glorious in the might
Of heaven-born freedom on thy being's height,
Why with such earnest pains dost thou provoke
The years to bring the inevitable yoke,
　　　　　—WILLIAM WORDSWORTH
　　　　　　"Ode on Intimations of Immortality"

6

In the fall of 1964, Judith fell in love with Randall Fisher. Until then, she had only casual boyfriends, but was more annoyed than aroused by their passions. She was waiting for some dramatic sign that would tell her she had found the person she wanted. Her first encounter with Randall was dramatic, but hardly what she expected.

She met Randall when she enrolled in a Greek drama class. Well, not met exactly. He was a sullen young teaching assistant who gave no indication that he even liked the work under discussion. Occasionally, she caught him glancing at her with the same practiced disdain he showed during the professor's more enthusiastic lectures on Greek literature.

Then one day he dropped her paper on her desk as if he were shedding an irritating burden and said in an eastern-accented voice, "I believe this is yours." Across the top of her paper, he had scrawled: *Miss Gregory, dutiful daughters are a bore. Antigone died to prove she was capable of her own heroic actions, not because she was trying to be a good girl. You will make a fine wife and mother—but a hero, never. If you have any questions, check my office hours and make an appointment.* Under his comment he had jotted a dismissive C.

Judith was still smarting from Randall's comment when she showed the paper to Sara. "I struggled for weeks on this assignment," she told her roommate. "It may not be brilliant, but it's not bad enough to justify his snotty remarks."

Sara read Randall's note and laughed. "I know him," she said. "He's your typical Jewish genius from New York. He thinks the gods tempted him with a fellowship in this barbaric land and then punished him for accepting it." Sara handed Judith back the paper. "Tell him to go screw himself," she said, switching from the language of finishing-school debutante to that of the streetwise ghetto survivor. Judith often wondered which language she had learned first, but never asked.

The next morning when Judith walked into Randall's office, he was sitting at his desk wearing his fixed bored expression. Judith didn't think he was particularly handsome, with his dark uneven features and his tall, painfully thin body. "So you want to argue about *Antigone,*" he said, hardly looking up.

His world-weary pretentions irritated Judith. After all, he was only a few years older than she was. "No, I have no quarrel with *Antigone.* I think I understand the play."

Randall looked at her with amused tolerance. "Oh really, do you identify with the heroine? Did your father marry his own mother, beget children from an incestuous bed, and then blind himself to expiate his sins?"

Judith ignored the unmistakable sarcasm. "No, but I don't have a problem accepting the idea that family loyalty can be heroic."

"And would you have dug up your brother's rotting body just to give it a proper burial?"

She knew he was making fun of her, and she felt her indignation giving way to embarrassment. "Maybe not, but I'd like to think I might."

"You're on the swim team, aren't you," he said, changing the subject so abruptly that she was thrown off balance.

"Yes."

"It figures. And then what? Off to the Olympics and later to teach young Americans how to develop their Grecian bodies?"

"I'm majoring in Physical Education, if that's what you mean," she said, trying to sound proud, but knowing it had more the ring of apology.

"That's what I mean. Noble ambition."

"I want to talk about my paper. I'm not challenging you. I just want to learn something," she said, trying to match his sardonic tone.

"Why not challenge me? What can you lose?" he asked.

"There wouldn't be much point in arguing. My father says, 'The pen is mightier than the sword,' and you hold the pen."

"Original fellow, your dad."

Judith felt her anger rising. It was one thing for him to attack her paper. It was unforgivable that he belittle her father.

Before Judith could think of the words that would match her fury, Randall continued. "At any rate, if we may borrow from your father's insight, Antigone faced both the pen *and* the sword, but she argued anyway. You, on the other hand, have an option. You can request a second reading of your paper. I understand our spellbinding professor is easy on the tight-skinned coeds."

Judith stepped back, stunned by his contempt, raw and pointed. Swallowing against the lump in her throat, she willed the tears clouding her vision to vanish. No one had ever spoken to her this way, directing such venom at her. She resented it, was fascinated by it, wanted to control it, change it. At that moment she was a Greek hero on the side of right, he a villain on the side of corruption. She would win. "I don't need to have anyone else read my paper! I'll fight my own battles."

Randall looked at her and smiled. "So, the Breck Girl is a hero. You do look like a shampoo ad, you know."

Furious, Judith advanced, leaning across his desk. "I've heard about you. I wrote a good paper, but you don't want to hear anything you don't agree with. So you give me a C and a lot of crap about what shampoo I use!" The tears, until now captive, escaped, fleeing down her face, demanding revenge. Without thinking, Judith hurled her paper in the air and sobbed, "And you can go screw yourself!"

Judith turned and ran, leaving both her dignity and her paper floating somewhere above Randall's head.

"Don't give the bastard the satisfaction of quitting," Sara said after Judith had fled Randall's office. She handed Judith some Kleenex. "And stop crying. Take it from me, quitting may look like the easy way now, but somewhere down the line it costs too much."

Sara never got upset. In Washington, a street repairman wearing a bright yellow vest called her an uppity nigger. "I don't think he likes the way I dress," Sara had shrugged casually. It was true. Sara looked more like an exotic fashion model than a struggling college student determined to be a doctor. Judith had come to rely on Sara's advice, partly because she was Judith's senior by three years. But today Judith didn't think her friend grasped the magnitude of the situation. "But he hates me," Judith sobbed, "and I don't even know why."

"Some people don't need a reason," Sara said, patting her friend's shoulder. "I've met your dad and brother, so I figure this is the first time anybody has ever said an unkind thing to you. But that jus' ain't the way life is. If we'd quit when they turned the hoses on us, we'd still be riding the back of the bus." Even though Sara had become like the older sister Judith never had, Judith knew she wasn't included in that "we."

*   *   *

The next day, Judith found her paper in her mailbox with the old comment scratched out and a new one written in the margin: *The grade has been reconsidered based on the quality of your writing and the support you bring to your argument—albeit an unoriginal one.* The C had been replaced with an A –.

Judith might have found consolation in the revised grade had it not been for the little, round, sunshiny face Randall had drawn underneath it that laughed out at her.

Judith returned to the class two days later, her heart beating even faster than it did when she swam a last lap, straining for victory. She held her books tightly so her sweating hands wouldn't shake and held her head as high as she dared without appearing the caricature of a proud martyr. But it was all without effect. Her nemesis was nowhere in sight.

She tried to concentrate on the professor's lecture, but his words faded into a humming sound, and Judith found herself angry that Randall was not there to witness her courage.

Judith felt her body grow heavy and awkward as she climbed up out of the pool. She always hated the moment when she had to leave the custody of the water.

"You're really good," he said, as Judith reached for her towel.

Judith didn't have to turn to know who had spoken. She picked up her towel and moved away from the voice.

"Wait a minute," Randall said, coming up beside her. "I don't usually say I'm sorry. And I'm not sure I will now, unless you promise you'll smile and tell me no apologies are necessary."

Judith hoped he would think her shivering was the natural result of being dripping wet. "I won't say that," she said, quickening her pace to reach the sanctuary of the locker room.

"Then I guess I won't say I'm sorry—too risky for my ego."

Judith ignored this last remark, and, pushing open a door marked WOMEN, she left her enemy behind. A few minutes later, Judith stepped into the shower, turned the water on as hot as she could stand it, and forced herself to concentrate on how ridiculous Randall had looked in his ragged, cutoff blue jeans that carelessly accentuated his long, skinny, white legs. Nothing about him harmonized—his blue eyes were paled by his olive complexion, and his ears fought against his dark, curly hair. How could she have been intimidated by him, she wondered? He looked pathetic. She resisted the word "vulnerable." When she stepped out of the shower, she was still shaking.

Randall was nowhere in sight when Judith walked out of the gym. By the time she had crossed the campus and turned toward her apartment, her apprehension had drifted into curiosity. He had sounded almost decent. Then she saw him leaning against a tree.

"I'll give you one last chance to make a fool of me," he said as he walked toward her.

"You're doing a pretty good job without my help." But she couldn't bring herself to sound convincing.

"Look, where I come from you have to be crazy to let your guard down, but I'm going to do it anyway," he said, stepping in front of her, blocking her advance. "I'm sorry. Forgive me. I acted like an asshole."

"Where do you come from?" she asked, trying to decide how to handle his apology.

Randall smiled. "That's hardly absolution, but I'll settle. I come from the Bronx. And I really am sorry for the way I acted the other day. It's a conditioned response when I have to sit in a classroom with a beautiful blonde who I know would reject me if I asked her out." Then, after a moment, he added, "My God, your paper read like Cinderella in chains. Are you really that pure of heart?"

Judith remembered how disturbed she had been when

Eddie was so critical of *King Lear*. She could almost hear her brother saying, "It was Antigone's own fault. If she had disowned her father and let her brother rot, she'd be alive today." Judith smiled. Randall would like Eddie. "If you thought it was that bad, why did you change the grade?"

"Because I had to admit it was well written. And because I had to admit you were right—not about the paper, but about making it personal. I was punishing you for not being in love with me."

The first time Judith went out with Randall, she stayed alert, waiting for the caustic, young teaching assistant to reappear. Instead, she found herself sitting across from an intense young man who spoke to her earnestly about his desires and concerns. When his grant expired, he wanted to go back to New York. "To do what?" she asked.

"I'm not sure. Not to teach. I don't have the patience or temperament," he confided. Judith agreed, but didn't say so.

She was surprised at how the conversation drifted easily from one subject to another. Even though he was too old to be drafted, he was worried about the escalating war in Viet Nam. "It's one we can't win."

When President Kennedy was assassinated the year before, Judith grieved as though it had been her own father. She didn't like to think Kennedy had started something that couldn't be won. "Everybody says it will be over soon. It's only a small group of communists," she said, relying on President Johnson's latest reports. She thought of Eddie. Thank God no one in her family would ever be involved.

"That small group of communists kicked the shit out of the French," he said grimly. "We've got no business being there. Do you have any brothers?" he asked as though he knew what she had been thinking.

"Just one, but he's only twelve." Judith welcomed the change of subject. She enjoyed talking about her family. "His name is Eddie, and he's incredibly bright. He was the one who inherited all my father's brains. I have a sister who is a year older than Eddie. She's shy and sensitive. I think she's going to be an artist."

"What about your mother?"

"What about her?" Judith asked, assuming that Randall was being polite.

"Well, so far we have one incredibly bright brother who takes after your incredibly bright father, and one sister who is shy, sensitive, and talented. I just wondered where your mother fit into this domestic success story. What's she like?"

Judith tensed at his insinuating tone. She had heard it before. "My mother's just a housewife." Judith felt she was leaving something out. There was more that needed to be said. "She never says much." There was still something missing, but Judith couldn't imagine what. "I guess I've never given it much thought," she conceded.

Judith was relieved when Randall made no comment. He just nodded his head and ordered more wine.

It took almost a month for Judith to realize that the dramatic sign she had been waiting for had already happened. She was in love.

The first time Randall made love to Judith, he confessed he was actually terrified. "Are you serious? You've really never done this before?" he asked. Randall shook his head at her. "I'm not sure I want the responsibility of teaching you."

He did teach her though, carefully, patiently, respecting her inexperience. He led her to the bed, and when she resisted his hand on her blouse, he politely turned his back while she undressed. Lying next to her, he made sure the sheet she covered herself with stayed in place. His hand moved leisurely across her breast and down to her flat, tight stomach. "Relax," he said. "It's enough just to feel you next to me. You're built like a lovely thoroughbred." Then he added, proudly, "Who would have believed I'd ever be making love to Miss America?"

Judith closed her eyes and experienced herself drifting—weightless and graceful, and luxurious. His touch outlined her body, and for the first time she became aware of her firm leanness. Pride battled modesty. Were her legs really that long? Did her waist actually curve in so dramatically? She wanted to discover every inch of herself through his touch. Slowly, her body defeated her mind's embarrassment and began making its own demands. She found herself bound to the heat above her, moving with it like a dancer drawn to music.

She smelled the lubricating dampness spreading between them, aiding the rhythm, making it effortless. She tasted the salt on his body and thirsted for more. He was everywhere, his breath, his weight, his admiring hands. Then Randall stopped being Randall and became a coalescing force, invading her body, driving unexpected pleasures into every nerve and muscle. She was alone, plunging into a sea of sensation, drowning. She tried to save herself by riding the cresting wave that mercilessly swelled inside her. Finally, a hot surge swept her up, lifting her to safety.

Randall stroked her wet hair and made soothing noises. "My God," he said. "Forgive me. You're exactly who you pretend to be."

For Judith, there was nothing to forgive. She remembered her father saying that this was nature's way of letting men and women love each other and have children. She smiled. Her father forgot to mention that it was also an exquisitely simple thing to do. "You're a good teacher," she said.

Three months later, Judith hurried across campus already late for the rally. On the way she passed students who lounged under the trees studying and others who moved with purpose in and out of adjoining buildings, either ignorant of the restless force growing around them or unconcerned about it. Since meeting Randall, she found herself caught in a suspended dimension, slipping in and out of two worlds: one of swimming meets and study groups, the other of protest rallies and mounting anger. Alone together and naked, she and Randall were complete. It was only in the outside world that doubts took over, and she felt herself caught in a void that even Randall couldn't fill, especially when she was among Randall's friends.

Almost every night Randall's small apartment was jammed with people who talked about "the establishment" and how to battle it. She had seen students like this on campus, their clothes carefully designed to show contempt for order. Some sat around all evening drinking cheap wine or smoking pot, chanting the new adage, "Do your own thing." Yet, when she refused the smoldering joint they passed her way, they looked at her with suspicion or scorn. She learned quickly that they expected "your own thing" to be like theirs. Eventually, she began to disguise herself as one of them, letting her hair grow and shopping in secondhand stores. But she still felt uneasy and out of place.

Randall had tried to make it easier. "Don't take all this so seriously," he told her after everyone had finally gone. "Some of these kids have a lot to say. Others are just along for the ride. Look around. The world is changing, and kids like Mario are changing it."

Judith had heard Mario Savio speak. She agreed with him. Students should have the same right to speak out on issues as everyone else. What bothered her were the ones who turned the subject into an excuse for a party. "I think we can change things without burning down buildings," she said.

"Sounds like something your father might say."

"You've never even met my father. Why don't you like him?" she demanded. She wasn't about to admit those were indeed her father's words.

"How could I dislike him?" he asked. "Like you say, I've never even met him. Just be yourself," he cautioned her.

"Now *you* sound just like my father," she said

"Forgive me," Randall said. But not with the sincerity he had said those words the first night they made love.

Now Judith was on her way to hear Mario Savio speak

again. She reached Sproul Hall just as the speeches were warming up. Moving through the crowd, Judith searched for Randall and eventually found him sitting next to Sara on the steps of the administration building. Wiggling into the place they had reserved for her, Judith laughed. "I'm surprised to see you two together," she said.

Sara frowned. "We try to book a place near each other so we can argue about the relative values of these demonstrations."

Randall put his arm around Judith. "Your friend seems to think we have usurped civil protest and turned it into a middle-class pastime. She's got a point."

Sara turned to Randall. "I support freedom of speech. I'd just like to see it start at the bottom and work its way to the top where they already have it. Unlike you, I can't afford the luxury of getting excited over every chic cause."

Randall gave Sara a look of appraisal from head to foot. "That's strange. You look about as chic as they come," he said with more admiration than sarcasm.

It was true. Sara dressed like the cover of *Vogue*. Yet she looked more comfortable here than most of the others who wore emblematic T-shirts advertising their collegiate wit with slogans like I AM NOT NOW NOR HAVE I EVER BEEN A MEMBER OF THE HOUSE UN-AMERICAN ACTIVITIES COMMITTEE. A vague, septic envy crept into Judith's consciousness. She turned away, trying to avoid the quick repartee that passed between her best friend and her lover. "Sounds like you're becoming friends."

Sara feigned surprise. "We're not," she said.

"No matter how I try," Randall quipped.

Judith moved closer to Randall. "Sometimes I don't think you try very hard."

"Take pity on the poor, exiled bastard," Sara said consolingly. "What can you expect from someone who measures culture by the height of buildings? Do you realize that millions of ordinarily normal people in Manhattan became neurotic overnight because they heard a rumor that Chicago might build the highest building in the world?"

As they sat and listened to the speeches, Judith had the uneasy feeling that it was the confrontation, not the winning, that excited so many people. Then the loudspeakers directed the faithful to move in an orderly manner into Sproul Hall and remain there until the administration had met their demands. Judith rose.

"Where do you think you're going?" Randall asked.

Judith was puzzled. She hadn't even considered he might not follow her. "Aren't you going?" she asked.

"Are you kidding? I'm here on a grant. Not that I love it here, but at least I've found you," he said, kissing her lightly. "I understand your overwhelming urge to be a hero, my love, but you don't want to sacrifice me to your cause, do you?"

Judith was confused. "I thought it was your cause too."

"You misunderstood me. I applaud what is happening here. I welcome change. But I'm no hero. If I march in there, I'll probably be sent packing within a week. Do you want that to happen?"

"I guess not," Judith said, disappointed. "How about you, Sara?"

"Not me. This is a white issue."

Judith was shocked. Sara could philosophize all she wanted about this being a "white issue," but it was still a betrayal of their friendship. In Washington, Judith had been moved by the look of desperate hope and determination on the weary black faces that sang the same songs Judith had heard in her grandmother's church. But no one in her grandmother's church had been forced to sleep in public parks and endure the mean-spirited jeering from people who bore an uncomfortable resemblance to people she had known all her life. Judith had never considered telling Sara she wouldn't go to Washington because it was a "black issue."

The crowd began to drift apart. "Screw you, Sara. I'll go by myself," Judith said angrily.

Her friend took it in stride. "Hey, sister Judith, cheer down. Someday you'll need all your energy to fight your own battles. Then you'll understand why I didn't go with you today."

Judith turned her back on both deserters. She marched with resolution toward the administration building, as Joan Baez sang "We Shall Overcome." Being a hero wasn't as difficult as the poets pretended.

When Judith appeared in court the next morning, she turned to see Margaret Gregory standing next to Sara. Judith had always considered her mother's contrasting features one of nature's sad jokes, but now she appreciated their unsettling effect. Margaret's eyes reflected an even deeper darkness than her ebony companion's.

"You didn't have to come all the way up here," Judith said as she walked out of the courtroom. And then, against her mother's silence, Judith's defiance escaped into defensiveness. "It's no big deal. They just kept us overnight and then released us." Actually, the scene had been fairly pedestrian. Judith was just one of many called, charged with failure to disperse, and then dismissed to go home. The authorities even offered transportation from the Oakland city jail back to Berkeley, as though it were an authorized school field trip.

Her mother's flat, even voice bore no relationship to her strained, anxious look when she said, "I want you to come home." Then, turning to Sara, Margaret's words found emotion. "Thank you for everything. I appreciate all your help."

Judith couldn't imagine what help Sara might have rendered or why her mother sounded almost humble when she spoke to her. Judith was still angry with her friend for refusing to join her in defying the school administration. Judith watched Sara reach out and shake her mother's hand and was astonished when her mother pressed Sara's shoulder in a half-embrace. There was more affection in that intimate gesture than Judith could remember her mother ever showing.

Just as unsettling was Sara's genuine return of Margaret's warmth. It made no sense why these two women, who stood there ignoring her as though she were a tiresome child, should like each other. Her mother never had an opinion on anything, while her father was at least intelligent—there were times when she would even have said brilliant. Yet her father and Sara clearly had not liked each other when they met two years ago. Judith still flinched when she thought about the unpleasant undercurrent of hostility that day. Fortunately, Eddie's presence had eased the tension and given the combatants something neutral to concentrate on.

After Sara and her mother had said their farewells, Judith was content to let her mother drive. It had been a long, weary night, and she was grateful just to sit back and be a passenger in her own car. On the way home, she watched the green northern hills begin to fade away, and eventually the dry, brown, patchy land ahead announced the approaching Southern California sprawl. Until she met Randall, she had never paid much attention to the land around her. "There are no colors," he had said. "No subtle shades of green. Just unending variations of brown. That's why you people paint everything in faded pinks and blues. You're color-starved." When Randall said "you people," Judith knew he meant her, as though she had painted every pastel house in California all by herself. Actually, Judith's house was a two-story white house, and so were most that surrounded it. And her grandmother's flower garden was ablaze with color year round. But even that Randall found fault with. "Without seasons nothing looks real. There's something obscene about flowers growing in December," he had complained.

It was December, and Judith thought about the bright red poinsettias and winter English primroses that would be growing in her grandmother's garden. She found herself looking forward to being home again.

Her mother didn't take her eyes from the road as she gripped the wheel, every nerve intent on mastering the highway. Judith assumed her mother must be nervous about driving an unfamiliar car. She almost didn't hear her mother's quiet "Do you feel like talking?"

"Why didn't Father come up?" Judith asked.

"He was upset," she said, looking at her daughter for the first time since they started their journey home.

"I'll bet," Judith said. But the sarcastic tone she had attempted didn't sound quite right. Judith watched her mother's hands tighten even more around the steering wheel. Remembering the momentary show of affection between her mother and Sara, Judith was tempted to tell her mother that everything had disappointed her lately. First Randall, then Sara, and finally her father, who had not come to Berkeley when she needed him. Instead, it was her mother who was there. In fact, her mother was always where she was supposed to be, doing what she was expected to do. "Why did you come up?" she asked her mother.

"Because Sara said you might need someone. She was worried. She's a good friend. You're lucky to have her. Does it disappoint you that I came up?" her mother asked.

Judith remembered the first night she had gone out with Randall and realized that she should have at least told him that her mother was dependable. "No, I'm not disappointed. I'm glad you came," she said, regretting her casual tone.

When Judith walked into the house, she was still wearing the same clothes she had worn the day before. Her long, uncombed hair hung in strings to her shoulders. Her father didn't even move to shake her hand. He just looked at her and asked, "What kind of an example do you think you're setting for your brother and sister?"

More disturbing than her father's greeting was her little sister's glare of suspicion. Judith wanted to put her arms around Christine and tell her that nothing had changed, that she was the same big sister who had always loved her, but Christine backed away from her as though she were a dangerous intruder. But Eddie hugged her and laughed, "You look like Cinderella before her godmother cleaned her up."

Judith suddenly realized how silly she must look standing there in her straggling skirt and careless, unmatched blouse.

She had come to think of her clothes as a litmus test, revealing who was open-minded, who was loving, who was secure. And to her dismay, her family was failing the test. She wanted to cry, to run up to her old room, to return in one of her pretty dresses, to call her father "Daddy," and to ask him why everything was changing. "I'll go upstairs and change," she said.

Eddie followed his sister up the stairs. "I'm glad you're home," he said when they reached the top of the stairs.

Judith looked at the tall, skinny boy who was about to become handsome. "So am I," she said, giving her brother an impulsive hug. For the first time in months, she realized how much she had missed her family. She thought about Randall and was annoyed at his cynicism. Why shouldn't she be a dutiful daughter? It's what she wanted to be. She was tired of the constant anger and the endless protest speeches. "Do you have some Levis and a shirt I can borrow? You must think I look like hell."

"It doesn't matter to me how you look," Eddie said. Then, hesitating, he asked, "If you think you look like hell, why do you dress that way?"

"I thought I was making a statement."

"What kind of a statement?"

Eddie studied her carefully, awaiting an answer. But she didn't have one. What did the way she dressed have to do with free speech or civil rights? She could just as well have marched off to jail in a pinafore. Under her brother's serious gaze, she felt like an idiot. "I thought I knew yesterday, but now that I'm home, I'm not sure anymore," she said.

Judith showered quickly. She could smell her grandmother's Sunday chicken cooking downstairs and was impressed that her sister had been able to cope with the complicated recipe. Judith pulled her wet hair back into the ponytail she had worn as a child, slipped into her brother's worn clothes, and joined her family at the dinner table. She was about to compliment Christine on the meal when her father said, "I still don't understand. You have nothing to complain about. You're beautiful and bright, and you have a family that loves you."

Those were almost exactly the same phrases Randall used when he referred to her. But from Randall it was a criticism of what she was; from her father it was a criticism of what she was forgetting to be. Which of her critics was right?

Her father looked across the table. "I want to understand," he said quietly. "What did you think you would accomplish by getting yourself arrested?"

Judith heard the deep sadness in her father's voice when he spoke and wished he wouldn't pursue the subject. "My God, Dad. We didn't kill anybody, all we did was sit up all night in a building demanding the right to free speech. You of all people should support what we did. Besides, I made a commitment to my friends." Judith thought about Sara and Randall and was embarrassed for the lie.

"Terrific friends," he said, as though he were reading Judith's mind. "Is it really necessary that you join the new class of humanoids?"

Judith was suddenly aware that Eddie was watching her intently and she felt the need to defend herself. "Why do you have to criticize me just because I don't look like the image of the perfect middle-class daughter?"

"Just remember, young lady, if it hadn't been for this middle-class life you criticize so much, we couldn't have sent you to that damn school."

Why was he acting like this? Couldn't he see how glad she was to be back home? "You didn't 'send' me. I earned a scholarship, and you were proud of me, as I recall," she said, aware that she was ruining the dinner, yet unable to soften her voice and show how much she cared about all of them.

"Maybe we should talk about this later," her mother said.

For once, Judith wished her father would heed her mother's warning but instead he said, "No, I think we should talk about it now. Then he sighed, "I'm still proud of you. I just don't understand your attitude. Why can't you change the world without condemning ours? What are you trying to prove?"

There was something she was missing, something she was angry about that had nothing to do with civil rights or the human condition. Judith felt herself rushing forward, separating herself from the family she had loved and respected. "I'm not trying to prove anything. I don't have to. Not anymore."

"What's *that* supposed to mean?"

"It means I'm doing what you used to say was important—I am being myself."

"Do you think you're being yourself by looking like a tramp and spouting the latest gibberish from illiterate folk songs?"

Why was she was pressing the issue so far? But she knew the answer. She wanted a fight, one that would force her to move forward into the new world she was afraid of. She felt power and drove herself to use it against him. At the same time, she hated herself for winning and hated him for letting her.

"Fuck you."

After he slapped her, Judith ran from the room. With each step, she felt all the good things in her life flooding out of her like blood from a self-inflicted wound.

Judith drove through the darkness with the determined numbness that usually accommodates the grief-stricken directly after a death. By the time she arrived at Randall's apartment, it was nearly daybreak. "What the hell's the matter? What time is it?" he asked, answering the door half-awake. Then, more alert, he reached out and gently put his arm around her. "Come in."

Randall's drowsy touch invited the tears that until that moment had remained deceptively absent. "Damn him!" Judith sobbed. "He can go to hell."

Randall cradled her in his arms like a patient guardian,

soothing her with "hush" and "everything's going to be okay," asking no questions, offering no caustic observations, no pompous judgments. Unlike her father, he loved her.

For over a year, Judith convinced herself that she had never been happier. She was finally free of indecision, ambivalence, guilt. She was grown-up. And if the sacrifice for her new maturity was parental approval, so be it. Even Randall, although he had never declared it in so many words, seemed to regard her with more respect. He no longer made sardonic references to her Breck Girl image and her Pollyanna complex. In fact, he had avoided any mention of her estrangement from her family. That made it even more surprising when, after making love, Randall rolled over, lit a cigarette, and said, "I think it's time you made it up with your family."

"What brought that up all of a sudden?" she asked, apprehension crowding out the contentment that follows well-spent passion.

"Nothing in particular. I just think it's time to stop punishing him."

Judith didn't like the suggestion in his words. "You sound like you think he's right and I'm wrong."

"Unlike you, I don't believe in innate justice and cosmic rightness."

Judith tried to ignore the glowing ash that clung precariously to the end of his cigarette above her face. "Don't you believe in anything?" she asked, glad to have the conversation turned away from her family, but uneasy about where it was leading.

"Like a good existentialist, I believe the universe is absurd. To think that I can alter a world that has no plan in the first place requires an even greater ego than mine." Resting on his elbow, the cigarette smoldering in his free hand, Randall looked down at her. "But I do believe in choices," he continued. "I decided to fall in love with you, but I labor under no illusion that my love was fated. It was simply a personal choice on my part."

Judith remembered the soothing reassurances he had murmured the night she fled her father's house and sought refuge in his arms, reassurances of a believer in innate justice and cosmic rightness. That night he had altered at least Judith's world. "I don't care if it was fate or choice. I'm just glad you love me," she said.

Mercifully, Randall extinguished his cigarette and turned his attention to smoothing Judith's hair. "You see the world as a place where perfection is possible, and God help anyone who doesn't live up to the challenge. Your exegesis frightens me."

Judith hated it when Randall assumed the professorial air that had so infuriated her the first day they spoke, but she couldn't help wanting to ask him how to spell "exegesis" so she could look it up. One thing she could say about her affair with Randall, her vocabulary had grown. "I can't believe anything frightens you."

"Your expectations do. Look at how pissed you are at your father because he couldn't keep the world the way you wanted it to be. You believed you were a perfect princess in a perfect world and you'd go on reigning in a perfect land. When your father walked into your bedroom and saw you playing with your tits, he realized you were becoming a woman. So he pushed you off his lap into a not-so-perfect world and began shaking your hand. You never forgave him."

Judith remembered the day she and Randall laughed about her father's unannounced entrance into her bedroom. "It must have been a shock when your dad walked in and saw his little princess blossoming before his very eyes," Randall had laughed. Now he was using that story against her. Why? "You're wrong. I don't expect the world to be perfect, and I never did," she said.

"I hope you really mean that. I said I fell in love with you out of choice. It was an easy decision. I wish the one I have to tell you about now were as easy. I've decided to go back to New York. My grant wasn't extended."

There had been no hesitation in his voice, no consideration of what she might feel. They had just made love; he had told her he loved her. He had no right, damn it . . . Judith shut her eyes, hoping to shield herself from his image and his words. From a great distance, she heard her voice offer a faint, polite "When?"

"As soon as the term ends. Maybe before."

"Is this your way of pushing me off your lap?" she asked, attempting to sound casual and failing.

Then she felt his quick, playful kiss. Opening her eyes, she saw him smiling above her. "Come with me," he said. "We can starve together in a civilized environment."

Until now, Randall had never mentioned a life together. Judith felt a rush of air fill her body and realized she had been holding her breath for what seemed like hours. "Oh yes," she said, giving vent to pure relief. "I'd love to live in New York. But I want to get married here. Not a big wedding, just a small one in my grandmother's church with Sara as my maid of honor."

Randall's "Jude, for God's sake, stop it!" failed to quell her excitement. She had been offered the opportunity to put everything right. "It will be a great chance to start all over again. Things will be like they used to be. I know the family will like you."

Randall got up without another word and started to dress. "Where are you going?" she asked, a small alarm sounding in the back of her mind. "You don't have a class until this afternoon."

"I hate to fight with no clothes on. It makes slamming out the door difficult." Randall's smile reflected more sadness than humor.

Judith tried to bring her feelings into line with Randall's new tone. "Why are we going to fight? I'm happy!"

"You're happy for the wrong reasons. I asked you to come to New York with me. I didn't say anything about getting married."

"But you can't expect me to give up my scholarship and just go running after you to New York."

"I don't 'expect' anything from you. I want you to do what you feel like doing. I love you, and I want you to be with me. But only if that's what you decide is best for you. I can't think of getting married and settling down to domestic bliss. I've decided that teaching isn't for me. I'm going to seek my fame and fortune, and that could mean bussing dishes for the rest of my life."

Judith found herself plunging toward the predicted fight. "And what do I do for the rest of my life while you're finding yourself?"

"The same thing you would do if we were married. Get a job and finish school."

The image of Christine and Edward flashed through Judith's mind, their questions and her inability to answer them. Her mother's silent disappointment and her father's not-so-silent judgment. The last night she had seen her father he said he was still proud of her. If she left like this, there was no chance of ever putting her world together again. Her life would be shattered pieces of Randall's life and her family's. "Oh please, don't ask me to do that," she moaned, afraid to add "without getting married."

"I'm not asking you to do anything," Randall said. "And you mustn't ask me to either. So far things have been great between us. But I don't kid myself. You expect everybody to live up to your standards. Look at your poor old dad. One crack in his shining armor and you tell him to go fuck himself."

"I never used that word until I met you," Judith said defensively. "In fact, there are a lot of things I never did until I met you."

"Grow up, Jude. Stop blaming other people for causing the walls of your ivory tower to crumble."

Judith felt fear give way to fulminating rage. "Who made you so damn superior? That ivory tower is where I came from. It was where the best part of me lived. But the minute I let you into it, you started destroying it because you couldn't stand the idea that there might be a part of me that you couldn't contaminate. I don't understand. Explain to me, oh great intellectual, how can you criticize me for the very same reasons you fell in love with me, damn it?"

Randall picked up his coat and walked to the door. "See what I mean about dressing for a fight? If I were naked, I couldn't do this." Randall turned and closed the door quietly behind him.

Sara marched around waving her arms, almost knocking over the only good lamp in their apartment. Judith had never seen her friend so furious. "How could you let this happen?"

"I just forgot to take the stupid pill."

Sara glanced at Judith suspiciously. "That's not like you."

"Dear God, Sara, do you think I did this on purpose? It was an accident."

"Freud says there are no accidents, only wishes."

"I'm sorry you got accepted to med school," Judith said, irritated by the superior tone her friend was taking. "I need a friend right now, not a would-be shrink. And you know what you can do with Freud."

In frustration, Sara flung herself into a chair opposite Judith and said with forced calm, "You have to listen to reason. This isn't some romantic, gothic novel where the heroine overcomes being done wrong by giving birth to the future king of England. Do you realize what this means? We're talking about a baby, not a goddamn puppy."

"I know the difference," Judith said defiantly.

"Okay, okay," Sara sighed, accepting defeat. "If you insist on going through with this, at least tell Randall. He has a right to know."

Randall had been gone over a month, leaving nothing behind except a note. Judith could recite it by heart:

April 10, 1966

Dear Jude,

I didn't want it to end this way, but I suppose it couldn't have been otherwise. You insist on a world where everything is possible. You have some innate belief that there is justice in the universe and that if you just play some cosmic cards right, good things will happen. I, on the other hand, consider man truly tragic. Optimism, except in a very limited and individual sense, or as a purely regulative principle, is certainly one of the most destructive elements in the whole American personality. However, the optimism of fantasy I can accommodate quite easily, which is probably why I decided to fall in love with you. Fantasized optimism doesn't promise anything except what is patently impossible, and above all, it doesn't deny anything except what is patently revolting. I am tempted to join you in the fantasy that we could settle down in some cramped little apartment made comfortable by our boundless love. We could dine out in little inexpensive restaurants where there are no electric lights, no closing hours, no orthodoxy, and not many people. (The last is an absolute condition upon which the fantasy is founded.) The night offers virtual infinities—music, wine, and love-making.

But morning comes when the eyes are forced to open and see a small, cramped apartment, no money to eat out on, and two people jammed together with diametrically opposed views of the world.

Randall hadn't signed the letter, much less left a forwarding address. "I wouldn't know how to get in touch with him even if I wanted to," Judith pointed out.

"You could trace him through the school. He had to leave a forwarding address," Sara advised.

"And then what? Force him to make an honest woman of me? Now who sounds like a gothic novel?"

"All right, you win. What are you going to do?"

"Have a baby," Judith laughed. "I graduate in June. Do you mind living with a scarlet woman until then?"

Sara shook her head and sighed. "I guess I can handle that. I just hope you know what you're doing."

Judith considered the irony of quoting Randall. "I'm going

to try to play my cosmic cards right. Who knows? Maybe everything will turn out beautifully."

During the months following Randall's departure, Judith learned that the universe operates on simple principles established by clichés formulated over the millennia of human experience. In Judith's case, the cliché about expectant mothers assuming an inner contentment to the exclusion of all others was essentially valid.

After Randall wrote what she referred to as his farewell lecture, Judith felt betrayed and alone. But as soon as she found out she was going to have his child, Randall's reason for existing seemed fulfilled and he ceased to be important. Eventually, she hardly remembered what Randall looked like; nor could she understand her rapacious appetite for their nightly passions. Now she was consumed with the thought of being the perfect parent—both mother and father—never deserting the child she alone was creating, never disappointing it, never making the same mistakes that the world's parental predecessors had made. And that probably accounted for Judith's faith in the validity of a second cliché—"blood is thicker than water."

Judith wrote to her grandmother, stated she was pregnant, and asked if she could stay with her until the baby was born. Her letter offered no explanation or excuses. Her grandmother answered promptly, demanding neither answers nor justification. In fact she bordered on the sanguine:

May 3, 1966

Dearest Judith,

The spring flowers are all in bloom, and the weather is lovely. Eddie drops by almost every day to help me weed the garden and then stays for cookies and milk. I feel wicked knowing that he is doing the dirty work while I sit back enjoying the fruits of his labor. But I am getting older, and running a house becomes more difficult as time passes. Thank you for suggesting that you stay with me. It will be very helpful having someone to share the housework with. The spare bedroom is ready any time you are.

Your loving grandmother

When Judith showed the letter to Sara, her friend said, "She makes it sound like you're doing her a favor? Are you sure she understood what you were telling her?"

Judith laughed. "She understood."

Until now Sara had avoided asking the obvious. "What do you think your parents are going to say?"

"I don't know," Judith said without rancor.

A few days later Margaret wrote to Judith providing the answer.

Dear Judith,

Please reconsider. Both your father and I want you to come home to have the baby. It is where you belong.

Mother

"I'll say one thing about the women in your family," Sara commented. "They're not big on long-winded discussions."

Judith suspected being a mother had something to do with not needing a lot of words. She was beginning to understand her own mother a little better.

When Judith answered the door, she saw her brother standing on the porch waiting to be invited in. "Come on in," she said. "Grandma just went to the store." Judith lumbered into the living room, her brother following. While she lowered herself awkwardly in her grandmother's overstuffed chair, Edward put his books down and picked up an oatmeal cookie from the plate that always awaited him. Judith became aware of Edward's appraising stare. "Do you like being pregnant?" he asked.

Judith's legs hurt constantly, and lately the bones around

her pelvic area felt like they were being pried apart. It was impossible to believe that she had ever skimmed gracefully through the water or that her waist had curved so firmly under Randall's touch. "Would you believe I hate it?" Judith laughed, amused by how her body had finally sent her a message she had been trying to ignore.

"Then why didn't you go to Mexico and have an abortion?"

"You certainly know a lot more than I did at fourteen. But then at fourteen, I didn't know anything." Annoyance at her childhood ignorance put a slight edge in her voice. Her father had always had the answers to all her questions. She just hadn't had sense enough to ask the right ones.

Judith saw her brother flush and regretted whatever words had discomforted him. Was she already making the same mistakes that other adults before her had made, mistakes she vowed never to make with her own child? Had she cast Edward in the role of little brother only to enhance her role as big sister? Was part of her irritation because she could no longer dress him up and lead him by the hand down the street? Are we destined to protect ourselves by insisting the world remain static? she wondered. Judith leaned toward her brother. "Do you think I should have gone to Mexico?" she asked, wanting to make amends for resenting his growing up.

Her brother looked pleased at being consulted. "Heck no. I like the idea of being an uncle. But if you didn't want to have a baby, I just wondered why you didn't do something."

The day Judith found out she was pregnant she had dismissed the idea of an abortion without ever really considering it. Without trying to persuade her one way or another, Sara had assured Judith that if she wanted one, it could be arranged without resorting to the butchery of San Francisco abortionists or the danger of Tijuana's back alley clinics. Judith appreciated Sara's concern, but refused. Not that she had any moral objection to abortion. She didn't. It was simply that she wanted the baby.

"I didn't say I didn't want the baby. I'm just not in love with being pregnant. It's not all it's cracked up to be," she laughed. "You've been reading too much Hemingway."

Judith saw Edward blush and wondered if he might be embarrassed by his bookishness. When he was just a little boy, he had been the only one in the family who understood *King Lear.* By what literary standards was he judging reality now that he was becoming a man? Judith watched him studying her swollen stomach, and she knew what he was going to ask and how difficult the answer would be for both of them. "Why didn't you get married?"

"Probably because I wasn't asked," she answered, respecting his right to the truth. Besides, Eddie's simple, direct questions forced her to face the unpleasant realities that awaited her outside the comfortable safety of her grandmother's house. When her mother came to visit, she acted as though anticipating an illegitimate grandchild were a common occurrence. She never asked questions that demanded accusations or denials. But this morning, her mother had sounded a warning when she said, "Soon you'll have someone demanding your total loyalty, just as your father demands mine. When that time comes, I hope you'll understand why I can't visit you again unless it is as a family. I love your father as much as you will love your child. Your father needs me as much as your child will need you."

Judith didn't know how to tell her mother that she had long since concluded that the battle with her father was more complex than a stubborn difference of opinion. Not that she accepted Randall's complicated Freudian explanation of Oedipal conflict and Electra response. She was sure the answer was simpler than Randall or Freud would have her believe. "I can't go home," she told her mother, "at least not for a while." After her mother had gone, Judith felt the acute pain of estrangement.

Now Judith looked at her brother and had the urge to say, "Let's go home." Instead she asked, "How are things at home?"

"Things are okay," he said. "You know Dad's pissed, but he won't say anything. He's upset because you don't want to live at home."

"He'd be even more upset if I did," she said. "I couldn't give him what he needs, even if I wanted to."

"What do you think he needs?"

Judith knew that whatever battle they were engaged in, it was not over yet. Judith shrugged her shoulders. "Atonement, I guess."

"Whose atonement?" he asked.

Judith sat back and looked at him curiously. Until now it had not occurred to her that she had anything to atone for. But she was beginning to have great respect for her brother's insights, and she was not willing to dismiss him with a quick answer. "That's a very interesting question, Eddie. But I don't know the answer."

The first pain taught Judith that pregnancy was only the down-payment on motherhood and the long grueling labor that followed, the first of many payments. The pain was colorless, white. It had no meaning. She tried to concentrate on her mother's reassurances and her grandmother's muffled prayers, but everything around her disappeared into blind agony. She imagined a sadistic giant strangling her body between his hands, squeezing out her insides like toothpaste from a tube.

"It's all right. It'll be over soon," her mother said, stroking her hair and occasionally wiping her brow.

Judith vaguely remembered her mother rushing into the house after her grandmother's telephone call. And later, when they put her in a wheelchair and installed her in the white and chrome room that made agony a sterile procedure, her mother had insisted she and her grandmother be allowed to follow. "Remember, my mother was with me when Judith was born," she told Dr. Davis. "And I intend to be with Judith when her baby is born." The doctor Judith had known all her life did not argue.

Judith heard a voice she hadn't used for years scream out "Momma" and then felt a cool hand caress her face.

"Shhhhh. It's all right. I'm here. Grandmother and I are here."

A man's voice intruded. "It's time."

Someone was singing. The white pain grew dark. What had she done wrong in the middle of the night that would make them leave her with a strange voice? She tried to remember the words to the song she learned in Sunday school. Her grandmother told her that if she believed in that song nothing bad could happen to her. And then through the darkness she saw a bright light shining above her and she tried to see the tiny clown's face hiding behind it.

7

After dinner Robert Gregory sank into his chair and tried to escape into his evening newspaper. But escape was impossible. At least once a week his wife insisted on displaying some new gift she had bought for Judith's coming child and, worse, expected him to pass approval. Margaret's obvious enthusiasm over Judith's condition irritated him. "I don't know what she's going to do," he would say. "What would she do if you or her grandmother weren't there?" And Margaret would casually respond, "She'd manage."

Robert hadn't seen Judith since she returned home to live with her grandmother. Even though he knew she wouldn't call, Robert's hand trembled each time he answered the phone or opened the front door. Today he had even taken the long way home, driving past his mother-in-law's house, hoping to catch a glimpse of Judith. Not to talk to her, of course, just to see if she looked all right.

At first, Margaret had made it plain that she expected him to make the first gesture, to go to Judith and tell her he was sorry. But what should he say he was sorry about? He honestly couldn't think of anything he had done wrong or anything he would have done differently. He had always loved his children, especially, he had to admit, Judith. She had made him feel proud, special, important. She was so beautiful and sure of herself. She was the one who had changed, not he.

Robert felt his indignation grow. What right did Judith and her friends have to dress up like unwashed freaks and act like they had a monopoly on moral outrage? Robert had tried to convince himself that his daughter had been caught up in an atmosphere she was too young and naïve to handle. He imagined some semi-literate, barefoot young man sporting the latest fashion of beard and beads brainwashing his daughter into believing that she shouldn't trust anyone over thirty. It has nothing to do with me, he told himself. Judith has always been impressionable.

Tonight Robert noticed that Christine, who was normally docile, bordered on the contentious. "Why is it okay for Judith to do anything she wants, and I can't even go out on a date in a car?" she whined at her mother.

"You'll have plenty of time to decide what you want," her mother told her. "And when you do, you will have to live with those decisions for the rest of your life."

"And so will we," Robert added, picking up the evening paper and trying not to think about what surprises Christine's future decisions might hold.

"Well, I'm ashamed of her, even if you're not," Christine sulked.

Even Robert was annoyed by Christine's attitude. Regardless of whatever else he had felt, not once was Robert ashamed of Judith. Even at work, where he was certain everyone knew his daughter was going to be a husbandless mother, Robert didn't consider explaining or apologizing away her condition. He admitted he was upset with Judith, even hurt, but that was between the two of them. She had shut him out, made it seem his fault that the world was going to hell in a handbasket. Even when she needed help, she showed her contempt for him by not coming home where she belonged.

Robert was about to point out to Christine that she was not her sister's keeper and therefore had nothing to be ashamed of. But Margaret interrupted his intentions with a sharp reprimand. "Don't you ever say anything like that again. She's your sister."

Christine didn't sound impressed by her mother's argument. "It isn't fair," she said. "Judith gets away with whatever she wants. Maybe I should rob a bank or something."

Her brother looked up from the book he was reading. "You don't have the nerve."

Edward was making a lot of enigmatic comments lately that made Robert uneasy. A few weeks ago, when his son announced he wanted to be a writer, Robert had tried to warn him about pursuing hopeless fantasies. "I thought I wanted to be a writer when I was your age," he had advised his son. "You'll get over it. You've got a good mind. Don't think of wasting it on romantic dreams." Edward had responded as though he resented Robert's concern instead of appreciating it. "Maybe it takes a good mind to have a really good dream." Now Edward sat intently reading, and Robert wondered what new romantic dreams his book was eliciting.

Christine's counterattack was jolting. "At least I don't sneak around reading dirty books and writing weird stories," she snarled at her brother.

"You should. It might do you some good," her brother said without looking up from his book.

Robert couldn't understand what was happening to his family. Christine, usually so sweet and manageable, had taken to sulking around the house like the victim of constant insult. And his son, always so quiet and bright, now cast disquieting looks of appraisal at everybody.

Robert looked over at his son. "What are you reading, Ed?"

"D. H. Lawrence."

Edward was only fourteen years old. Where the hell had he gotten a copy of D. H. Lawrence? But Robert refrained from criticizing his son's literary choices. He prided himself on his disapproval of censorship. Just two months ago he had approved headlines that read JAMES MEREDITH SHOT DOWN IN COLD BLOOD. The owner of the paper, remembering last year's riots in Watts, wanted to kill the story because it was too inflammatory. But Robert had held firm. "It's a national disgrace," he had argued. "Four years ago Meredith needed the help of five hundred and thirty-eight U.S. marshals and twenty-two thousand combat troops just to attend school. He's earned the right to walk through the South without being shot down just because he's black." Robert was surprised at his own use of the word "black."

Edward put his book down. "He's a good writer," he said in defense of Lawrence.

D. H. Lawrence certainly wasn't to Robert's taste, but he had to admit he was a respected writer. Besides, to comment on his son's reading habits was to invite the accusation that he was just another member of the present repressive generation. "So they say," Robert said, returning to his newspaper.

The headlines read FOURTH TIME AMERICAN CASUALTIES EXCEED NORTH VIETNAMESE. Robert glanced at the article. He already knew its contents. The death toll in this so-called "conflict" had reached an all-time high: 970 in the past week. Robert glanced at his son and felt enraged. Surely this madness would stop before Edward was old enough to be involved. What was going wrong in this country, anyway? Almost one thousand American boys die in combat, and the politicians can't even decide to call it a goddamn war, he thought angrily. Well, by God, when he saw a wrong, he tried to right it— and without resorting to bomb-throwing or flag-burning. And he was flexible too. If Negroes wanted to be called "black," he would respect their feelings.

It was Margaret who finally put a stop to the escalating battle between brother and sister. "Christine," her mother said, "we are a family. If none of us had faults, we wouldn't need each other. But that's not the way life is. There may come a time when you have trouble. And if that time ever comes, the only people you can count on to take care of business will be your family. Remember that!"

Only the vehemence of Margaret's voice prevented Robert from disagreeing. After all, Robert had never known a family when he was growing up. Yet, as Margaret liked to say, he had "managed." Robert wanted to suggest that she deliver that speech to her older daughter.

Robert waited for his wife to come to bed. In the twenty-four years they had been married, Margaret had never varied her nightly ritual. She would undress, shower, put on her nightgown, and then quietly enter the children's rooms after they were asleep. Even now, Robert could imagine her standing over her half-grown children like someone who had neglected to deliver an important message and was debating on whether to awaken them to relay it. Then she would lean over and give each one the kiss she never gave when they were awake.

Margaret returned to the bedroom, the hall light silhouetting her nude body through her gown. Robert pulled back the covers for her, realizing it had been a long time since he had been fully aware of his wife's maturing beauty. "Are you tired?" he asked.

Margaret slipped in beside him. "Not really," she answered, putting her head on his shoulder and pulling the sheet up under her arms. "I wish you would change your mind and go see Judith," she said.

"If Judith wants to see me, she can come here. She's much too old for me to drag home."

"I'm not suggesting you 'drag her home.' I just think you should go visit her."

Robert wondered why it had taken Margaret so long to press the issue. It wasn't like her to give up anything she had set her mind to. But this was one time he was as determined as his wife. He was not the offending party, turning against his family, using obscene language. Good Lord, what did Judith expect, congratulations that she had been arrested and sent home, praise that she was carrying a fatherless child and refused to even discuss her situation? He didn't deny that the silence between himself and Judith was painful. But he had to draw the line somewhere. The night Rose had announced Judith's return, Robert made it clear that unless she came home where she belonged, he refused to discuss it further. Until now, Margaret had not tried to change his mind. Instead, she visited Judith almost every day, taking with her baby gifts, and returning home to report on how healthy their daughter looked and how happy she appeared. Occasionally, Robert resented his wife's divided loyalties, but that was a small price to pay for keeping track of Judith's welfare.

"I think you should visit Judith less and concentrate on the two we have at home. Is it my imagination, or do Eddie and Christine seem more difficult lately?" he asked, edging the conversation onto more constructive ground.

As usual, Margaret didn't resist the shift in subject. "Growing up is difficult," she said.

"For whom?"

Margaret laughed. "Mother used to say children were like puppies: the hardest part is watching them growing into their feet."

"As I recall, my feet grew at the same rate the rest of

me did. I certainly didn't feel the necessity to make everyone around me pay for every inch."

Robert thought Margaret's silence signaled her intention to sleep. Then she turned over and faced him. "When I was young, I thought the whole world was conspiring to take away everything I cared about."

"Like what?" he asked, more to prolong the companionship of conversation than to explore the subject.

"Like my father," she said. "As young as I was, I still remember being surprised that such a big, rough man could have such a quiet voice. Every day he came home smelling like a day's hard work. As tired as he was, he always had time for my mother and me. And then one day he wasn't there anymore. That's when I knew I had to constantly guard against life's conspiracies."

Robert tried to remember something specific about his own childhood and was surprised to find he had no memory at all. "I know it was hard on you and Rose."

Margaret stroked her husband's face. "No, you don't understand. I was lucky. I knew what love was from the minute I felt those big hands lift me up and carry me through the house. The love didn't disappear when he did. It got deeper and more desperate. My mother used to tell me it was a sin to waste things. When I met you, I knew I had a lot of love just sitting in empty space going to waste. Love's like anything else. If it has any value at all, it has to be put to use." Margaret turned over and snapped off the bedlamp. "Do you feel like putting a little to use tonight?" she asked.

In some ways, Margaret had become even more desirable. Her skin had softened around her dark eyes, relaxing the fearful intensity of their scrutiny. She was still thin, but now the hollows of her angular body had filled in, blunting her sharp, chiseled bone structure. Lately, when they made love, Robert noticed that she was more relaxed, gentle, almost kind. Sometimes he missed being able to orchestrate her old explosive passion. But he assumed that women inevitably lost the ability to respond. Actually, he was just as happy with the way things were. It was rather nice not having to concentrate so hard on what might arouse her.

Tonight Margaret's passion needed no tutoring. She pushed him back and whispered, "Let me love you."

At first Robert experienced a kind of emotional vertigo. They were her hands reaching out, not his; her mouth exploring. Like a sailor gaining his balance in a stormy sea, Robert slowly adjusted to being an accessory to passion, began to welcome it, and eventually found himself anxious to feed on her sudden exoticism.

Afterward, he clung to her, imagining that during his final thrusts toward released passion, she had whispered a secret. For a long time, he lay sleepless, desperately trying to remember what it was.

Robert reached out of a deep, satisfied sleep and picked up the phone. Rose Harris's voice sounded an alarm. "Let me speak to Margaret," she said without explanation.

It took Robert a moment to realize that Rose didn't make unimportant telephone calls in the middle of the night. "What's the matter?" he asked.

"It's Judith's time. I think Margaret should come."

Margaret had already turned on the light and was getting dressed. "Is it Judith?" she whispered.

Robert nodded his head, slightly annoyed that his mother-in-law automatically assumed it should be Margaret who would want to be with Judith at a time like this. "We'll both come," he said.

"May I speak to Margaret?" Rose asked.

Robert handed the phone to his wife, then reached for his robe. His wife listened for a moment, then said, "All right," and hung up the phone. Raising her hand, she halted Robert's journey to the closet. "I'll go," she told him.

"Don't be silly. I'll go with you."

"Robert, this is no time for reunions. Judith is going to have to concentrate on having a baby. She mustn't have any emotional distractions."

"Why am I considered a 'distraction' and not you?" he asked, knowing he sounded like a petulant child.

"Believe me, darling. This has nothing to do with you. I loved you when Judith was born, but the night I gave birth to her I didn't think of you until it was all over. It helped having my mother with me because I knew she had been through it and would know what I was feeling."

"Of course. You're right. Call me when it's over," he said, remembering that he hadn't been anxious to attend his own children's births.

Just before Margaret closed the door behind her, she said, "Judith will be coming home soon. I promise."

When Robert opened the front door and saw Judith standing on the porch, he was struck by how she had changed. She was older than the girl who had left his house over two years ago. In fact, "girl" sounded silly. She was a mature woman whose watchful look reminded him of his wife. He had known that eventually his daughter would come home, had always pictured them gathered as though nothing had happened. But he had never rehearsed what he would say at the reunion and was now embarrassed by his lack of words. He decided that the safest subject would be the small, lacy bundle she was holding in her arms. "So this is what everyone's talking about," he said, pulling back the triangle tip of the blanket that hid his granddaughter's face.

Emma looked up at Robert, her eyes shut tight in protest against her wide yawn. There was nothing about this child that looked like Judith. Her hair was darker than her mother's and tightly curled. Her nose was long and majestic, and even though she was not yet four months old, the bone structure was already suggesting sharp angles, clearly Margaret's gift to the new family member.

Judith held the baby out to Robert almost as an offering. "Would you like to hold her?"

Robert continued to inspect the baby, not quite sure how to respond. "I was never much good with babies," he said. "I'm afraid they'll break."

"You should have learned by now that they don't," Judith said.

Robert was relieved that his daughter's voice held no animosity, no hesitation. He reached out and took the infant from Judith's arms. Judith followed him as he carried the baby into the house.

Later that night, Robert kissed his wife good night and turned off the light. "Everything is going to be all right now," he assured Margaret, settling into the dark comfort with an easy sigh. "Thank God all this trouble is finished." He accepted Margaret's silence as assent.

CODA

Her husband kissed her good night and then reached out and snapped off the light. Through the darkness, she heard him say, "Everything is going to be all right now. Thank God all this trouble is finished."

Margaret Harris Gregory viewed trouble as a natural element like wind or water. It might be managed or contained, but never started or finished. She had begun measuring her life by the ebb and flow of trouble after it swept in and carried away her father. From that time on, she counted herself lucky when it receded and life moved along smoothly. But she was never deceived by the calm. She watched vigilantly for any ripple that signaled danger, listened for any tocsin. A sore throat might disguise crippling polio; a stomach ache could conceal a ruptured appendix; and an unkept promise would tempt vengeance.

Margaret had been reared by Rose Harris, a laconic woman with simple values. Rose believed in two things—her daughter and Jesus. It was implicit that neither would fail her. Margaret and her mother were alike in most ways save one. They worshipped a different God. Rose had struck a bargain with her God. She had given her soul to him in return for His assurance that He was always right. No matter what happened, there was always a reason, mysterious as it might be. It was "God's way." Even after her young, hardworking husband keeled over without warning and died in her arms, Rose accepted it as a divine plan. "The Lord wanted your father to come to him," she told Margaret with the absolute confidence of someone reading an engraved invitation inviting her husband to Heaven. At the funeral, Rose looked almost joyful as she sang "The Old Rugged Cross" while Margaret stood next to her weeping bitterly. Years later, Margaret believed that her mother found joy in God because as long as she kept her part of the bargain He couldn't die.

Margaret was not willing to make such a bargain. Like the vestal virgins of ancient Rome, Margaret was consecrated to a deity that demanded the service of perpetual watchfulness. But unlike her historical sisters, Margaret had learned that her deity was quixotic, that He might extinguish the flame of life whether she was watching or not, just as He had her first son's, even before it had a chance to burn.

Of course Margaret didn't think of herself in such abstract terms. She had little knowledge of what the ancients believed, or the moderns for that matter. Her philosophy, or perhaps religion was more accurate, was quite simple—hang on to what you have for dear life, and if trouble rips part of it away from you, hang on to what is left.

Now Margaret lay in bed next to her husband and thought about the tides in her life. She considered herself fortunate that Robert Gregory had come to the five-and-dime so many years ago. She remembered his pretending to inspect that ugly woolen scarf and dropping it instantly when she said,

"It's a bad buy." Even if there hadn't been that harmless fire, she knew he would have found a reason to return to the store. And he did return a few days later, flushed with the excitement of his first published article. When he asked, "Well? What did you think of it?" she was puzzled by his need for her approval. Why did he care what she thought? She didn't know anything about writing, or Tolstoy, or almost anything else he seemed to care about. Tall, red-haired, ungainly, anxious for praise, he reminded her of an overgrown Irish setter puppy her father once had. She would wait until he asked her the one question she was qualified to answer. Until then, she would have to answer the unimportant questions. "Yes. I liked it," she had smiled.

Later, when the United States Army threatened to tear her husband away from her, Margaret realized she had to insure his replacement. Robert had released all her love so long imprisoned in her father's tomb. If she lost him now, that love would be buried again. Her only safety was in numbers. "The war will be ending soon. I want to get pregnant now so we will have a family by the time you get home," she announced one night when he was home on leave. She felt his hesitation, his reluctance as she drew him near her. Why did the idea of creating a child frighten him so? Wasn't that what he wanted to do with his writing—create people? Was it easier for him to make up a person on paper than to make one up from their love? Margaret pressed her body next to his until she felt his desire harden against her. He responded, his hands caressing her, his mouth seeking her breasts the way her child would. He towered above her, and she felt the warmth inside as he entered her. She concentrated on the growing heat, moving carefully to intensify it, to spread it the way she had learned to stoke a fire. All she had to do was keep moving, and she would have the explosive release her body demanded. Afterward, she felt wetness trickling between her legs and willed it to seek a different course, to plant life deep inside her. Then he asked, "Why don't you ever say, 'I love you'?" the same way he had asked, "Well? What did you think of it?" after he had written his article. She didn't understand. Hadn't her body given its approval, its applause? Why did he need the words? She moved closer to him. "I just did. Couldn't you tell?"

For months after Judith was born, Margaret had never known such perfect intimacy. She was almost glad when Robert appeared to reject his infant daughter after his return from the army. It meant she didn't have to relinquish her hold on her child. But when Judith spoke the word "Daddy," Margaret knew she had lost her daughter to a competitor who needed words to assure himself that he was loved and who used words to return that assurance.

Margaret understood that Robert had no frame of reference, no history to make him alert to the possibility of losing what he felt was his. He had lost a mother and father he had never known, been deprived of the chance to learn he needed them, loved them. His memory lacked the luxury of grief. Margaret could still reach out and feel the pain of her father's absence and the weight of her mother's love. But she sensed that her husband's loss was greater than hers because he had never understood what his loss was, what it meant. She had been wrong to try and confine Judith's love. Love should be spread out, shared, made safe. She insisted that the numbers increase.

And they did increase. There was nothing she could do when she failed to deliver the son who would have balanced Judith, a son who might have given Robert the chance to recreate himself in the home he never had. But she hung on to what she had, and eventually she succeeded in duplicating Judith with Christine. And after that, when Edward was born, she felt she had struck a perfect balance. She didn't mind that her children gave their outward affection to Robert. It never occurred to her to feel jealous. After all, her need was to get rid of her love, not balance it with a system of credits and debits. Besides, Robert absorbed his children's adoration, fed on it. And since Robert loved her, Margaret felt four times loved.

Margaret thought about the long periods of calm when, though she still kept careful watch, trouble seemed defeated by her happiness. Judith, so beautiful, so trusting. Margaret was content to devour the sight of her husband and her daughter growing in each other's admiration. She should have been more alert to their need for the deception of words. She had tried to caution him against the danger of always having the answers for his daughter. "Why can't you just tell her you don't know the answer?" she had warned. And again, "Some day Judith may not be able to accept the fact that you don't have all the answers." But Robert viewed it as a harmless game and couldn't understand her monition. Margaret didn't think in analogous terms, so she couldn't explain to Robert that he had become like Rose's God. That, like Rose, Judith had struck a bargain with him. She had given him her soul in return for his always being right. The only difference was that Rose's God was safely tucked away in Heaven, unable to be tested.

And then there were Christine and Edward. Each required special watching—Christine, so unsure of herself, so fearful, and so resentful of being both; and her son, trying not to be drawn into the sphere of Margaret's protection, staying out of reach, living in his private world of books. Edward worried Margaret most because, of all the children, he was the one that Robert responded to least. She had been wrong to think that every man wanted to duplicate himself, to have the chance to recreate himself the way he had wanted to be. Instead of applauding Edward when he announced he wanted to be a writer, Robert had dismissed him, saying, "You'll get over it." Was he afraid Edward would experience the same disappointment of failure he had? Or worse, was he afraid his son would feel the joy of success that had eluded him?

Tonight Judith had come home, bringing her own child with her. Judith, who had expected too much of her father and, from what Sara had said, of her lover as well. Would Judith finally discover, before Emma started to grow, that credits and debits didn't guarantee balance?

Margaret had wanted a family so they could protect each other from loss. Now, as she rolled over and forced her mind toward sleep, she had to admit that she had been wrong. There was no safety in numbers, just increased dangers.

8

Christine was alarmed when she arrived home from the gallery and found her mother sitting in the living room leisurely sipping white wine while she visited with Judith. Absent were the subtly spiced aromas offering hints of what baked in the oven or simmered on the stove. In fact, there was no suggestion that dinner had been planned at all. On the sofa next to Judith, Emma lay sleeping, her head buried in her mother's lap. Judith seldom stopped by during the week, and it was unheard of for her mother to relax with a drink before dinner, or any other time for that matter. Then Christine noticed that her sister looked tired or ill, or both. "Is anything wrong?" she asked.

"Judith's going to the cabin," her mother said, as if that explained both her abrupt departure from a lifelong schedule as well as her daughter's dissipated appearance.

"What on earth for?" Christine had never liked the family's trips to the mountains. She was always bored there, with Eddie reading book after book, and her sister and father playing around in the water. The only thing left to her was trudging behind her mother, wordlessly prowling the surrounding woods looking for God knew what.

The expression on her mother's face was even stranger than her explanation. If it wasn't so preposterous, Christine would have suspected she was a little drunk. "Do you want me to start dinner?" she asked, hoping to verify her mother's sobriety.

"It can wait. Your father won't be home. He's working on that story about the actress and her friends who were murdered."

Christine cringed. Each day some grisly new detail of Sharon Tate's murder found its way into the news. There was even gossip about Tate's movie director husband being implicated. Christine wouldn't be surprised. She had seen his grotesque *Rosemary's Baby* and considered it the work of a sick mind. She didn't want to think about the mutilated bodies, much less speculate about the identity of the maniac who was still on the loose. Moving away from further discussion of the bloody massacre in Benedict Canyon, Christine turned to her sister. "Are you going with someone?"

"With an old college friend." Then, as though Judith didn't like this topic any more than Christine had the previous one, her sister asked, "How are the wedding plans going?"

They both appeared to be negotiating a safe subject, and Christine was alert to the dangers of this one. She braced herself for yet another of her sister's endless speeches about Bill's complicity in the war. Judith had become a symbol of the country's hostility toward the man Christine was about to marry, counseling young men on how to avoid the draft, encouraging them to break the law. Even her own father had turned against the war and therefore, as far as Christine was concerned, against her fiancé. "Everything is great. The wedding is going to be beautiful," she said, affecting defiance.

"As long as you're happy. That's the important thing," Judith said with unexpected fondness.

Even though she resented Judith's attitude toward Bill's military service, Christine had felt compelled to ask her to be maid of honor, or was it matron? How did one refer to a young, unmarried mother? "I've designed your dress. Do you want to see it?"

"No. I'm sure it will be lovely," Judith said, stroking her sleeping daughter's hair with absentminded tenderness.

Christine refused to be lulled by her sister's flattery. If Judith didn't have time for a fitting, then maybe she didn't have time to be her "whatever" of honor. She was about to say so when her mother intervened. "Christine. Sit down." It was a command, not an invitation. As Christine reluctantly sought a chair, Margaret Gregory poured another glass of wine and said, "We'll be taking care of Emma for a few days."

Nothing about this scene made sense to Christine. First her mother's odd behavior, then her sister acting like she approved of the wedding, and now Judith actually asking them to take care of Emma—something she had never done. When Judith was around, things had a way of tipping off balance. She cautioned herself to keep up her guard. "Aren't you afraid we'll corrupt her?" she asked, nodding toward her sleeping niece.

"I'll take my chances," her sister smiled. "I was just telling Mom that Sara has decided to join the army and see the world."

Christine couldn't believe that her radical sister actually sounded like they should applaud Sara's decision. "Whose army?" she asked sarcastically.

Judith smiled. "Ours. The Army Medical Corps." Judith had fought her own sister's marriage every step of the way for no other reason than that Bill was in the army. But she had no criticism for her friend. "Did you give Sara your standard speech about the immorality of participation? Or do your friends get a special dispensation?" Christine sneered, glad that Sara had finally given her a weapon to defend Bill.

"No. This time it was Sara who gave *me* a speech. But I was lucky. She also granted me a dispensation."

"Christine, d'you wanna glass of wine?" her mother interrupted with a slight slur. Without waiting for an answer, Margaret Gregory raised her glass. "To dispensations."

The photographer approached the family grouping, rearranging Margaret and Robert Gregory and placing Emma in the center. As he moved Edward and Judith next to Christine and her new husband, he said, "All right now, let's have the best man and the maid, uh, your sister next to each other."

Today was the happiest day of Christine's life, and nothing could spoil it. This morning Christine had been the triumphant bride, the center of her family's pride, and, though ashamed to admit it, she hoped the object of her sister's envy. Now all she wanted was for the entire world to be as happy as she was, including her sister. She even found the photographer's predicament amusing. Enjoying a moment of sibling conspiracy, she winked at Judith and whispered, "Sorry about that."

As the family struck a pose, Christine heard Eddie whisper to Judith, "This proves a picture isn't worth a thousand words," and assumed he was referring to how perfect the family looked. As if agreeing with Eddie, she heard the photographer's voice announce behind a flash of light, "Perfect. A beautiful family."

The band started playing "We've Only Just Begun," signaling the bride and groom to begin the first dance. Christine took Bill's hand and led him, like a reluctant child, onto the floor. It was "their song," and it promised everything. *We've only just begun to live. White lace and promises. A kiss for luck and we're on our way,* she sang softly as they danced self-conciously around the floor. Bill tightened his embrace, throwing her out of step with the music. "I love you," he breathed into her ear.

Then, on cue, her mother and father joined them on the floor, following the music with such assurance that Christine suddenly felt awkward. For a guilty instant, Christine was relieved when her father handed Margaret Gregory over to the groom and then swept Christine up in his arms. The sureness with which her father commanded her steps allowed Christine to relax, to enjoy the rhythm instead of concentrate on it. And she noticed that Bill seemed more graceful, more sure of himself with his arms around her mother. Someday, she and Bill would look like that; they just needed more practice. *So much of life ahead. We'll find a place where there's room to grow,* she hummed.

Her father smiled with pride. "That's a very pretty song. And you're a very beautiful bride. Bill's a lucky fellow."

As Christine and her father continued to dance, Judith and Edward joined others on the floor. Her brother and sister looked handsome together, dancing and talking like two best friends. Christine wondered why Judith and Edward had always gotten along so well, much better than she had with either one. She could understand why she and Judith had never been particularly close—there was too great an age difference. And it was natural for a brother and sister to have different interests. But for those very reasons, it didn't make sense for her older sister and younger brother to be so devoted to each other. That was why it was surprising when she saw Judith step back from her brother as though he had just struck her. Christine held her breath. Judith wouldn't dare start an argument in front of all these people. Fortunately, the band picked up the tempo of a new piece, and her brother turned to leave the floor, Judith following.

"I think it's time I gave you back to your husband," her father said, leading her toward Bill and Margaret who were valiantly trying to keep up with The Doors' latest hit. Handing the bride over to Bill, Robert Gregory took his wife's arm. "Let's leave the calisthenics to the younger generation."

Her mother pressed Bill's hand. "Thank you. That was fun." Then, without further comment, she followed her husband to the bar.

"I like your mom. She's really nice," Bill said, resuming his duty as dance partner.

"How can you tell? She never says anything. Sometimes wonder if Dad ever gets bored not having someone to talk to."

"I doubt it. They seem pretty happy together."

Christine had never thought about whether her mother and father were actually happy together. She considered their relationship static, in place to serve a purpose, to have a family and provide comfort and security. Her father was the architect, her mother the manager responsible for the maintenance of his master plan. "We'll be happy together," she whispered, as she laid her head on his shoulder. "We'll do things together and share everything, even after we have a family of our own."

Bill pulled her close to him, halting her movement mid-step, almost causing her to lose her balance. "When can we be alone?"

In the time she had known Bill, she had been tempted to satisfy their desires, to finish what they had started so many times when they were alone together. But she remained determined not to end up like Judith, not to make the mistake of releasing her body to someone else's dictates before it was insured by commitment. Christine had implored her fiancé to endure his hunger until they were married. She interpreted his acquiescence as proof of his love, a sign that he shared her desire for whetting anticipation and ritual consummation. "It will be perfect after we're married," she had promised. A few hours later, when she and Bill retreated under a hail of rice to their honeymoon in San Francisco, Christine looked forward to the adventure of fulfilling her promise.

Christine lay next to Bill, relieved that their lovemaking had ended. For years she had been excited by artistic renderings of man's consummate passion with woman. She had imagined herself posed in a hundred paintings, the object of either frenzied, violent lust or ecstatic, spiritual purity. But no artist had prepared her for the frenetic, exhausting clumsiness that now left her feeling more absurd than frustrated, more shamed than exalted.

She hoped Bill was asleep and was disappointed when he said, "I'm sorry. I've wanted you for so long, I guess I was too anxious. I didn't hurt you, did I?"

Christine hadn't minded the grinding pain as much as the gracelessness of the act. She was as embarrassed by this moment of postcoital awkwardness as she had been by their fumbling performance. "I'm all right," she said, wishing he wouldn't say more.

He remained motionless, not touching her. "Are you sorry you got married?"

"No. Of course not," she said. And she meant it. She wouldn't trade his gentle shyness for all the sexual technique in the world. He made her feel safe. He would never desert her as Judith's lover had. "What happened isn't important. It hasn't got anything to do with the way I feel about you."

"I love you," he said, sounding more hurt than reassured. "No matter what happens, I would never do anything to upset you."

Christine didn't want to make their failed act an issue. "I'm tired," she said, curling up next to him like a child seeking protection. "Let's go to sleep so we can get up early. I'd love to ride the cable cars tomorrow and then go to Fisherman's Wharf."

Actually what Christine wanted was to go home. Things would be better there. Bill had agreed to live with her parents until he finished the service. By that time, Christine was sure she would be used to the idea of being married. They just needed more time to get to know each other. She would learn how to manage these intimate moments, become more experienced. She thought about talking to her mother when she got home, but rejected the idea. She couldn't visualize her mother ever being tangled up in sweaty sheets. Much as she hated the idea, Christine knew she should talk to her sister.

*   *   *

After she and and Bill returned home, Christine welcomed the relief of old routines: her work at the gallery, the dinner prepared when she arrived home, her father's thoughtful "How did the day go?" She had even looked forward to the monthly Sunday night dinner with Judith and Emma, hoping it might afford her the opportunity to speak to her sister alone. After their first night together, Bill had tried to make love to Christine again, touching her like a wary shoplifter. But when he tried to enter her, his rigid body went limp, this time leaving Christine not just embarrassed, but humiliated, and something else too. Angry. New sensations had been stirred, demanded growth, then been denied. Her body felt as if it were starving after being tantalized by some unknown, exotic food. From that night on, Bill had been kind and affectionate, but had made no further attempts. Now, in less than a month, he was due to leave for Viet Nam, and Christine was sure he would not want to come home to her. She had no choice. Judith was her only chance.

But after the family had finished dinner, Christine's resolve faded. She found herself aggravated by the noisy game of dog and cat that Emma had coaxed Bill into playing. The game's only goal seemed to be Bill's continual pursuit of Emma as he scurried around the floor on hands and knees making barking noises while Emma, feigning terror one minute and screeching with laughter the next, managed to stay just out of her playful tormentor's reach. It was the first time Christine had seen her husband laughing and playful since the wedding almost a month ago. As a matter of fact, it was the first time she had ever seen Emma in a state of uninhibited jubilance. For the past three weeks, Christine had been working on Emma's portrait. It was amazing how long the child would sit patiently without saying a word. There was a sad quality to Emma's expression, but so far, Christine hadn't been able to capture it.

Now, watching her husband and her niece romp around her feet, Christine saw no trace of sadness in either face and envied each for the ability to provide the other such happiness. She wished Judith would reprimand her daughter and quell the noise, but admitted that it was her own husband who was responsible, and in fairness Judith couldn't find Emma guilty without also indicting Bill. Besides, no one else seemed to mind. Her mother and sister were busy in the kitchen preparing dessert, and her father was reading the paper, apparently oblivious to the commotion.

"Hey, you two animals. How about some ice cream?" Judith said, appearing from the kitchen, a bowl in each hand.

Emma eyed the interfering bowl. "No! We're playing."

"Come on, cats are supposed to like ice cream," Bill instructed his playmate. "And it's chocolate. My favorite."

"We're playing," Emma pleaded, as though repetition carried authority.

"So I see. But it's a little loud, and Granddad is trying to read," Judith said, standing above both man and child, the frozen bribes still in hand.

Bill straightened up sheepishly and turned to his father-in-law. "I'm sorry, Mr. Gregory. I guess we got a little carried away."

"Don't worry about it. Raising three kids, I learned how to tune out noise. Otherwise, the last current event I would have read about would have been the Second World War," Robert said, picking up his paper again with what Christine imagined was a sigh of relief.

"Eat on the floor!" Emma commanded her now reluctant playmate.

Bill glanced at Judith. "Is it all right? We'll both be careful not to spill, won't we?" he said, turning to Emma for confirmation.

"Please, Momma," Emma teased.

Judith handed both bowls of ice cream to Bill. "You're awfully good with children. Christine's right. You'll be a good teacher."

"I'm glad you think I'm right about something," Christine said, resentful that Judith had never shown much respect for Bill. Now that he had captured Emma's affection, he had apparently captured Judith's as well. "He's a good soldier, and he'll be a great teacher," Christine said, reminding her sister that Bill's occupation hadn't changed in the past few minutes.

"I have no doubt you're right on both counts," Judith smiled, as though she had conceded one point and now intended to attack another. Turning to Bill, Judith asked, "What made you join the army? You could have had a deferment as a teacher."

"ROTC," Bill said without a trace of the anger or defensiveness Christine felt when her sister brought up the subject of the war. "It helped get me through school. I didn't want my sister to help me out more than she already had. Besides, I figured I owed it to the country that was giving me an education."

Christine waited for her sister's predictable diatribe, but Judith's response was uncharacteristically warm. "I respect that. I guess we all have to pay back what we feel we owe." Judith's unexpected remark must have caught her father's attention too, because he lowered the paper, which until now had held his attention even in the midst of deafening frolic. It was obvious that Judith's audience expected more, and she obliged them by adding, "But it's a shame you can't repay the country for your education by using it. Our priorities stink."

It wasn't the expected diatribe, but it had an old, familiar ring. Robert Gregory smiled and resumed his reading; Judith reached down and wiped Emma's sticky brown chin; and for just an instant, Christine thought they welcomed predictability more than compassion. But that was silly. Why would anyone prefer contention to calm, criticism to acceptance? "Would you like to see Emma's portrait?" Christine asked, rejecting the idea that contention and criticism might be what she too was seeking.

"I'd love to, if you think we can leave these two alone," Judith laughed, nodding to where Bill and Emma sat quietly together, cross-legged on the floor eating their dessert.

As Christine led her sister into the converted studio, Judith stopped to look at the sketches covering the wall.

"These are really good. Who is this for?" she asked, pointing to a series of studies for a three-piece suit.

Christine had begun designing clothes in her spare time because it wasn't demanding and didn't seem to require much talent. "It's for Mom. It's a surprise for her birthday."

Her sister seemed genuinely enthusiastic. "It's perfect for her. You ought to think of going into the business. If I can ever afford it, will you design something for me?"

Christine was flattered. It wasn't often she met with so much approval from her sister. "I'd love to. It will be my Christmas gift." She didn't want to spoil the moment by stating she had no intention of being a glorified seamstress. She wanted to be an artist. Lifting the sheet that covered Emma's portrait, Christine asked, "Well? What do you think?"

Judith examined the picture thoughtfully. "How did you match the color of her hair so perfectly? It looks exactly like her."

Judith probably didn't know it, but that was faint praise. "That's the trouble. It looks too much like a photograph. A portrait should reflect the inside as much as the outside. But when I try to paint what I think is there, it goes away."

"Maybe it doesn't go away. Maybe you just don't understand what it is you're seeing. I'm finally learning the important thing is to keep looking." Then, as if to explain what she meant, Judith asked, "How do you like being married?"

"I'm a little afraid," she confided. "I suppose you're going to say 'I told you so.' "

Judith sat down on the bed that each child had slept in after graduating from the crib. "Why would I say that? I'm not against Bill. I'm against the war. But I don't want you to be afraid."

It was true that Judith hadn't mentioned Bill's military service since Sara announced she was joining the Army Medical Corps. Tonight she had even acted like she really liked Bill. Now the warmth in Judith's voice encouraged confession. "I didn't mean I was afraid of the war. I meant I was afraid of being married. You said I was too young, remember?"

Judith's silence invited more, but how could Christine explain that one part of her loved Bill without reservation and another part blamed him for awakened desires and unsatisfied needs. "I don't think I make him happy."

"Are you happy?"

"It's not me I'm worried about," she said, knowing that was only half true. She was sorry now that she had brought up the subject. She and her sister had not been close for years. Besides, how could Judith know what it was like to be in love and want to stay that way forever.

As if to argue with what Christine was thinking, Judith said, "You can't hold on to someone if you're unhappy."

Christine turned away, feeling like one of those Indian women who won't let a doctor touch her and is forced to use a doll to indicate where she hurts. "What was it like when you first made love to Emma's father?" she asked, pointing to her pain.

Christine had broached a forbidden topic, and when she turned around, she anticipated her sister's ire. Instead Judith was smiling. "I was very lucky. It was wonderful. For others, it takes a little time. Especially when they are shy, and sensitive, and artistic—three things neither Randall nor I was."

Randall. It was the first time Christine had ever heard a name to describe the phantom that was Emma's father. Named, he became a man, with a man's desires. Her sister's lover. She wanted to ask Judith a million questions. "Sit down," Judith said quietly, patting the bed. Christine moved obediently next to her sister. Judith continued, as though beginning a bedtime story. "At your wedding, Eddie reminded me of something that happened when you were a little girl. Do you remember when my dog died and Mom invited some of my friends to a wake after we buried him?"

Christine didn't know what Judith was talking about, but apparently that didn't matter, because she didn't wait for Christine's response. "Afterward, my friends and I took you outside and danced around you, singing and teasing. You sat on the ground terrified. The louder you cried, the louder we sang."

Christine had a vague, uneasy memory, but no picture came with the sensation. "It can't have been very important if I don't even remember."

"That's the point. You didn't understand what was happening. You were too young to know that *we* were the ones who were frightened. It was *our* fear that made you cry, not your own." Judith put her arm around her sister. "Maybe you're still too young to know who the frightened one is. Maybe it's Bill who's scared. It might be *his* fear you're feeling. He could be the one who is afraid of losing you."

Wondering if Judith had ever been afraid of losing (now she could give him a name) Randall, she asked, "So what can I do?"

"Tell him that you want him. Put everything out of your mind except that want. And when he comes to you, close your eyes and let your body do the thinking. It'll know what to do. And believe me, Bill's body will feel yours and forget it was afraid." Judith put her arms around Christine. "It's fun," she said, hugging her. Then she laughed. "And for heaven's sake, remember. Whatever you do, don't think about what a picture you make."

Christine was glad for the first time that she had an older sister who had had a wonderful love affair with someone named Randall.

Christine waited until the Sunday dinner was finished before she read Bill's letter to her family:

William Wolfe 1Lt.
101st Airborne Division
American Division, I Corps

February 13, 1970

Dearest Christine,
    We arrived in Saigon. It's hard to believe there's a

war going on in the countryside. Some of my buddies have warned me that everybody here is either a VC sympathizer or out to get my money. But from what I have seen, that's not true. Everybody seems to really like Americans. It's not like I expected at all. Of course I haven't seen much so far.

And the weather here is terrific. If there weren't a war here, I'll bet it could be a resort like Hawaii.

As you can see, I've been assigned to the 101st Airborne. I'll be leaving for Phu Bai in a few days. You may read about the unit in the papers because they have had a lot of KIAs (killed in action) but I don't want you to worry about me. The 101st has a lot of seasoned guys and they know what they're doing. In fact, they say that the fighting is winding down because of Nixon's Vietnamization policy. The ARVN (South Vietnamese Regular Army) is doing most of the fighting now.

I'm glad that you are living with your parents and that you won't be alone. That way I won't worry so much about my not being there to take care of you.

I don't know why you should be surprised that people think your designs are good. I knew the minute I met you that you were not only beautiful, you were talented. Those people are lucky to have you waste your time on them. I wish I had your talent. I may never get rich being a teacher, but I know I can make you happy.

Give my love to Mom and Dad, and tell Judith I send my regards. Tell her that I haven't forgotten about trying to see her friend if I can.

I love you more than ever,
Bill

When Christine finished reading the letter, her father said, "The 'hundred and first is a pretty tough outfit."

For a moment, the concern in his voice frightened Christine. "What do you mean? Is that bad? Do you think he's in real danger?" She couldn't stand the thought that anything might happen to Bill. The last two weeks they had spent together had been wonderful. For a change, Judith had been right. Her body had known how to make the aching feeling grow, flower, and yield fruit. All she had to do was weed out the mind's inhibitions. Now, neither her body nor her mind could accept losing Bill.

In a comforting voice she hadn't heard since she was a child, her father said, "Don't worry, darling, he's going to be fine. I wouldn't be surprised if this mess was over in a few months. Bill might be home sooner than any of us thinks."

Relieved, Christine turned to her sister. "See. Sara must be exaggerating. Bill doesn't seem to think he's hated, and Dad thinks it will be over before we know it."

Christine wondered if Judith was paying attention because, instead of arguing, she said, "The next time you write to Bill, tell him I send my love." But she didn't look at Christine when she said it. She looked at her father.

March 20, 1970

My Darling Bill,

I love and miss you too. I'm glad you are going to be with men who have experience. I promise, I won't worry about you. But I can't help missing you.

Everybody in the family sends their love—including Judith. Not that she's changed her mind about the war. The other day she dragged Emma off to a so-called peace march that turned violent. Judith got pushed to the ground, and she almost lost Emma in the crowd. And guess who gave her hell for it. Nope, you're wrong. Not Dad. It was Mom. She told Judith that it was her job to protect Emma, not endanger her. Her exact words were "Emma will have to face enough threats in life without you providing them for her." That's pretty strong stuff for Mom. The funny thing is, Judith kept her mouth shut and took it. She's getting more like Mom that way— she keeps quiet instead of jumping on people for every

little thing. Ever since she went away to Arrowhead,
she's acted different. But then my sister can change overnight for no reason.

I called your sister in Chicago and read your letter
to her (not the personal parts). I asked her to send me
her measurements and a picture of her so that I could
design a dress for her. I hope I can meet her when you
get home. We can go to Chicago for vacation.

I finished Emma's portrait last week. Everyone says
it looks just like her and I suppose that means they like
it. But I know it's not very good. Actually, I'm beginning
to like designing clothes better than painting. It's like
doing a cloth frame for a portrait, instead of doing the
portrait itself. I guess this won't make much sense, but
I'm pretty good at knowing what a person should look
like on the outside, even though I can't see what the
inside is like.

I love you so much and miss you. Please write to
me every chance you get. I'll do the same.

Your loving wife,
Christine

And at first they did write to each other every day. She,
constantly searching for interesting bits of news that would
make him feel closer to home—*As usual, Judith is up in
arms about the war. This time it's the bombing of Cambodia.
You'd think she was a military expert*—and avoiding the
unpleasant—*Grandmother Rose's garden is in full bloom.*
He, giving daily descriptions of the weather— *I've changed
my mind, the heat, rain, and constant humidity are terrible*—and offering anecdotal reports of his army buddies' ex-
ploits—*The other night someone swiped a pig, greased it,
and set it loose in camp. We had pork chops for dinner.*
Lately, though, his letters seemed to dwell on subjects that
meant little to Christine—*Sometimes I can't tell who the
good guys really are.* And—*A lot of guys are hooked on junk*

here. I can't blame them. Most of us will do almost anything to dull the reality of this place. In one letter he described his own means of escape. *I saw Sara again. I look forward to going out on Med Caps with her (remember, the medical service I told you about that volunteers to help in the villages). I like working with the kids. It's the one bright spot over here. No matter how rough they have it, these pathetic children still manage to smile and even play. I wish this were my regular duty.*

As time passed, Christine became less sure of how to respond.

April 3, 1970

Dearest Bill,

I'm glad you had a chance to see Sara again. I only met her a few times, so I guess I didn't see that side of her. She didn't seem particularly sweet or sensitive to me. In fact, there were times when I thought she was laughing at all of us. But I think it's really wonderful of you to spend your free time going to the villages to help. It sounds so sad, all those children just wandering around with no parents and no place to live. If you send us a list of things they could use, I'll send whatever I can. I worry that you may not be getting enough rest. Maybe you shouldn't spend so much time volunteering for things.

There's not a lot of news here. The busier Judith gets (her law practice is growing) the more time Emma spends here. She's getting more beautiful every day and I think Dad's secretly pleased when Judith leaves her here. He's become very fond of her. And Emma adores him. He's like a father to her. She's a sweet little girl, but brooding. I have the feeling that she blames all of us for not telling her anything about her father.

Please don't let the sad things there upset you too much. Remember, you're fighting for your country and I'm proud of you.

I love you. And every night I imagine you are next to me.

Love, Christine

April 30, 1970

Dearest Christine,

I've seen my first real combat. We're just outside of Hue. We lost over eleven men, and God knows how many were wounded. The NVR pounded us for four straight days. It wouldn't be so hard to take if I could figure out what we were trying to capture. There was nothing but mountains and jungle. Nothing looked important enough to kill and maim for. I'm afraid no one here really thinks Nixon's policy is working. Thousands of the ARVN are deserting, and so are a lot of our guys. I know I shouldn't say this, but I can't blame them.

The 1st Lt. was killed, and presto, I got promoted. I'm so afraid. I was a recruiter. I don't know anything about leading men. I'm going to take my R&R at the Evac. Hospital. It'll be good to see Sara and talk about home and the people we love. It makes me feel closer to you, and I enjoy helping out with the village kids when I can. But sometimes even there I feel like I'm in the enemy camp. We're hated everywhere.

You're the only thing that makes sense to me right now. I think of you all the time.

I love you so much. You're
all I really care about.
Bill

Christine's letters continued to reflect her pride and love. She was worried, of course. But it was all so far away. Every day the politicians promised that American forces were being withdrawn and that the real fighting was being turned over to the South Vietnamese. She refused to watch the evening news, which continued to show the isolated incidents of American casualties. The media insisted on sensationalizing everything.

June 5, 1970

My Dearest Bill,

All I can think of is that you will be with me soon. The papers are filled with Nixon's promise to bring all the American troops home and leave the fighting to the Vietnamese. I pray that will happen soon and we can begin our life together.

I've started looking for a house for us. Yesterday I found one not too far from Mom and Dad's. It reminds me of Grandma Rose's house. It's small and old and it needs work, but I think we would have fun fixing it up. Considering the price of houses these days, it's not too expensive. I've saved every penny you've sent home, along with the extra money I've made designing dresses. And Dad says he'll help with the downpayment if we need more. Just think. Next year we could be celebrating the holidays together in our own place.

Darling, please write to me as soon as possible. The only time I really worry is when I don't hear from you.

Don't think about what's going on there. Just think of how we will be together soon.

I love you so much,
Christine

July 30, 1970

Dear Christine,

I don't know how to describe it here. Every day either we're surrounded by artillery, mortars, and air bombardment, or we're slogging through rice paddies looking for an enemy who never shows himself. Every time I hear a duster, I know some poor guy is being hauled off either dead or ripped to bits, and I start to shake. What scares me most is that I'm afraid I'm going to get a lot of kids killed (and they are kids, most of them are only nineteen and twenty years old). So far I've been lucky, but I don't know how long that luck is going to last.

I know I shouldn't write any of this stuff to you, but I need to tell someone what it's like here. Knowing that you love me, and that I can tell you how I feel, is the only thing that seems to make me feel I can survive this terrible place.

Tell Judith that Sara has been transferred to the Evac. Hospital in Oui Nhon. If I'm lucky, I'll get out of this hole long enough to see her.

I love and need you more than ever.

Bill

July 28, 1970

My Dearest Husband,

I was so worried when I didn't hear from you. Then Judith said she got a letter from Sara, and she said you two managed to meet again. You can't imagine how relieved I was to know that you were all right. But now that I do know, I'm a little upset that I had to hear it from someone besides you. Are you angry? Is it the house? Do you think it's too expensive? If you don't want me to buy it, just tell me.

Love xxxxes
Christine

August 20, 1970

Dear Christine,

I know you've been worried, but I'm all right. I just needed a little time to get over what happened last month. My platoon lost seven men in less than five minutes. It was unreal. One minute I was leading them through a "friendly" village, and the next we were being blown apart. I don't even know if they were NVA, Cong, or armed peasants. All I know is that no matter what the Captain says, it was my fault. I led them into that trap because those fucking people looked like they were glad to see us. Sara told me that I should write to you and be honest about my feelings. But that's hard to do because I'm not sure what those feelings are anymore. No matter what we throw at these people, they just won't give up. They just keep coming and coming. Christine, what if they never give up? We'll just have to keep killing them forever and ever. I have to get out.

I got the packages you and the family sent. As soon as I got them, I locked them up because I know everything will be stolen. Everybody steals here, but it's okay because if murder is all right, so is everything else. Anyway, thanks for the stuff.

Christine, I love you so much. I can't stand being away from you, especially at Christmas. I feel like I'm falling apart and I need you so much. At first when I came here I thought the women looked delicate and sad. Now I know they're either sneaky whores or Cong. They say Bob Hope comes here during the holidays. The show is supposed to be terrific. So I guess Christmas will be okay.

Bill

PS. Do whatever you want about the house. I just want to come home.

Christine put this last letter down. She had read it over and over, each time with a different response. At first she was angry. Bill was beginning to sound like some of the men he had invited to the wedding—coarse and mean. Then she was afraid. Maybe he didn't really miss her at all; otherwise why would he mention other women? And finally, she felt despair. The man who wrote this letter didn't make sense. It wasn't her husband. One minute talking about stealing and whores, the next about Bob Hope and Christmas, when the holidays were almost six months away. By that time he was due to come home. And he didn't sound like he cared about the house one way or the other.

She wanted to show the letter to her father, but she was ashamed of it. And she wouldn't give her sister the satisfaction that she might have been right all along.

Bill's letters didn't come regularly after that, and when they did come, they stopped saying much of anything. They were sometimes no more than a single sentence—*I'm all right.* Or—*Don't worry, I'm going to make it.* One of the last ones read:

> September 3, 1970
>
> Christine,
>
> Send me all the news you can about Mylai. They don't tell us the truth here. Funny isn't it, how upset everybody is. They shouldn't be. It happens all the time here. Did you notice that Lt. William Calley and I have the same first name and rank?
>
> Lt. William Wolfe

And finally—*I'm being discharged early.*

Christine had worked months preparing for this moment, designing and sewing curtains and drapes and bedspreads. But she had not actually moved into the new house until today, promising herself that their first night in the house would be spent together.

Against Judith's advice, Christine had planned a homecoming party. Christine simply couldn't bear to face her husband alone until she was sure he was all right. She refused to feel guilty, regardless of Judith's admonition about their father picking Bill up at the airport. It would be easier if other people were around when she first saw him again. Judith had finally agreed to take the day off and bring Emma. And even

Edward was home for the Thanksgiving vacation. Christine was sure Bill would like seeing everybody together again; he had always said he felt like a regular member of the family. Everything was ready for him—his favorite fried chicken and potato salad, his old civilian clothes, even his old faded robe in case he just wanted to sit and relax.

When she opened the door, Christine was prepared to see that her husband had changed, that his hair had thinned or grayed, that he had lost weight or gained it, that he had at least aged. But the man who stood on the porch next to her father was the same man who had kissed her good-bye almost a year ago. His hair was the same unruly brown, his body still lean and gawky, and his face still boyish and shy. She threw her arms around him and rained kisses on him, weeping with relief that he had returned home, not just whole, but unchanged. She should have known he was all right. Otherwise, they wouldn't have released him from the hospital. Dragging him by the hand, she pulled him into the house after her. "Darling, come in and see our new house. Everyone's here."

Christine was overcome with pride as she stood amidst her family. "Well? How do you like it?"

Bill looked around, appearing not quite sure of where he was, and said, "It's nice," as if trying to humor a pestering child.

Christine tried to conceal her disappointment at Bill's obvious lack of enthusiasm and was relieved when her mother appeared next to Bill and put her hand on his shoulder. "It's good to have you back with us. Are you tired? Would you like something to eat?"

Bill backed away from Margaret Gregory as if she had just offered him poison. "What?"

"Are you hungry?" her mother repeated.

"Uh, no, ma'am. Thank you," he said, apparently remembering his manners.

Edward joined his mother and shook Bill's hand. "Welcome home."

For a moment, Christine thought she might have to remind Bill who Eddie was. Then he responded, "Oh, Edward.
How have you been?"

Finally Judith stepped forward and said, "It's good to
have you home, Bill. We'll only stay for a few minutes." Christine felt a momentary panic. She wasn't ready to be alone
with someone who didn't seem to recognize anyone, who
acted like he didn't belong where he was standing. He might
look like the man she had married, but he wasn't acting like
him. Then, for the first time, Bill's eyes seemed to focus, and
he smiled. "Judith! I'm glad you're here. Don't go. I have a
message from Sara. She told me to tell you that she was wrong.
There's no such thing as a black or white issue. There are
just issues. Does that make sense to you?"

"You bet it does," her sister said, embracing Bill. "Thanks."

As Christine watched her husband return Judith's embrace, relief battled annoyance. Relief that Bill was responding
in his old, gentle way, and annoyance that it was Judith, not
she, who had elicited that response. When Christine saw their
mutual tears of a secret, shared complicity, annoyance was
the victor.

The doctors told Christine that it was perfectly normal for
her husband to have brief periods of depression. After all, he
had seen some pretty unpleasant things. Not more than most
combat soldiers, of course. But it took some longer to forget
the experience than others. She should just be grateful that
her husband had come home in one piece. Others had not
been so fortunate. They were the ones who needed help.
Money was tight, and there just weren't enough facilities to
help people like Bill. Be patient, give him time, he'll get over
it, they said.

"He'll get over it?" Judith fumed. "We don't mind spending this country into bankruptcy and killing God knows how
many people before this is through. And you're telling me
they can't afford to provide hospital care. I don't believe it.
Did you tell them how serious this was?"

Christine had called her sister in the middle of the night. Bill had locked himself in the bathroom and refused to come out. The only one he would listen to was Judith. When her sister arrived, she coaxed him out, and then they spent the remainder of the night huddled together talking. Eventually, Christine had gone to bed, feeling that her presence was not only unnecessary, but unwanted.

Now Christine stood opposite her sister arguing in hushed tones, careful not to awaken her exhausted husband. "But they say it's not serious. It's normal."

"Normal my ass. Christine, you have to do something. He's been home almost a year, and he's getting worse. Can't you see it?"

Christine choked back her tears of frustration. "Most of the time he's fine. Maybe not like he used to be, but not crazy." Holding out proof that the experts knew more than her sister, Christine said, "They say he's not even sick enough to be eligible for disability." Then, she called on her last witness to testify that there was hope. "Even Bill says he'll be all right. He says all he needs is to forget about the army. He refuses to go to the hospital."

"If he won't go to the VA, then get him to a private doctor. Make him go!"

Christine flung herself onto the sofa sobbing. "I can't. He won't talk to me about it. He won't talk to me about anything. I beg him to tell me what he's thinking, but he won't. You're the only one he'll talk to."

Judith stood towering above her, her fists clenched. "Maybe that's because he knows you don't really want to hear. It might upset you," she said contemptuously.

Christine wanted to jump up and hit her sister. What did she know about being awakened in the middle of the night by the piercing screams of a nightmare-ridden husband. About holding him in her arms until his shaking subsided. About reassuring him over and over that she loved him and that he was safe now. About begging him not to think about it. And about submitting to desperate lovemaking that had less do to with passion than it did with panic. How could Judith think she hadn't tried to do everything she could? "That's not fair. I can't help it if he would rather tell you his war stories. Sharing your little secrets about what he and Sara did over there. You enjoy them." Christine couldn't hold back the flood of anger that had been building since the first day Bill returned to smile at his sister-in-law instead of his wife. How dare Judith steal her husband's love and trust and then accuse her of being the accomplice to Bill's despair. Christine stood up to dramatize her attack. "You love every minute of this. It makes you feel so self-righteous. It's just one more thing you can feel smug about, looking down on me, laughing at me behind my back. I'll bet you two have a great time discussing his whores. Or did Sara fill that need for him?"

Christine tried not to shrink from Judith's raised hand, welcoming the final victory that her sister's violence would provide. But Judith's hand stalled in midair, faltered, then dropped powerlessly beside her, declining the invited anger, offering instead only humiliating patience. "You should be ashamed of yourself," Judith said, the way a mother might scold a naughty child. "Bill loves you more than anything in the world. Do you think he *wants* to act like this? He's drowning, and he's terrified that if he grabs on to you, he'll take you down with him. He talks to me because I'm his one connection with someone who is still over there. Sara was his lifeline. His link to us. Now she's his lifeline to the past, and so am I. You can't believe the things you've just said."

Christine knew that Bill loved her, that he had never stopped loving her from the time they first met. But what good was his love if he was too frightened or too sick to show it? And what good was hers if she couldn't use it to help. For the first time in her life, Christine felt fear, real fear. Not the kind that comes with a spurt of adrenaline and an outcry of "I'm afraid." This was a slow, unnamed terror that was drifting into her, invading her body, threatening to wrap itself around her love, choking it, leaving nothing behind— not love, not anger, not even hope. She reached out to her sister and allowed herself to be folded into the comfortable shelter of Judith's arms. "He's not going to get better, is he?"

Judith's silence threatened a verdict. "Is he?" Christine persisted.

Her sister's embrace tightened. "Yes, he is. I promise. He's going to get better."

And Bill did get better. Her father asked Dr. Davis to recommend a specialist to treat Bill, and Judith convinced him to go. Eventually, Bill's nightmares came less often and with less severity. True, occasionally he still awoke clinging to her half asleep, bathed in sweat and weeping softly. But the terrifying moments of not recognizing where he was or who he was with had stopped. He began accepting substitute teaching assignments, coming home with stories about the antics of his preadolescent pupils. He was even considering a permanent teaching position at the local grade school. And Christine no longer resented her sister's visits because Bill appeared to welcome them as a friendly social call, not a frantic need. Tonight, as she and Bill joined the family for their regular Sunday dinner, Christine felt happy and secure. Things were back to normal.

"How's the job going, Bill?" her father asked halfway through dinner.

Christine warmed to her husband's enthusiasm. "Great. Kids sure are more uninhibited than we were at that age. Nothing seems to embarrass them."

"I'm not so sure that's a good thing," her father said.

Judith looked up at her father. "You think it's healthy for a child to be embarrassed?" It was more an accusation than a question.

Robert Gregory either didn't notice or chose to ignore his daughter's tone. Patting his five-year-old granddaughter, he said, "Emma is a good example of proper modesty. She'd have sense enough to be embarrassed if the situation warranted."

"I try to teach Emma that there is never a subject that

is too embarrassing to discuss. Sometimes modesty is just an excuse for not facing things squarely."

Christine knew that he and Judith were embarking on their old, familiar struggle of wills when her father said, "Really? I notice there are some subjects that you seem to be avoid."

Christine was annoyed at both of them. She wasn't going to let them spoil the announcement she had planned. "I'd like to make a toast," she said, raising her glass. Waiting until the attention focused on her, she continued, "Well? Who's going to join me?"

"I never turn down a toast," her father smiled, turning away from his older daughter. "What's the occasion?"

"Tonight is special. I'd like to drink to my wonderful husband."

Bill looked at his wife, puzzled and a bit uncomfortable. "Thank you."

"Don't you want to know why this is a special night?" she asked playfully, savoring the pride and joy that was about to greet her.

"I'll ask," Judith said calmly, as if she already knew the answer and wasn't anxious to have it celebrated.

"Because tonight, it is official. My husband is going to be a father."

Robert Gregory was the first to react, raising his glass, touching it gently against Christine's. "That's wonderful! Congratulations!"

Her mother reached over and covered her daughter's free hand. "Are you sure?" she asked with an irritating lack of excitement.

Judith sat, holding her goblet frozen in midair, until Emma cried, "Me too!" Then, imitating her grandfather's gesture, Emma smashed her glass of milk into Judith's glass with shattering force.

Judith jumped to her daughter. "Oh God, did you cut yourself?"

Before Judith had the opportunity to inspect Emma for possible injuries, Robert Gregory reached over and picked up his granddaughter, checked her hand, found nothing. Just as Emma's tears began to express her fear, Robert laughed, "I think you've had too much to drink. How about some dessert, sweetheart?"

Emma rejected Judith's attempt to retrieve her. Wrapping herself around her grandfather's neck in a child's death grip, she cried, "I want to sit on Grampa's lap."

Only when Judith reluctantly returned to her seat did Christine realize her mother had not moved. Instead, Margaret Gregory sat rigidly staring directly across the table. Christine followed her mother's intent gaze to where Bill sat motionless, his amnesic eyes unfocused on the commotion.

Three weeks later Christine found herself banging frantically on her parents' door in the middle of the night. When her father appeared, his bathrobe haphazardly tied over his rumpled pajamas, Christine threw herself sobbing into his arms. "Bill's gone crazy. He's crawling around on the floor, knocking over furniture, shouting 'Get down. They're killing us.' He's tearing the whole house apart. He ripped out the phone. Daddy—do something."

As her father helped her into the house, Christine heard her mother's voice from the stairs. "What's wrong?"

Guiding Christine to a chair, he reported, "It's Bill."

Without further inquiry, her mother said, "I'll call Judith."

"No!" Christine screamed. "She caused this. It's her fault."

"Christine, don't say such a thing," her mother said, already dialing the phone. In a moment Margaret Gregory was speaking to her unseen daughter. "Judith. Christine just came here. It's Bill. Can you go to him?" After a moment's silence, she said, "I'll ask." Her mother turned to Christine. "Did you tell Bill about Sara?"

Judith had warned her not to mention Sara to Bill, promising she would break the news to him as soon as she, Judith, was under more control. But who was Judith to tell a wife what she could say and what she couldn't to her own husband.

This was Christine's opportunity to share something with Bill, to be there when he needed her. Maybe even to use the news to snap him out of his most recent silence. But she had never considered how the news would affect him. After all, Sara wasn't a member of the family or an old friend. He had only known her a short time. "Yes. I told him," she said defensively, imagining her sister's accusing voice on the other end of the line.

Her mother turned her attention to the phone. "He knows." Then after a moment's silence, she said, "I'll tell her." Margaret Gregory replaced the receiver and walked over to Christine. She knelt down and grasped her daughter's shaking hands. "Bill shouldn't be left alone. We'll get dressed and drive you."

Christine allowed her hysteria to grow, welcoming its power to obliterate the memory of the scene that had almost paralyzed her. "I can't," she cried. "He hates me because of the baby. Ever since that night at dinner, he's hardly spoken to me. He sits and stares out of the window all day. He won't even come to bed at night. I thought if I told him about Sara, he might talk to me. But he didn't. He just sat there and kept whispering 'Poor Judith.' Then he started screaming and tearing things apart. Mother, please. I can't go back there. He doesn't want me there. He wants Judith. Let her go. He'll listen to her."

"Maybe we should wait until we hear from Judith," her father said. "In Christine's condition . . ."

There was no mistaking the impatience in her mother's statement as she stood up and moved toward the stairs. "She belongs with her husband. I'll get dressed and we'll go together."

Her mother never understood how other people felt. Christine used to be furious at her mother when she insisted Christine go to school unprepared for an exam or forced her to go out on a date when she was nervous and wanted to break it. Her mother never showed any emotions. Maybe she didn't have any. But she didn't have the right to ignore other people's. Her father was different. Christine remembered she had even seen him cry once. "Please, Daddy. Don't make me go."

Robert Gregory stopped his wife's exit. "Margaret. Wait! Christine's too upset. I'll go. If Bill has calmed down, I'll find a phone and call. Then you can bring Christine along." Patting his daughter's hand protectively, her father said, "Don't worry, honey. Everything's going to be all right. I promise."

Less than two hours later, Judith and her father returned. The moment Christine saw their faces, she knew neither one of them had been able to keep the promises they had made.

9

Judith's three-year-old daughter sat next to her on the front seat of the car chattering away. "Let's go see Grampa."

After graduating from Berkeley, Judith had kept in touch with Sara, exchanging occasional letters and visits. Today, she was again reminded of how fortunate it was that Sara had decided to finish her residency in Los Angeles. Not only had Judith reunited with her best friend, but she had prevailed upon her to be Emma's doctor. "First, we're going to see Aunt Sara at the hospital. After that, maybe we can stop and have ice cream."

Judith didn't like the idea of bribing her daughter. On the other hand, it was a half-hour drive to the UCLA Medical Center, and she didn't want Emma to start fidgeting. She knew her daughter wasn't too crazy about being examined, even if it was by someone she called Aunt. Judith glanced at the clock on the dashboard. She didn't want to take advantage of the relationship with her friend by being late for her daughter's appointment.

Concentrating on the winding canyon road that led to the beach, Judith increased her speed. Topanga Canyon was only fifteen miles from the urban sprawl of Los Angeles, but much of it was still unspoiled wilderness. The canyon cut through the mountains that separated the Pacific Ocean from the desert floor of the San Fernando Valley, snidely referred to as the bedroom of Los Angeles, not for its sexual attraction but for its inexpensive suburban real estate. Judith had moved into Topanga when an ex-law student's failing grades lost him his enviable deferment. "It's all yours," he had said, handing her the keys to her new home. "Enjoy." That afternoon he left for Canada.

Robert Gregory called the canyon Hippie Heaven, and he was partially right. While the canyon was a refuge for serious writers, musicians, and painters, it was also a haven for drugged-out flower children, pseudo philosophers, and alienated dropouts. Judith fit into no group but was welcomed by all. She learned quickly that, although most of the canyon's denizens claimed to reject society's values, they were always embroiled in them. Judith contributed to the commune spirit with free legal service in exchange for being accepted as an unwed mother and, she hoped, for treating Emma as just one more member of the varied population.

"Where'd water go, Momma?" her daughter asked, raising herself to a kneeling stance.

Judith braked the car slightly and looked past Emma's questioning fist to the dry river bed that last year had carried torrents of raging water, mud, and debris down, out of the mountains, and into the ocean. Now, a hot, dry summer had left no more than an empty, cracked gully. "The sun has dried it all up for the summer," Judith explained as she reached over and pulled Emma back into a safe, sitting position. As a diversionary tactic, Judith decided to play their familiar "word for the day" game. "It's called e-vap-o-ra-tion," Judith said. "Can you say that?"

"Eeeev-por-tion," Emma repeated slowly, trying out the the new word that sounded like three.

"And what does it mean?" Judith asked. One of the rules in this game was to know the definition as well as the sound.

"No more water."

"That's close enough," Judith laughed.

Emma began to rock back and forth, her head pounding against the back of the seat. "Eeev," bounce, "por," bounce, "tion," bounce. Judith was tempted to repeat the word, emphasizing Emma's missing syllables, but decided against it. Experience told her that her daughter's rhythmic bouncing was a sign of either fatigue or worry. "Are you tired?" she asked Emma.

"I'm hot," Emma complained.

Judith felt guilty for not accepting her father's offer to install air conditioning in the car. It was one thing to endure a little discomfort to dramatize her independence; it was another to make her daughter suffer the sweltering heat of the canyon ride. "We'll be near the ocean soon. It will be cooler then."

Emma rested her head against the seat. "I wanna go to Grampa's," she scolded, as if blaming the heat on her mother's selfish pride.

Although she had reconciled with her father, Judith still felt the sting of his resigned disappointment in her. And in spite of herself, she found herself craving his approval. Even when she knew that she was not the target of his criticism, she responded like a testy child. She remembered the phone call last year that interrupted a family dinner to inform her father that Sirhan Bishara Sirhan had walked into the Ambassador Hotel and shot Robert Kennedy. Before rushing to his office, he had railed, "What the hell's going on in this country?" Judith was so shocked and angry with the news that she struck back without thinking. "You ought to be used to it by now.

In this country, if we don't like what someone says, we shoot
him. We can't stand to see our middle-class platitudes challenged." She was ashamed of her words even before she had
finished them. Worse, she resented his not challenging her
fatuous outburst. It was a sign that he didn't care much what
she thought anymore. She had lost even the power to irritate
him.

"I wanna go to Grampa's," Emma whined. "Let's live with
Gramma Rose. It's hot here."

"We have our own home now," Judith said, aware that
Emma loved her great-grandmother's house and its proximity
to her grandparents. And Judith missed the convenience of
prepared dinners and easy babysitters. But she was determined that her daughter grow up in the real world, free from
illusions that were sure to disappoint her eventually.

The air inside the car cooled, signaling their approach
to the Pacific Ocean. Judith was continually amazed when
the rough, curving road made its final turn and the vastness
of the sea sprang up before her. Emma seemed to share Judith's sense of anticipation, halting her head in midbounce
until she could see the blue water underlined by the white
surf pounding on the beach. How had Eliot described it?
Mermaids "Combing the white hair of the waves blown back..."
Judith hadn't thought of Randall in months, but recalled now
that *The Love Song of J. Alfred Prufrock* was one of his favorite
poems. Only a few weeks before he disappeared from her
life, he had lain next to her and recited:

I grow old... I grow old...
I shall wear the bottoms of my trousers rolled.

Shall I part my hair behind? Do I dare to eat a peach?
I shall wear white flannel trousers, and walk upon
the beach.
I have heard the mermaids singing, each to each.

I do not think that they will sing to me.

Afterward he looked at her and said, "Actually, you're the only mermaid I've ever known. Will you sing to me when I grow old and walk upon the beach?" At the time, Judith had been touched and somewhat embarrassed by her lover's unusual melancholic tone. She had grown used to their caustic romance. "I don't sing," she laughed uneasily. "And you hate the water." Judith recalled his disappointed expression when he said prophetically, "Not the stuff of poetry, are we."

Suddenly Emma jerked her hand back from the radio and the silence was broken by an announcer's voice, too loud for its gravity. "Actress Sharon Tate was the wife of director Roman Polanski. She was found murdered in her Benedict Canyon home Saturday morning, along with coffee heiress Abigail Folger and prominent hairstylist Jay Sebring. Tate was eight months pregnant, and it has been revealed that she received multiple stab wounds to the abdomen. We will keep you informed as more facts become available." Before Judith could reach the volume control, the enthusiastic voices of The Fifth Dimension had already begun heralding the long awaited dawning of the age of Aquarius.

Judith switched off the radio. She had already heard about the murders, but now the details were being reported, piece by gruesome piece. Judith tried to deny the essence of this new report, concentrating instead on the announcer's reference to the murdered actress as "Tate." She considered the possible reasons. He probably didn't know whether to call her Miss or Mrs. since she was married but didn't use her husband's name. Judith grew furious with the loud, serious voice that hadn't used Ms. as Sharon Tate would probably have wanted. After all, she was a beautiful, progressive, young woman who had kept her own professional name, proving . . . Judith fought desperately against the image forming in her mind. "My God, why? She was pregnant!" Judith cried, angrily pounding the steering wheel.

Emma had resumed bouncing back and forth, her hands

covering her ears. "It got loud by itself," Emma whimpered. "I didn't do it."

Judith sensed her daughter's terrified confusion. Emma had touched one of the forbidden controls and now her mother was angry. Pulling Emma next to her, Judith stroked her hair and soothed her with "It's all right. Shhhhhhhh. Don't worry. You didn't do anything."

Tears blurred Judith's vision as she turned the car south on the Coast Highway. Gripping the steering wheel, she muttered, "What the hell's going on in this country?" and was startled by her own question.

Judith was still shaken when she arrived with Emma at the UCLA Medical Center. "Did you hear?" she asked Sara as she soon as she walked into the examining room.

Sara, who managed to look elegant even in a standard, white starched smock, glanced up from the medical chart she was reading. "I heard," she said, putting the chart down.

"How could anyone do something like that? I can't believe it."

"I can." Without further comment, Sara swept Emma up and plunked her on the examining table. She handed one end of her stethoscope to Emma and held the other end to her own chest. "Okay, you get to listen first; then it's my turn."

Emma listened, first with serious study, then with playful curiosity. "I hear your heart," she giggled.

"Some people say I don't have one," Sara said, winking at Judith.

A few minutes later, Sara tickled Emma's stomach. "That's it, kiddo. Aunt Sara can't find a single thing wrong with you. You're perfect." Then, turning to Judith, Sara instructed, "In a month she'll need booster s-h-o-t-s."

Judith wanted her daughter treated with candor, even when it might be unpleasant. "Emma knows she has to have shots," she said, pronouncing the last word clearly.

The word was not lost on Emma. "I don't want shots," she pouted.

Sara ignored Judith's implied admonition. "I'm going away for a while, and I've instructed the nurse to give you the name of a good pediatrician. I'll explain later." Then she turned back to Emma. "You're going to meet a new doctor. He's a nice man, and he gives a cherry sucker to every little girl that visits him."

Emma didn't look impressed. "Is he black?"

The last time Emma had seen Sara she had asked, "Why isn't Aunt Christine black?" and Sara explained, "Because my momma and daddy are black. Aunt Christine's momma and daddy are white. Children look like their parents." Emma had obviously discarded the idea that all aunts are black and was testing a new theory about doctors. Apparently, Sara understood Emma's logic. "Not all doctors are black, honey. In fact, this one looks just like Santa Claus."

"Santa Claus is a fairy tale grown-ups make up," Emma recited looking at her mother.

Sara picked Emma up and gave her a hug. "Who told you that?"

"Momma."

Sara shook her head sadly. "Maybe your momma just hasn't seen him for a long time." She gave Emma a final squeeze and put her down. "Why don't you go out and ask the nurse to give you the box that's all wrapped up and has your name on it. Then you can go down and play in the toy room."

"Are you going on vacation?" Judith asked as Emma headed for the door.

Sara closed the door behind Emma. "We'll talk about that later." Then, so quietly that Judith almost couldn't hear, Sara said, "I saw Randall."

It had been a long time since Judith had heard the name spoken aloud. "Who?" she asked as though she was having trouble placing the name with a face.

"Randall. You remember him, don't you? Emma's father.

I ran into him Tuesday at the theater. It was a Pinter play."

Judith pushed her trembling hands into her jacket pockets and tried to match Sara's chatty tone. "How is he?"

"Aren't you going to ask how he liked the play, Mrs. Lincoln? He did. Personally, I think Pinter is pretentious. As usual, we argued."

Judith didn't enjoy Sara's wit at her expense. "Are you going to tell me about it, or do I have to beg first? All right. I want to know."

"He's running a little theater in New York—experimental, he calls it—I got the whole lecture on what's happening in New York theater. He's in California to talk to a young playwright he's interested in."

Judith craved information like an addict who hated herself for needing what was unhealthy, dangerous. "Did he ask about me? And I hope to God you didn't say anything about Emma."

Sara put her hand on Judith's shoulder. "Yes, he asked about you. And no, I didn't mention Emma."

Judith shook off her friend's hand. "Just tell me what he's doing here and how much he knows."

Sara dropped her hand and leaned against the examining table. "He asked if I'd seen you, and I said yes. Don't worry. I didn't give anything but your name, rank, and serial number. I told him you were an attorney. That you were considered the Clarence Darrow of lost causes, which is a bit of an exaggeration, and that you never talked about him, which is true. He wanted to know if I thought you'd see him. I said I'd ask. So I'm asking: do you want to see him?"

Judith still felt something for Randall, but she couldn't put a name to the feeling. Sometimes, in the middle of the night, Judith would awaken surprised to find she had been dreaming of him, of having him inside her again, fulfilling needs she thought she no longer had. It angered her that even in sleeping fantasy, Randall could arouse greater passion and sexual release than she had experienced in the few brief affairs she had allowed herself since Emma's birth. Now she was being offered the opportunity to exchange fantasy for reality, to let him invade her territory, challenge her isolation. Suddenly, the name that only a little while ago recalled a poetic ex-lover now warned of a dangerous intruder. Panic, more than conviction, prompted Judith's "No!"

"I thought you'd say that. So did Randall. He told me to tell you that he'd understand if you said no and respect your decision. He's changed. Mellowed out. The bitterness is gone. Of course that makes him less interesting, but it happens to the best of us when we get older." Sara held out a card. "Here. He wanted me to give you this. It's his number at the hotel. He says to call if you feel like it. You can reach him there."

Judith waved away the offending card. "I'm not interested."

"Take it anyway. You might change your mind," Sara said, dropping the card in Judith's purse. "How long can you go on pretending Randall doesn't exist? If you're not going to be honest with yourself, what about Emma?"

Judith was annoyed with Sara's implied criticism. "I've already told Emma that she has a father. That he lives far away and doesn't even know he has a little girl. I'll make sure she knows it was my decision not to tell him. So don't accuse me of being dishonest. Not with Emma. And not with myself. I'm not going to let Emma wait around for Randall to show up once a year like Santa Claus, making promises he can't keep."

"Do you think depriving a child of her illusions means she'll grow up strong and self-reliant?" Sara asked with the professional tone of a doctor taking a medical history. "Did you happen to see Emma's face when she said 'Santa Claus is a fairy tale grown-ups make up'? She wants to believe in the same things other kids do."

"I don't happen to think that it's necessary to believe in fairy tales," Judith said defensively.

Sara turned and busied herself disposing of the used tongue depressors and tissues. "Just be careful. Some day

Emma might resent you for not letting her believe in fairy tales. Just like she might resent you for not letting her believe in her father." Sara turned, walked over to the sink, and washed her hands. As she reached for the towel, she asked casually, "Do you hate him that much?"

Judith felt her irritation mounting. Since when did Sara feel such loyalty to Randall? "This has nothing to do with Randall. I don't hate him. I don't even dislike him. Actually, I haven't thought about him in months," she lied. "I just want him to stay out of my life, and Emma's. We don't need a father popping in and out of our lives when the mood suits him."

"*We* don't need a father?" Sara insinuated.

Judith's anger came without thought, uninvited. "Get off it, Sara. Spare me the psychological crap. If I'd listened to you, Emma would have been flushed down the toilet in some back-alley clinic. So don't take that uppity 'I'm a doctor' tone with me."

Sara removed a pack of cigarettes from her white smock, lit one, and inhaled slowly, her face hardening into the chiseled mask of contempt she had once turned on Judith's father so many years ago. "Would you feel more comfortable if I took my 'I'm juss'en ol nigger' tone?" She exhaled behind the smoke.

Judith was mystified by Sara's sudden counterattack, but didn't retreat. It was an avenue of escape away from the subject of Randall. "What the hell's that supposed to mean?" she demanded.

"I used to wonder why this young, white, middle-class coed who looked like—what did Randall call you?—oh yes, the Breck girl, would chase after a black woman who couldn't get into a sorority if she were the Queen of Sheba. Then it began to dawn on me. You loved the idea of the privileged white and the oppressed black becoming sisters. It had such a nice, universal goodness about it. Hey, Sister Woman, I be curious. Would y'all a'been ma friend if'n I was white?" she asked mockingly.

Judith shrank from the tiny, glittering nugget of truth lying among Sara's dark, angry words. It was true that when she first met Sara, Judith had been struck by her uniqueness, by her emancipated strength, but she would have felt the same toward her if she had been white, or purple for that matter. Didn't that prove the injustice of Sara's accusation, even enhance the bond between them? "Sara! Please don't. I've never thought anything like that, and you know it. You were my first real friend, the only person in the world I was able to talk to."

"Then talk to me," her friend said with unrelenting calm. "You can tell me I'm wrong about you. About Randall. About everything. Or you can even tell me it's none of my business. But don't you ever dismiss me like I was an uppity nigger."

Judith knew that the history of their friendship was being written, and she must say something now that would not invite the final chapter. But how could Judith explain, even to her best friend, that when a child believed in something or someone, forever and ever afterward it hurt not to be able to recapture that belief. To give herself more time, Judith asked, "Can I have a cigarette?"

"You don't smoke."

"I do now," Judith said, taking a cigarette from the offered pack and lighting it. Judith took a drag on the cigarette, then exhaled both smoke and explanation. "I'm trying to be a good mother, and it scares me when you say that may not be enough."

Sara remained unmoved, the magisterial speaker. "I'll give you even odds that your mother feels the same way. Probably even your father. So what makes you so unique?"

"They're different. They don't question anything. I was taught that the world was 'mud luscious and puddle wonderful.' I was never prepared for anything. You know what? Last month I took Emma to Disneyland. Walking through the Magic Castle, I heard Cinderella sing, 'Some day my prince will come,' and I almost cried. You know why? Because I still want to believe it and can't. At least I'd like to spare my daughter that." Judith took another drag on her cigarette and coughed.

"If you're going to smoke that way, you'll get bad breath, stained fingers, and no pleasure." Sara removed the cigarette from Judith's hand, took a drag, then crushed it in an empty urine cup. Judith almost didn't hear, "Your mother knows about Randall. She's known for years."

At first Judith didn't think she had heard correctly. "What?"

Sara led Judith to a chair. "Sit down. You look like shit. I'm tempted to take your blood pressure." After she pushed Judith into a chair, she said, "I told her about Randall the day she flew to Berkeley to bail you out of jail. I had to do something. You were running around getting yourself arrested. I was afraid you were going to screw up your whole life. This time I suppose you have a right to be pissed at me."

Judith was too confused to be angry. "She never said a word. Why?"

"You'd have to ask her that question. But I know one thing. You underestimate her. Believe me, she knows the world isn't 'mud luscious and puddle wonderful.'" Then, as if it were a logical progression, she said, "I always wondered why you never asked me about *my* parents."

"I didn't think you wanted to talk about them."

She went on as if she still didn't want to talk about them, but had no choice. "I lived with my daddy in Maryland not far from the Chesapeake," Sara said, her rigid expression melting into the anguish of remembrance. "He was everything I bet you imagine a noble, oppressed black should be—a poor dirt farmer who slaved night and day to give me a decent, God-fearing life. We didn't have much, but Santa Claus managed to leave a present every Christmas Eve."

Reluctantly, Judith left the the subject of her own mother behind. "What about your mother?"

"Daddy said she died when I was born. He used to tell me grand stories about her—what a good singer she was, how she loved Sarah Vaughn, and how she wanted me named after her. She neglected to spell it for him. He always told me my momma had gone off to Heaven and that someday I'd meet her there. But I didn't have to wait that long. I met her the day I graduated from high school. She came all decked out in silks and jewelry."

"Where had she been?" Judith asked, knowing from Sara's voice that it definitely wasn't Heaven.

"Working the streets. My mother was a whore," Sara announced with the offhand modesty of a daughter who didn't want to brag about her mother's accomplishments. "Funny isn't it. After all those years of hard work, it wasn't my father who could afford to send me away to a big, fancy, liberal university. It was my mother."

It took Judith a moment to register Sara's words, and when she did, Judith didn't know what she was expected to do with the information. "Where is she now?" Judith asked, unsure it was the right question.

"When she got too old to make money on the streets, she set up a little business on the outskirts of town. She convinced a lot of little black girls that they'd be better off working in her cathouse than cleaning other people's toilets. Who knows? Maybe she's right."

"What about your father?"

"He died a year after Big Momma showed up. I think the shame killed him more than the hard work." Sara lit another cigarette, took a few drags, and looked directly at her friend for the first time since she had started her story. "I guess what I'm trying to say is that I can't afford your morality. You see, I loved my daddy with all his high ideals, but don't kid yourself, I'm glad a whore gave me the chance to be a doctor."

"Do you, uh . . . keep in touch with her?"

"You mean, do I still have anything to do with her? The answer is yes. She's my mother. She came through for me in the end. I guess it takes all kinds to raise a kid." She laughed.

Judith laughed too, relieved that the threat of estrangement now lay behind them. "Okay, let me get this straight. I should tell Randall about Emma just in case she wants to be a doctor and needs help with her education, right?"

"Terrific. I knew you'd get my point," Sara said, the irony in her voice assuring Judith that the bond of friendship was still intact.

"Actually, I'm not sure I do, but I'll think about it. Now what's this about your going away?" Judith asked. "Can't I bring Emma in when you get back?"

"I'm not coming back. At least not for a long time. I've decided to join the army and see the world."

Judith stared at her friend, not believing what she had heard. Brilliant, stylish Sara standing there, the beauty of her blackness contrasting with her white jacket, saying she was joining the army. It was a bad joke. "You don't look good in khaki. It washes out your color."

"I leave this month. Want to come along?"

"You can't be serious. It's crazy. Why? I thought you hated this war as much as I do."

"I do."

"Then would you mind explaining what you think you're doing," Judith pressed, not really wanting to hear the words that would make her friend's decision a reality.

Sara shook her head and sighed, but there was no anger in her voice when she said, "There you go again. Do you remember how pissed you were at me that day at Berkeley when I refused to march into that building and get myself arrested?"

The memory still irritated Judith. "I remember. You said it was a 'white issue.' "

"Well, right now you have that same look of outraged betrayal that you had that day."

"I had a right to be angry with you that day, and I have a right to be angry with you now. God almighty, Sara, how can you be so inconsistent? Five years ago you agreed the establishment was wrong, but you didn't join us. Now you say the war stinks, but you're going to be part of it. Why?"

Sara was quiet for a moment, and Judith was afraid she had once again threatened the relationship. But when Sara spoke, there was no trace of rancor. "Like I told Emma, I'm the same color as my mama and daddy. I have to go. Do you understand what I'm trying to say? I've chosen my battle. This time it's a black issue."

Judith was more than aware that the worst of the fighting was being done by minorities, but that was just one more reason to hate this war. "What good will it do to join them? Stay here and fight."

"Do you also remember that day at Berkeley I told you that someday you'd need all your energy to fight your own battles? You were always running around fighting wars you didn't understand. You didn't even know who was on your side—like your mom." Judith started to defend herself, but Sara wasn't going to be interrupted. "Your problem is you can't figure out which fights are whose, so you embrace them all and criticize the rest of us for being choosy. A few weeks ago we landed on the moon and you hardly mentioned it. But today you marched in here looking whiter than usual and shaking like a leaf because some crazy asshole decided to commit mayhem. Why do you take everything so personally? Not everything in this world is intended as a personal attack on your sensibilities. It's not all black or white—no pun intended. Some things just happen."

"The war didn't just happen."

"This time you're right. There're a half-million boys getting the shit kicked out of them over there. Have you noticed who most of those kids are, Sister Woman?"

Judith was beginning to understand why Sara hadn't joined her so long ago. "On you, an army uniform will look great."

"Does that mean I'm forgiven?" Sara asked, wrapping her strong, graceful arm around Judith's shoulders.

"I'll forgive you, if you'll forgive me," Judith said, so grateful for the friendship that she had almost forgotten the original subject that had endangered it.

Judith dragged Emma behind her as she approached her parents' front door. The throbbing pain just behind Judith's eyes threatened to cause brain damage, and her stomach responded to her every step as though it were trying to adjust to a violent storm at sea. Usually, she enjoyed Emma's precocious banter, but today she clenched her teeth against the tempting command to shut up and leave her alone. "Never again," Judith vowed. "Never again." It was a vow she knew she would have little trouble keeping. She seldom drank more than an occasional glass of wine. Last night had been the exception.

Without knocking, Judith opened the door and entered her parents' house, almost pushing Emma in front of her. She needn't have worried about the impatient gesture, because her daughter increased her entry speed, rushing away from her mother in search of her grandparents.

Judith caught up with Emma in the backyard garden, where Margaret Gregory was intent on trimming her prize roses. "After what happened to Sharon Tate, I'm surprised you still keep the door unlocked," Judith said, knowing that a simple threat of multiple murder would not change a lifetime habit of an open-door policy. Only after it was time for the inhabitants to sleep did Robert Gregory throw the bolt on the front door.

"If someone wants in badly enough, a locked door won't stop them," her mother said, still on her knees. "Locked doors only make it difficult for my family to come in."

Emma gave her grandmother a perfunctory kiss on the cheek that had been turned without apparent emotion to her own children a generation ago. As a child, Judith had considered her mother's gesture an act of tolerance; now she realized it was more one of supplication—like a peasant, head bowed, content to receive the sacrament.

Having bestowed her tiresome blessing, Emma chirped, "Where's Grampa?"

Watching history repeat itself, Judith muttered, "Some things never change, do they?"

"Some things shouldn't," her mother said as she straightened up and removed her gardening gloves. Margaret studied her daughter for a moment. "You don't look well. Is there something the matter?"

From the instant the blinding light of day had painfully awakened her, Judith had rehearsed this moment. But now she was not so sure she wanted to pursue the plan that last night had seemed so drunkenly logical. "You know about Randall."

Margaret looked at Emma, who was running amuck through her small vegetable patch, picking the last of the summer tomatoes. "I'll fix some lunch for Emma. Would you like something."

"Did you hear what I said?" Judith asked, exasperated that her mother never registered surprise, even when caught unaware.

"I heard you. Did you hear me? I asked if you would like something to eat?"

"I'll settle for an aspirin," Judith said, accepting defeat. Her mother had just set the schedule. Judith would have to wait until Emma had eaten and the moment was right before she would have her mother's full attention.

A few minutes later her mother handed Judith a Bloody Mary. "Here, drink this while I fix lunch. Your father says these help."

After the first sip of the thick red juice, Judith was sure her mother was trying to punish her for last night's transgressions. The Tabasco was like a blowtorch, blasting away all sediment it encountered on its journey from tongue to stomach. And she was pretty sure there was equal part vodka to tomato juice. She couldn't tell if it was the hot sauce or the alcohol causing her sinuses to dilate and her eyes to tear. "My God. Are you trying to kill me?" Judith managed to gasp.

"I think your father calls it 'a hair of the dog that bit you.'"

"This is more like the teeth of the dog that attacked you," Judith managed to smile. Actually, after the liquid's initial shock, Judith welcomed the cure.

An hour later Judith sat next to her drowsy daughter on the couch while her mother cleaned up the last of the lunch debris. Judith was fairly recovered when her mother joined her, carrying a chilled bottle of white wine and two glasses. Margaret filled both glasses to capacity and handed one to her daughter. Then, as though only a moment had passed since Judith first mentioned the name, her mother said, "Yes. I know about Randall."

Judith checked to make sure Emma was asleep before asking, "Does Dad know?"

"No. It wasn't my place to tell him. It was yours. It still is, for that matter."

"Why didn't you ever say anything?"

"What should I have said?"

Judith didn't have an answer. She knew her mother was right. Nothing she could have said would have made any difference at the time. "I'd like to talk about it now." When her mother didn't respond, Judith forced herself to plunge forward, telling her mother how she and Randall had met at Berkeley and how they had finally parted. She concentrated on presenting the story as she might a legal brief, leaving nothing out, but, like most lawyers, unable to avoid shading the facts to her advantage. "He didn't know about Emma, and as far as I know he still doesn't. It wouldn't have been right for me to use Emma to hold on to him—even if I could have."

"Besides, it's easier not having to share her. It's safer,"

her mother said, as though that summed up Judith's rationale. Margaret didn't wait for Judith's argument, asking, "Why are you telling me all this now?"

"Because I saw Sara yesterday, and she told me you knew who Emma's father was. Or at least you probably suspected. She says I should tell Randall about Emma. What do you think?"

Refilling their now empty glasses, Margaret said, "I think it's more important what you tell Emma. You and Randall aren't the important ones—she is. I agree that it wouldn't do to introduce Emma to a man who doesn't want to be her father. But you won't know what he wants if you don't ask."

Judith wasn't ready to tell her mother that last night, after she had tucked Emma into bed and kissed her good night, she had sought out the fifth of Scotch that she had received in lieu of a fee. After her first drink, she sorted through her old records, masochistically selecting ones that brought back memories of her affair with Randall. She couldn't remember how many hours or how many drinks later she found herself talking to him on the phone. It must have been very late, because she dimly recalled that the hotel operator hesitated to put through a call at that hour. "I'm thinking of seeing him," Judith told her mother.

"You're thinking of seeing him, or you've decided to see him?"

Judith sensed that her mother had waited patiently for almost five years, knowing that eventually they would have this discussion. And Judith was surprised that talking to her mother seemed the most natural thing in the world because she too had always known this conversation would take place. "I talked to him last night. He wants to see me. Do you think I should?"

"Judith, my child. He's Emma's father. Don't you think it's a little late for you to want my permission to see him? What's past is past. Now you must decide what you want to do about the future. Not your future, Emma's. Do you still care for him?" her mother asked, almost as an afterthought.

Each time Judith thought of Randall, his title changed—first affair, unrequited love, Emma's father. "I'm not sure how I feel about him. He's become a ghost. I suppose that's one reason I've decided to see him in the flesh. I'm afraid of ghosts." The wine was numbing the pain in Judith's head, relaxing her, giving her confidence. "If it's all right with you, I've invited Randall to go to the cabin with me this weekend."

Her mother's eyes were losing their usual dark intentness. "That sounds nice. When you were a baby, I decided I wanted to have a place where we could all be alone together without interruption. Your father was always so busy at the paper, and you were already beginning to have other interests. Then Christine and Eddie came along, each with their different lives. At the cabin there is no choice. We had to be alone together. It was the one place I could watch you all together and know you were all safe." Margaret Gregory sipped the last of her second glass of wine and then asked, "Would you like us to take care of Emma while you're gone?"

Judith was amused. Was her conventional mother actually encouraging her to go away with Randall, or was it the two full glasses of wine speaking? "Are you telling me you think it's a good idea to spend the weekend with him?"

"There are three bedrooms there. Unless, of course, you don't think your Randall will be a gentleman."

Judith considered the possibility of an ulterior motive in her mother's suggestion and then rejected the idea. Her mother didn't operate that way. Or did she? How much of her watchful silence was deceptive purpose? Judith smiled. "I never thought of him as a gentleman, much less as 'my' Randall. But I suppose he wouldn't take advantage of a poor, defenseless woman."

"Tell me about Sara," her mother said, apparently considering the subject of Judith's life closed.

Judith detailed her conversation with Sara, leaving nothing out. As she recounted the story of Sara's childhood, Judith sensed her mother had heard it all before. "You know all this, don't you?" Judith said, remembering the day she first saw Sara and her mother together. Now she began to understand the odd courtroom embrace her mother and friend had shared. "You knew all about Sara's parents, didn't you? My God, you know more about my best friend than I do. Why didn't she tell me?"

"Because you weren't ready to see the similarities."

"Similarities! What similarities? Our families are completely different."

Margaret poured another glass of wine. The bottle was almost empty. Judith started to caution her mother on the evils of excess when Margaret looked at her. "Do you know why your father didn't like Sara?" Before Judith could give her standard answer about Sara challenging her father's values, her mother answered for her. "He couldn't see the similarities either."

"Neither can I," Judith said, just at the moment Christine arrived home from work.

Christine entered the living room, then stopped dead. "Is anything wrong?" she asked, looking around suspiciously, as though a hidden intruder were holding Judith and her mother hostage on the sofa.

Judith didn't blame her sister for looking wary. Seeing her mother and her sister sitting around getting drunk in the afternoon wasn't an everyday occurrence. Judith was about to offer some implausible excuse for seducing her mother when Margaret Gregory said, "Judith's going to the cabin."

Judith almost laughed. Her mother didn't go for the implausible; she went for the inexplicable.

August was usually the hottest month in Los Angeles, with the sun forcing the pollution back down into the city's sprawling basin, and the muddy brown air spreading across the foothills, obliterating them like a dirty eraser. It was a good time to get out of town.

Judith wasn't sure what she expected when she met Randall again, but it wasn't the prematurely gray, conservatively dressed man who was waiting for her in front of the Century Plaza Hotel, suitcase in hand. Nor was she prepared for the polite pleasantries he offered as she got out of the car and opened the trunk. "It's good to see you again. You haven't changed a bit," he said.

Judith almost said, You have. You've put on weight, cut your hair, and donned the mantle of respectability. "Neither have you."

"How've you been?" he asked, tossing his overnight bag into the trunk.

Why should this acceptable, conventional banter make her feel so contentious? "Fine," she said.

"If you hadn't called, I would have been forced to wander around the city alone until Monday. I don't know Los Angeles very well."

Judith braced herself for the old, caustic observations about the cultural wasteland of Southern California, almost welcomed them. She felt deprived of familiarity when none were forthcoming. "There's not much to do. Compared to New York, that is," she said, offering him another chance to recite his old litany.

But Randall was apparently bent on cordial inquiry. "Did you ever get to New York after . . ."

"You left," Judith finished for him as she climbed into the driver's seat and slammed the door. As soon as Randall joined her in the car, she sought control by deliberately starting the engine and an argument. "I've still never been to New York. But even in the hinterlands of Los Angeles we get the *New Yorker.* Occasionally I like to punish myself by reading what I'm missing."

Either Randall didn't hear the gauntlet when it was thrown down, or he chose not to pick it up. "You're not missing so much. We have theater and museums. You have the sun and the mountains. It's a trade-off."

Randall's condescension disarmed her. "Who can tell with all this smog?" she complained, irritated with herself for assuming the role of unwilling critic.

The silence next to her teased her into sneaking a surreptitious glance at her passenger, and she found herself caught in Randall's unabashed stare. "Did you invite me for the weekend so that we could finish the fight?" he asked pleasantly.

Damn, Judith thought. Why am I on the defensive with him? "No. I'm sorry."

"Why *did* you invite me?"

"I've already told you. Sara said you wanted to see me. I couldn't think of a good reason to say no."

"You've already told me that. I mean the cabin, and all this," he said, waving his hand in the general vicinity of the mountains. "Not that I'm not happy. But I didn't even expect you to call, much less suggest a weekend alone."

Judith felt the blood creep into her face and hoped Randall would consider it a blush of anger, not coyness. What *had* she hoped to accomplish by this reunion? Packing her diaphragm along with her toothbrush, she had planned for any possibility, a fight, a renewed love affair, an opportunity for a future, a final ending, something, anything. She had wanted to show him how she had changed, grown strong, independent, could handle anything. But she wasn't prepared for this exercise in superficial civility. It didn't even afford the opportunity of a final, unpleasant argument, depriving her of the chance of closure. "I've already assured you I have no intention of jumping into bed with you. I just thought you might enjoy getting out of the city and relaxing for a couple of days. I was planning on going alone," she said, adding the final lie.

"I'm sorry. I didn't mean to suggest you had anything else in mind."

Judith maneuvered through freeway traffic effortlessly, wondering who this soft-spoken, conventional, even thoughtful man was. He was doing a terrible job of impersonating

Randall. "I'm sorry," she said, realizing how unfair it was to punish this stranger for not meeting expectations even she couldn't define. Then she laughed. "It's going to be a little boring if we're going to spend the next two days apologizing to each other. Tell me what you've been doing for the past four years. Three-and-a-half to be exact," Judith said.

As they headed out the San Bernardino Freeway, Randall avoided any further mention of his departure from Berkeley. Instead, he related his slow progress toward managing a small theater on the Upper West Side. At one point, Judith imagined an unspoken "I told you so," as he recounted his many jobs, from the predicted busboy to bellhop. He had haunted the theaters during every free moment, volunteering to do everything from painting scenery to reading hundreds of dreadful scripts by hopeful amateurs. Eventually, he found one young man who had some real talent, a black vet who had lost his legs somewhere on the outskirts of Da Nang. Randall worked with him to shape his play, then banged on every door in New York. Finally, he cornered the owner of a rat-infested theater on the edge of Harlem, who agreed to let him produce it. The play received enough attention from the critics to warrant moving it to a small, reputable theater in the Village. After that, he had a string of critical successes. Not big productions. No Broadway smash hits, of course. But he couldn't complain. "I may not have creative talent myself," he said. "But I know it when I see it in others. That's why I'm out here. There's a kid who sent me his play. It's not bad. I think we may be able to do something with it."

Not once during his long recitation did Judith detect any vestige of the cocky attitude she had come to identify with Randall. To her surprise, the prospect of spending a pleasant, uneventful weekend with this mild-mannered person next to her was more frightening than the possibility of risking a recapitulation of their painful affair. Taking the Mountain Resorts off-ramp, Judith headed east. "How long will you be in Los Angeles?" she inquired politely.

"I leave Tuesday. We're in rehearsals on a new play. One by the black vet I mentioned." Randall pulled a pack of cigarettes from his pocket. "Do you mind if I smoke?"

"I don't recall your ever asking before. I thought maybe you'd quit."

"What about you?" he asked, ignoring Judith's reference to the past. "Sara tells me you're a successful, crusading lawyer."

"Not if success is measured by money." Stepping carefully around her pregnancy and Emma's birth, Judith broadly outlined the years following her graduation from Berkeley, the move to her grandmother's while she attended law school, and her work as a paralegal at a storefront legal clinic in the East Los Angeles barrio. "Most of my clients can't afford to pay much, if anything. But we eat well. I get rice balls wrapped in seaweed from my Japanese customers, stuffed chilies from the Chicanos, and fried chicken from the blacks. Once in a while I get a rich kid whose parents don't want to see him in the army, so I can pay my rent."

"Who's the 'we' in 'we eat well'? Sara didn't say much about your personal life. Are you living with someone?"

Judith made a mental note to be more careful about how she phrased things. It wasn't going to be easy. She didn't think of herself as 'I' anymore. "If you mean 'do I have a man in my life,' the answer is no."

"I guess that's what I meant. I know I don't have a right to ask, but I can't deny I'm curious about what's been happening with you."

"Since you left?"

"That's the second time you've filled that in for me. Yes, since I left. I'd like to explain that."

Judith finally experienced a tangible reaction, one she could give a name. Resignation. "There's no need. You write a good farewell note. I got the message. Let's forget it."

They rode in silence as they climbed out of the flat, arid

San Bernardino valley, leaving behind the scraggly scrub brush and the dry, rocky arroyos that appeared deceptively benign, but in a quick, unexpected downpour filled instantly, channeling torrential death and destruction toward anything standing in their way. By the time they reached Crestline Drive, the landscape had changed. The ugly shades of brown gave way to the soft greens, yellows, and reds that predicted the ripening autumn. As Judith negotiated a hairpin curve, there was a moment's spectacular view through the crystal mountain air, down four thousand feet to where the valley below was shrouded in the muddy mist of smog. The scent of pine prompted Judith's "We're almost there."

Fifteen minutes later, Randall and Judith gathered their sparse luggage from the trunk and entered the cabin. It took no time to whisk away the sheets that covered the furniture and inspect the kitchen's provisions. The cupboards and the refrigerator were fully stocked. "It looks like we could hole up here for a month," Randall observed.

"My mother has a way of arranging things."

Randall sounded truly shocked. "Does your mother know *I'm* here?"

Judith relished Randall's sudden prudish tone. "Yes. Why not?" she asked casually.

"A lot has changed since—and don't finish this for me—I left."

"It certainly has," Judith smiled. "Your room is the last one on the left. Mine is upstairs."

The rest of the first day was spent walking in the woods, reminiscing about old college acquaintances, recounting forgotten incidents, and assiduously avoiding mention of their long-ended love affair. That evening, as they finished dinner, they had run out of light gossip and superficial remembrances and lapsed into uncomfortable stretches of silence. As Judith rose to clear the table, she said, "You must be tired. Don't let me keep you up if you feel like turning in."

"Can I help you clean up?" he asked like a grudging teenager anxious to leave the table but forced to mind his manners.

Judith heard his lack of enthusiasm and thought he probably regretted this boring reunion as much as she did. "No. Please. Just relax," she said, trying not to convey the "just go away" she actually meant.

"I guess I am a little tired. Besides, I've got a couple of new plays I have to read." Randall pushed his chair back without reluctance. "It's been a nice day. I'll see you in the morning," he said before disappearing down the hallway.

After he left, Judith made slow work of cleaning up the kitchen. She was restless and dreaded the prospect of a sleepless night. Maybe a walk would help ease the tension, take the edge off her restlessness. Reaching for one of the old sweaters that always hung on the large wooden peg next to the door, she turned off the light and slipped out quietly.

It was a cool, pleasant evening, the kind Judith remembered from her childhood. The pine trees caught the shimmering moonlight, tossed it back and forth between their swaying boughs, then let it drop into the lapping water of Lake Arrowhead. How many years had it been since she had swum in that lake? Ten, at least.

When she reached the dock, she sat down, took off her shoes, and let her feet dangle in the water. The lake had held its summer warmth despite an unseasonable frost last week. As naturally as getting ready for her nightly bath, Judith undressed and slipped noiselessly into the water. Against the chill of the night air, the water seemed comfortable, protective. With a feeling of freedom she hadn't experienced in years, Judith began a slow, steady stroke out and away from the dock. She had forgotten the pleasure of gliding through the water, weightless and alone. It was the closest man could come to flying, offering more solitude than soaring at great heights because there was no distraction of sights below. Why had she deprived herself of this pleasure for so long? She should have come here alone. Or better, she should have brought Emma, who was now old enough to share this experience.

The cadence of her steady strokes lulled her thoughts. She wasn't sure how long she had been swimming or how far she had gone when she noticed the light no longer danced on the rippling water. She was surrounded by watery darkness. Rolling over, she floated on her back. Above her, the breeze had drawn a dark cloudy blanket over the night lights of moon and stars. When she turned back, she could no longer see the dock. There were only a few cabins on her side of the lake and the residents of those had turned off their lights and gone to bed hours ago. She had no lights to guide her. Damn. Why hadn't she left a light on in the cabin?

Turning around, she saw the lights from the village across the lake, off to the west, but she didn't relish the thought of showing up on someone's doorstep dripping wet and naked. This was ridiculous. The lake was only two miles at its widest and she had swum it hundreds of times as a child. She should be able to find the cabin blindfolded. In fact, that's what she would do. Pretend she was blindfolded. She took a last look at the lights across the lake, judged herself to be a little more than half a mile west from where she had started, positioned herself, shut her eyes, and kicked forward toward the dark.

She had not realized how out of shape she was. Each time her arms passed her body preparing for another stroke they felt heavier and she sank a little deeper into the water. After several minutes, she stopped to check her bearings and discovered the lights had moved directly behind her. When had she veered off course? Had she made any progress, or had she just moved farther away from safety? She lay quietly on the water, floating until the growing panic subsided. Then she heard a familiar sound she couldn't quite place. She strained to listen and finally identified the distant lap of water against graveled shore. Judith reached out, cupped her hand around the water and pulled herself toward the sound. To steady her strokes, she imagined herself out in front of an able opponent, the lapping water the sound of applause congratulating her for being a certain winner in the competition. In her exhilaration, she didn't notice that the water again danced with moonlight. The cloud had passed.

Finally, she saw the ripple sparkle against the shore, and her feet touched the muddy bottom. The cold air hit her as she pulled herself waist high out of the water. She had missed the dock by more than a hundred yards. Better to stay in the shallow water until she could reach the warmth and comfort of her clothes.

Just as she was about to submerge again for her final crawl to the dock, Judith saw a figure step out of the shadows to the water's edge holding a bundle that was hers. The polite voice she had heard all day offered, "I thought you might need these."

Relief rivaled embarrassment and lost, not just because she was helplessly naked, but because she hated the idea that he had witnessed the dangerous miscalculation of her destination. Sinking shoulder-high into the protective water, she ordered, "Leave them there and turn around."

For the first time, the impostor's voice betrayed his real identity. "Why? Have you acquired new modesty or do you look different from the last time I saw you bare-assed naked?"

Judith thought of the telltale stretch marks across her abdomen and breasts. "Goddamn it, Randall. I'm freezing. Would you mind, just once, doing what I asked you to do?"

"Not this time. Maybe later. After the stupid stunt you just pulled, you don't have a right to give orders."

Defeated, Judith climbed out of the water, trying to control her body, which was shaking with fatigue, cold, and fury. "Fuck you!" she hissed.

Randall flung the old sweater around Judith's shoulders and began to rub her back vigorously. "Just what in the hell did you think you were doing out there?"

"Swimming," she said, slipping into her pants and buttoning up her sweater. "You ought to learn how to do it sometime."

"Right after I learn how to eat poison. You look like you could use a drink. Is there any brandy in the house?"

"I'm fine," she said, unable to stop shivering.

"Well, I'm not. Do you mind?"

"I think there's some Scotch. Will that do?" she said sardonically, already anxious to feel the burning liquid warm her from the inside out.

As they started back toward the cabin, Randall said casually, "By the way, you look even better than the last time I saw you bare-assed naked."

It had almost cost her her life to flush out the old Randall. "Thanks. You don't know how that makes my day," she laughed.

An hour later, after taking a long hot shower, Judith sat wrapped in a blanket, her hands cupping a mug of hot coffee. "Feeling better?" he asked, lacing the coffee with liquor.

"Yes," she said gratefully.

Randall sat down opposite her. "You know, you really scared the shit out of me tonight."

"I didn't mean to. I thought you were asleep."

"I could just see myself calling your family and saying, 'Excuse me, we've never met, but I'm an old boyfriend of Judy's, and I think you ought to know she decided to drown herself rather than spend another day with me.' "

Judith smiled. "My mother would have felt guilty because she encouraged this weekend, and my father would have been furious because I disobeyed the first command he ever gave me and went swimming alone. It would have been ironic if I'd died doing the only thing I was ever really good at."

"As I recall, you're the only person I ever met who resented having the perfect childhood. How *is* your family?" he asked.

"They're the same," she said. But that wasn't true. Or maybe it was true, and she was only beginning to learn what 'the same' meant. The apprehension she used to feel when she discussed her family with Randall returned. Only this time it stemmed from her own inability to make a judgment rather than from her defensiveness at his anticipated one.

"All is forgiven, I assume."

"We've made our peace. Or maybe negotiated a ceasefire is more accurate. Eddie's going to school in New York, and Christine is going to marry a nice guy. He's a lieutenant in the army."

"You must have had a thing or two to say about that."

"I did. Not anymore. Sara gave me a lesson in not fighting other people's battles."

"I can't imagine it. Lord, you were determined to be perfect. I always wanted to ask, do all gentile girls flush the toilet to hide the fact that they pee?" Randall set his drink down. "I want to make love to you," he said abruptly.

In spite of herself, Judith felt the warmth of desire and liquor mingle. "For old times' sake?" she asked, trying to keep the moment light.

"Nostalgia's always been a turn-on," he said, escorting their easy banter through a hazardous subject. "Before you answer, remember, I have a suicidal reaction to rejection. I've been afraid of it all day."

It had been a long time since Judith had made love. She had even given up taking the pill, unwilling to bear the side effects of headaches and gained weight in exchange for the occasional night of attempted passion that was seldom rewarded with gratification. Looking at Randall, she told herself that the increasing rate of her heartbeat and the spreading moisture between her legs were the punitive responses of abstinence. This was the moment when she could have the final word, the one denied her by his parting letter. He was vulnerable. She could fling the rejection he so feared, and deserved, in his face. On the other hand, the diaphragm tucked away with her shampoo, soap, and mouthwash, argued against the righteousness of her retribution. She conceded her hypocrisy. At that moment, she wanted him more than she wanted revenge. That too might offer a sense of closure, a final word. "Give me a minute," she said as she arose and headed toward the stairs that led toward the bedroom of her childhood vacations.

They made love twice, first with the frenzied appetite of the starving who gorge themselves without regard to manners or appearance. Then later, they joined with the familiarity of two old, considerate friends seeking to delight each other with recalled pleasures. Finally, Judith lay next to him content and satisfied, all thoughts of anger and revenge destroyed in the explosive climax of their lovemaking. Perhaps there were never any final words, no endings. Maybe there were only beginnings.

Randall brushed his hand across her breast gently. "I really don't think you have any idea how beautiful you are. I used to watch you when you were sleeping, and it made me feel handsome just to be lying next to you. I guess it's a little late to tell you now, but I'm still in love with you. I have been since the day you threw your paper in my face. Do you understand why I left?"

This morning Judith had anticipated this question in one form or another, been ready for it, would have said it didn't matter, there was no need to explain, it had all worked out for the best. "No," she said. "Tell me."

"I was frightened, so I ran away."

"From what?"

"From the fear of losing you. From a girl who wanted to be perfect, who wanted the world to be perfect, who expected me to be as good as she was. You had such a sense of moral indignation about every damn imperfection in the world. Every problem was your problem. I was afraid to be around when you found out the truth."

"What truth?" Judith asked, trying to understand what she was being accused of.

"That I wasn't perfect. That one day you'd wake up next

to me and realize that I didn't measure up to your standards. That, in fact, I didn't give a shit about most of the problems in the world. I doubt a day has gone by that I don't regret that cowardice. Come to New York with me," he whispered. "I think we could make it now."

"You're not afraid anymore?" she asked, thinking about Emma.

"Tonight, when I watched you slip out of sight and I thought I might lose you again, I made up my mind that I'd take a chance on asking you to forgive me, to come with me. So I'm asking."

Would this invitation be withdrawn, she wondered, if he knew it included a ready-made family? "I'm not sure exactly what it is you *are* asking. What's changed?"

"I've changed. And so have you. I ran away from a beautiful young girl who expected me to take the place of her father. I was afraid I'd disappoint you and end up losing you, the way he had. Today I met a grown-up woman who has built a life for herself. Somehow you've managed to keep the best of that young girl and get rid of the worst. You still care about the world, but you seem willing to understand and forgive that it isn't perfect. I could see it when you talked about your sister marrying a soldier. A few years ago you would have disowned her. I know I walked out on you, and I wouldn't blame you if you told me to get stuffed. Hell, I don't even know if you still even care. But if you do, I was hoping you might be strong enough to forgive me too."

Judith tried to keep her voice steady. "I seem to remember a similar invitation. Then all I had to do was leave my family and give up school. Now all I have to do is walk away from my career."

"As far as your career is concerned, there are a lot of poor people in New York who won't pay you as much as they don't pay you here. It's different this time," he said. "I'm willing to pay for my past sins by making it respectable. That is, if you still want the offer to include marriage."

Judith caught an edge in Randall's voice that she once thought signaled sarcasm and now understood camouflaged anxiety. Why couldn't he have said these words the last time they were together? She wanted to say yes. Yes, I'll go wherever you want. I admit I've missed you. But you walked out and left someone you claimed to love. How can I be sure you wouldn't do that again? And worse, even if you knew about Emma, said you wanted her, how can I be sure you wouldn't do that to Emma? "Are you sure you're ready for a wife and children?" she tested.

When Randall moved away from her, Judith almost expected him to command, "Jude, for God's sake, stop it." Instead, he chose to plead. "The theater is just getting started. I'm building a reputation. I think we could have a good life together, just the two of us," he said, failing the test.

"No children?" she asked, wanting him to see his error, to demand he be given another chance to answer the question that would make everything right.

"Marriage yes. But not children," he said cautiously. "Jude, I grew up the hard way. You were lucky. I remember when I first met you. My God, you were the product of a perfect family. I was jealous of the way you talked about them, especially the way you talked about your father. I wanted you to love me more than them, more than him. But when you showed up on my doorstep and said you didn't want to see him anymore, I felt guilty. I knew I had helped destroy something you cared about, just because I had never had it, couldn't ever have it."

Somewhere in what Randall had said was the answer to more than she had asked. "What are you talking about?"

"I'm trying to tell you that I'd make a lousy father. I don't trust the American Dream. My father walked out and left us. My mother survived on welfare. Actually, she didn't survive. After she died, I was pushed around from relative to relative who couldn't afford to have me around any more than my mother could. I don't think I can remember one family that I lived with who had a day of happiness. All I can remember is yelling and struggling. I think we have a good chance to make it together, but if I'm wrong, I don't want some kid fucked up. I don't want the responsibility."

Looking out the window, Judith could see the sky. What had her father said when she was a little girl? That here the stars were brighter because they didn't have to compete with other lights. But tonight the stars weren't as bright as she remembered them from her childhood, and there weren't as many. "Things have changed," she said. "And I can't tell you how sorry I am about that."

Sara Wallace, Capt.
71st Evac. Hospital, Pleiku

November 20, 1969

Dear Sara,

I can't believe I'm actually sending this letter to Viet Nam, and to a *Captain* Wallace no less. At least I'm relieved that you landed safely, but you make it sound even worse than I imagined. God, I worry about you. Please be careful.

I suppose by now you've heard about the march in Washington. There were 250,000 people, including me. And the very next day the papers reported that a massacre occurred in a place called Mylai last year and the army hushed the whole thing up. If it's true, how will this country ever recover from the shame?

On my way back, I flew to New York to visit Eddie and was tempted to see Randall. There's no use denying that I still have feelings about him. When I think back to Berkeley, all I can remember are the arguments and the sex. As he once said, we weren't the stuff of poetry. But after the weekend at the cabin, I find myself wanting to be with him out of bed as much as in. I did see the new play he's doing, and it's good. I'm glad he's finally doing what he wants.

I'm so sorry you're going to miss Christine's wedding. Eddie's flying in to be best man. Mom sends her love and says to tell you that she will write to you soon.

Your best friend,

Jude

Judith had not slept in her parents' house for almost five years and was surprised to find that she enjoyed the family noises of doors slamming, water running, and music playing. Nothing seemed changed. The room that was once a nursery welcomed Emma as though it had been waiting for a child to arrive and claim title to it by plugging in the nightlight that had been removed so many years ago. Even the animals on the walls invited Emma to name them, as Judith had done years ago, and after Judith, Christine, and then Eddie.

Judith had agreed to stay at her parents' house in deference to her mother's request that the family gather together for Christine's wedding. Edward was due home from New York in a few hours, and there was a mood of festive anticipation.

Judith was helping Christine and her mother clear the table when Edward walked in and surprised them. Everyone moved to welcome him, but his greeting went to Emma. "What a little beauty you are," he said, picking her up and tossing her into the air.

It had been almost a year since Emma had seen her uncle, and memory fades quickly in a three-year-old. Concerned by the look of suspicion on her daughter's face, Judith reassured her with, "You remember Uncle Edward. He lives a long way from here and now he's home for a visit."

When Emma looked down from Edward's extended arms and asked cautiously, "Are you my daddy?" all family noises stopped. Margaret wiped her dry hands on her apron. Christine retreated to her seat as if obeying an inner command.

And Robert Gregory stood, his arm fixed in an unfinished handshake. For a moment Judith imagined they were all playing a children's game of Statue and Emma was the leader, swinging them around and fixing them with the command "Freeze!"

Edward broke the silence. Giving his tiny niece a final animated toss, he laughed, "No. I'm not your daddy. If I were, we'd all be in real trouble."

After being lowered to the floor, Emma looked up at Edward. "Momma says my daddy lives a long way from here. Do you know him?"

Edward blushed at being the center of Emma's attention. "No, honey. I don't know him."

Judith sensed her family's silent reproach and, this time, thought it might be deserved.

"All right now, let's have the best man and the maid, uh, your sister next to each other." Judith tried not to smile at the photographer's stumbling attempt at tact.

Christine caught the moment, winking at Judith. "Sorry about that," she whispered, stepping next to her new husband. As Judith returned her sister's conspiratorial gesture with a nod, she experienced a vague sensation of loss. Christine was renouncing the title of "baby sister," demanding equal status. The wedding gown Christine had designed for herself was her mantle of womanhood. Judith had seen Christine's sketches of the dress, but wasn't prepared for its dramatic effect. It was cut to suggest, but not emphasize, her firm, full breasts, then tapered to accentuate her contrasting, diminutive waist. Judith was equally impressed with the dress Christine had created for her. Like the bridal gown, it was designed for the body it would cover, its soft, pale green silk draped loosely, moving gracefully against Judith's slim hips. Even Emma's tiny flower girl costume made her toddler's stomach look fashionable.

Only the groom looked ill-fitted, wearing his tuxedo

with the same, shy discomfort with which he wore his army uniform. No one in Bill's family had journeyed from Chicago for the wedding. His widowed mother was in failing health, and his older sister was required to stay home and look after her. The only evidence of the groom's family was the word CONGRATULATIONS in gold lettering sprawled across a wide, white ribbon draped on a small flower arrangement. Here and there, a few men lounged with drinks in their hands, their uniforms testimony that they represented Bill.

"Okay, everybody, look this way and relax," the photographer commanded.

Edward spoke quietly into Judith's ear. "This proves a picture isn't worth a thousand words."

Holding a fixed smile for the camera, Judith resisted the temptation to turn, to look at her brother and read his meaning. Then, behind a flashing light, as if arguing with Edward, the photographer said, "Perfect. A beautiful family." He had explained what Edward meant.

A few minutes later, the band began to play "We've Only Just Begun," and the family took their positions as rehearsed. As soon as the bride and groom had moved around the floor a few times, Robert Gregory turned to his wife. "I think it's our turn," he said. Taking Margaret's hand, he escorted her to the center of the floor.

Judith watched the two couples dance, noting the difference in their performances. Bill moved with self-conscious awkwardness, holding Christine like a delicate prize he had just won. In contrast, the bride's parents danced with the confidence of experience. Robert Gregory moved, if not gracefully, at least with authority, his arms relaxed around his wife. Margaret followed her husband precisely, making every step look easy. Judith wondered which one was really in control. "They're so different. How can they look so good together?" Judith said, more to herself than to Edward, who stood next to her.

"I take it you're not talking about the bride and groom," her brother said.

"They're beautiful too," Judith said, aware that Edward was watching her.

"But not so different, I'm afraid. It's hard to dance well when both partners want to follow."

There was a warning, a prediction in Edward's words, and Judith feared them. "Do you think Christine is making a mistake?"

"If I did, who would listen?"

From the time Edward was a little boy, Judith suspected him of possessing the powers of Cassandra, of being cursed with divination and of knowing his revelations would be met with either disbelief or derision. "I was the one who talked Dad into letting Christine live at home instead of going away to school," she said. "I told him she wasn't ready to grow up yet. We had a big argument about it."

"What did Dad say?"

"He said he always listened to what his children had to say and then asked me why Christine hadn't come to him. I told him that listening doesn't count if you don't take what you hear seriously."

"You're pretty hard on him."

"I seem to recall he didn't pay much attention to your dreams of being a writer," she said defensively. Judith decided not to tell Edward that the argument had ended when her father asked, "Did I ever ask you to be something you weren't?" and she had responded bitterly, "Yes. You asked me to be perfect." Remembering that scene reminded Judith of how right Randall had been. Trying to be perfect had its drawbacks.

"They make everyone look good," Edward said, nodding toward the dance floor, where Bill and Christine had just switched partners, the bride sweeping around the floor on her father's arm, the groom growing more confident, more graceful as his new mother-in-law slipped into step with him.

Edward took Judith's hand. "Come on, let's show them a really pretty couple," he said, pulling her toward the dance floor.

Last night, after her father and brother returned from the bachelor party, Judith had started downstairs for a glass of milk. Unobserved, she had watched as her brother sought out the brandy and carried it to his room. And today, in spite of his handsome youth, he looked tired. "I'm surprised you're not whimpering after last night's debauch," Judith said, arranging herself in her brother's arms.

"One, two three. One, two three," he intoned with the music. "Don't remind me. I'm trying to recover."

They danced easily together until her brother stopped abruptly and stood in front of her, not moving. "Did you have a dog that died?" he asked.

At first she didn't understand the question. "What?"

"Did you have a dog that was killed?" he repeated.

"What? Yes. Don't you remember? You called him Puppy. Not very original for a little kid who started reading when he was three."

"No. I mean, did you have a dog before that one?"

Judith thought back to the morning her father had backed out of the driveway. "Yes. Why do you ask?"

"Did Dad have it killed?"

Judith was stunned. "Of course not! I left the kitchen door open and he got run over. It was my fault. What ever made you think Dad would do something like that?"

"Because he thinks you blame him. Do you?"

"Edward, what the hell are you talking about?"

The music started again, switching to a faster tempo. "I don't know," he said. "Let's get a drink."

"Don't you think you had enough last night to last you for a while?" she asked, annoyed at almost being dragged from the dance floor.

"Just a little hair of the puppy," her brother laughed.

*   *   *

Judith's correspondence with Sara crisscrossed in the mail, questions asked and answered, advice sought and received too soon or too late.

December 5, 1970

Dear Jude,

If you've made up your mind not to tell Randall about Emma, so be it. But don't be tempted to play games. It was different when you didn't know where he was. If you see him again, you don't have any excuse not to tell him about Emma. What would you say to him if he found out (and he probably would)? I can hear you now, "Gee Randall, I meant to tell you about your daughter, but it kept slipping my mind." Take my advice, kiddo, either tell him if you're going to see him anymore or don't see him again. You can't have it both ways.

Write and tell me about the wedding (knowing you, you probably have already—the mails are slow). I crave news from home. Give my love to your mom, and kiss Emma for me.

Always your friend,
Sara

Sara was right. Judith had written about the wedding— *It was beautiful, but I'm apprehensive about Christine's fragility.* She related her fear of Edward's strange omniscience about the family—*I think he sees things no one else does, and the fact that he can't change what he sees makes him feel impotent.* Sara also learned that her warning about Randall was unnecessary. Had she waited a few days, she would have learned that Judith had come to the same conclusion:

I know now that I can't ever see Randall again. If I told him about Emma, he'd run. Worse, he'd play the trapped gentleman and offer to marry me. Either way, we'd all lose—me, him, Emma. He made it clear that he couldn't handle the idea of a child. When Emma asked Eddie if he was her father, I realized how dangerous it would be to try and have my cake and eat it too. Anyway, for whatever it's worth, I've made my life.

And like most intimate friends, they used each other as sounding boards. Their letters became vehicles for their anger, fear, and despair.

January 5, 1970
Dear Jude,

I hate to write you another depressing letter, but who can I complain to here? We're all in the same boat. I can just see myself turning to the kid they brought in here last night and saying, "You just lost your legs for nothing, kid. This war stinks and we're going to lose it."

What a crummy holiday we've had here. Bob Hope romps in here bringing a little tit and ass with him and makes jokes about army life. When the show is over, all these little kids we call soldiers get drunk, or stoned, or both, and try to forget that there's a good chance they're going to die tomorrow.

I'll be glad to do whatever I can for your brother-in-law if I hear from him. Like most of the men here, he'll probably be homesick. You say he likes kids. If we can hook up when he has a pass, maybe he'd like to tag along when we go out on Med Vac. The kids here need all the help they can get. I'll write as soon as I've seen him.

Always your friend,
Sara

May 30, 1970
Dear Sara,

Please read the enclosed letter that twenty soldiers

wrote to a small hometown paper in Ohio. My dad clipped it out and handed it to me without comment. Do you think it's possible that what we're doing here is causing more harm than good? All I could think of was Bill when I read it.

"We speak for a lot of guys when we say that we've had a gut full of you marchers and so-called protestors. A lot of people call you bleeding hearts, but we know what bleeding hearts are, because we see them on the battlefield every day along with bleeding heads, ripped-out guts, and maimed bodies. The sad thing is that the men who are bleeding over here are doing it for all you traitors who don't give a damn about your own country or the men who are dying for it.

"We read about all the memorial services given for those kids who were killed at Kent State in Ohio. We're sorry about that, but what about all the thousands of young men who are killed in the name of democracy here? What's going on in our own country when criminals are given memorial services and brave soldiers are condemned for doing their duty? Why isn't anyone marching for all the good, loyal Americans who have died? Every goddamn time there is a protest, you're saying that we're dying over here for nothing. Well, we know better! We're dying to protect your butts. All we ask in return for doing our duty is respect, and all we get is garbage thrown in our faces.

"Almost every man here has seen a buddy blown to bits or picked off by some Commie scum hiding in the bushes. If we're not bitching and dissenting, why the hell should the safe and sound college kids, hiding in their nice clean middle-class houses? Even when we're crawling through the mud getting blown apart, we know what we are doing is right and would spit on our own families if they joined you in your treason.

"Just remember all you worthless radicals and friends of the communist enemy, we've learned to use our guns and bayonets and hands. Someday we'll come home and demand answers from all you marchers and followers of traitors like the Chicago Seven and the SDS. Let's see how good you are at protesting us to our faces. Beware, because we've learned to hate you even more than we hate the VC and the NVA. So go on, keep marching and protesting and yelling how wrong we are. You'll need the exercise to keep in shape for the day we come home and fight you, our real enemies—America's traitors! Let's see if you're as brave when you're facing us as you are when we're thousands of miles away fighting your battles. Beware, you're going to learn what it feels like to be in Nam."

June 15, 1970

Dear Jude,

I got your letter a couple days ago, but this is the first chance I've had to collect my thoughts. The answer to your question is: keep doing what you're doing. Most of the guys here would call you and your friends cowards and traitors, and you can't blame them. They're the ones getting their asses shot off. They don't want to hear that a quarter of a million people marched into Washington to say it's all for nothing. They have to believe what they are doing is right; otherwise, they couldn't make it. I don't regret coming here—at least I can patch some of them up and send them home. But don't feel guilty about what you're doing. For every kid you smuggle out to Canada or prove is a conscientious objector (funny isn't it, just objecting isn't enough) is one that won't get blown to bits, hooked on drugs, or picked off by a sniper.

When those kids were killed at Kent State last month, the general feeling was that they probably deserved it.

I know how that must sound to you, but I don't think anyone can understand the profound bitterness some of these kids feel, and I guess their parents and friends at home must feel just as bitter. So be careful.

Their letters continued to cross each other, but now took on a personal urgency, concentrating on Bill's gradual breakdown. It was as if each friend were waging a war to save him. For Sara, salvaging this one soul would provide a victory, no matter how small—*Jude, make your sister understand that he needs to talk to her. She writes to him and tells him not to worry. What the hell does she think this is over here, a picnic? If she can't do it, then you must.* For Judith, it became a delicate act of diplomacy, negotiating between her sister's confidence in Bill's stability and her brother-in-law's ever increasing disintegration—*Sara, I got another letter from Bill. It's almost incoherent. I feel so helpless. Can't something more be done? I don't think the time he spent in the hospital has helped. I'm writing to him today, but what can I say? All I can really do is encourage him to keep writing, keep acknowledging the horrors.* And then finally—*Christine received Bill's letter (if you can call it that). You were right. He's coming home.*

Judith watched the black jungle looming beneath her as the helicopter floated downward like a feather. Her hysteria seemed incongruous against the machine's slow, graceful fall. Judith screamed at Sara to take her hand, to jump with her to safety, but her friend stubbornly refused. In the distance, Judith heard a ringing and prayed that it wouldn't stop, that it was someone signaling a rescue, that if she could reach the source, the agony of the nightmare would end and her friend would be safe. Still half in the dream world of fatal descent, Judith picked up the phone. The urgency of her mother's voice wiped away the sleeping terror. Judith listened as a waking nightmare began. "Judith. Christine just came here. It's Bill. Can you go to him?"

"Does he know about Sara?" Judith asked.

"I'll ask."

Judith waited, not wanting to hear the answer. She was going to tell Bill. But not yet. Not so soon. She couldn't face him, not until she adjusted to the news herself. She had needed time after Sara's mother called this morning to say, "Sara used to write me 'bout you. I know y'all was good friends." It was the black woman's flat, dead voice more than her use of the past tense that made Judith know what had to be said. She couldn't know the particulars, of course, not that Sara was killed when her helicopter was shot down, not that it happened while she was on a Med Vac. Those details would come slowly, painfully, not from an aged whore, but from a grieving mother.

Margaret Gregory's answer came quietly. "He knows."

Damn Christine! Damn her. "Tell Christine I'll go straight to her house. She should go too. Bill needs to see that she's all right."

But Christine didn't go, and it was just as well. When Judith arrived, her father was already there, standing in front of the garage door. "I've called the police," he called helplessly. "I can't get in."

Judith ran to the garage door. Nothing responded to her pounding fists or her shouts. "The car!" she yelled at her father. "Use the car."

Understanding, Robert Gregory pushed Judith aside, sprang to his car, started the engine, and rammed the door. Once inside, Judith watched her father desperately trying to breathe life into a body that refused to be awakened to more suffering.

Part Four

Though nothing can bring back the hour
Of splendour in the grass, of glory in the flower;
  We will grieve not, rather find
  Strength in what remains behind;
  In the primal sympathy
  Which having been must ever be;
  In the soothing thoughts that spring
  Out of human suffering;
  In the faith that look through death,
In the years that bring the philosophic mind.
         —WILLIAM WORDSWORTH
              "Ode on Intimations of Immortality"

10

Edward flew home immediately after his father called to tell him about Bill's suicide. The morning he arrived, he found Christine inconsolable, stubbornly refusing to leave her room, pushing away all offers of food and comfort. Not even Margaret Gregory could induce her daughter to leave her room by scolding—"I know this is terrible for you. But you must get on with life. You have no choice." When Edward tried to comfort her, Christine turned her face away and moaned to the wall, "It was an accident. I don't care what anyone says. He wouldn't leave me like this."

That afternoon Edward sought out his father at the newspaper and expressed his concern for Christine. "She's lost weight. I'm really worried about her."

"That's why she mustn't see this yet," his father said, reaching into the top drawer of his desk and handing Edward a neatly folded piece of paper. "We found it in Bill's pocket. The police know about it, of course. But I persuaded them to let me show it to her after the funeral, when she's over the shock. Since there was no question about what happened, they agreed to let me handle it."

The suicide note was written on heavily lined, white paper, the kind Edward remembered using when he was in elementary school. It was painstakingly printed in the hand of a conscientious child:

> My Darling Christine,
>
> I wanted to be a good husband. I really tried. I didn't mean to scare you tonight. No matter what you think, I never wanted to hurt you. But I'm afraid I might someday. I've done things that you would never be able to forgive me for. I can't forgive myself. Please don't hate me too much or think that I'm being a coward. I'm doing this because I love you and I want you to have a happy life. I know that you will be all right. Your family is wonderful and will take better care of you and the baby than I could.
>
> Remember, no matter what else you think, I love you.
>
> > Forgive me,
> > Bill

"I found this in Bill's pocket too," his father said, producing another piece of paper. "I haven't shown it to anyone, not even the police. It's not as if it were important evidence."

The second note appeared to be torn at the last minute from the same pad of paper, and the barely decipherable script bore the appearance of last-minute desperation. *Jude, you're the only one I can depend on. Take care of Christine and the baby. Sara should have made it, not me.*

"I don't understand why Bill didn't ask me to take care

of things. After all, it's my daughter and grandchild he left."
Robert Gregory returned the notes to the safety of his drawer.
"Would you like some lunch? I have a few minutes."

Edward felt the need of a drink, but alone. He couldn't
chance a momentary alcoholic temptation to rebuke his father
for quarreling over the spoils of war. "I don't think you should
show the note to Christine," Edward said.

"It's addressed to her. Sooner or later she's entitled to
see it."

"I didn't mean that note," Edward said.

At the funeral, Edward watched his sisters mourn—Christine
choked with gasping, sporadic sobs; Judith immobilized by
unutterable, inert grief. He wanted to reach out, to absorb
their agonies like a blotter soaking up desperation, guilt, fear,
and sorrow. Each sister had suffered a double loss: Christine
wept for the husband she had been too frightened to help
and for the unborn child that husband had been too frightened to know; Judith mourned for a friend she could never
replace and a brother she had adopted too late.

In deference to Bill's sister, who had traveled from Chicago, the nondenominational service was brief and simple.
"We aren't a religious family," Edna Wolfe had informed Robert Gregory when he called to break the news of her brother's
death and to seek her opinion on preparations for the burial.
Although she didn't say so directly, Bill's sister didn't approve
of a religious service, advising Robert, "God didn't help my
brother much when he was alive, so I don't guess there's
much use asking Him to help now."

Christine had wanted to overrule her sister-in-law's wishes.
Like so many others devastated by death, Christine sought
comfort in her childhood religion and wanted to hold the
funeral in her grandmother's church. It was Margaret Gregory
who counseled against it, arguing, "Bill's sister will be alone
among strangers, don't make it more uncomfortable for her
than it already is." Even Christine's grandmother gently urged,

"Bury him as his mother and sister want. It's not like he was a member of our church, my child."

Strangely enough, it was Edna Wolfe who, after she arrived, had finally prevailed upon Christine to relent and guard her health, admonishing her, "The baby's all we have of Bill. You wouldn't want to do him harm." Perhaps his sister heard the same unspoken "like you did Bill" that Edward imagined he had heard, because afterward Christine joined the family at dinner, accepting small portions of food and making heroic efforts at small talk.

Now Edna Wolfe, whom the family had never met until yesterday, was saying her good-byes as Robert Gregory opened the car door and helped her settle into the front seat next to Edward. As she had since her arrival, Bill's sister offered only those phrases appropriate to the occasion. To Robert Gregory, "I wish I could stay longer too, but I have to get back to Mother." To Margaret Gregory, "You've been very kind. Thank you for putting me up." To Christine, "Yes, we'll all miss him. Yes, we'll keep in touch," and "You take care of yourself and that baby of yours." And finally, to Edward, "I hate to make you drive me to the airport. I could have taken a cab."

"I'm happy to do it," Edward said truthfully. He had no desire to hurry back to the house for the post-funeral festivities, which would be attended mostly by family friends and neighbors. He wondered if Bill's sister had noticed the absence of young men at the funeral. Only one had attended, the same sergeant that Edward had met at Bill's bachelor party, and even he had shown up late, stood in the back of the funeral parlor, and then left without a word before the service ended.

As the car door slammed shut on the family her brother had become part of, Edna Wolfe said, "Bill liked your family. I can see why. You're like those TV families. You know, like 'Father Knows Best' or 'Leave It to Beaver.' "

Edward tried to see his family through this poor woman's

eyes. Yes, his father projected that handsome, easy assurance that had made Robert Young the nation's father figure. And, although his mother didn't come to the table wearing a single strand of pearls to accent a demure but stylish dress, Edward could see how Edna might confuse his mother's intense watchfulness with dutiful adoration. Even Christine could be considered network pretty, and Judith all-American beautiful. How much did this woman know about his family? Or had Bill, like Edna, seen only domestic tranquility instead of determined truce? Perhaps all families looked ideal to an outsider. "We're not much different from most," he said, alarmed that he might be right.

"Bill wrote me about you. He thought you were a genius," she said with simple midwest frankness.

Her ingenuousness discouraged embarrassment. "I fool a lot of people," he laughed.

"Do you miss living at home?" she inquired.

Edward accepted the invitation to engage in casual conversation. "Sometimes. But I'm pretty busy. I work part-time as a teaching assistant while I'm in graduate school. I get homesick once in a while," he said, relaxing into the comfort of exchanging meaningless and harmlessly inaccurate information. "But I still come home for the holidays."

"And funerals," she added ruefully. There was a moment's awkward silence before she reissued her previous invitation to friendly discourse. "Do you like teaching?"

Edward framed the expected lie, then surprised himself by rejecting it. "No. I don't."

"What would you like to do?"

Edward felt guilty discussing his problems when she had not complained of her own. Yet he found himself compelled to tell this stranger what he had not revealed to his own family. "I write when I have time. I'd like to quit school and do nothing but write."

"Why don't you?"

"Because I'm not sure I'm any good. Besides, I don't

think my father would be too happy about my giving up the chance at a respectable career just to become a starving playwright. He wanted to be a writer once. He knows the chances of making it are pretty slim."

"Funny, isn't it? Bill always wanted to be a teacher and never really had the chance. It's going to be hard getting used to the idea he's gone. I raised him, did you know that?" Edward knew she didn't expect an answer. It was now her turn to testify to pain. "Dad died when he was a baby. Mother's been sick for years—arthritis, emphysema. She was too old when he was born. Not much of a family for a little boy. Not like yours anyway." With a weariness that comes from resigning oneself to the burden of loss, she said, "Your sister's very beautiful."

Since she could have meant either one of his sisters, Edward felt safe in agreeing. "Yes, she is."

"My brother should have married her," she said, identifying which sister she meant. "He wrote me about her. He called her Jude. I thought it was her nickname, but I didn't hear anybody in your family call her that. Anyway, she tried to help him. Not that it did any good, but at least she tried. And that friend of hers, what's her name?"

"Sara?" he prompted.

"Yes, that's her name. Sara. She tried too. Everybody did. Except his own wife." Her polite, controlled voice gave way to angry despair, and Edward knew he would be unable to stop the words that only someone outside the family would ever dare to speak aloud. "He married a baby. Why didn't someone stop them? What was she thinking of, buying a house and getting pregnant? He was too sick to deal with any of that. He was too weak. He needed somebody strong. Instead, he married somebody weaker than he was. I should have known from her letters, talking about designing me a dress and fixing up her house. She was a little girl playing at being married. Didn't she understand how sick Bill was?"

Edward listened like a silent chronicler. What did this

woman expect him to do with this information? Take it back home? Deliver it to Christine, to the family? Didn't she know what happened to the messenger who brought bad news?

"I'm not blaming her," she said, before Edward had to choose between defending his own sister or sympathizing with Bill's. "If there hadn't been the war, they might have made it together, but I doubt it. Maybe he wouldn't have killed himself, but sooner or later they both would have realized they weren't good for each other. Not that he didn't love her. He did. I suppose she loved him too. But love isn't enough, is it?" she asked, looking to Edward for confirmation.

When Edward glanced to acknowledge her question, he was struck by her weariness. Edna Wolfe looked years older than what he guessed was her actual age, older even than his mother. She was a plain-looking woman whose solid features had been worn away with years of hard work and worry. How much it must have cost her to be a mother without a title, a daughter without a childhood. "I'm sorry," Edward said helplessly. "I didn't know your brother very well, but I liked him. "If there's anything I can do . . ."

"Thank you. That's very nice," she said graciously, the way a condescending adult receives a child's nonsensical gift. Then, after a few moments of silence, Edna retreated into the protection of past memories. "He was such a sweet little boy, quiet and shy. He couldn't stand to hurt anything. He never had a chance. No father. An invalid mother. And an old maid sister who worried about him all the time. I suppose that's why he joined the army. He wanted to get away from us. Look what that got him."

Edward heard her swallow the tears that were beginning to season her words and felt obligated to offer solace, no matter how trite, defense, no matter how weak. "At least they had a little happiness together. It's more than a lot of people have who live a lifetime together. Maybe you're right—maybe Christine was too young. But she'll grow up."

Edna Wolfe slumped over her purse and rummaged around

until she produced a clean, starched handkerchief folded rigidly into the shape of a one-dimensional ice cream cone. "She better grow up fast," she said, twisting the soft linen around her fingers like a miniature tourniquet. "She's going to be a mother."

Two hours later, Edward tried to steady himself as he maneuvered his way up the sidewalk leading to his parents' house. Turning up the walk, he almost collided with the postman, whom he had known most of his life. The old man reached out to offer a handshake of condolence. "Good to see you, Eddie. Real sorry to hear about the family's trouble. Don't blame you for having a drink," he sniffed, his senses benefiting from being downwind of Edward's breath. "Times like this, it helps to take a little nip."

Edward had had quite a few little nips after he dropped Edna off at the airport. He had hoped the gum and the Binaca would disguise his transgression, cover his detour to the seedy bar where ordering double whiskeys in rapid succession was met with admiration, not derision. Now the old postman had exposed him for the sickly-sweet-smelling impostor he was. Edward moved away from the subject, nodding at Mat's heavy mail pouch. "Neither sleet, nor rain, nor . . ." Edward couldn't remember the rest.

"Funny about that motto. Nobody ever gets it right. It's 'Neither snow, nor rain, nor heat, nor gloom of night stays these couriers from the swift completion of their appointed rounds,' " the courier recited without pause.

"Is that for us, Mat?" Edward asked impatiently, nodding toward a letter in the mailman's hand.

"It's for Judith. Don't get much mail for her anymore. It's from Viet Nam. You see she gets it, you hear."

Edward glanced at the name of the sender and wondered what kind of cruel joke the United States Postal Service had decided to play. Whatever it was, this was not the time to find out. He shoved the letter in his jacket pocket. "I'll deliver it," he said, pushing past the old man with polite determination.

Once inside the house, Edward avoided the solemn gathering of those who had carried all manner of cakes, breads, roasts, and casseroles to the house like caterers hired to make sure the bereaved were free to host a grim party. He marveled that they had managed not to duplicate each other, one bringing mounds of cheese, another providing bread and crackers, still others coordinating assorted meats and salads. Later, these organized, well-meaning accomplices in the macabre would retrieve their dirty dishes, wrap and put away the leftovers, then depart, leaving the family to concentrate on their suffering. As he passed through the crowd, Edward's father headed toward him. "What happened? Did you have any trouble?"

"No trouble," he reported as he headed directly toward the liquor cabinet. "Okay if I have a drink?" Edward asked, pouring himself a drink just as his father joined him. It was an expedient way to mask the evidence that lingered on his breath.

"It's a little early, son. But I think I'll join you," his father said, pouring less than a shot of brandy into a large snifter. "Did you wait to see Edna off?"

"Yes." At least this was partly true. Edna had traveled lightly, carrying only a small overnight case. Edward escorted her to the boarding lounge, where she shook his hand and then dismissed him politely with "There's no need for you to wait. We don't have any more to say. Thank you for bringing me this far."

Robert Gregory swirled the brandy around in his snifter, held it to his nose, and then breathed deeply. "She hardly said a thing while she was here, but I had the feeling she blamed us in some way for what happened. Did she say anything to you?"

Edward spoke slowly, shaping his words carefully to overcompensate for the thickness of his tongue. "You'll be happy to know that she thinks we're the perfect family."

*   *   *

True to form, Margaret Gregory had stayed up "to put the house right," as she said. Dr. Davis had given Christine a mild sedative. Judith had refused the doctor's offer of a similar sleeping agent, but did agree to let Emma spend the night with Grandmother Rose. Edward had claimed a headache and retired early. Eventually, he heard his father throw the dead bolt on the front door, a signal that the day's activities were ended. A few minutes later, Edward lay listening to the silence and wondered how many others in the house were staring into the darkness trying to make sense of the past few days.

Edward reached under his pillow and retrieved the letter he had placed there hours earlier. "Neither snow, nor rain, nor heat . . ." he whispered, as he felt his way down the darkened hall, "but gloom of night is a pretty damn good reason to stay me from the swift completion of my appointed round." Reaching the old nursery, he rapped lightly on the door. He was startled by how quickly Judith appeared.

His sister put her forefinger to her lips like she used to when she played hide-and-seek with him and Christine. "I'm glad you came," she whispered. "I couldn't sleep."

Judith closed the door noiselessly and led him into her room. She was barefooted and wore an old, faded robe that was too big for her. She had loosened her hair from its French twist, and now it hung unkempt and slightly oily to her shoulders. As he passed by her, he smelled her exhaustion. Edward remembered the time she had come home from Berkeley looking like this in her carefully contrived hippie costume and her straggling hair. That day, he hadn't understood when she explained that she looked that way because she wanted to make a statement. Tonight, he clearly understood the statement her appearance made, and he was reluctant to complete his mission. "I couldn't sleep either. Are you all right?"

"Not really. But I will be. I don't have any choice." There was an echo behind her declaration that he couldn't identify. When she added, "Poor Christine," he knew it was the echo of his mother's voice he heard.

"Not everyone feels sorry for Christine. Edna blames her," he said.

For the first time since Edward's arrival, Judith was alert. "Did she say that?"

"No. Not outright. But that's what she meant. By the way, Edna thinks you're beautiful. She says you're the one Bill should have married."

"That's ridiculous, and you know it!"

Edward welcomed her anger. It was easier to deal with than grief. "There's a lot I don't know. Like, why did Bill do it? What happened?"

"I thought Dad told you."

"No, I mean what *really* happened. I know Bill was disturbed, but I thought he was getting better. What pushed him over. Was it the baby?"

"It was the war," she recited as though she had rehearsed the answer a hundred times and was bored with the repeating.

Edward needed more to go on before he delivered the letter he carried in the pocket of his bathrobe. "Come on, Judy, lots of guys went through hell in Nam, some of them as sensitive and fragile as Bill. They didn't all come home and kill themselves. You were the one he talked to. What made him do it?"

She looked down at her hands as though she couldn't quite see the answer they held. "I'm not sure. Lots of things, I suppose. He talked to me, but I always had the feeling that there was something he was holding back. Something he hadn't told anyone. He saw some horrible things. All I really did was listen. Maybe Christine was right. Maybe it was my fault for listening instead of insisting he put it all behind him."

Edward put his arm around his sister and guided her to the bed, where she let him gently seat her. He picked up a small chair from the child's desk where he used to study, turned it around, and straddled it, facing Judith. "Tell me about Sara," he said softly.

Judith absentmindedly reached for the pillow next to

her and cradled it like a child on her lap. "She could have left over a year ago, but she decided to stay on until they had taken everybody out. I don't think anybody knows what happened for sure. It was a madhouse when the North started across the demilitarized zone. Someone said it was the biggest attack in four years. Sara's mother told me Sara volunteered for some rescue mission. They're not even sure if the helicopter was shot down or not. It crashed in the jungle." Judith gave her report slowly, accurately, between deep breaths. "I wrote to her a few weeks ago to get advice about Bill. She always had the right answers. When she thought I was wrong, she used to really let me have it. Who's going to tell me when I do something wrong now?"

"Don't worry. There's always someone around who'll be happy to supply that information," he said, slipping on the armor of humor to defend against her misery. Edward reached over and held his sister's hand, hesitated, then said, "I have something to tell you."

Edward's caution must have alarmed her because she dropped the pillow and stood up. "What? Is it Christine? Is the baby all right?" she asked too loudly.

This was no time to arouse the family. "Shhh. No. Please, sit down. Everyone's fine. They're all asleep."

Judith sat back down, retrieving her bundle of downy security. "What's the matter?"

"I bumped into Mat as he was about to deliver this," Edward said, pulling the letter from his pocket. "I told him I'd give it to you." Edward held the letter out to his sister. "It's from Sara."

For a moment, Judith stared at the flimsy blue envelope in Edward's hand. "That's not possible," she said, drawing back. "It's postmarked the day before . . ."

Judith reached out and took the letter, her hands remarkably steady. "Thank you," she smiled, as if accepting an unexpected gift.

"Do you want me to leave?" he asked.

"No. I'd like you to stay," she said, carefully lifting the flap on the envelope that contained what Sara couldn't have known was to be her final letter to Judith.

Edward watched as his sister began listening to her friend's silent words. She ignored the tears that escaped so swiftly they had no time to impair her vision, only heeding them when they threatened to drop on the printed page. Edward sat transfixed, like a frustrated voyeur, unable to penetrate the spectacle of this final intimate moment between friends. When Judith finished, she dropped the letter next to her and lay back on the bed, her arm covering her eyes. "She answered my letter," she said with an exhausted sigh. "I think you should read it. It answers your question. She mentions you too. I think she knew this family better than any of us did. Maybe it's impossible to understand something you're part of."

Edward picked up the letter. The handwriting was strong, sure, just as he imagined it would be:

March 30, 1972

Dear Jude,

I'm sending this to your mom's house because you said you were there every day, and I'm enclosing a note to Bill so you can give it to him. All hell is breaking loose here since the North crossed the DMZ. People are scurrying at the last minute either to escape or to make a final buck. There are a lot of children here who are up a creek. Their American fathers, a lot of them black, have either deserted them or have been killed. The combination of black, French, and oriental has thrown off some incredibly beautiful human beings. I don't know how many we can get out of here before the communists take over the country, but I'm going to try to get as many as I can. Something tells me they won't be too

popular with their lovely kinky hair and their large al-
mond eyes.

I got your letter yesterday. Bill sounds bad. Worse
than you described when he first got home. Like you, I
was hoping he would eventually begin to cope with what
happened to him here. You asked what you could do.
I'm not sure you can do anything. He was broken here,
and no matter how the doctors try to mend him, he may
break again under the least little pressure. There's something I never told you because Bill made me promise
never to. For his sake, I'm going to break that promise.
For the past year you and your family have been treating
Bill as though he were a victim of this war. And believe
me he is. But if that was all, I think he could handle it.
What you don't know is that he was also a victimizer.
And that's what he may never be able to live with. You
mustn't condemn him for what I'm going to tell you. It
happened all too often here. When he led his men into
that village almost two years ago, he thought it was just
a routine scouting mission into a friendly village. Well,
it wasn't routine. The place was crawling with VC. When
they opened fire, seven kids caught it right away. Bill
started shooting anything and anybody that moved. So
did everybody else. Afterward, he found a whole family
had been killed—mother, father, and five children. No
one knew who fired the shots that killed them, and no
one cared. No one except Bill. It was the children that
drove him crazy. The higher-ups declared that the parents were VC and patted Bill on the back for his heroic
performance. Bill didn't buy it. He was smart. He knew
that babies don't make war. In some ways, that's to his
credit. In others, it's what might destroy him. Talk to
him Judith. I write to him as often as I can, and I know
he trusts you. I know it's tough for you kiddo, but *no
judgments.* Just try to understand what it's like here.

My guess is that when Christine said she was going

to have a baby, he couldn't handle it. In some sick way, he may feel that he doesn't deserve to have a child.

You've got a strange family, my friend. You all love each other, but you don't read each other very well. (I take that back—your mom does, but she's just trying to hold you all together.) I remember that day your dad brought Eddie to school. Lord, what a disaster. You, sitting there trying out all your new liberal ideas, and your dad, devastated because he was afraid you were rejecting him. And your poor little brother, what a dynamite kid he was. He knew everything that was going on at that table, but he didn't dare say a word. No wonder he's drinking too much. I would too if I had to live a life I thought someone else had made up for me.

I'm going to get some sleep now. I'm catching a copter out of here early to snag a few kids. Tell Bill I'll be home in a few months. Tell him to hang on.

Love, Sara

Edward put the letter down with an involuntary "Shit."

Judith still lay with her arm fixed over her eyes. "Is she right? Have we made up your life for you?"

This was the second time today that Edward felt guilty exposing feelings that weighed so lightly compared to the moment. "Maybe then. Not now," he lied.

Judith sat up and looked at her brother. "Are you sure?"

Edward avoided answering her question. "What are you going to do?" he asked.

"About what?" she asked, successfully distracted.

"About this," he said, extending the letter to her.

Judith recoiled. "Tear it up. And tear this up too," she commanded, handing Edward the unopened note Sara had written to Bill.

Edward hesitated to destroy the evidence that had been presented so eloquently and explained so much. "Are you sure?" he asked.

"There's just so much truth we need," she said. "Too much, and we drown in it."

Early the next morning, Edward was already packed and anxious to fly to the safety of the East Coast. He was on his way to Christine's room to say good-bye when he heard her bitter attack. "Don't tell me what to do. I don't need your advice. You've already done enough talking. If it weren't for you, Bill might still be alive. You're the one who said everything would be all right. Leave me alone."

Edward wanted to scurry past the door, to avoid this scene that promised to settle so many accounts for his widowed sister. But after reading Sara's letter last night, he had become an accessory to the hidden truth and felt he could not desert the recipient of Christine's attack. Opening the door, he saw his sisters facing each other in a tableau of violent frustration. "Hi. My plane leaves in a little while. I wanted to say good-bye," he said, feeling like a kid whistling to keep away the bogeyman.

"Make her leave me alone," Christine pleaded.

Edward turned to Judith. "What's the matter?"

"That's right! Ask her, not me. You always think our big sister knows everything. Well, she doesn't. Just once, why don't you ask *me* what's the matter?"

Edward turned away from Judith, hoping she understood his desertion to the other side. "Okay. What's the matter?"

"She says I can't stay here. She wants me to go live in that house by myself. She wants me to make all the same mistakes she's made. What right does she have to tell me what to do? This isn't her house. Dad says I can live here as long as I want."

Edward turned to the "she" of Christine's accusations. "Maybe it's too soon."

Judith chose either to ignore or to reject Edward's mediation, challenging Christine, "If you don't learn to take care of yourself, how in God's name are you going to take care of a baby? Dad can't protect you for the rest of your life. Mom would probably say the same thing, except she doesn't want to force Dad to confront you."

"You're just jealous because Dad wants me to stay. You can't stand the idea that you're not the favorite one anymore."

"Christine, don't be such a bitch," Edward said, hoping his feint would decoy her attack. It worked.

Christine turned the full force of her anger toward her brother. "Who the hell do you think you are? You come wandering home once in a blue moon and act like we're all beneath your contempt. I know what you think behind those silent know-it-all looks. You think that Bill killed himself because I didn't understand him. That if I had just listened to our brilliant sister here and not told him about Sara, he'd still be alive. Well, you're wrong. He loved me, and Judith only made matters worse. I don't know how he got locked in that garage, but he wouldn't have deserted me and his baby for anything, no matter how sick he was."

Behind him, Edward heard his mother's stern command, "Stop this!" All three of her children turned in stunned silence. "Christine, it's time you saw this," she said, holding out a lined piece of paper that Edward recognized.

"What is it?" Christine asked.

"It's a note Bill left for you. You're father didn't want you to see it until after the funeral," his mother said.

Christine stepped back from her mother's extended hand as though it held a lethal weapon. "What does it say?"

"It says you're wrong about a great many things, child. It's true that Bill loved you, but love's not always enough. You made a mistake thinking it was. If life was that easy, there wouldn't be a family in the world with problems. You didn't cause Bill's death, but you weren't grown-up enough to understand his life very well either. Ever since you were a little girl, you've run away from things that you didn't think were pretty. I suppose we're all to blame for that. We let you do it. Now it's time to learn some pictures can't be made pretty no matter how many ways you try to paint them." His mother's hand now insisted that the note be taken from it. "Read it," she ordered.

Christine obediently reached out and accepted the paper. As she read, her audience watched in anxious silence. Edward braced himself against the expected sobs that would come with written confirmation of the truth. But his mother apparently had no intention of allowing her daughter the luxury of either self-pity or indignation. Instead, Margaret Gregory pulled a second piece of paper from her pocket. "Bill meant this for Judith. You weren't intended to see it, but now I think you should," she said, placing the small scrap of paper in Christine's shaking hand.

Before Christine had time to defend against the implication of her husband's final words, Margaret Gregory turned on her other two children. "Shame on you both. Edward, don't let me ever hear you call anyone in this family names again. Not ever! And you, Judith. Don't speak for your father and me. We can do our own talking. Your life isn't so perfect that you can tell others how to live theirs."

For a moment all three stood like naughty children awaiting the verdict of parental justice. When it came, it was swift. "Edward, your father's waiting to take you to the airport. Judith, it's time you picked up Emma." Even her newly widowed daughter was not to be spared. "Christine, it's finished. It's time you started planning for the baby. When you're ready, I'll take you home." Edward realized that his mother had found her children guilty of destruction, of waste. And the punishment was banishment.

For the next three years, Edward hid out in New York, visiting only when no excuse to do otherwise was plausible, or, as Christine had accused, "once in a blue moon." Today he was glad he had lacked an excuse for not visiting before the fall term started. It was one of those unusual September days in Southern California when the hot Santa Ana winds swept out of the dry desert valleys, pushing the smog and soot away from the foothills, cleaning out the city, and depositing the polluted debris miles out over the ocean. As he sat on the beach and watched his family at play, Edward nodded politely to the couple who were busy spreading their beach towels near him, enthusiastically demanding he share their appreciation of the air's sparkling clarity. On days like these, newcomers to the Los Angeles area often marveled that it was so clear they could see Catalina Island clearly outlined on the horizon. He didn't have the heart to tell these happy young tourists that the spectacle was courtesy of the dirty air, which hung like a dark shroud beyond the little land mass, lending contrast, giving the illusion of a pristine view. Instead, he smiled and agreed that it was indeed an exceptional day.

Next to Edward, on the old, worn blanket that had served similar purposes a generation ago, his mother sat dozing under a wide-brimmed hat. He settled back and fed on the scene before him. The desert wind had not only scoured the air; it also assisted the ebbing tide, blowing the water back, smoothing it, calming it, making it a safe place for his sisters' children to sit just beyond the water's reach and build their castle under the direction of their grandfather. Christine's son, Eric, already three years old, fetched and carried the building material for the wet feudal structure without complaint. He was a handsome boy, with his father's blue eyes and lanky body, and his mother's full sensual mouth and dark hair. Unfortunately, Eric had inherited his grandfather's fair skin, and even the sunscreen his mother had meticulously applied was not preventing his toddler's nose from turning bright pink. At almost nine years old, Emma was fulfilling her promise to be a beautiful woman. Tall and graceful, with deep green eyes, Emma resembled her mother, but her olive skin and long, dark, curly hair insinuated an exotic paternal influence.

Edward noted with amusement the pecking order of the building project. His father was the architect of the already crumbling alcazar; Emma, his faithful contractor; Eric, her adoring crew. After triumphantly delivering each pailful of wet sand, Eric stood waiting for his reward. Edward watched Emma's pantomime of praise, a casual hug and a pat for a job well done. Satisfied, Eric was happily back digging and hauling more building material for his idolized cousin. Edward thought of Judith and the reverence he had had for his own surrogate mother. He wondered if all little boys gluttonously craved female affection. And if so, did all little girls, realizing this was their one moment of total superiority, sate that craving? Nature may have made a big mistake in not providing enough mothers for its male offspring.

Edward turned his attention toward his sisters, the foam gently swirling around their ankles as they kept an eye on their young master builders. Tragedy and motherhood, or perhaps merely survival, had strengthened both of his sisters. After the war ended, Judith had continued to fight for her causes, and her reputation as a civil rights attorney had grown. She had taken on three junior partners to assist her in the various battles she waged against both federal and local government, one minute opposing the CIA's infiltration of agents into black, antiwar, and political movements, the next defending the rights of the Nazi party to hold public meetings. No one could accuse her of a consistent knee jerk.

And Christine. She had met her exile three years ago with an "I'll show you" attitude that Edward suspected was motivated first by anger, then necessity, and eventually maturity. She had used her talent for designing clothes and worked hard to build a clientele. Last year she opened a small shop in Santa Monica and seemed proud of her modest accomplishments. Would either sister have done so well if she had not been forced to leave the protection of her father's home and care for her fatherless child? Edward smiled. For women, Nature may have made a big mistake in providing too many fathers for its female offspring.

"Your father's getting burned," his mother said, once again awake and alert.

Edward wasn't sure if his mother intended a warning or a simple observation. "Do you want me to go tell him?" he asked.

"No. They're having such a good time."

Edward sensed his mother had weighed cost against value and decided the discomfort of a peeling nose was a small price to pay for the happiness of the moment. Remembering Edna Wolfe comparing his family to a television version of domestic bliss, Edward glanced out at Robert Young at play with Bud and Princess. Somewhere Edward had heard the rumor that the young actor who had played Bud was fighting to overcome a drug problem. So much for the illusion of the perfect family. "Eric's turning into quite a little man," Edward observed. "I'm surprised his Aunt Edna hasn't come out to visit him. Have you heard from her since her mother died?"

"Yes. When her mother died, she sold the house and took up with a younger man. He left her in Florida after she ran out of money. Poor woman. She never had much of a life. I suppose she just wanted a little happiness."

Edward tried to visualize that worn, plain woman flinging caution aside with one final passionate toss. That day in the car, she had told Eddie that love wasn't enough. He wondered if, after having a respite from a life of drudgery, she had changed her mind. "I hope she found it," he said.

"Have you found it, Dr. Gregory?" his mother smiled.

"What?" he asked, unprepared for the question.

"Happiness."

He had finally become Dr. Edward Gregory, an expert in neoclassic criticism and one of the youngest instructors at NYU. He tried to be a conscientious teacher, but knew the most he could aspire to was mediocrity. He had settled into his life in New York, content to live in his old, one-bedroom brownstone apartment in the Village, with its Georgian wainscoting, Indian rugs casually scattered on the hardwood floor, and lovely arched window that overlooked Washington Square.

It was an ideal place for an alien to retreat to from the relentless energy of Manhattan. For over a year, he had divided his time between fulfilling his teaching obligations and finishing the play he was writing. There was no time left over for social conquests and drinking bouts. He missed neither. "Yes. I suppose I'm happy. Not ecstatic, but happy."

His mother nodded, more with relief than approval. "I wish she wouldn't go so far out," her mother said, squinting toward the horizon.

Far beyond the surf line, Edward saw flashes of Judith's white bathing cap. "She'll be all right. She knows what she's doing."

"Sometimes I wonder," his mother said as Christine joined them on the blanket.

"You two haven't moved all day," Christine said. "You should cool off in the water. It's wonderful today."

Margaret Gregory reached out and began rummaging through her big, ancient straw bag that over the years had transported needlepoint canvases, children's cast-off jackets and sweaters, and light picnic lunches. Today it held towels, beach shoes, cover-ups, and sunscreen. Edward remembered when she had bought that bag from a vendor in Tijuana years ago and could still see her standing there pointing to this bag amid hundreds of exact copies as though her name had been invisibly woven into it. Now, watching her, he was reminded that it was he who had insisted on visiting that Mexican border town when he still had childish "go out night" fantasies of finding a place where they would be happy together, where they would renounce their silences and confess their mutual needs. So much had happened since that day, and Edward marveled that both the bag and his family had survived the wear and tear of all those years.

"Your father and Eric need to put more of this on," she said, extracting the sought-after protective lotion. Reaching up and accepting Christine's offered hand, Margaret Gregory heaved herself up. "Oh Lord," she grunted, "I'm getting old."

Age had consented to replace his mother's youthful beauty with handsomeness. "You don't look it," Edward said honestly.

"You know you're getting old when your knees start to wrinkle and they don't bend like they used to," she said before striding off toward the construction project.

Christine dropped down next to him on the sandy blanket. "Well, Dr. Gregory, it's been a long time. How do we all seem to you?"

"The same," he said, picking up sand and letting it run through his fingers. It brought back memories of other days on the beach, other times when he and his sisters would bury each other in a mound of hot earth and then laugh to see the victim struggle out. "I take that back. You all seem better. Especially you."

"Thank you for noticing. I *am* better. I didn't think I would be after Bill died, but I am."

Edward remembered the day his mother delivered Bill's last words to Christine, and he wanted to tell her that he was sorry he ever accused her of not having nerve. "You've done a good job. You have a terrific-looking son there," he said, gesturing toward his nephew.

Christine acknowledged the compliment with a smiling glance at her son, then said, "I suppose Judith was right to tell me I should start living my own life, on my own. I know you agreed with her too. But sometimes, when I think of that last note Bill scribbled to her, I still feel resentment. I hated the thought that Bill's last thoughts were directed to Judith. Good old reliable Judith. She screws up her own life and somehow that makes her our resident guru. I didn't speak to her for almost a year. Did she tell you that?"

"No. Judith only writes about things she thinks will make me happy. She told me how well you were doing."

Christine followed Edward's example, and began running sand through her fingers. "Everything's okay now. I've forgiven her."

"How did you two make it up?" Edward asked, trying to visualize Christine forgiving, and unable to imagine it.

"I don't know. You know how things are in this family. Mother says come to dinner Sunday. I go. Judith and I are barely polite. Dinners come and go. And then one Sunday we start talking about babies, about which is easier to raise, boys or girls, and finally everything seems back to normal. Except normal used to mean I was always angry about something Judith would do or say. Now she doesn't seem to do or say annoying things anymore, or maybe she does and they just don't bother me anymore—I'm not sure which. I suppose I never understood how close she and Sara were and what that meant to Bill. I still don't understand, but I don't hate Judith anymore for what happened. I guess she was just trying to help."

Edward sensed this was as close to forgiveness as Christine would ever come. "I'm glad things are working out for you," he said.

"I've met someone," Christine said without preliminary explanation.

"Who is he?" Edward asked, knowing she meant a man, a man who was being considered to replace Bill.

"His name's Dale Reed. He's a businessman. Retail marketing. He's giving me lots of ideas on how to build my business. And he's wonderful with Eric. He's strong and so sure of himself. I don't know what I'd do without him. I hope you like him."

Edward thought of Bill. Quiet, decent, and so unsure of himself. "I'm sure I'll like him," he said.

"Are you glad to be home?" she asked, once she had established Dale Reed's credentials.

Edward had avoided visits home because he had finally realized it was dangerous territory, a place, unlike New York, where he couldn't insulate himself from estrangement. He bore his family no grudge, admitting he was a member of this domestic coalition united in a conspiracy never to divulge who they were. Today, he found he had missed his coconspirators and was glad he had lacked an excuse for not visiting before the fall term started. "Yes," he told his sister, glad that he could be honest. "It's good to be home."

Edward had invited his date to his apartment for what he hoped would be more than the suggested quick nightcap. Her name was Deborah, and he liked the fact that she didn't permit herself to be called "Debbie." She was a graduate student who, like Edward, was a transplant from another world. She was from Ypsilanti, Michigan. She wasn't beautiful, at least not in the way his sisters were beautiful. But she had a sturdy midwest quality that belied her intelligence and sensitivity. He had enjoyed the few times they had spent together, and tonight that enjoyment promised to be even greater.

As he unlocked his apartment door, he heard the phone ringing. "Aren't you going to answer it?" she asked, as Edward walked past the phone toward his kitchen and the bottle of wine chilling in the refrigerator. "It might be something important."

Important things didn't happen to him here. "It'll keep."

The phone continued to ring. "I think you should answer it," Deborah said. "An unanswered phone offends my Puritan ethic."

The smile he wore for Deborah faded when he heard Judith's voice. "Edward. Mom had surgery today. It's not good news."

"How bad?" he asked, ashamed that he resented the intrusion.

"A year at the most."

"I'll come home."

"No. She'll be out of the hospital in a week, and she'll be fine for the next several months. There's nothing you can do, so there's no point in your coming home. You know that's what Mother would say, so let's do what she would want."

As he hung up, Edward realized he had been deceived.

He saw now that he had been teased into contentment by a few years of calm. Misery thrives on complacency; like torture, it needs relief or it begins to go unnoticed. Constant pain dulls itself. Why hadn't he paid more attention to Lear's warning that "As flies to wanton boys, are we to th' gods. / They kill us for their sport." "From the minute we're born, it's a setup," he said bitterly.

"Is there anything I can do," his forgotten guest asked.

"Can we make it another time?"

After Deborah left, Edward opened the wine. He doubted there would be another time.

Edward dreamed someone was shaking him awake, criticizing him for his drugged escape into sleep. He tried to roll over and pursue another more pleasant unconscious scenario, but the shaking and chastising continued. "Edward, wake up!" It was a woman's familiar voice. He was used to various members of his family invading his dreams. This time his subconscious had assigned Judith the starring role.

"Damn it, Eddie. Wake up and pay attention."

Finally, Edward gave in to the aggressive actress in his groggy play and opened his eyes. "You can't be here. This is New York, not California," he said after Judith swam into focus.

"I'll make some coffee. We need to talk," his real, live sister said, already moving away from him.

Edward pulled himself up and tried to sit on the edge of the sofa, where he had passed out a few hours ago. He was only partially successful. For a moment, he thought he might be sick, then remembered, or perhaps forgot is more accurate, that he hadn't eaten for the past . . . he wasn't sure how long. Lowering his head to his hands, he tried to sort things out. It couldn't be his mother; he had just spoken to the family on Sunday morning (early enough to be fairly sober). There was no indication that his mother was ahead of her one-year death sentence. In fact, she had sounded better than the rest of them. Behind closed eyes, he asked, "What time is it? How did you get here?"

The only answer was a cupboard opening, water running, a pan banging on the stove, and, finally, "Get up and take a shower."

In his condition, retreat was easier than defense. Edward steadied himself and then with monumental effort stumbled toward his only sanctum. Behind the locked bathroom door, he managed to turn on the shower and crawl under the spray. "Cold," he told himself. "Take your punishment and make it cold." A few minutes later, more chilled than refreshed, he was ready to face his next trial. "To what do I owe this honor?" he asked as he entered the arena where his sister stood, steaming coffee in hand.

"Drink this," she ordered.

Edward accepted the offered cup resentfully. "You know, so far you've answered every question with a command. That's not a nice way for a houseguest to act."

"You're not funny, little brother. As far as being a houseguest, you have to be kidding. I'm probably the only one you know who would consent to stay in this pigsty."

Edward looked around. She had a point. Over the past months, the floors and scattered Indian rugs (what you could see of them under the mess) had taken on a grimy, abused look, and the window had filmed, obscuring the view of the park. It hadn't looked like this last year when Judith had visited. He regretted giving her a duplicate key. "The maid quit," he said, sitting down at what served as both desk and dining room table. "Now. What brings you here?"

"You're what brings me here. I called the university. They said you were on a permanent leave, whatever the hell that means."

"It means I left permanently. More precisely, it means I got fired. But you know how they are in academia. 'Fired' has such a plebeian ring to it. They don't like to think in terms of intellectuals being fired; they prefer to think of them as leaving, albeit permanently."

"What happened?"

"Why does something always have to have happened? I'm a drunk. It's that simple. Things happen to drunks. They screw up, they lose their friends, they get fired, they run away from their families." Edward didn't tell her that, guilty as drunks are, sometimes they end up paying for their sins when they are innocent. How could he tell her? He wasn't sure himself how it all happened. After he learned about his mother, he got drunk and stayed that way to one degree or another. Then there was the faculty party, the invitation by the dean to see the manuscript he was about to publish (something about originality not being a valid criterion in literary criticism), more brandy, the dean kneeling, caressing, stroking, trying to sober Edward's drunken penis, which insisted on sleeping. Edward vaguely remembered apologizing to that kind old man who had so often looked the other way when Edward staggered into his classes unprepared. He had not wanted to reject the man, to hurt his feelings. In fact, he wanted to tell him that he appreciated the gesture of love but that, drunk or sober, he couldn't return the favor. He was spared that ordeal and offered another.

"Was it your drinking?" Judith pressed.

"Not entirely. There's always a place in the hallowed halls for a devotee of the grape, as long as you don't insult the dean's wife at a cocktail party." But, of course, that was exactly what Edward had done without meaning to. Worse than spilling a drink on her dress or making an unwelcome advance, Edward had spilled one on the dean in return for his unwelcome advance just as the dean's wife was walking into the den to find her husband. Naturally, she assumed the insult was to her, not to the two men who at that moment would gladly have given their lives to be anywhere but where they were. "Seniority works in mysterious ways," Edward instructed his sister.

"Eddie, please. Would you mind not being a supercilious asshole for a minute, and tell me what's going on."

Edward looked at this marauder who had swept in, occupying his territory, blocking his escape. "I can't. I probably could if I were drunk, but you've shut off that avenue of free-flowing, open communication."

Judith walked across the room and retrieved the half-empty bottle of brandy that had rolled under the couch after it had slipped out of Edward's hand a few hours earlier. "Well, then, be my guest," she said, slamming the bottle down on the table.

Edward decided shame would have to wait and poured as much brandy as his coffee mug would permit. "Here's looking at you, kid," he toasted, before bringing the shaking cup to his lips. Judith sat impassively as he poured another, draining the last of the bottle. Edward thanked lack of food, sleep, and an already established level of alcohol in his system for the sudden, merciful numbness he felt spreading throughout his body. He wasn't drunk yet, but with a little more effort . . . His sister's face floated closer to his. "Why are you doing this to yourself? Talk to me, Eddie. Let me help."

"You can't. Leave me alone." He had witnessed this same scene years ago. Only this time he had the starring role. "Now I know how Christine felt," he said, venting his brandied anger.

Edward saw Judith swimming toward him, reaching out, touching his face. "Sara was right, wasn't she? We all made up a life for you that you didn't want. Why did you listen to us, Eddie? Why didn't you tell us?"

"I tried to tell you in this," he blurted out, picking up the scattered pages of his manuscript that had been rejected so often with the standard phrases—"Shows promise but not what we were looking for"; or, "Lacks vitality"; and, "If you try something else, keep us in mind." Edward had to agree. His characters had outsmarted him, kept him from knowing their secrets, laughed at his counterfeit talent. His father had been vindicated. It came in a rush, unexpected, unintended. He threw the pages at his sister. "I'm a goddamn spectator, impotent. I know what's going on, but I can't do anything about it. I open up my mouth to scream, to warn all of you, but nothing comes out. Now it's too late. Everyone's leaving." He wasn't surprised to find himself welcoming the protective embrace he had loved as a child. He wept against her softness. "Why does so much love cause so much suffering, so much pain?"

Edward awoke to a find a stranger sitting in the living room reading the manuscript he vaguely remembered throwing at his sister the night before. Or had that been a dream? If it was, then dreaming had its advantages. The apartment was clean and ordered, and the view through the bay window was once again sharp and clear.

The man's deep brown, sad eyes looked out over a nose that was just a little too large for the thin face, and his ears extended a little too far beyond the dark, thinning hair that showed traces of gray. Taken individually, his features would be thought unattractive; together, they blended into one harmonious whole. Not handsome, Edward noted, but correct. "Your sister went out shopping. She thought you'd sleep until she got back. I just finished reading your play," the stranger offered, as though that explained his foreign presence.

Edward wasn't sure what politeness demanded. Gesturing toward the manuscript that had been laid aside, he asked, "What did you think of it?"

"Do you want me to be gentle or blunt?"

Curiously, Edward valued this stranger's opinion. "I have a feeling you'd be more comfortable being blunt."

When the man smiled, his forehead wrinkled, and the sad look in his eyes changed to amused comradeship. "Your work lacks courage. You write like your head and your balls are miles apart. Your characters refuse to reveal themselves, which means you refuse to do it for them."

Edward felt he should be angry, or at least defensive, but he wasn't. He actually wanted to hear more. "And?"

"You have talent. If you ever find the nerve to put your feelings on the line, then I think you could be a good—maybe even a great playwright. It's probably just as well that you're out of the academic scene for a while. You ought to think about doing a little fieldwork. That usually starts with a job in a restaurant."

The phone rang before Edward had the chance to respond. The voice on the other end had changed, matured, was approaching womanhood. "Hi, Uncle Edward. Is Mom there?" Emma asked without bothering to identify herself.

"No. Your mom went out shopping. Is anything the matter?"

"No. Just tell her I'm driving up to Arrowhead with Grandma and Granddad. We'll be gone for the weekend. How's everything going?"

Edward glanced at his guest. "Everything's going fine. I'll give her the message." Edward gave an uncle's "Be a good girl" and hung up. He turned his attention back to the man sitting opposite him. "That was Emma," he said. "Judith's daughter," he added, to clarify his unsolicited explanation of the interruption.

Edward heard the door open and turned to see his sister, laden with bags, struggling to keep them in balance. When she saw him, she looked relieved. "Oh good, you're up. I see you two have met."

"Not formally," Edward said.

Randall looked up at Judith. "The last time I saw you, you didn't mention that you were married and had a child."

In that moment, Edward knew that Judith and Randall had been lovers, that Randall was Emma's father, and that Randall was the only one in the room who didn't know the truth. "I'm starved. What's for breakfast?" Edward asked, as he took the bags from Judith's hands.

Judith returned to California the next day, and Edward went with her for the Christmas holidays. Two weeks later, when he returned to New York, Randall helped Edward get a job working in a small theater on the outskirts of Harlem. Randall's idea of "fieldwork" included everything from painting scenery to scraping gum from the bottoms of chairs. Edward wondered if Randall had befriended him because he was Judith's brother or because he had talent. But within a year, Edward had finished his second play, and Randall had more than praised it—he had produced it in that same tiny Harlem theater. Edward had never been happier.

Four months later, his father called to announce, "Your mother's dead. And you may as well know now, Judith has been arrested. She won't even defend herself. It's all so stupid . . . your mother . . . she wouldn't have lived much longer. I just can't understand why your sister . . ."

Without a word to anyone, Edward went home.

11

Judith sat with her father and Christine in the sterile hospital waiting room. Her mother had been in surgery for almost two hours, during which time words were avoided, fears unexpressed. The bright fluorescent light above made everything seem harsh, old, stark. Judith's back was cramped from the rigid, modern plastic and metal chair that was not designed to accommodate anxiety. She wished Christine would stop pacing like a caged animal frustrated at not being able to pounce on her prey. Her father had settled into a chair that must have been donated by someone who thought it would offer homey comfort, pacific calm to this otherwise barren room where people were condemned to await a medical verdict. Judith was worried about her father. He sat like a young boy who had been deserted among strangers set adrift without direction. "Dad, go have a drink. Chris and I will wait here."

"I don't think Dad wants to be alone right now," Christine snapped before her father had the chance to consider the offer.

Judith accepted Christine's hostility, knew that much of it was deserved. Judith had to admit that the various roles she had played in her sister's life had hardly engendered affection: the condescending big sister; the overbearing, self-righteous young mother; and the unqualified counselor who failed to prevent Bill's death. It was she who had first challenged Christine to confront life apart from the shelter of her childhood home. But Judith took some comfort in the possibility that because of, rather than in spite of, these past grievances, Christine had managed to grow, to become self-sufficient, confident. Judith was glad her sister had found a man who promised to be both a partner in business and in marriage. His name was Dale Reed, an extroverted marketing expert, handsome, sure of himself, and demanding. Under his management, Christine's business had nearly doubled in less than a year. Surprisingly, Christine seemed to feed on her new lover's aggressiveness, learn from it, become expert in it. As vulnerable as she had been with Bill, that's how secure she was with her new lover.

When Dr. Davis finally appeared, Judith saw her father struggle to stand. For some reason, it was important to Judith that her father stand up to this man who had the power of life and death. Slipping her hand under her father's arm, she tugged him roughly to an upright position and felt him falter. My God. He's not a young man anymore, she thought. Why haven't I noticed that?

Judith listened as this messenger from the underworld, disguised as a healer in white, delivered his death sentence.

"Do you think we should tell her?" Robert Gregory asked, like a child waiting to be told what to do.

How could her father ask such a stupid question? Why was he permitting this aging medical fraud to get away with this? Why didn't he put up a fight? Judith wanted to shout,

"Do something! Years ago you could do anything. Why can't you now?"

Insensitive to her thoughts, the doctor addressed the future widower, who stood passively waiting to be told what to do. "That's your decision to make with the children. But I think she's strong enough to handle the truth. Besides, if I know Margaret, she won't let us get away with less."

None of this was possible. It was true that her mother had lost weight over the past few months. But Judith believed her mother's guarantee that "everything will be all right." Now Dr. Davis was not honoring that guarantee. He was cheating, saying that it was good for only "a year. Perhaps a little longer. We can never be sure about these things."

Why were they standing there so calmly, her sister gently touching her father's arm like she wanted to make a casual observation, a light remark? And her father looked preoccupied, as though he were trying to remember where he had left something. Judith had to do something. She couldn't just stand there, paralyzed by the hysteria she felt mounting into a scream. But her scream was calmly deceptive. "I'll go call Eddie."

When her mother asked Judith to move back home, Judith seized the chance to be the daughter she had not been as a child. She had been guilty too long of not making her mother's life easier. But it wasn't like her mother to suggest that she couldn't manage things on her own. In fact, her mother gave every appearance of being perfectly healthy. "If you think I can help," Judith said.

Her mother looked irritated. "I don't need a nurse, Judith. I need some company. With Eddie away and Christine traveling all over with Eric, I miss having a child around. Besides, it will give Emma a place to come to after school. Grandma Rose is getting too old to watch out for a young girl. It won't hurt her to live with the people she calls family. I've discussed it with your father, and he thinks it's a good idea."

Actually, Emma had started coming to her grandfather's house after school against Judith's wishes. "All right. I'd like to be home again. And you're probably right. It would be better for Emma," Judith said, not sure she believed it would.

Two weeks after Judith moved in with her parents, her mother asked her to call Edward. "I've tried to call him at home, but I don't get an answer. We haven't heard from him in over a month. I want to make sure he's made his plans for Christmas."

"I'll call him at the university when I get to the office. It may take a while to get through to him," Judith said, picking up her briefcase. "Tell Emma to get a move on it—she's going to be late for school. I've got to be in court today. I'll try to come straight home afterward." As Judith left the house, she realized she had forgotten the purpose of her returning to her parents' house and wondered who was taking care of whom.

As soon as she let herself into Edward's apartment, Judith's stomach rose up against the smell of rotting food, unflushed water, and stale alcohol. At first, she was frightened when she saw her brother's lifeless body sprawled out on the sofa, then relieved that it was drunken oblivion not malignant illness that had immobilized him, and finally angered by his soured brandy groans when she awakened him. Moving into the filthy kitchen, Judith found an opened can of coffee, prayed to the preservative gods, and searched for a clean pan. She settled for a crusted pan and trusted to boiled water. "Get up and take a shower," she ordered through the air to what used to be her clean, well-ordered brother.

A few minutes later, Edward emerged, looking slightly better. "To what do I owe this honor?" he asked, a semblance of his comforting sarcasm returning.

"Drink this," she said, giving way to the hope that coffee would solve all his problems.

"You know, so far you've answered every question with

a command. That's not a nice way for a houseguest to act."

With the bribery of more drink, Edward finally dropped his guard. He was not on leave, he had been fired—reason withheld, transgressions unexplained. As his shaking hand reached out for the bottle of brandy, Judith imagined her brother shrinking hopelessly into drugged oblivion. She was losing him as surely as she had lost Sara and Bill, as she was now losing her mother, and maybe even her own daughter. Everything was falling apart. "Why are you doing this to yourself? Talk to me, Eddie. Let me help."

Her brother pushed her away. "You can't. Leave me alone. Now I know how Christine felt."

What did he mean, he knew how Christine felt? Was he blaming her for his failed life? What had she done to him? She always loved him, took care of him, was proud of him. But she had never really ever understood him, listened to him. Was that her sin against her brother? "Sara was right, wasn't she? We all made up a life for you that you didn't want. Why did you listen to us, Eddie? Why didn't you tell us?"

Drunkenly, Edward swept up the sheets of paper scattered on the table and hurled his despair at her. He wept something about being a spectator, impotent, trying to warn them. Judith tried to understand his cries, but in the end, she could only hold him. She had no answer to the question she had asked herself so many times. "Why does so much love cause so much suffering, so much pain?"

Judith put Edward to bed sometime after midnight. She had become used to the generalized odors that pervaded the apartment, but there was no way to shut her eyes to the disheveled mess around her. She spent the rest of the night scrubbing the kitchen, emptying mounds of garbage, and returning the apartment to some semblance of order. She didn't even notice her hands scraping pans and mopping floors—they were simply moving instruments that accompanied her thoughts. She vaguely remembered telling Christine years ago

in that tumbled canyon shack decorated with such pretentious disarray that she didn't hate chaos, so she had no particular need to impose order on it. Now she knew she had
been wrong. To survive one had to continually tidy up. Each
day she began to understand her mother better.

Without conscious effort, Judith had already worked out
a plan. By the time she heard the predawn garbage trucks
prowling the streets, collecting the city's cast-off debris, she
knew it was time to call Randall. She was prepared to accept
his rejection of her "Please come. I need help," but he didn't
even ask why he was being summoned five years after their
last parting. "What's the address?" was all he asked.

When Randall arrived, Edward was still asleep and the
apartment was at least presentable. In his mid-forties, Randall
had become almost handsome. His features had stopped war-
ring with each other, accustomed themselves to the face that
wore them, blended, looked kindly together, content. "I'm
glad you came," she said, ushering him in.

"How could I refuse? It's the first time I ever heard you
ask for help."

"I'm learning," Judith said, handing Randall Edward's
manuscript. "My brother wrote this. Would you read it?"

"And if I think it's bad . . . ?"

"I'll respect that. I just want your opinion. Straight and
honest."

"Where is the author?"

Judith considered confiding in Randall, but decided that
she had no right to ask him to be both nursemaid and critic.
Besides, Randall had never been noted for his bedside manner.
"Asleep," she said. "I'd offer you breakfast, but there's nothing
here. If you can wait, I'm going to run to the store."

"Go ahead. I prefer reading without an audience," he
said, making himself comfortable, manuscript in hand.

Judith took more time than necessary to find the few
things she needed at the little deli less than a block away.
She wanted to give Randall a chance to finish the manuscript
and herself enough time to consider what to do next. She

wasn't concerned about the possibility of her brother's giving away the secret of Emma. It wasn't in his nature to volunteer information. Last night, she had even thought of telling Randall herself. But not now. Not yet. Not with her mother dying and her brother so disturbed. She had to believe she had been right five years ago when she refused to see him again. How could she? He would have felt trapped by the responsibility of a daughter? What good would it do now to add even more chaos to everyone's life? Perhaps later, when both father and daughter were older, when responsibility would be a matter of choice and not obligation, then she could tell them both.

Judith returned to the apartment a little more than an hour later, her arms heavy with groceries. Edward was up and dressed, sitting opposite Randall. "Oh good, you're up. I see you two have met."

"Not formally," Edward said.

Randall's eyes searched Judith's face with mingled confusion and anger. "The last time I saw you, you didn't mention that you were married and had a child."

"Don't you think you ought to tell me about your daughter?" Randall asked, barely concealing his hostility. Fortunately, he had not pursued the subject in front of Edward. Instead, he had helped Judith unpack the groceries and, after a quick, strained breakfast, had invited her for a walk. Judith had to gather her information carefully in order to choose the correct path, the one that would lead all the way to the truth. "How much did Edward say?"

"Just that you have a daughter named Emma. You must have had a daughter named Emma the last time I saw you, unless of course she was born afterward. In which case, she's pretty young to be making long-distance phone calls," he said sarcastically.

A sudden gust of cold autumn wind blew, cutting through Judith's light California coat, but she felt only the suffocating heat of being buried under years of deceit. "Emma's beautiful. You'd like her."

"Would I like her father too? You haven't mentioned him yet. Now I'm beginning to understand our little weekend rendezvous, just the two of us tucked away where no one would see. No wonder you wouldn't even discuss coming to New York. It might have been a little crowded with a child and a husband."

Judith swallowed her anger. Righteous indignation might taste good, but she knew it would leave her hungry. "Emma's father has changed a lot. I think you'd like him too."

"Are you still married?"

She warned herself now, as she had so often warned her clients who were about to be deposed, never to volunteer information, only to answer the questions asked. "No, I'm not married."

Randall's anger breathed steamy white against the icy air. "When were you divorced? Before or after our interlude in the mountains?"

"I was never married."

Randall stopped walking and faced her. "You mean he deserted you?"

The truth came as suddenly as the gust of wind that whipped against her face, just as unpredictable, just as cold. "I thought he did. Now I realize we deserted each other, both for our own selfish reasons. The wonder of it is, Emma turned out to be terrific in spite of us. You'd be proud of your daughter, Randall," Judith said, betraying her own advice about volunteering information.

"Let's walk," Randall said, setting not only Judith's body in motion, but her old fears as well. Had he believed her? Did he think she was trying to trap him after all these years? Was he trying to think of a way to deny the possibility of fatherhood?

Wordlessly, he led her into one of the coffeehouses Eddie had delighted in telling her about. The pungent smell of hot coffee floated across the room. At one table, several young men were engaged in heated debate about the fairness of Patty Hearst's coming trial. "First she's a victim of the left wing nuts, now she's a victim of the right wing nuts," came wafting across the room. Another group opposite them were arguing the merits of a new Broadway play. Even the few strays who lounged over their exotic brews were reading the morning papers as if in silent argument. How odd, Judith thought. My mother is dying, my brother is making a mess of his life, I've just threatened my future with Emma, and all I can think of right now is how different New York is from Los Angeles.

"What would you like?" Randall inquired politely, as though being a gentleman were the most important thing on his mind.

"Plain coffee," Judith responded, aware that at this moment, being civilized was the one thing they could safely share.

Randall waited until the order was taken and the coffee served before he said, "All right. Talk to me."

Judith told Randall everything that had happened since he left her at Berkeley. She told him about Sara, about Bill, about Christine, and finally about her mother. She left nothing out. "I wanted to tell you the last time I saw you, but you had so many plans. You said you didn't want children. I knew if I told you, you'd feel the decision had already been made for you."

Randall studied her for a while before he said, "Bullshit."

Judith had been prepared for almost any response but this. The eyes of the caustic young professor she had first met and feared as a young coed glared at her. And it was that young girl who cried, "Randall. Please. You have no right."

"The hell I don't. You didn't tell me about my daughter because I might have wanted her. That would have deprived you of being the heroine you always wanted to be. How could you be the proud unwed mother, the big independent lawyer, the self-sacrificing sister and daughter if I had made demands on you? Maybe you're right. Maybe I wouldn't have been thrilled at the idea of being a father. I probably wouldn't have been. I might even have felt trapped into being a teacher for the rest of my life. Or I might have run away just like I did. The point is, you didn't have a right to make those decisions for me."

Now it was Judith's turn to say "Bullshit," with all the fury of a woman who had been condemned by half-truths. "I wasn't worried about your making demands. Why should I have been? All I ever heard from you was a lot of existential crap about choices. Demands mean commitment. You didn't make any then, and you have no right to start making any now. It must feel wonderful to feel so indignant about being saved. Admit it!" she said, her voice rising above the civilized pitch they had observed. "It's worked out wonderfully for you. Nothing has stood in your way. Not me. Not Emma. Not even another woman, I notice. It must have made it easier to tell yourself you were still in love with me. That way you never had to commit yourself to anyone else who might have held you back. At Berkeley, you were so frightened of commitment you didn't even hang around to say good-bye. You just dropped that masterpiece of intellectual crap and ran. You didn't even bother to sign it, you son of a bitch. And then at the lake, I gave you every chance to show me you were willing to make a commitment, no strings attached. But you always had conditions. First, it was come with me, but no marriage. Then, it was come with me, but no children. Now you have the nerve to sit there and feel betrayed. I don't buy it!"

Randall appeared to fit her half-truths into his and then resign himself to the whole truth. "You're right," he sighed. "Would you mind telling me about our daughter?"

"Of course not. What do you want to know?"

"Oh, the usual things a father might find interesting. What she looks like. Her interests. Thoughts. I don't know. I'm rather new at this line of questioning."

Judith realized that describing Emma's looks and interests would be easy. Her daughter's thoughts were another matter. Emma was beginning to shut Judith out, withdraw. She confided only in her grandfather, embraced only him, smiled only for him. Judith was powerless against her daughter's "Grampa says this..." and "Grampa told me that..." Judith knew this was neither the time nor the place to discuss the possibly damaging effects of being raised without a father. "She looks like the best of both of us. My eyes, tall, with your dark curly hair. She loves to read, and she's a darn good tennis player. But she's quiet. That quality must be due to a genetic throwback."

"I want to see her," Randall said quietly.

"Not now. It isn't the right time."

"What if I demand it?"

Damn him, Judith thought. Why did he always say the wrong thing. "You'd look a little silly demanding parental rights for a child you've never seen, especially if the mother denies that you're the father. Suddenly realizing you have an undying desire to have a child strikes me as a little ludicrous. And so does threatening me with demands. That doesn't work with me anymore."

"It never did. And you're right, I have no right to make demands. But I think I have the right to ask a question." There was no trace of anger, only defeat. "Do you have any feelings left for me? Or was what happened at the lake just a trip down memory lane?"

Judith had at one time or another wanted to offer Randall love, hate, revenge, reconciliation. This was the first time she wanted to offer him comfort. "Yes. But right now they're all mixed up."

"Don't ask me why, but even after this, I guess I still love you. I want to know my daughter, and I want to try and make a life together. No strings attached. It's up to you."

These were the words Judith had always wanted to hear, but now they brought with them new reasons to say no. "Randall. Try to understand. My mother is dying. My brother is in a lot of trouble. My family needs me. I'm not trying to be a hero. It's just that I can't think about us right now. Wait, please. Give me time to sort things out."

"There will always be a reason why you can't," he said,

picking up the bill. "I could try to force you to let me see my daughter. But I'm surprised to find that even though I don't know her, I love her too much to put her in the middle of that kind of fight. And I can't force you to believe things could be good for us. I think I've mentioned that I have a lot of difficulty handling rejection. This one hurts the most. I guess I have to admit I'm not man enough to keep trying. I'll stay out of your life."

Before Randall walked away and left her sitting alone, he said, "By the way, your brother has talent. I'll try to help him for his sake, not yours."

For almost a year, Judith forced herself not to think about Randall and the sadness he left behind when he walked away that day in New York. He did call her once after, but the conversation ended much as it had that day in the coffee-house. "I love you because you had the strength to do what you did, and I hate you because you could," he had said just before he hung up. After that, Judith concentrated on assisting her mother out of life, just as her mother had assisted her into it.

Judith wasn't sure when she began to notice that her father was absent more than she could remember him ever being. "He's an important member of the community now," her mother would say proudly. "You should admire him for his work." Or, "I insisted he attend that meeting." When other rationales failed, she simply declared, "I want him to make that speech."

As her mother's pain grew more obvious, so did Judith's resentment of her father's absences. Again he was late when Judith bent over her mother, helpless to ease the agony that came with an unexpected moan. "Please, Mother. You have to let them give you something for this."

Behind her Judith heard her tardy father. "What is it?" Robert asked, pushing Judith aside and kneeling next to Margaret.

Her mother smiled at her husband. "Just a little pain. Nothing serious."

"I want you to go to the hospital!" he said.

"I'm all right," Margaret whispered.

Once again her mother implored him to leave her bed and seek a peaceful night's rest away from her. And once again, Judith found it odd that, after all the evidence pointed to his wanting relief from the atmosphere of sickness, he still refused. "I want to stay with you," he said, lifting his wife from the sofa. "Let me help you upstairs."

Later, her father joined Judith and Emma in the kitchen. "Smells good. Who's the cook?"

"I am," Emma announced proudly.

In fact, Emma had contributed to the meal, peeling potatoes, washing lettuce, and setting the table. Judith wondered if her daughter would have been so obliging had it just been for the two of them. "Well, then, let me give the chef a kiss," Robert said, lifting his beautiful eleven-year-old granddaughter onto his lap.

As Judith watched, she realized that Emma was entering that void between childhood and womanhood. She envied her daughter the protective arms that encircled her. "Big girls don't sit on their grandfathers' laps," Judith instructed.

"Sure they do," Robert said, giving Emma a hug.

Judith felt a rush of resentment she couldn't target. Was it aimed at her daughter or her father? "Emma. Get down this instant!" she commanded. Then, with embarrassment more than regret, she added, "Your grandfather must be tired. He's worked all night. Let him eat in peace."

Her father aimlessly pushed the food around on the plate. "Don't you like the meatloaf?" she asked.

"I guess I'm not very hungry," he said.

No wonder her father hardly ate a bite. How could he when she stood there acting like a neurotic fishwife? "Dad, you must try and eat. It would upset Mom if she thought you weren't taking care of yourself."

Emma slithered off her grandfather's lap and took the fork from his hand. "Let me feed you like you used to feed me," she said, scooping a glob of potatoes from his plate. "Now open wide. And innnnnnnn it goes."

Robert watched hypnotically, opening his mouth on command. Judith forgave all when her father reported, "Thank you, honey. I feel better now. I don't know what I'd do without you and your mom to help me out."

In the final stage of her illness, her mother could no longer hide her agony. Robert begged his wife to go to the hospital. "I can't stand to watch your mother suffer," he told Judith one night. "You have to help me convince her to go to the hospital."

Judith suspected her father of wanting the convenience of an antiseptic environment where he would not have to contend with the ever-present reminder that death lived in his house. Since the day Dr. Davis had rendered his verdict of his patient's condition, her father had not admitted the inevitable, acted as though it were a temporary condition. Not that he actually denied it; he simply refused to discuss it. Her mother had said more than once that she hated the confinement of a hospital room. "I can live with pain. Or in this case die with it. But here, where I belong," she had told Judith.

"She wants to die at home," Judith said.

"She told you that?"

"Yes. Many times. She wants to be where she can control things. In the hospital, she knows she'll be at their mercy."

"Why hasn't she discussed this with me?" her father asked indignantly.

Judith felt her old resentments mount. "I suppose it's because she knows the subject would upset you. You don't want to talk about dying. You haven't even discussed it with me."

"That's because . . ." he faltered. "It's . . ."

"So final," Judith finished for him. She controlled her

impulse to shake him. "Don't you understand? She wants to talk about it. It's her death and it's important to her. But you keep denying her the chance to tell you how she feels about it. She never could stand to see you upset."

"Please, Judith. She can't stand much more pain."

Judith felt the ambivalence of disgust and pity. "I guess you can't either. I'll talk to her," Judith said wearily.

The day the ambulance finally carried Margaret Gregory off to the hospital, she insisted on dressing herself in the suit, now far too large for her, that Christine had designed. "And my straw bag," she instructed Robert as Judith stood by ready to help. "I must have it."

Robert picked up the bag, which was overflowing with yarn and knitting needles. "You won't be there long enough to work on this. As soon as they find the right medication, you're going to be back home. I don't see why you need this beat-up old bag. Let me buy you a new one."

"Damn it, Robert. Can't you just once give me what I want!" Then more gently, her mother said, "It has everything I'll need for the hospital. When I get home, we'll pick out a new one together."

Judith spent every night at the hospital visiting with her mother. They talked about Eddie and Christine, how well both were doing, how beautiful and bright Emma and Eric were. The last night of her mother's life, Judith waited until after Christine and her fiancé had paid their usual early evening visit— Christine the independent one, asking no quarter and giving none, while Judith had become almost immobilized by doubt. Had everything she had done since Emma's birth been wrong? Was she about to make one final mistake? Sara had been right once again; the past was never far behind.

Judith was in no rush to hurry the evening along. Instead, she stopped at her father's favorite restaurant, an unusual gesture befitting the beginning of an exceptional evening. That night Judith concentrated all her efforts on ordering the appropriate wine for each course. She ate and drank slowly, observing a couple who sat across the room from her. The woman was short, her expensively bleached hair sprayed into the overcombed style of the early sixties. Judith regarded her jewelry as rich but gaudy, and her clothes were tailored for a woman half her age. The man she was with apparently found no such flaws. Judith watched as the woman reached out and caressed her admirer's hand intimately.

When she finished her meal, Judith walked over and stood facing this woman she found so objectionable. "Yes. Is there something you want?" the woman asked.

It amused Judith that the woman's voice sounded like she looked, artificial, flawed. Judith thought it might be post-nasal drip. "Maybe I should ask you that question," Judith said.

The woman's companion turned around with a look of startled guilt. "Judith, I'd like you to meet Joan Ashland. She's uh . . ."

"Your fortune teller?" Judith nodded to Joan's still out-stretched hand. "I thought she might be reading your palm."

"And you are . . . ?" the woman drawled with under-played drama.

Judith gestured toward the man who was half-sitting, half-standing. "I'm sure my father will tell you all about me," Judith said, as she turned and walked away. She was already late for her promised appointment at the hospital.

12

Robert Gregory felt the numb tingling that comes with being held motionless, unable to exercise the necessary nerves and muscles, but he couldn't summon the energy to extricate himself from the overstuffed chair that held him. Besides, movement might stimulate his daughters to conversation, and right now he had no comfort to offer them. All he could think of was Margaret, who, after two hours, was still not out of surgery.

"Dad, go have a drink. Chris and I will wait here," Judith said, suggesting she neither needed nor wanted his withheld comfort. Robert looked at his daughter and found no trace of the child who had once responded to him with unqualified devotion. Instead, he saw a woman who years ago had charged him with an unnamed crime, found him guilty, and commuted his sentence from a lifetime of alienation to a lifetime of tolerance. He was tempted by the offer to escape to the anonymity of a comfortable bar where no one would criticize him for not measuring up to impossible standards. Of course, that would only add desertion to Judith's charges.

Before Robert could reject Judith's offer, and thereby deny her the opportunity to again prove him unworthy of her, Christine said, "I don't think Dad wants to be alone right now."

There was more challenge than concern in his younger daughter's tone. He wasn't about to be the battleground for a family fight. Nor would he referee it. "Thanks, darling, but I think we should all stay here until the doctor comes," he advised Judith.

Robert lost track of the time while they waited together in silence. Finally, Dr. Davis appeared and patiently explained the surgeon's findings, answering their questions, spinning the web of death that would soon ensnare his wife. Robert's first thought was the inconvenience death caused. How could he manage his job and . . . ? These concerns, lodged unspoken in his mouth, tasted so guilty that Robert felt a rush of nausea. He was being told that the woman he had lived with, loved, depended on for almost forty years, was going to leave him. He reached for a feeling and found emptiness. "Do you think we should tell her?" Robert asked when he realized that he was required to make some sort of response.

Dr. Davis accepted the assigned role of family counselor, granting Robert the right to withhold the truth from Margaret, but reminding him that Margaret was not one to keep bad news waiting. "How long?" Robert asked.

"A year. Perhaps a little longer. We can never be sure about these things."

Robert felt Christine's hand touch his shoulder lightly, while Judith showed no sign of caring, made no move toward comforting. Hadn't she heard what had just been said?

"I'll go call Eddie," she said in her usual efficient voice.

*   *   *

After Margaret came home from the hospital, it was business as usual. Robert suggested a trip, maybe to Europe. Margaret declined. Christmas was near. Shopping had to be done. Edward would be visiting. It was impossible to believe that his wife had suffered anything more than minor surgery as she prepared for the annual holiday festivities with a minimum of effort.

When the family gathered on Christmas Eve, Robert was surprised to see how their family had grown. There were eight now, nine if you included Dale Reed, the man Christine had been seeing steadily for over a year. Dale swung Eric up and settled him on his shoulders. With his free hand he accepted the eggnog that Robert was offering him. "Thanks, Bob," Dale said. "I want to thank you for including me in your Christmas celebration."

When Christine had introduced Robert as "my father, Robert Gregory," Dale had responded heartily, "Glad to know you, Bob." Not "Mr. Gregory," or "May I call you Robert?" To Dale, Robert was simply "Bob," no permission asked, none given. With Margaret, however, Dale took a safer path. "Does anyone call you Maggie?" he had inquired. And she had responded honestly, "Not anyone I have ever liked." From that day on it was Bob and Mrs. Gregory. And though that had irritated Robert at first, he no longer minded because Christine seemed to want this slightly loud, domineering man. "I'm glad you could be with us, Dale," Robert said, half-truthfully.

"Did Christine tell you I'm opening another store for her in Beverly Hills? She's become the darling of the fashionable set. With her talent and my know-how, we're going to make it big. Marketing, that's what counts."

"Fine, fine. I'm glad to hear that," Robert said, wanting to move away from this energetic young man. It was one thing to be successful, another to make it the main subject of conversation. Still, he seemed exactly what Christine needed, a strong, steady hand. Bill had been a nice young man, but obviously too weak to bear up under the demands of a wife and family. Robert never knew what had prompted Christine's sudden departure from the house the day after Bill's funeral, and Margaret apparently had no idea either, offering only "It's best." When Robert suggested that Christine move back home until after Eric was born, no one seemed to think it was a good idea. He needn't have worried, though, because Christine had become a competent, devoted mother. A little too protective of Eric, perhaps, but that was to be expected. Mothers made that mistake with sons. And as a businesswoman, Christine had exceeded all expectations, opening three of her "Christine's Clothes" line in Southern California. Robert admired Christine for seeing where her talent lay and then making the best of it. It was what he had done years ago.

Edward, on the other hand, still had a lot to learn about accepting his limitations. He had arrived home with the news that he was on leave from the university and was trying his hand at writing. Well, he was young and would get over it. Maybe it was better to get it out of his system now. Afterward, he could settle down to a secure position and then a family.

And Judith. Even Judith had made something of herself. She seemed respected in her profession. Her name appeared often in the paper as Judith Gregory, the civil rights attorney. And, although some of the cases she undertook were either frivolous or controversial, or both, like suing for the right of homosexuals to dance together on public dance floors, Robert was still proud of her. And she certainly had nothing to apologize for with Emma. His granddaughter was a beautiful, adoring little girl, the one great pleasure in his life. Emma dispensed her love without question or judgment. She reminded him of Judith before . . .

"Isn't it time for your eggnog, Robert?" Rose Harris asked as she had for the past thirty or so years. Rose was old now, almost eighty. But she seemed in perfect health and was not about to give up this one yearly ritual that permitted her to taste alcohol without breaking her covenant with God. Eggnog was for celebrating the Son of God's birthday; martinis were a sin. Robert always wondered why Rose thought God exempted one and condemned the other. Probably because, in eggnog, alcohol was almost tolerable. Robert served everyone, including the children, then raised his glass. "Here's to my family. Merry Christmas."

"Merry Christmas," they returned in chorus.

Robert relaxed into the familiarity of the night. There were the roast beef and turkey to be carved. The dressing to be spooned. "Edward, dark meat?" he asked, and without waiting for the answer, "Christine, white?" Without consulting the rest, he sliced and dished and received his expected nods of approval for the correct selections and portions. Afterward, when everyone had eaten their fill, he sat back. "I'm stuffed. What do you think we should do now?" Emma and Eric eyed the Christmas tree greedily. "I think there are a few things under the tree that should be opened," he announced.

Before the adults could make it from their chairs, the children were already heading for the piles of brightly wrapped boxes. One by one, gifts were presented: first the children undoing hours of careful wrapping in one greedy instant; then later, the adults, slowly, with appreciation, opening gifts selected with care. "Specially designed for you," Christine said, handing Judith a large package.

Judith carefully unwrapped the box, folded the paper, and handed it to her grandmother for next year's use. Removing a dress that matched her green eyes and holding it against her body, Judith twirled around. "It's beautiful, Christine."

"Be careful. I had to make it a half-size bigger than last year," Christine smiled.

Judith offered her sister a package in exchange for the affectionate insult. "For you. The salesman said it's what every successful businesswoman needs," she explained.

Christine lifted a leather date book from the box. "I became successful to spite Judith," Christine confided to the group. Robert frowned until he heard Judith laugh. No insult intended, none received. His daughters finally seemed at peace.

"This one's for you, Grampa," Emma said, handing him a large leather album adorned only with a single, wide, white ribbon. "I went through all of Grandma's old pictures and put them in order. I found everybody. Uncle Eddie and Aunt Christine when they were babies. You and Momma at the swimming pool. Momma holding her prize after she won a race. There's even one of you and Grandma the day you got married. Look!," she commanded, opening the album for Robert and pointing at a yellowing picture. "Grandma was beautiful, and so were you. Grandma Rose even let me have pictures of her and Grandma's daddy. See, that's Grandma when she was just a little girl standing next to her daddy and Grandma Rose." Emma relinquished control of her priceless gift. "I wish I could have found some of you with your mother and father, but there weren't any, so I left one page blank. Someday, maybe, I'll find pictures of my daddy and yours too. Do you like it?"

Robert opened the bound history of his life. It began here, with the first picture taken of him and Margaret together. He had no memory of anything coming before that. "I love it, sweetheart," he assured his granddaughter.

Looking at his family around him, he couldn't imagine this scene not being played out for all eternity.

The doctor had been wrong. It was almost two years before Margaret died. And during that time, unbidden, an entire battery of defense mechanisms came to Robert's rescue. First, of course, was denial. Margaret seemed so well after she left the hospital. The doctor had to be wrong. There would be many more good years together. He would make her happy as he had never made her before. Next came anger. As Margaret showed the first signs of weakness, Robert stormed at

the doctor to do something, to put a stop to all this. He
couldn't bear to see his wife suffer. He needed the mute
strength that was being drained from her. He hated the doctor
for not rescuing Margaret, and he hated Margaret for allowing
this attack on her body. When all else failed, he hated Judith
for his growing dependency on her. And then there was guilt.
Guilt that he had somehow brought on this catastrophe; guilt
that he was powerless to stay it. When he forgot for a moment
that Margaret was dying and found himself enjoying his work
or laughing at a colleague's joke, he felt guilty. The worst
guilt was for his inability to sustain his remorse.

And, finally, there was survival.

More and more Robert gave in and sought refuge in the
demands of his work. Margaret made his escape from hope-
lessness easier by requesting that Judith and Emma come
home to live and then insisting that he meet his professional
obligations. "What good will it do for you to stay home today?"
she would ask after she had an unusually bad night. Or, "Judith
will be home this evening. You promised to deliver that speech.
You must go. I'll be all right."

He had no intention of seeking a replacement for his
wife, and when he met one, he had no intention of pursuing
her. In fact, the day he met Joan Ashland, he found her irritating. She was an aggressive, short woman with a nasal voice
and an affected drawl that suggested boarding school conditioning. By Robert's standards, she was still young, probably
in her late forties. He disapproved of her flawless makeup,
her expensive jewelry. Margaret had never needed such trap-
pings. She had come to his office on behalf of the chamber
of commerce to "plead" with him to deliver a dinner speech
on bias in journalism. They needed someone of his stature
to speak and as chairman of the program committee she was
desperate, she told Robert. "Please," she said, "you simply
can't refuse. After Watergate and all, the public is interested
in knowing just how objective the press is."

Robert suspected the chamber of commerce was just the tip of the committee iceberg that Joan Ashland floated on. He reluctantly agreed. As editor of the local paper, he felt obligated to community duties as well as professional. These were, after all, the people who read what he printed.

"It would be my pleasure," he told her.

Three weeks later, after he had given his speech and the tiresome dinner was finished, Robert accepted the customary "you were wonderful's" and the "so informative's." As he tried gracefully to take his leave, Joan Ashland appeared. "Please, you must let me reward you with an expensive brandy."

Robert was tired, and this woman promised to add to that fatigue. "Thank you, but I have to be getting home. My wife's ill."

"Yes. I know," this stranger said.

It was a small community, and if one lived here long enough and traveled in wide-enough circles, knowing things wasn't difficult. He ignored the temptation to ask how she knew about Margaret. In answer to his silence, Joan Ashland answered the question he hadn't asked. "My maid belongs to your mother-in-law's church. When she heard you were speaking tonight, she told me about your wife. Apparently, the whole congregation is praying for her."

Robert was unaware that any request for divine intervention had been made and was annoyed to hear about it from a program committee chairman. "I'm sorry. I really must be going," he said curtly.

When Joan Ashland phoned him a few weeks later, her nasal voice, made more prominent by the absence of her distracting, bejeweled hand movements, identified her as much as her "This is Joan Ashland. I hope you remember me."

"I do indeed," Robert said politely. "What can I do for you?"

"Forgive me for bothering you. I know how busy you

are, but I was hoping you could find time to see me in the next week or so."

It might have been possible to say no to a specific request of meeting today, or three days from now. But Robert couldn't pretend that every minute of every day was scheduled for the next week and whatever "or so" meant. "Would tomorrow be convenient?" he asked.

"Could we make it for lunch? I feel so much more comfortable discussing things when I have a drink in my hand."

Robert wanted to ask what "things," but felt it could wait. "Lunch sounds fine," he said, already planning to eat and run.

The next day, when Joan settled into the booth across from him, Robert noticed that she was dressed more simply, almost conservatively, and that she wore less makeup. Without invitation, she put her now unadorned hand over his with a familiarity that made him uncomfortable. "It was so good of you to meet me."

"Would you like a drink?" he inquired, freeing his hand from hers under the guise of signaling the waiter.

"A vodka martini," she smiled.

He tried not to show his disapproval at consuming hard liquor before five o'clock in the afternoon. He never ordered anything other than an appropriate glass of wine during working hours. Robert ordered the drinks, anxious to get whatever business she had on her mind out of the way as quickly as possible. "Well," he asked, "how can I be of service to you?"

Joan Ashland lowered her eyes like she had been caught in a lie. "You can forgive me."

What on earth was this woman talking about? He hadn't been thrilled by the honor of addressing the chamber of commerce, but she hardly had to beg his forgiveness for arranging it. He wished she had simply phoned in whatever apology her insecurities demanded instead of insisting it be done in person. "I can't imagine what you might have done that would require my forgiveness," her told her politely.

"Oh, but I do," she said too loudly. "I sounded so un-caring about your wife. You see, I'm a widow. I've been through what you're going through."

Robert thought she had borne her tragedy bravely, all traces of grief having disappeared. He had no intention of spending lunch exchanging morbid insights on how to sur-vive the loss of a loved one, especially with this woman who was now engaged in sucking the pimiento out of her olive. "Please. You have nothing to apologize for. Would you care to order lunch now?" he asked, hoping to hurry the encounter along.

During lunch, Joan made no further mention of Margaret and her illness. Instead, she inquired about Robert's work, his interests, his opinions. With each answer, she either nod-ded gravely or smiled approvingly. Gradually, Robert relaxed and began to enjoy himself. It had been a long time since he'd allowed himself the luxury of idle conversation. He even consented to an unaccustomed second glass of wine.

By the time coffee was served, he realized that he had monopolized the conversation and attempted to acknowl-edge his social impropriety. "I'm sorry. I haven't asked you anything about yourself."

"I love hearing you talk," she assured him. "I miss the company of an interesting person. I hope you invite me to have lunch again soon."

An hour ago, Robert would have been irritated by her version of how the invitation originated. Now he found her female inaccuracy slightly endearing. "It would be my plea-sure," he smiled. "And next time, it will be my turn to ask the questions."

Over the next several months, as Margaret's health grew steadily worse, Robert turned to Joan Ashland for the innocent plea-sure of casual company, considering their luncheon inter-ludes no more than a harmless escape, a temporary anesthesia for pain, he told himself. Usually, Joan avoided the subject of

Robert's private life, concentrating instead on his every word about world affairs and the running of a newspaper. Occasionally, she would ask casually about his children, and, although he usually avoided discussing his private affairs with someone he still considered an outsider, Robert proudly alluded to his children's successes with comments like "Christine's quite a businesswoman" and "Judith has become a rather well-known attorney, specializing in federal law." He didn't add that Joan might not approve of some of Judith's clients. And finally, "Edward has a play running in New York. Some critics say he may be what they call a 'new voice' in American drama."

"Oh, I'm so happy for him! That's very exciting," Joan said, as though Edward were her own creative progeny. "Tell me, what's it about?"

Robert didn't have the faintest notion of what Edward's play was about. He had asked Edward to send him a copy several times, and when it finally arrived, Robert read it and was baffled. It had none of the required dramatic elements: no story with a beginning, middle, and end; no heroes or villains; no good or evil; no right or wrong. It simply presented a group of actors rehearsing a play about a family while engaging in endless arguments about what the characters really intended when they spoke their lines—although the family's dialogue didn't appear to have anything to do with what the actors thought the characters meant. Robert remembered one scene in particular, where an actor playing the part of the son asks if his family wants to go to a movie. Instead of answering the boy, each member of the family turns away from him and addresses the audience, enumerating all the reasons why they in fact hate the idea of going to a movie. Then, abruptly, they face the son and in unison shout, "Yes. Of course we want to go. Now, do you love us?" Next, without warning, his sister stops being a character and becomes the actress playing the part, criticizing the other actors for their inability to understand the scene that has just been played.

And to confuse things further, the director periodically marches on stage and chastises the entire cast for not being able to keep their characters under control. "Just make them say their lines," he orders. "It's not up to you to decide what the character really means. And it's not up to them either. I'm the only one who knows what the play means, and if I tell, the game's over and there's no play. So stop arguing and get on with it." The only thing that Robert could be certain of was that no one on that stage understood anyone else: not the actors; not the characters; not the director; and, Robert thought, not the audience either. It was strange, though, for all the jumbled confusion about who was who and who meant what, Robert found the play strangely compelling. He felt pity for the characters and actors alike, perhaps because they seemed to be missing the point of the play as much as Robert did. And like all of them, he felt there really was a point and missing it was a tragedy. "It's about a family," Robert told Joan.

"What's it called? I'd love to get a copy."

"*The Perfect Family,*" he said.

"What an interesting title."

"Eddie said he wanted to call it *Splendor in the Grass,* but it had already been used. My son's not always easy to understand."

As their friendship, for that was what Robert considered their relationship, progressed, he learned that Joan had been married young to a much older man (his own age in fact), and that her husband had died five years ago. As he had guessed, she was well-off, active in every recognized charity, and a member of the social world he knew only from reading his own newspaper. Since Margaret was the only woman he had ever known intimately, he found Joan Ashland an alien being, vocal, aggressive, and involved in affairs that had nothing to do with domestic duty. She appeared to consider their time together just one more enjoyable but insignificant social occasion. She was, Robert decided, the soul of propriety. Had she indicated otherwise, he, of course, would have declined further encounters. As it was, he saw no harm in extending an invitation now and then to dinner when he was required to work into the evening.

It was after one of those dinners that Robert came home to find Judith bending over Margaret, who was lying on the sofa. He felt the panic that was always just beneath the surface emerge when he heard Judith plead, "Please, Mother. You have to let them give you something for this."

"What is it?" Robert asked, pushing Judith aside and kneeling next to Margaret.

"Just a little pain. Nothing serious," Margaret reassured him. His wife had steadfastly refused drugs that would mask her pain. She demanded alertness at the price of comfort. Her only concession was to the Seconal tablets that afforded her a few hours of uninterrupted sleep and therefore offered Robert a night's rest as well.

Robert reached out and covered Margaret's thin body with the afghan she had just finished knitting. "I want you to go to the hospital!"

"I'm all right," Margaret whispered. "But I wish you'd think about moving into the nursery. You have to get your rest or you won't be any good to me or anyone else. If you're worried, Judith can sleep on a cot in our room."

They had had this argument before, and he always prevailed. He knew she was right: they each worried about the other and therefore guaranteed restless nights for each. But he couldn't stand the idea of crawling off to a room each night by himself. He had no difficulty leaving her during the day: between Rose and Judith, she was well cared for. But he was ashamed to tell her why he stubbornly refused to be parted from her at night. Certainly, it wasn't sensible. He couldn't admit that since her illness he was terrified of the darkness he had known as a child. For Robert, the dark was a return to the void in his life before Margaret and the children, a darkness where the parents he had never known floundered in the icy water, clinging to their valuable stringed instruments while half-empty lifeboats swept past them, leaving them to be pulled slowly under the sea. He would not leave her and return to that void. "I want to stay with you," he said, lifting the the weakened body that had always exuded force. "Let me help you upstairs," he said.

He laid her gently on the bed. "Do you want a Seconal?" he asked, handing her the small bottle she kept by the side of the bed.

"In a while," she said. "Judith's prepared your dinner. I feel like needlepointing for a while. Would you hand me my straw bag?"

"Why don't you get a proper sewing bag? This one is disgraceful," he smiled, knowing she would never part with her bargained conquest from Tijuana.

"Maybe some day. Now, why don't you go downstairs and get something to eat."

Robert started to confide that he had already eaten, but decided against it. Not because he had anything to hide, he told himself. He had done nothing more than accept Joan's invitation to join him after he was through working. "Come on, it's Washington's birthday. The least we can do is give him a birthday toast," Joan had teased.

"I'll just grab a bite and be back," he told his wife, who was already jabbing her needle expertly back and forth through the designed webbing she held in front of her. "What are you making this time?" he asked before leaving.

"A cover for Emma's tennis racket. I hope I can finish it on time."

Robert hated it when his wife sounded like she was scheduling her death the way she might any other unimportant appointment. "Damn it," Robert said. "Don't talk like that."

"I meant I want to finish it before Emma's tournament starts," Margaret said, correcting his first impression.

A few minutes later, Robert joined Judith and Emma in the kitchen. "Smells good. Who's the cook?"

"I am," Emma announced.

"Well, then, let me give the chef a kiss," Robert said, picking up his beautiful eleven-year-old granddaughter and setting her on his lap.

"Big girls don't sit on their grandfathers' laps," Judith said as she set a plate of food in front of her father.

"Sure they do," Robert said, giving Emma a hug.

Judith's voice bordered on punitive when she ordered, "Emma. Get down this instant!" But when she added, "Your grandfather must be tired. He's worked all night. Let him eat in peace," Robert realized that Judith was just worried about him, and he was momentarily touched and grateful that his daughter and granddaughter had decided to live with them during this time. Each day Judith came home and took over the household duties from Rose. The house ran as smoothly as it had when Margaret was in charge, and Judith actually seemed to enjoy her role as nurse and maid. Not since she was a young girl had she been so easy to get along with. But there were times when Robert had the uneasy feeling she was watching him, waiting for him to make a mistake.

"Don't you like the meatloaf?" Judith asked.

Robert looked at his untouched plate. He had eaten a full meal only an hour before coming home, and he couldn't manage all she had placed before him. "I guess I'm not very hungry," he said.

"Dad, you must try and eat. It would upset Mom if she thought you weren't taking care of yourself."

Emma took the fork from his hand and said, "Let me feed you like you used to feed me." Scooping a glob of potatoes from his plate, she commanded, "Now open wide." And then she swept the spoon through the air, gliding ever closer toward Robert's face. "And innnnnnnn it goes," she said.

Remembering the times he had cajoled this child with

294

the same game, Robert obeyed and opened his mouth. As he chewed his unwanted vegetable, he wondered at the American obsession with force-feeding. Even for this adolescent dietitian, eating seemed to be an affirmation of life. Something like, "If you eat this, you'll be all right, you can't die." Robert played the game obediently, finishing all his food. When he was through, he felt sick. "Thank you, honey. I feel better now. I don't know what I'd do without you and your mom to help me out," he lied to his beloved torturer.

The day the ambulance came for Margaret, she insisted on dressing herself in the suit, now far too large for her, that Christine had designed. "And my straw bag," she instructed Robert. "I must have it."

Robert picked up the bag overflowing with yarn and knitting needles. "You won't be there long enough to work on this. As soon as they find the right medication, you're going to be back home. I don't see why you need this beat-up old bag. Let me buy you a new one."

"Damn it, Robert. Can't you just once give me what I want!" Robert felt the slap of Margaret's outburst. She had never spoken to him like that before. What had he said? And what did she mean, "just once give me what I want?" He had never denied her anything. Then he remembered that only a few days ago Judith had accused him of denying Margaret the chance to talk about dying. Did either of them think he didn't care? Didn't they know the very thought was so terrible that he couldn't hold on to it, much less give it voice? He was incapable of discussing death as though it were a simple matter of reaching a mutual understanding, coming to terms. He didn't want to hear how she felt about dying, because if she told him, it meant she was admitting defeat, and he couldn't picture his wife being defeated by anything, not even cancer. He might not be religious, but he needed hope. Without it, how could they get through all this?

Margaret reached out and took the bag from Robert's

hand. "It has everything I'll need for the hospital," she explained. "When I get home, we'll pick out a new one together."

The anger in her voice was gone, replaced by the familiar, simple declarations he had always expected. It must have been the pain speaking a moment ago, not Margaret. She didn't want to talk about dying; she wanted to talk about coming home. He was exonerated.

For the next week, Robert visited his wife every afternoon and every evening at the hospital. After that, he let Dr. Davis convince him to let his daughters take over once in a while. "This could go on for a long time," the doctor told him. "Most people wouldn't have lived as long as Margaret has, but she has the heart of a lion. It could go on beating for a long time. She's making it hard on herself by refusing to let me give her heavy medication. She says she wants to be alert enough to enjoy your visits. I'm sorry, Robert. I know this is difficult for you."

Almost three weeks later, Robert gave in to the need to breathe air that didn't smell of medicine and death. He agreed to meet Joan Ashland for dinner. He refused to entertain guilt. Why should he? It was Margaret who suggested he not return to the hospital that night. He had been with her most of the day, and she claimed it would give her a chance to visit with the children, who planned to be there later. He chose a popular restaurant frequented by familiar faces. He would not be accused of sneaking around. They were both respected members of the community and had nothing to hide. If Margaret knew they were dining together, she would understand; hers was the only opinion that counted. As they finished dinner, Joan listened to Robert quietly, her hand covering his in a gesture of empathy as he discussed his inconsolable loss. "I can't stand to see her in so much pain," he told Joan.

Instead of her usual sympathetic consolation, he caught the impatience in her voice. "Yes. Is there something you want?" Joan asked, looking up, past Robert at some unannounced intruder.

"Maybe I should ask you that question," Judith said, the nasty implication clear.

Robert pulled his hand from Joan's protection. "Judith, I'd like you to meet Joan Ashland. She's uh . . ."

"Your fortune teller?" Judith nodded to Joan's still outstretched hand. "I thought she might be reading your palm."

Robert was confused, but Joan appeared in complete control. "And you are . . . ?"

"I'm sure my father will tell you all about me," Judith said as she turned on her heel and walked away.

Later, when Robert arrived home, he found Judith's note: *I think it would be better if Emma and I stayed at Grandmother Rose's house.*

Early the next morning, the hospital informed Robert that his wife was dead. And the following evening, the police informed him that his daughter had been arrested and charged with second-degree murder in the death of Margaret Gregory.

Today was the second day of Judith's trial. Yesterday, when Robert testified, he had tried to defend his daughter, answering questions without actually perjuring himself: Yes, he had seen her the night Margaret died. No, she didn't seem upset or nervous. In fact, she had gone out of her way to stop and visit his table at the restaurant where he was dining. No, he knew of no reason to believe his daughter had either the motive or the will to end his wife's life. He didn't mention the note she had left or the fact that he had not spoken to her since the night she saw him with Joan. Throughout his testimony, Judith stared at him so strangely that he felt it was he, not his daughter, who was on trial.

As Robert prepared to leave for court he heard the doorbell ring. On the front porch he found Rose Harris arm in arm with Emma. Rose stood remarkably erect for a woman in her eighties, and it was difficult to tell whose arm supported whom as granddaughter and great-grandmother stood side by side. "Rose, how on earth did you get here? Why didn't you call? I was just on my way to pick up Emma."

"I walked," his mother-in-law said, her voice as strong as he remembered it the first day he had met her. "Emma was exploring, looking through some of her mother's keepsakes that I stored in an old bureau." Rose pulled a black leather book with gold-leafed edging from the frayed handbag she always carried. "Judith must have put this away along with the other things I've kept of hers throughout the years. It's the Bible I gave Judith when she was a little girl. Don't blame Emma; she wasn't prying. I told her she could play with whatever she found."

Robert was irritated by Rose's unsolicited defense of his granddaughter. He had never questioned Emma's trustworthiness. Was this just the prattling of an old woman, or was this Rose's way of suggesting that Judith had strayed from the path of righteousness because he had not participated in her religious training? Whatever, he had more important things to think about today than the unearthing of Judith's childhood mementos. "Rose, we're going to be late. The trial starts in an hour."

"It will have to start without us. Can I come in?"

Robert was uneasy. Until now, Rose had refused to attend the trial. She said the whole idea of holding Judith responsible for Margaret's death was silly, and she would have nothing to do with such a ridiculous spectacle. Robert had no desire to worry Rose with the seriousness of Judith's predicament, so he had not argued with her. But she couldn't be so unconcerned that she thought Robert had no duty to attend. "What is it, Rose?" he asked, settling her in a chair. "Is something the matter?"

When the old woman looked up at Robert, he couldn't tell if the dampness in her eyes was tears or just the water of old age. "I never thought I would outlive my daughter. It's the worst thing that can happen to a parent. Even though Margaret was almost sixty, I still feel the loss of a child."

Robert wanted to comfort Rose, to say something that would make the loss of Margaret less painful. At the same time, he was irritated that she had taken this time to seek his consolation. He didn't think it would help Judith's case if her own father were not there to show support. "Rose, you've always believed that things happen because it's God's will. Why would you question that now?"

Rose looked at Robert and smiled. "I'm glad that you've finally found a time when mentioning His name is useful. You're right. I shouldn't question His wisdom, but I can't help feeling the pain of it. And I think you should know that sometimes God puts the truth into our hands and then lets us decide what to do with it." Rose reached down and removed an envelope from the Bible she had been holding and handed it to Robert. "There's something you should read. After that, you have a decision to make."

Part Five

The Clouds that gather round the setting sun
Do take a sober colouring from an eye
That hath kept watch o'er man's mortality;
Another race hath been, and other palms are won.
Thanks to the human heart by which we live,
Thanks to its tenderness, its joys, and fears,
To me the meanest flower that blows can give
Thoughts that do often lie too deep for tears.
—WILLIAM WORDSWORTH
"Ode on Intimations of Immortality"

has failed her mother's final wish, betrayed it, made things worse. She should have destroyed that letter; instead, she had hidden it, unable to obliterate her mother's last testimony. It was a long letter, probably written during the long, painful hours the last week of her life. Her mother had given it to her the night she died, instructing weakly, "Open it tomorrow. It's only for you to read." Judith knew it by heart:

Dearest Daughter,

I realize these final weeks have been terrible for you, and I had no right to ask you to be with me when I decided it was time to die. But I was so afraid that after I took the pills the night nurse might find out and feel obligated to pump what's left of my stomach. I knew that even if you didn't agree with what I intended to do, you would understand. And to be honest, I wanted at least one of my family with me at the end. But that was selfish of me.

This is not the only time I have been selfish. I let you look out for Christine and Eddie because I didn't know how to tell them to fix their lives. Eddie hated it that we weren't perfect and hated himself for not being able to make us what he wanted. The poor child kept running away from us, drinking and hiding. And Christine couldn't grow up, so like a little girl, she caused terrible damage. You had learned how to take care of yourself, and I thought you might teach them. But all you did was bury yourself in our lives instead of facing your own. Now your sister and brother are going to be all right, but I'm afraid you might not be.

I should have tried to persuade you to tell Randall the truth. Even if he didn't want the responsibility of a family, it wasn't right to keep him from knowing about Emma. Maybe I helped keep your secret because I was afraid Randall would take you and Emma away. That was wrong of me.

It would be even more wrong of me to leave you without saying what I should have said a long time ago. It's time you realized that your father is a good man and has loved us as much as he knew how to. You must not judge him. He needs acceptance from you most of all. It was always you that he looked to for approval, never your brother and sister, or even me. You were the first child he loved, and the first who rejected him. You couldn't forgive him for not staying the big, strong man who held you high above his head, keeping you safe from the water. After you turned away from him, I don't think he had the heart to really love his other children completely. Perhaps that is why I kept silent and let you look out for Edward and Christine so often. It was your father who needed all my support.

When I found out I was going to die, I was worried about what would become of your father. I couldn't bear the thought of his being alone. That would be terrible for everybody. Eddie would feel guilty because he is so far away; Christine would resent feeling obligated. You would be the one who would have to care for him. That would mean a life with none of you living up to each other's expectations.

I have found peace of mind knowing that your father has found someone to care for him. Her name is Joan Ashland, and her maid tells your grandmother that she is a nice person. Perhaps you might not like her, but that is not your business. The important thing is your father's welfare. This is your chance to rescue not only your father but yourself as well. Make him understand that you don't blame him for wanting a few years of happiness. Perhaps if you can understand why *he* deserves it, you'll be able to understand why *you* do too. You only have the responsibility of loving your family, not of living their lives or judging them.

her father who had convinced the judge to spare his children the same pain he must have felt when he read it. Whatever the truth is, she realizes that it is his to decide, to explain or not to explain, as he chooses. *He is, after all, head of this family, regardless of what his children think.*

Judith moves through the crowd toward her father, automatically reaching out for the long-practiced handshake that had always seemed a betrayal, a barrier, a denial of protection, affection. Why had she ever seen this gesture as rejection? Shyness perhaps, or embarrassment, or even insensitivity, but surely not rejection.

Had she ever looked directly at her father, at her brother and sister? Or had she watched them all these years like reflections moving behind her in a mirror, seeing them only through the eyes of her own reflection, her own image of herself? Long ago, she considered being pushed from her father's lap an act of treason, so she saw her father as a traitor. For years, Judith defied both father and lover, so she demanded Christine follow her example or suffer scorn. Judith had battled her imagined tormentors, so Eddie was to be pitied for concealing his wounds.

Judith reaches for her father's extended hand, holds it, exchanges it for an embrace. "I'm so sorry. Forgive me," she whispers into her father's shoulder. "I love you."

When Robert Gregory steps back, awkwardly, Judith almost laughs. By risking so much for her, this man has already proven himself; she no longer needs a little girl's assurance of hugs and kisses. She has no right to demand them. "I did care about the puppy," she tells her father. "I just didn't think I deserved to have another one. But I was wrong. We don't lose our right to love things just because we make a mistake."

Now her whole family surrounds her, relieved, offering her reassurances, happy that she is safe. As though she were once again her little sister, Christine is crying. "I never blamed you. Not really." Judith doesn't know if Christine is talking about their mother's death, or Bill's, but it doesn't matter.

They will never be close friends, but they are sisters. They are part of a family.

Next it is Eddie's turn to embrace, to congratulate. But he holds back. "Remember a long time ago? I asked you who you thought needed atonement."

"I remember," Judith said, recalling the young boy sitting across from her, asking "Whose atonement?" "I know the answer now," she tells her brother.

Eddie smiles. "There's a seven o'clock flight. We could make it together."

If she hurries, she and Emma might have enough time to make it. Judith can already imagine herself folding the fabric of guilt that she has so painstakingly woven over the years. She will have to pack it, along with the rest of the things she will carry with her.

Emma is beside her, bewildered, holding Judith's hand as though in danger of being lost. "It's time for you to meet your daddy," she whispers to her daughter.

At first Emma looks suspicious. "Really?"

"Really," Judith promises.

Emma holds her breath as though she is about to dive into the depths of unfamiliar waters, regardless of how dangerous. "When?"

Judith knows that she has lost the right to expect another chance. It may be too late. But, thankfully, she has finally learned she can't afford not to find out. Judith holds Emma's hand. "Now," Judith says. "It's time to go."

I love you very much and pray you will make peace
with yourself by making peace with others.
Your loving mother

That last night at the hospital, Judith had begged her
mother not to leave her, not to shorten the time they had
together. But her mother made it clear that she had no intention of passively accepting life by clinging to dripping
tubes and noisy machines. Judith knew the moment had come
to say good-bye when her mother opened the old straw bag
that, along with needlepoint canvases, blue stationery, and
reading materials, also contained small orange pills—pills that
her mother had methodically stored away for a time when
she would make her own decision about how they were to
be used. "I can live with pain, or in this case die with it,"
Margaret Gregory said. "But I cannot stand the waste that
will ruin the family financially and emotionally. It wouldn't
be fair to your father."

Judith had been outraged that her mother's last thoughts
were of sparing her husband the time-consuming business of
comforting the dying. Her mother's letter had made her
ashamed of that outrage.

Neither mother nor daughter had foreseen that Margaret
Gregory's decision would be considered anything more than
the final act of a terminal patient in pain concerned about
being a burden to her family. It had never occurred to either
one that Judith would be accused of administering the lethal
dose. And after she was accused, how could she defend herself
without revealing that letter that, for all its good intentions,
would expose her father to public gossip, perhaps even scandal; her brother and sister to the humiliation of her mother's
judgment; and worst of all, present the truth of Randall's long
absence to the impersonal judgment of strangers and the not-
so-impersonal condemnation of Emma herself.

Now they have her mother's letter, and all this has been

for nothing. And the final irony is that her father had produced the evidence, in spite of gossip, in spite of the possible scandal. He is, after all, more concerned about her welfare than his own, than Eddie's, or Christine's, or even Emma's. And for the first time in her life, Judith knows real shame. Now Judith braces herself for the moment that all those she loves will hear her mother's words echoing throughout the courtroom, words that were lovingly intended but would be devastatingly destructive. In a moment, her father will be commanded to read, to explain, to reveal.

But there is no command. Instead, she hears the quiet voice of the black-robed judge inquire, "Does the state wish to make a statement?"

Judith recognizes this question. She has heard it before many times. She knows it calls for an answer that has already been rehearsed by all the parties in the judge's chambers, an answer that occasionally recognizes the innocence of those not on trial.

As if relieved, the prosecutor announces, "In the interest of justice, the state wishes to withdraw its complaint against the defendant. And it further agrees to the stipulation that the evidence presented in chambers be sealed." The rest of the legal litany is swift and predictable: *No objection; so stipulated; the court agrees.* Judith hardly hears the attorney's congratulatory "You're free to go."

Emma is there, watching her, wondering what it all means; Edward, Christine, smiling the relief that for the moment has canceled their curiosity about what has wrought this legal miracle; and her father, waiting, apprehensive, standing in her path ready for whatever words are to be said, if any. There will come a time when the excitement of the trial is over, when the mind begins to replay events, when each of them will want to know what had happened here today. But it is not her right or responsibility to tell them—it is her father's. Perhaps he will never tell them what is in the letter the judge has so wisely sealed from their knowledge. Perhaps it was